When You Dance with the Devil

GWYNNE FORSTER

When You Dance with the Devil

KENSINGTON PUBLISHING CORP.
http://www.kensingtonbooks.com

DAFINA BOOKS are published by

Kensington Publishing Corp.
850 Third Avenue
New York, NY 10022

All Kensington titles, imprints and distributed lines are available at special quantity discounts for bulk purchases for sales promotion, premiums, fund-raising, educational or institutional use.

Special book excerpts or customized printings can also be created to fit specific needs. For details, write or phone the office of the Kensington Special Sales Manager: Kensington Publishing Corp., 850 Third Avenue, New York, NY 10022. Attn. Special Sales Department. Phone: 1-800-221-2647.

Dafina and the Dafina logo Reg. U.S. Pat. & TM Off.

ISBN 0-7582-1308-5

First Kensington Trade Paperback Printing: August 2006
10 9 8 7 6 5 4 3 2 1

Printed in the United States of America

ACKNOWLEDGMENTS

To Carole K., Carol S., Chloe G., Donna H., Ingrid K., and Melissa F., who have supported and encouraged me during my decade as a published author, I cherish each of you.

To my editor, Karen Thomas, whose helpfulness, graciousness and professionalism make my work a joy, and to Kristine V. Mills-Noble, whose wonderful cover designs for *When You Dance with the Devil* and my previous two Kensington/Dafina novels enhance their salability. I am also grateful to my husband for his unfailing support.

As always, I thank God for the talent He has given me and for the opportunities to use it.

Chapter One

In the darkening mist of that cold December afternoon, Sara Jolene Tilman stared down at her mother, reposing peacefully amidst red and yellow carnations—flowers suggestive of joy rather than sorrow—and whispered, "Yes, Mama." She had avoided burying her mother beneath a blanket of white flowers for, to her, white symbolized purity, and nothing—not even death—would lead her to link Emma Tilman with purity. To her mind, meanness was incompatible with purity, and meanness was the one word that, since her early childhood, she had always associated with her mother.

"Yes, Mama," she said, almost sneering, turned away dry-eyed, and left Emma Tilman to the undertaker and grave tenders.

Sara, do this and Sara, do that. Sara, bring me this. Pick up that. Sara, come here. Sara, go there. Commands that she would never hear again, and that she would not miss.

From the little she had seen of other children with their mothers—so little because Emma did not allow her to visit other children—kindness was the least she should have received from Emma Tilman. Kindness? She pulled cold air through her teeth. If Emma had ever smiled at her, Sara Jolene had not been looking. But Emma had been adept at mental torture. She didn't engage in abuse, at least not the kind that bruised the skin; she used her tongue to inflict the punishment.

"You're not worth the lard that goes into the biscuits you eat," Emma would say when Sara Jolene asked her mother for shoes or other basic necessities. "You're useless." She would never forget the times when, in one of her frequent rages, Emma would scream at her. "Go hide your ugly face. I wish I had never seen your daddy. I couldn't even abort you, hard as I tried." Maybe now, the hatred and resentment she felt for her mother would cease hammering at her head, like day-long migraines, and churning in her chest like acid reflux.

Tears? She had no tears for Emma Tilman. For five long years she had nursed and cared for her bedridden mother, and not one word of thanks, not one gesture of appreciation. But as she stumbled away from the grave, she dabbed at the brine dripping from beneath her eyelids, blinding her as she walked. The tears that finally streamed from her eyes were tears not of mourning but of relief, and tears for the dark unknown that lay ahead of her.

Sara Jolene was not afraid. The hard life she'd lived had inured her to anxiety about possible calamities. Before her mother's seemingly interminable illness, for six terrible years she'd had the burden of caring for her stroke bound and bed-ridden maternal grandmother, a woman every bit as domineering, mean, and lacking in feeling and warmth as Emma Tilman.

She threaded her way past tombstones and crosses, over ground hardened by Hagerstown, Maryland's icy winter, struggling with her shoulders hunched forward until she reached the black Cadillac where her mother's pastor detained her.

He grasped her upper arm. "I'm truly sorry, Sara Jolene. I know this has been difficult for you."

Sorry about what? Neither he nor his parishioners had done a thing to ease the burden she'd struggled under all those years. She looked over toward the small group of people walking down the hill and raised her hand in a weak wave at the seven individuals who had cared enough to tell her mother—a woman without friends—goodbye. "I'm no worse right now, Reverend Coles, than I ever was. This is just different."

"But you're all alone now."

"Wasn't I always alone?" She attempted to move on, but he detained her.

"I know. You can make a fresh start now, if you will. Move to another town and do something with your life. If you don't get out of that old house, you'll waste away, a bitter woman like your mother and your grandmother." She watched as he wrote a few lines on a card and handed it to her. "My sister has a place on the Atlantic Ocean not too far from Ocean City. You can make a living over there. Just tell her I sent you."

She looked at the card before slipping it into her pocketbook. "Thank you, sir. I may need it."

"Use it," he called after her, "and be careful, now."

Careful, huh? He didn't have to worry about that. From now on, she was looking after number one.

She walked into the house, turned on the hall light and closed the door behind her. Maybe the preacher was right. She had no reason to remain in Hagerstown. When she hung up her coat, the cold seeped into her. She started to her room, shivering, to get a sweater and remembered that there was no one to tell her she couldn't turn up the heat. As the room warmed, she walked through the house turning on all the lights, banishing what seemed to her like eons of darkness. Then she turned on the radio, unable to remember when she had last heard music in that house. Laughter poured out of her until, in tears, she collapsed into a dining room chair.

"Don't you want to keep some souvenirs of your mother?" the real estate agent asked Sara Jolene three months later when she sold the house with everything in it except her clothes.

"You'd be surprised at the souvenirs I have," she said, ignoring his quizzical expression. "I wish I could give you the memories that go along with the house."

"Too bad. Where can I reach you if I have any problems?"

She stared at him. "What kind of problems you expecting? We just closed the deal. I got my money and that's all I want from you." At his expression of surprise, she added. "And my house is all you're getting from me."

"Why, Miss Tilman, I can't believe we're having this conversation."

"Everybody knows I'm on my own for the first time, but maybe y'all don't know that I'm not dancing to anybody's tune but mine. When they buried mama, they threw dirt on the last person who's going to exploit *me*. I've met all the conditions of sale. The house is broom clean. I had the chimneys swept, new locks put on the doors and the back steps repaired. So, mister, you don't need to get in touch with me for a frigging thing. My business with you is finished."

If he thought her fair game, she'd show him. She knew people believed her to be timid, even cowardly, but she wasn't; she was Emma Tilman's unwilling victim. Not even the local sheriff stood up to her mother, and Emma got off scot-free when, in anger, she'd dashed hot water on a neighbor, leaving the woman permanently scarred.

The preacher's car approached, and she was certain that he would continue on, wherever he started, but he parked in front of the house she'd just sold. She walked toward him.

"I just closed the sale at the bank this morning. Your sister is expecting me tomorrow, sir."

"Yes. She called to tell me. I'm glad you decided to go there. I don't think you'll be sorry. God bless you." His gaze roamed over her for a second, and then he started the engine and drove away. She wondered at his interest. He visited her mother only to bring communion once every three months, and hadn't visited but once, for a short while, during her last days. Well, few people had seemed able to tolerate her mother's company. And who could blame them? She quickened her steps and headed for the inn where she would spend the night and where she'd left her few belongings.

Thirty-five years and not a thing to show for them. Well, that's all in the past. Tomorrow, I'll start finding out what life is really like.

The following afternoon, Sara Jolene opened the back door of the taxi, went around to the trunk and unloaded her three suitcases and two shopping bags. Then, she went to the driver's side of the taxi and gave the man sixteen dollars and eighty cents, the amount on the taxi meter.

"Don't you people tip?" he asked, his face red with anger and his blue eyes flashing with what she didn't doubt was scorn.

"We tip when *you* people get off your behinds and earn it," she said, looking directly into his face, a face mottled with fury. "I'm not paying you to sit on your behind while I lug these heavy suitcases from the trunk of your taxi. Being black doesn't mean being stupid." Lord, how good it felt to speak her mind. She was through with "yessing" people.

A tall, brown-skinned woman with large brown eyes, a pointed nose and pouting bottom lip, Sara Jolene wore arrogance easily, though she wouldn't have defined her attitude as such. Her good looks had never interested her; any effort she'd made on her own behalf had been directed toward the simple matter of existing. With her mama gone, she easily found avenues for her lifelong resentment.

When the taxi driver drove off with a powerful burst of energy and speed, Sara Jolene had a feeling of immense satisfaction because she had infuriated the man. Looking up at the big white wooden structure, its green shutters gleaming as if they had all been painted that morning, and at the white rocking chairs scattered along the front porch beckoning like the "house by the side of the road," a shiver or two shot through her body. Undaunted, she picked up the heaviest suitcase and started up the walk. The front door opened, and a stocky African-American man of about thirty rushed out to meet her.

"Afternoon, ma'am. I'm Rodger. Miss Johnson is expecting you. I'll get your things up to your room."

"Thank you, Rodger. You'd a thought that taxi driver would at least have taken my things out of the trunk for me."

"No, ma'am. I wouldn't. They take your money, but they sure don't do much for it. You go on in. I'll look after this."

She wanted to ask Rodger who he was and what he did at the Thank the Lord Boarding House, but the bite of her mother's tongue had taught her that it was best not to ask questions.

A matronly woman about five feet, six inches tall and who bore no resemblance to the Reverend Philip Coles met her at the front door. "Welcome, Miss Tilman. I'm Fannie Johnson. Your room's right at the top of the stairs, and it's on the front.

Course, if you want to face the bay, it's fifty dollars more per month."

She imagined Fannie Johnson's age to be somewhere between fifty and sixty, although her prudish appearance might have added more years than she had earned.

Sara Jolene stared at the woman, wondering if she was going to like her. "I don't have fifty dollars to throw away. I'll take the front room."

"Come on. After I show you your room, I'll get you a sandwich. You must be tired and hungry after your trip. I sure hope you're not a vegetarian. And no smoking. If you do, you'll be responsible for cleaning your own room and bath. No liquor in public rooms, other than wine with dinner at the table, if you want it, and no bad language. No men in your bedroom, but they can visit you in the lounge, and if you want to invite a guest for dinner, it'll cost you ten dollars. Try to get along with the other residents. We're a happy family. If you get sick, we'll take good care of you. Breakfast at seven-thirty, lunch at one, but let the cook know you'll be taking it, and supper at seven. As of now, there are no roaches and no bedbugs in this house. I hope you didn't bring any."

What a mouth! Sara Jolene looked hard at the woman, deciding whether to be insulted and tell her off or to bide her time and see whether she wanted to stay. She did neither. "Miss Johnson, I just buried my mother. For thirty-five years, I did as she commanded. When I left her grave, I vowed never to let anybody else treat me as if I'm a child. I'd appreciate a sandwich and your apology. Thank you."

"No point in—"

"I'm not unpacking till you apologize for that crack about the roaches and bed bugs."

"Oh, all right. I'm a Christian woman, and I believe in peace. I apologize, and I'm glad to have you with us. Baked ham or turkey in your sandwich?"

Sara Jolene could feel her bottom lip drop. The woman could switch gears like a racing car driver. "Ham, please."

"It'll be on the dining room table in ten minutes." She started from the room, turned, walked back to Sara Jolene and put an arm around her shoulder. "I'm sorry about your mother. May the Lord let her rest in peace."

Unaccustomed to such gestures, Sara Jolene flinched at the woman's touch. "Not a chance," she muttered, and Fannie's eyebrows shot up.

Then, Fannie lifted her right shoulder in a long shrug. "Well . . . uh, what do you want us to call you? We use first names. I'm Fannie."

"My name's Sara Jolene, but I . . . uh . . . like to be called Jolene." She hoped she never heard the name Sara again. "This is a huge house, Fannie. How many boarders live here?"

"Ten with you, and I have one vacancy. When I'm full, there're twelve of us living here."

"Twelve. I hope I don't go out of my mind."

"You won't. You'll find them very friendly. The Lord put us all here together for a purpose. Just let him do his work, and you'll be happy."

As she watched Fannie trip down the stairs, Jolene couldn't help wondering if the Lord was doing his work all those years when first her grandmother and then her mother abused her continuously as if doing so was their right. She doubted it. What she didn't doubt was that, from then on, she was going to get some of her own and if that meant stepping on a few innocent toes, so be it.

She unpacked, shook out her clothes, and put them away. With pale yellow walls, white curtains and bedspread, and two comfortable over-stuffed chairs upholstered in pale yellow, the room appealed to Jolene, especially its cheerful and sunny appearance, it was a drastic change from the house in which she spent her first thirty-five years. When she went to wash her hands, she discovered that her bathroom was also yellow and white. She hurried down to the dining room where the sandwich, a glass of iced tea and an apple rested in the middle of a place setting. She blinked back the tears. At last, somebody had done something for her.

After she finished eating, Jolene took the dishes to the kitchen, where she encountered a surprised cook. "You don't have to bus your dishes, honey," the woman said. "You start doing that, and

Miss Fannie may decide she don't need some of the help. My name is Marilyn, and I'm the chief cook."

"Uh, sorry. I'm Jolene. It may take me a while to figure out how things work around here."

Marilyn stuck her right hand on her enormous right hip. "Ain't nothing to figure out. Just come to your meals on time, don't smoke, stay sober, and don't take your man to your room. If you can remember that, you'll be the apple of Miss Fannie's eye."

With no chores to do for the first time in memory and no commands to follow, Jolene wandered into the lounge where an older man and two women sat watching television. She hadn't ever watched an entire television show. She had rarely visited anyone, and Emma hadn't seen the need for a television nor had Emma's mother. Jolene sat in a chair some distance from the other boarders and watched. Fascinated.

"Judge Mathis is just leading that woman on, letting her hang herself," one woman said.

"He sure is," the old man said. "He's laughing and joking, and she's just digging her grave. But if you don't know the difference between virtue and immorality, and if you're so involved with yourself that you don't care, you get what the judge is about to lay on that woman."

"Come on, Judd," the woman replied, "it's just a television show."

Judd leaned back in the shaker rocker—the only one in the lounge and the seat that, by tacit consent, belonged to him. "It may be a TV show, but that woman is being her real self, arrogant and self-absorbed. I'm glad she's there and not here."

Jolene stood and headed for the door. "Is she the new one?" Jolene heard one of the women ask.

"Looks like it. She sure could use a little manners. Walk in here and don't say a word. Get up and leave just like she came. A dog would at least have wagged his tail."

Jolene realized they were talking about her, and wanted a place to hide. From the corner of her eye, she saw the old man and two women who she presumed to be the house gossips. The thin, pursed lips of one woman reminded her of her mama's attitude toward the rest of the world. "I'm not going to like that one." She said to herself. She dashed up to her room, closed the door and let it take her weight. What did they want from her? She didn't know them.

By supper time, she had become well acquainted with the view from her window. The park that faced her, a wide open space with scattered trees, a pond, flowers, a narrow, river-like stream that was host to a small bridge. And she could see the edge of the bay. It was a place where a person could be free to embrace the world.

"Don't be so fanciful," she admonished herself as twilight set in and, in the distance, she could see fireflies and hear croaking bullfrogs. "It looks good, but it may turn out to be like everything else: something to sap your will, eat up your energy, and consume you. I'm not getting attached to anybody or anything."

She dreaded supper for it meant meeting ten strangers, and after having seen three of them in the lounge, she'd as soon eat her food in her room. But that wasn't an option, so she washed her face and hands, added a lip gloss, combed out her hair— mama had insisted that she braid it or wear it in a knot at the back of her head—and trod down the stairs. The laughter and talking reached her before she got to the bottom step. After a deep breath, she laid her shoulders back and headed for the dining room. At the door, she saw an empty seat at one table, judged that to be her only option, and took it.

Total quiet ensued, and she gazed at the empty plate before her, certain that all ten of the boarders were staring at her. But when Fannie finished saying grace, the chatter resumed.

"That's my biscuit, Miss," a man beside her said. "Yours are over there on the left where your fork is."

Heat flushed her face and neck. "Sorry," she murmured.

"Oh, that's all right. Where're you from?"

"Hagerstown."

"That's a nice city. How long you staying?"

"I don't know."

"My name's Joe Tucker. What's yours?"

"Jolene," she said, barely loud enough for him to hear it. Joe turned his attention to Judd Walker, who she'd seen in the lounge that afternoon. What kind of man slicked his hair with conka-line? Her mama would have dismissed as worthless any black man who straightened his hair. She glanced at Joe's fingernails and wondered; they looked like the work of a manicurist. He was a big man, too, she mused, at least six feet four inches tall, and wearing a red corduroy shirt, at that. She shook her head from side to side. "Mama always said, 'It takes all kinds,' and maybe it does." She concentrated on her plate.

At least the food was tasty, Jolene thought and, even if it hadn't been, at least she didn't have to cook it. She focused on the food and didn't allow her gaze to meet anyone else's. As soon as she finished the strawberry shortcake, she left the table with the in-tention of escaping to her room. However, she remembered hav-ing seen newspapers in the lounge and went there to get one.

"Where're you going?" Fannie asked, effectively waylaying her. "We all sit here in the lounge after supper and have coffee or tea and watch the reality shows."

"Well . . . I've, uh . . . had a long day and—"

Fannie's knotted right fist went to her hip. "Listen, Jolene, if you're going to stay here with us, you must try to be friendlier. You walked in tonight and didn't say hello or anything else, and then you walked out without saying excuse me, good night, cat, dog or pig. And Jolene, please don't blot your lipstick with my napkins. It's hard to get it out."

Jolene's stomach began to churn the way it had when her mother berated her. She swallowed the liquid that accumulated in her mouth and reminded herself that Emma Tilman was gone.

"If I've done something to offend you, Fannie, please find a better way to let me know." She reached down, scooped up the newspaper and headed up the stairs. *Nobody is going to tongue lash me, and if Fannie tries it again, she'll find out what it's like.* She hadn't remembered that the napkins were linen because her mama used paper napkins, and she'd wiped her mouth auto-matically. Embroiled in misery, Jolene sat on the edge of the bed, holding her belly with both hands and rocking herself. She didn't

remember having eaten in the company of that many people before. What was she supposed to do and say? It had required all
the courage she could summon just to walk to that chair and sit
down. She took out her tablet and made some notes. *If I have to
learn how other people live*, she said to herself, *I'd better start now*.

Thousands of miles away in Geneva, Switzerland, Richard
Peterson sat alone in his elegant wood-paneled office eating lunch
at a mahogany desk that sprawled across more than one-quarter
of his thirty-foot wide office. Alone and staring at Mont Blanc, a
rare picture-perfect vision on a brilliant sunny day. Alone in the
flesh and alone in the spirit. Although born in Brooklyn near the
bottom of the heap, by the age of forty-five, tall, handsome, and
polished, Richard had scaled the top. However, on the way to
becoming an ambassador and, subsequently, executive-director
of one of the largest and most prestigious nongovernmental or-
ganizations, he ruthlessly trampled his competitors, ignored un-
derlings who needed his help, and used women for his own
ends without regard to their feelings or needs. He also became
a snob, a trim six-foot-four-inch, good-looking and flawlessly
dressed snob.

Richard recognized the justice of his own tragedy: a powerful
man with no interest in or will to use his power. He glanced at
the copy of the *New York Daily News* that his secretary placed beside his luncheon tray and saw the notice of Estelle Mitchell's
marriage. The account merely confirmed what he had known for
months: she was lost to him forever. He stopped eating, leaned
back in his swivel desk chair, and made a pyramid of his fingers.

Hadn't he brought it on himself with his craftiness, his insis-
tence on treating her as he had all other women, as a person un-
deserving of his integrity, a woman to be used? This, in spite of
the fact that she was his equal in status and position. But Estelle
Mitchell had not succumbed to his charm, nor was she bamboo-
zled by his lovemaking, and it was she with whom he had fallen
in love—and too late to correct his behavior. She wanted no part
of him.

"Come in." He sat up straight, brushed his fingers through his semi-straight curls and angled his square-jawed face toward the door.

"Mr. Pichat from France is here to see you sir. He has a two o'clock appointment." Marlene Gupp, his secretary, said.

He wiped his mouth with the white linen napkin, and gestured toward the tray. "Would you remove this, please Marlene? What does Pichat want? I don't remember."

Her eyebrows shot up in an expression of disbelief that he had witnessed often in recent weeks. "Sir, it's about our contribution to the five-year plan."

"Yes, of course."

He didn't see how he could continue the façade, the superficiality, the automatic grins and empty smiles, the shallow women. He no longer cared about the job. He dealt with important world problems that deserved more able attention than he or his cohorts were bringing to it. Oh, what the hell! It wasn't working, and he wanted out. Maybe he would regret it, but he was tired of it all. And to think of the things he'd done in order to sit in that chair, eat at that desk and see Mont Blanc from that window. He'd give anything if . . . He couldn't tolerate the man he had become.

He pasted a smile on his face and stood when Yves Pichat entered. "This is a pleasure, my friend," he said. "Would you like coffee, a glass of Chablis or something stronger?" More shamming. He'd done it so long and so well that he wasn't sure who he was.

Pichat took a seat. "Chablis would be fine. My wife wants to go to the Caribbean before it gets too warm, and you were ambassador to Jamaica. Where should she go and what should she take along?"

Wasn't it always the same? Important men in important jobs running errands for their wives when they should be working to relieve the world's poor. He let a grin expose his white teeth. "How's Michelle? I've got some fliers and brochures here that ought to do the trick." He opened the bottom desk drawer, gave the man the material and prayed that he would be satisfied and leave.

"I presume you've accepted the invitation to our official reception for the prime minister? If you're not there, the single women will want Michelle's head. Some of the married ones, too, I imagine."

Richard lifted his right shoulder and let it fall in a show of diffidence. "You give me too much credit, man."

Pichat left without mentioning the five-year plan or waiting for his Chablis. The man's visit reminded Richard of the reasons why he had begun to alter his way of life. Sick of its shallowness, he had begun to reject the high social life that he had once relished, indeed thrived on, to eat his lunch alone at his desk and to confine social interaction to what the job required. He stood at a precipice looking down at the great unknown, his life's great divide into periods BE and AE, the era before Estelle rejected him and the period after she walked out of his life for good. A watershed, and he had to live with it. If he had known the price would be so high, would he have lived differently? He thought so.

"What do you mean, you aren't going to seek reelection?" The executive-director of a sister nongovernmental organization asked Richard as they strolled along the banks of Lac Leman one March evening at sunset.

"Just that. I've had enough. I'm going back to the states."

"Hmm. Wouldn't have anything to do with a certain assistant S-G in New York, would it?"

"Only indirectly. She's in the past."

"Yes. I know."

"Where're you planning to settle?"

"A small town somewhere, preferably near the ocean or, at least near a large lake or big river. I need to live near the water."

"I know just the place. It's a small town in Maryland right on the Atlantic Ocean. I've vacationed there a couple of times, and when I retire I'm going to settle there." He wrote something on a card and handed it to Richard. "Don't let the name fool you. It's a great place if you don't want your own house or apartment."

"May be just what I'm looking for. Thanks, friend."

Lean, fit, and self-confident, as usual, Richard stepped out of the taxi—a bedraggled vehicle that had seen better days—and

looked up at the big white green-shuttered house before him. If
he got back in that automobile and headed for the luxury he
knew he'd find in Ocean City, he would defeat the purpose of
his trip. He'd try it for a few days.

"It's a nice place, sir," the driver, an aged and whiskered
black man, assured him. "We all know Miss Fannie, a good God-
fearing woman who'll mother any human she comes across.
She'll take good care of you. If I had time, I'd go in and see if I
could buy a few biscuits."

Richard counted out the fare and added a five dollar bill for a
tip. "She's a good cook?"

"Somebody there is." He tipped his old seaman's cap.
"Thank you kindly. If you need a ride, just ask Miss Fannie for
Dan. She'll call me."

Richard put a bag under his right arm, picked up another one
with his right hand, took a third one in his left hand and headed
up the walk. Just before he reached the door, Fannie stepped out.

"Glad you got here safe and sound, Mr. Peterson. I'm Fannie
Johnson." She reached for the bag in his left hand."

"Oh, I can manage this," he said, startled that she would attempt to relieve him of his heavy load. The women to whom he
had become accustomed wouldn't consider relieving a man of a
burden. "You just hold the door."

"I'll show you your room. We can talk on the way upstairs."
She punched what proved to be an intercom button. "Rodger,
would you please come and take Mr. Peterson's bags up to his
room."

He appreciated a business-like person, but the litany of regu-
lations that rolled off the woman's tongue made him nervous.
"At least I'm allowed to have wine with my dinner," he said, offering a mild protest.

"It's late for lunch, but I can get you a sandwich. Ham or
turkey?"

"If you have any warm biscuits, I'd like the ham."

"Be downstairs in fifteen minutes. Your food will be on the
dining room table. We use first names here. I'm Fannie. May we
call you Richard?"

Taken aback by her casual use of his first name, a frown clouded his face. "Uh, well . . . yes, of course."

She looked hard at him before adding "Been a long time since I had a full house." With that she strode out of the room and swished down the stairs singing, "How Great Thou Art," a religious song that he'd heard his mother sing at least a hundred times.

He looked at his suitcases and remembered that for the last ten years, his butler had packed and unpacked his bags, hung his clothes and seen to his laundry and dry cleaning. With a quick shrug, he walked over to the window for a view of his surroundings and gasped. There before him lay the vast expanse of ocean, or maybe it was a bay, but beyond the shore, he could see nothing but water. His gaze took in the room, a neat and graciously furnished, though not luxurious, chamber. Beige and white. He liked that. After inspecting the bathroom, he decided that if everything else suited him as well, he'd stay a while.

Richard ambled downstairs and wandered around until he found the dining room. He stood transfixed at the door, for seeing the twelve places set for a meal discombobulated him. He hadn't counted on being a member of a community of strangers. His plan had been to stow himself away in a quiet place, write his memoirs, and figure out what to do with the rest of his life, a life that didn't include Estelle Mitchell.

"Come on, sit down before these biscuits get cold," a plump and heavy-hipped black woman in a white dress and apron said to him. "You must be our new boarder. I'm Marilyn, and if you want to eat good, you got to treat me right." She flashed him a smile. A flirtatious smile. The weapon of a woman who knew how to handle men. "What's your name?"

"Peterson."

She put her hands on her hips and looked at him from beneath lowered lashes. "That your first name?"

As his gaze swept over her, he remembered that they didn't know who he was or how he was accustomed to being treated. "My first name is Richard."

Her white teeth glistened, and the dimple in her left cheek

winked at him. For a woman who had to be in her late fifties, this one was a piece of work. But she was also the kind of woman he'd played with in his philandering days, and before he realized what he was doing, his right arm went around her shoulder and the grin that had always accompanied his bursts of charisma captured his face.

"I plan to eat well," he said. "Very well." *What the hell am I doing encouraging this woman? This sort of thing is behind me.* He pulled a curtain of solemnity over his face. "I'd better get to those biscuits while they're still warm."

"Not to worry, honey. I can always heat 'em up." She left and returned with a glass of iced tea and a dish of raspberry cobbler. "Do you have any diet problems like no fat, no salt, vegetarian?" she asked.

"Uh, no. I eat anything except rhubarb, chitterlings, and brains." He thanked her for the food and, after eating, looked at the two new keys Fannie gave him and struck out for the beach. He'd heard it said that a leopard didn't change its spots but, by damn, his days of taking women for the sport of it were behind him.

With his shoes in his hands, Richard stood on the sandy beach and stared out at the ocean. He couldn't see anyone or anything but water. Shading his eyes from the sun's rays, his thoughts went to Estelle and what he wouldn't give to frolic there with her knowing that she was his. He shook himself out of it and headed back to the boarding house.

What did a man do with his spare time in Pike Hill? As he walked back to his new home, it occurred to him that he hadn't seen a building more than three stories high, no public transportation, and that there were very few moving automobiles. Well, he had wanted a change, and he had one now. The problem was what he'd do with it.

Over the last ten years, he had dressed for dinner every evening, and fifty percent of the time he wore a tuxedo. He shook the sand out of his socks, threw them on the closet floor, washed up and looked through a suitcase for something to put on. He settled on a blue dress shirt with the collar open and an oxford gray suit. He put a red tie in the pocket of his jacket in case he needed it, grabbed the second section of *The Maryland Journal* and walked down the stairs—he had always loved a winding staircase—to the dining room. A peep from where he stood at the door assured him that he didn't need the tie that, indeed, a pair of Wranglers would have been adequate.

He looked around for a place to sit, saw an empty table for two in the corner and rushed to claim it. Rodger, the porter who carried his bags to his room, had become a waiter, and he nodded slightly to the man who greeted him as would an old friend.

"How far'd you go down the bay this afternoon? I tried to ketch ya to tell you not to get your feet wet. We got a lot of jellyfish right now, and I tell you those buggers can sting. Fore you know it, you'll be hobbling back here with your feet feelin' like they on fire. Cook's got some mighty good shrimp soufflé to start, or would you rather have oyster chowder?"

"What? Does she serve things like that every evening?"

"Rodgers broad grin exposed his left, gold bicuspid. "If you like fish and seafood, the eatin' here is real good. Soul food ain't bad either. Marilyn's a fine cook, and she's got a real good helper."

"I'll take the chowder." Rodger left, and Richard opened his newspaper, as he would have done if dining alone in a restaurant.

A brown skirt appeared beside the table, and he looked up into Fannie's frowning face. "Richard, everybody's looking at you. This isn't a restaurant. We're all family here, and we don't read the paper during meals; we talk to each other. I'm gonna say grace, and then I'll introduce you and my other new boarder. A glance around the room and his gaze caught the other uncomfortable person in the room.

Fannie said the grace and added. "We have a full house now, thank the good Lord. I want you all to meet Jolene Tilman, who joined us yesterday. I neglected to introduce her last night at supper, and I apologize. This gentleman is Richard Peterson. He came to us all the way from Europe. Switzerland, I believe. Welcome both of you. Now, let's eat."

"No place left for me to sit but right here with you, Richard," Fannie said, "so you can read your newspaper later upstairs when you don't have anybody to talk to. These people may not have been to Europe and seen the world, but they're good folks, and if you let yourself get to know 'em, you'll like 'em and you may even learn something."

He had hoped not to have a dinner partner, but he suspected that he'd drawn the least disagreeable one. "Give me time to find my way here," he said, trying to keep the harshness out of his tone. "I'm a careful man."

"Maybe. Just make sure you don't look down on anybody. You can't look at a person and tell what he's like inside."

Marilyn appeared at the table, saving him the need for a response. "How's your chowder, Richard? You want some cornbread to go with it? My cornbread's so good it walks all by itself."

"I'll bet it does. The chowder is wonderful. I'll take the cornbread next time since I've just about finished this." He loved cornbread and he wanted it with the rest of his chowder, but he didn't want Marilyn in his hair, and he could see that she was primed for it.

When the cook left the table, he said to Fannie, seeking her estimation of the woman, "She's a nice person, very motherly."

Fannie's laugh startled him. "Motherly? Marilyn? That woman doesn't have a maternal bone in her body. Biggest hussy that ever walked. She's tried every man in here, except Judd, and I can see that you're next."

"Thanks for warning me."

"What you planning to do with your time? You can't spend all of it on the beach, 'less you want to look like a lobster. The school could use you. The library, too. You look like a person with a lot of good experience."

A person with good experience. What the hell! He had signed his letter to her with his title, executive-director. Didn't she know what that was, for heaven's sake? "I'm hoping to find the peace and quiet I need in which to write my memoirs, and this seems like the perfect place."

She rolled her eyes to the ceiling and pulled air through her front teeth. "Humph. So you planning to spend your time *on* yourself and *with* yourself. That has never brought anybody anything. You get something when you give something. I don't eat dessert. Enjoy yours."

She left the table, but her words stayed with him. For as long as he could remember, he had focused on himself, what he wanted, and how he'd get it. But when he finally reached the pinnacle, his trophy ran like water through his fingers, and only then had he realized what was really important to him. Too late. Much too late.

Encumbered by the weight of his past indiscretions, he climbed the stairs as if he had gained a ton since ambling down those same steps an hour earlier. He took out his cell phone and placed it on his night table. If he could only talk with her just once! He'd promised himself that he would never do it, but he opened the cell phone to call her and then slumped on the bed. It didn't work in that remote area. Thank God. He'd almost done the unpardonable, and he prayed he would never again be tempted.

Jolene could hardly hear her own voice when she slipped into her seat at supper that evening and said, "Hi," hoping that Joe and the woman on the other side of her whose name she didn't know would hear her. Neither responded, but she'd done her duty, and she contented herself with that fact. Still, with everyone around her telling tales in a jocular manner, she couldn't help feeling excluded. Alone. At least when mama's voice had sounded from the rafters, it was meant for her to hear and respond to. A woman across the table reached for the salt, and Jolene hastened to get it and hand it to her, and when she saw that only three squares of cornbread were left on the plate, she passed the plate to her neighbors hoping that they would respond in some way.

"I already had my share," Joe said. "Take one for yourself, or maybe Louvenia over there wants one."

"Sure is good," Louvenia said. "You know I cooked for years, Joe, but I can't say mine were any better than these. Marilyn knows what she's doing."

"She does that," he replied.

Jolene had a sense of defeat. Her gesture had sparked conversation, but it wasn't directed to her. Maybe she should take a course of some kind. As soon as she ate the last crumb of her apple pie, she said, "Excuse me," and got up from the table. She wasn't sure that Joe or Louvenia heard her.

"What a waste!" Jolene thought she heard Louvenia say. "Youth is wasted on women like that one."

As she started to walk away, Joe said, "Look, babe, when we leave the table, we push in our chair, so whoever passes won't stumble over it."

Mortified at having received another reprimand and angry at herself for provoking it, she stared down at him. "No . . . you look." She sucked in her breath. "Sorry. I didn't know it was a custom. Good night."

"Hey, I didn't mean to upset you. That's just the way I talk. Don't let nothing get to ya, babe. Life's too short. Good night."

"Good night," she repeated, loud enough for all those present to hear her. She got upstairs to her room as quickly as she could and stood for a long time at the window, staring out at the eerie shadows in the park that faced her. The next morning after breakfast, she received another surprise when Fannie asked whether she was planning to look for a job and whether she wanted any help.

"You ought to look for a church, too. I'll be glad to take you along to mine. People there will be glad to receive you. You and Richard need to learn how to get along with people. They're not gonna eat you. It's people who make your life good. I know just the person for you to meet."

"Who?" Maybe she would make a friend, someone who cared about her.

Fannie looked down at the floor. "How old are you?"

"Thirty-five. Why?"

"Come to church with me Sunday, and we'll let the Lord take it from there."

Chapter Two

Jolene wasn't anxious to go to church, not Fannie's or anyone else's. Before her mama became ill, she was in Mount Zion Church every time the doors opened, with her mama giving praise and testifying. But to Jolene's way of thinking, a more unrighteous woman probably had never been conceived. However, she needed a friend, any friend to whom she could feel close. At least she thought that was what she needed. The empty void inside of her was a new experience, or maybe it had always been there, and she'd been so harassed, so put upon that she hadn't had time for self-reflection. So, the following Sunday morning, she dressed in her gray and white, short-sleeved seersucker suit and went with Fannie to eleven o'clock service at Disciples Baptist Church on Martin Luther King Jr. Avenue, a twenty-minute walk from the boarding house.

"I'd ask Rodger to drive us," Fannie explained when Jolene wanted to know how much farther they had to walk, "but this is his Sunday off. Any way, it isn't much farther. Besides, Rodger's a good man, who can't seem to say no, not even in his own defense. I'm careful not to take advantage of him."

At the end of the long service, Fannie's friends crowded around them, welcoming Jolene and asking her to come to the church regularly. So profuse was their welcome that Jolene began to wonder if Fannie had programmed them. Just as she began to tire of the smile she'd placed on her face and of the hugs and handshakes, Fannie pulled her from the group.

"Gregory, this is Jolene who I've been telling you about. She's just come to Thank the Lord Boarding House, and she's such a joy to be around. Like cool, fresh air on a hot sticky day. Jolene Tilman, Gregory Hicks is one of our most faithful members, and we're very proud of him."

Jolene gazed at the man, tall enough—about five feet, eleven inches—and nice looking. Her mama didn't trust light skinned men, but she remembered that Emma Tilman didn't trust *any* man, and forgave Gregory Hicks for his fair skin.

When Hicks extended his hand, Jolene took it, but mainly because she didn't want Fannie to lecture her about her manners. "Glad to meet you, Mr. Hicks," she said.

"I'm certainly glad to meet you. Miss Fannie didn't tell me how pretty you are. I hope I'll be seeing a lot of you."

When Fannie's fist dug into her back, Jolene recovered her presence of mind and said, "That would be nice." She didn't think she was supposed to wilt just because a man smiled.

Gregory's eyes glistened as would a child's at the sight of a new toy. "If you don't mind, I'll call you tomorrow evening after supper time. It would be my pleasure to show you our little town and maybe take you over to Ocean Pines."

"Thank you," Jolene said. "So far, I haven't seen any of the place." Her interest quickened when it occurred to her that he could give her some pointers on getting a job and making a place for herself in the community. "I'll look to hear from you," she said, glanced at Fannie and saw that the woman wore her approval the way a prince displays his crown.

"Hmm. Looks like I'm pleasing all three of us," Jolene said to herself.

"You're smarter than I thought you were," Fannie said as they walked back home. "Gregory's a good catch. He's got a good job over in Ocean Pines, doesn't run around with a lot of loose women, and he saves his money. He's also a Christian. You won't find better anywhere around here."

It surprised her that Fannie assumed she was looking for a

man. The thought hadn't occurred to her. She wanted a job and some friends or companions that, from her earliest memory, her mother had denied her. And she wanted to be rid of that awful feeling deep in her gut that if she died, nobody would care. She wasn't averse to male company, but she didn't know how to act with a man. Mama said all they wanted was to empty themselves into you and leave you with the consequences. She wasn't sure mama was right; if she was, why did so many women attach themselves to a man?

Besides, her mama had never said one good thing about men. Indeed, she even refused to tell Jolene who her daddy was, claiming that she hated him so much that she refused to mention his name. It seemed to Jolene that she had a right to know. After her mama died, she went through all of her personal papers, but could find nothing that revealed her father's identity. As her mind pondered her mother's reasons, she accidentally bit the flesh on the inside of her right jaw and, not for the first time, knew the taste of her own blood. It occurred to her that not many people disliked their mothers, as she had and still did, and that she had her distaste for Emma since childhood.

She's dead, and I'm still not free of her.

"You're mighty quiet," Fannie said as they neared the boarding house.

"Yes, ma'am. Just thinking back about things."

That evening, Fannie called up to Jolene with the news that Gregory wanted to speak with her on the telephone. Shock reverberated from Jolene's scalp to the ends of her toes. She hadn't expected to hear from him so soon. Mindful of Fannie's strict house rules, she threw off her robe, donned an old house dress that she had worn during her mama's illness and raced down the stairs.

"Hello. This is Jolene." She hated that she sounded breathless and that he would know she ran to take his call.

"This is Gregory. There's an old movie about Dr. King showing at that movie house on Ocean Road near you. Would you like to go tomorrow evening about eight thirty? Supper ought to be over by then."

"Uh . . . yes. Thanks." As soon as she agreed, she had an attack of nerves, for she had no idea how to deal with a man. If mama was facing her eternal judgment, she had a lot to account for.

"Good. I'll be at Miss Fannie's place for you at eight o'clock sharp."

She hung up and turned to see Fannie standing nearby, folding and unfolding her hands. "He's coming here for you, isn't he?"

Jolene nodded and fled up the stairs. Shaken. She had agreed to go out with a man. A date. The first date she'd ever had. If the behavior of the church women was any measure, her date was a man who appealed to females. He certainly looked good to her, especially his big, grayish-brown eyes with their long, silky lashes. She guessed she was doing all right.

"I've been looking for a nice girl," Gregory said to Jolene, taking her hand as they left the movie theater, "and I'd like us to be friends."

Jolene let him hold her hand, because his grip gave her a warm, comfortable feeling. "I'd like it, too. Right now, I have to get a job."

"I'm a phone company supervisor over in Ocean Pines, but I hope that's temporary. It's my intention to manufacture sails. If you want to make money around here, you have to do something connected with water, and I've noticed that no one anywhere near here makes or repairs sails."

"Do you know how to make them?" she asked, her interest piqued.

"Sure." He seemed to dismiss the question as trite. "If you need a lift from time to time, I'll be glad to help during the weekends. Other days, I'm working till four-thirty."

Jolene thought for a minute. There was something he could help her with. A telephone company supervisor would be a trusted person. "I'm going to have trouble getting a job, because all I've done the past ten years is take care of my sick mother and grandmother, and I don't know anybody here except Fannie." She held her breath as she waited for his response and let it out slowly when a smile floated over his face.

"After all the good things Miss Fannie said about you, I can certainly give you a character reference." He wrote something on a card and handed it to her. "When you apply for a job, tell them to call Gregory Hicks."

"I sure do thank you, Gregory." If he worked at the phone company, maybe he could get her a phone.

"It's getting warm enough to swim," he said as they approached the boarding house. "We could go swimming Saturday afternoon, if you're not busy."

Her feeling of inadequacy was never far from her consciousness, and it returned with alacrity. She stopped walking, withdrew her hand from his and looked at him. "Gregory, I don't swim. My mama always saw to it that I didn't have a free moment for any kind of recreation. I can't even dance."

He took her hand again and started up the stone steps. "I'm going to enjoy teaching you to do both."

They entered the foyer, and he took a pad from his pocket, wrote his home and cell phone numbers on it, tore off the page, and handed it to her. "Here are my numbers, in case you need me for something."

This was her chance. "You shouldn't call me too often because the phone is down here in the hall, and Fannie or somebody has to call me to come downstairs." She hoped he'd take the hint, but he said nothing, kissed her on the cheek and left.

Gregory headed down the street to where he'd parked his white Ford Taurus. Invigorated. Wondering if his ship was about to dock. One look at Jolene Tilman and he'd fallen hard. It hadn't made sense, so he'd called immediately and asked for a date in order to test the attraction. Now, he knew. It was there, and it was solid. He wanted her: A woman who was simple, reserved, maybe even shy, plainly dressed but with large brown eyes that seemed to reflect the wisdom and secrets of the ages. Yes, and pain, too. Even as he acknowledged his introduction to her, he had imagined himself nestled in her arms, sucking at her pretty breasts and then losing himself inside of her. But he was in no hurry for that. He had learned the hard way not to let his penis lead him. Leaning against the shiny-white Taurus, his long El Greco-like silhouette spanning the width of Ocean Road, he made up his mind to have Jolene for himself. Maybe not permanently, but for as long as he wanted her.

Around three o'clock the following Saturday afternoon, he arrived at Thank the Lord Boarding House prepared to swim. "We're going to start in the pool," he told Jolene, referring to the public pool in the park that faced the boarding house. He hoped she'd wear a scanty bikini, but he doubted that she would. Still, the one-piece suit she wore allowed him to see enough of her high, firm breasts and rounded hips to whet his appetite.

"You have to trust me," he told her.

Her glance might have withered a weaker man. "If I didn't, do you think I'd be standing here in water up to my waist and nobody nearby to keep me from drowning but you?"

"Hardly. Would you mind smiling? I haven't seen you do it yet."

A startled expression slipped over her face and then, in a grudging way, her face creased into a smile. He looked away. *I'll be damned if I'll make a fool of myself over her.*

"We'll start with the breast stroke. It's easier than the crawl, or at least, it was for me."

After an hour, he suggested that they dress and go for a ride. "Unless you have something else you'd like to do."

"Not a thing. Thanks for the lesson. How'd I do?"

"You did well, but don't try it alone."

"Oh, I won't. I'll wait till you're free again."

They dried themselves in the warm sunshine, dressed and got into his car. "With this, you won't have any trouble getting my calls." He handed her a cellular phone. "I've already set it up for you, and I wrote the phone number on the box."

Her eyes widened, and he sucked in his breath when both of her arms reached for his neck. Quickly, he held her away from him. Plenty of time for that when he was ready.

"Thanks so much, Gregory. I didn't see how I could have af-

forded to put a phone in my room. This is the perfect solution."
She cradled the phone to her breasts. "Gee, thanks."

His frown lingered on his face for he thought he detected a
note of triumph in her voice, and then he shook his head as if
that would discard the notion. He might have imagined it, but
just in case he hadn't, he'd be careful.

"You stay to yourself, do you?" Judd Walker observed when
he entered the dining room the next morning and sat at a table
with Richard, deliberately with the intention of annoying him,
for Richard always sat alone at the little table for two, unless
Fannie joined him.

"I've found that a man travels fastest when he travels alone,"
Richard replied without moving his gaze from the front page of
The Maryland Journal.

"Where you in a hurry to get to? All I've seen you do is walk
along the beach. You don't have to hurry to get to that; it's been
there since the beginning of time, and it'll probably be there till
Judgment Day."

Richard put the paper aside and sipped his coffee. "I'm used
to being busy."

"I suppose you are. Everybody here's been busier than they
are now. All except Lila Mae Henry, the fourth grade teacher.
She's still working. And there's Percy Lucas. He still drives an
eighteen wheeler, though he's cut down to three days a week on
the East Coast. You're young. Why don't you go back to work?
You're not sick, are you?"

Richard leaned back and stared at the old man. "You don't
want my life history, do you?"

A rumble came out of Judd's throat in the form of a belly
laugh. "I'll bet it's interesting. Not many men your age would
try to give me my comeuppance. I'll be eighty-five before this
year is up."

Richard had thought the man at least ten years younger. "You
don't look it."

"That's because a glass of wine or one bottle of beer is m'

limit, I never smoked, never caroused, and I haven't made a fool of m'self over women."

"I can't say the same."

"I know you can't. What you running away from? Or should I ask *who* you running from? When I was your age, I owned and managed one of the biggest canneries in Cambridge, which is why I can do as I please now."

Richard suspected that his tolerance for the old man's meddling was about to expire, but he didn't want to be rude. Judd didn't know who he really was and that he was accustomed to some deference. People didn't sit at his table uninvited and didn't ask him personal questions, either. He decided to get some answers himself, since the man wanted to talk.

"Why don't we get some more coffee and drink it in the lounge?" he asked Judd, "So Rodger and Marilyn can straighten up the dining room."

"Don't mind if I do."

"How long have you been living here?" Richard asked after they settled in the lounge.

"Thirteen years. I've been here longer than any of the present boarders. Fannie opened it a few months before I came. Most of the folks have been here over five years. I couldn't ask for a better home because I don't have to do a thing for m'self unless I want to. The place is comfortable, the food is great, and I'm not by m'self. I'm with people I like."

"You . . . uh . . . never married?" Richard wanted to know how it felt to live one's life alone, and maybe lonely, as he was.

"I've been a widower for thirty-one years. We didn't have any children. I have a niece who keeps in touch with me and a nephew who comes by to see me at Christmas and calls from time to time. My family's here in this house."

He drained his coffee cup. "You're a remarkable man. I want to get some writing done this morning. See you at lunch."

"Looks like it's gonna rain, so I'll be down here if you get bored up there."

Richard lifted his hand in a slight wave and went up to his room. He had to admit that the conversation with Judd had been a satisfying one, even if it consisted mainly of Judd's quizzing him. He didn't have a single person with whom to discuss the situation in the Middle East, the reconstruction of Angola, pollution of the environment, or any of the other issues that had been a part of his daily concerns for the past dozen years. The people with whom he lived had no idea who he was or what he was capable of accomplishing and didn't care. Why had his Swiss friend thought that he would be content in such a place and among people who didn't think far beyond their next meal? A gust of wind sucked the curtain out of the window, and he hastened to close his room door. "You can't look at a book and judge its contents," Fannie had lectured, and he knew that, but these books seemed to have blank pages.

I have to find something to do before I go insane. If I could just tell somebody how I feel! Maybe the old man plays chess.

He closed his window and went back to the lounge where he found Judd reading a newspaper. "You don't happen to play chess, do you?"

Judd rested the paper on his right knee, fingered his chin and angled his face toward Richard. "We never did meet properly. M'name's Judd Walker. Chess? Don't know the first rule, but I'll go a few games of blackjack with you."

Richard walked up to Judd and extended his right hand. "I'm Richard Peterson, and I'm not very good at blackjack, but I expect you can give me some pointers."

"If I wasn't busy cooking your lunch, I'd take both of you to the cleaners in some cutthroat pinochle." Richard looked up to see Marilyn standing over him with a glass of lemonade. "It's pretty hot, Richard, and I figured you could use a little help cooling off."

"The air conditioning works fine for me," he said. "Maybe Judd needs it."

"I wouldn't mind some lemonade," Judd said, "but that's not the kind of cooling off Marilyn has in mind." He leaned back and fixed his gaze on her. "I'm old, but I ain't deaf or dumb, and m'memory's fine, so don't think your insinuations will pass over m' head. And another thing. M'daddy fathered his last child when he was eighty-seven."

"Yeah? I'll bet you scored a few in your day." She said to Judd, turned and left without looking at Richard.

Nearly a minute passed before Richard absorbed the import of Judd's words. "You're a cagey one. I thought she was actually talking about the climate."

Judd shrugged. "She's one you have to watch. If you're not careful, you'll be looking for another boardinghouse, though I don't think there's another good one anywhere around here."

"What's Fannie's reaction to having her boarders move because her cook crowds them a bit too closely?"

Judd's laugh did not reassure Richard. "Fannie's practical. A room never stays vacant more than a week or ten days, but where's she going to find another cook like Marilyn? The woman's cooking is legend in these parts, and she's completely dependable."

Richard didn't like what he was hearing. Estelle was the last woman he'd wanted, and a fire for her still burned hotly within him, but he knew himself well. If he got the itch, he'd let any woman who appealed to him scratch it, and Marilyn's age didn't detract from her blatant sexiness.

"She's too old to play games," he said to Judd.

"Don't fool yourself. She'll play, and so will you."

"Time was, but those days are behind me."

Judd reached down to the bottom sheif of the coffee table, picked up a pack of cards and shuffled them. "You can be certain of that when they lay you in a box." He shuffled the cards again. "Cut."

That afternoon, just before five o'clock, Jolene telephoned Gregory as he left his office. "I just wanted to try out my new phone on you. Where are you?"

He had expected her to call earlier, but it pleased him that she used discretion about contacting him while he was at work. "I've just left the office. If you're not busy, I could drive by your place, and we could spend a couple of hours together."

"I'd like that. I got two phone calls today about possible job opportunities, and I'm thinking about taking the job in Salisbury. How would I get there?"

"We'll talk about that when I see you, which should be in about twenty minutes."

To his surprise, she didn't wait for him to ring the doorbell but stepped out of the door as he parked in front of the house. He didn't know what to think of that and wasn't sure he liked it. However, he had no reason for suspicion, so he dismissed it, supposing that she was eager to be outside in the near-perfect weather.

He got out of the car and went to meet her, bent down and kissed her quickly on her lips. Her eyes widened, and she looked back toward the front door, leading him into a moment of self-examination. He asked himself why he'd kissed her on the mouth and didn't have an answer. Surely, he knew better than to be impulsive when it came to women. He also wanted to know who she thought might have seen the innocent kiss and whether that person had a special interest in it. He opened the passenger door for her, went around and seated himself.

"There's a bus going to Salisbury every hour on the hour daily, and from seven to nine mornings, it leaves on the half hour as well. You get it on the corner of Bay Avenue and Ocean Road right by Joe's Watering Hole."

"That's only two blocks from the boarding house."

"Right." That settled, he had some questions for her. "Where did you go to school, Jolene?" He pulled away from the curb and headed toward Ocean Pines.

"In Hagerstown where I grew up. I only finished high school. Mama said I didn't need to waste money on college. She wouldn't even buy me a prom dress."

He reached across her and flipped on the radio. "Something tells me I didn't miss anything important by not meeting her. She sounds like a hard woman." He noticed that Jolene played with her hands, lacing her fingers, buffing her nails on her thigh, and resting her hands intermittently on her knees, her belly, and in her lap. Yet, she hadn't spoken as if she were nervous.

"I've been blessed," he said, musing aloud. "As a child, my parents doted on me. They still do. We're a loving family. Very close and always there for each other. I doubt anybody had less money than we had. I wore shoes to school that had holes in them, and you could see all ten of my toes, but I was a happy child."

"Didn't your feet get cold?"

"What do you think? Sometimes I thought that they had frozen. But I didn't complain, because I knew that whenever my parents got a few cents to spare, they spent it on me. As long as I'm living, they won't want for anything. I'm building them a retirement home."

"Before you build a home for yourself?"

His head snapped around. "Why do you ask that?"

She moved from her slouched position and sat erect. "I think it means you're unusual."

"Maybe I am." He didn't like the turn of conversation, but he had to give her the benefit of the doubt. From what she'd told him, she hadn't had much experience with give and take, except that she gave, and her mother and grandmother took.

She seemed thoughtful, and he waited until she spoke. "I hope you don't mind my asking why you haven't married."

It was a fair question. "I borrowed every penny of my college tuition and, with the low-paying jobs I was able to get until recently, it took me ten years to repay the money. I got engaged a while after that, and it proved to be the biggest mistake of my life; she wasn't what I'd thought. I saw all the signs and ignored them, so you could say it was my fault I got mired in that relationship. Since then, I haven't allowed myself to step into the trough of romance. You might say I've been wary. The moral of the story is, never lower your standards." She didn't like that, but she didn't know why.

In Ocean Pines, he turned off Route 90 into Harpoon Road and stopped. "Want some ice cream?" he asked Jolene. "I can't resist an ice cream truck. When I was little, there wasn't any money for ice cream."

"Thanks. I'll have whatever you're having."

He bought them each a cone of butter pecan ice cream and, with the driver's door open, sat with one foot on the pavement and the other in the car while he ate his.

I've spent two afternoons with her, he thought, but I haven't

learned much more about her than I knew when I met her. I want her,
but if she wants me, she's damned clever at hiding it.

He put his left foot into the car, closed the door, started the
engine and headed back to Pike Hill and the Thank the Lord
Boarding House. Surely, a feeling as strong as his couldn't be
one-sided. Inside the foyer, he pressed his lips to her cheek.

"See you at church Sunday?" She nodded, but her gaze un-
settled him. He didn't try to decipher it. In due course, he'd
know what he needed to know. One thing was certain: He didn't
plan to come out of it the loser.

A glance at the big clock in the foyer told Jolene that she had
nearly an hour before supper, time to relax and wash up. Gregory
thought a lot of her, she was sure of it. Ambling upstairs, she
hummed, "In the Sweet Bye and Bye," one of her mama's favorite songs.

She stopped humming and turned around when Arnetha
Farrell, a retired nurse's aide, called to her. "Girl, you sure are a
fast worker," Arnetha said, a big grin exposing the gold that
framed her two upper front teeth. "I never would a thought it of
you. So quiet and all. But they say still waters run deep." A tall
woman with dark, ashy skin and in the habit of wearing more
makeup than would suit a teenager, Arnetha was both imposing
and comical.

"I don't know what you're talking about," Jolene said.

"Come on, now." Arnetha's voice dripped with honey and
warmth. "I saw Gregory Hicks kiss you right there in the foyer.
Half the young women at church are after him, but you been
here three weeks or so, and he's already kissing you. Girl, you
go get 'em."

"We're only friends," Jolene said, exasperation giving a
sharpness to her voice, and headed up the stairs.

"Only friends! Did you hear that? Only friends don't kiss,"
she heard Arnetha say to someone.

"You have to watch 'em nowadays," a female voice replied.
"I hope Fannie knows what she's doing letting everybody in

here. This has been a decent, peaceful place, but before you know it, the house will be crawling with every Tom, Dick, and Harry who's after a roll in the hay."

"You said it," Arnetha replied. "I don't know what these young people are coming to."

Jolene turned and walked back down the stairs. "How are you, Miss Arnetha? Miss Louvenia? After listening to you two, I've just decided not to go to church tomorrow. I always thought my mother was a big hypocrite, but the two of you make her seem saintly."

Without waiting for a reaction, she went to her room and called Gregory on her new cellular phone. "I've decided not to go to church tomorrow," she said after greeting him. "I'll explain it when we meet."

"I see. Well, there isn't much to do around here on Sundays except see a movie, and we've seen the one that's playing."

If he was trying to avoid seeing her, he could forget it. "Then let's drive over to Ocean City or maybe Salisbury."

His silence lasted too long for her comfort. "I'll be over right after church," he finally said, but she detected a change in his tone.

Maybe I should have gone to church, but I didn't feel like watching those two old biddies shouting and praising. They're as mean as my mama was."

"We've got company for supper tonight," Fannie announced that evening before saying the grace. "Joe Tucker's kid brother, Bob, is with us. Welcome, Bob. Let's bow our heads."

Bob Tucker, sitting between Jolene and his brother, Joe, fidgeted throughout the prayer. "You seem out of place in this bunch," he said to Jolene. "What're you doing here?"

She focused on the plate of soup in front of her. "Telling will take too long."

"In that case, how about going down to Joe's Watering Hole with me after we eat?"

"Not tonight, Bob."

"You got a date?"

"I have something to do." She wanted to go with him, but couldn't bring herself to risk it, and she knew he could read the eagerness on her face.

He put his spoon down and let his gaze roam over her face. "All right. How about next weekend and we go over to Baltimore and check out the scene? This place is dullsville."

Excitement coursed through her. "I'll let you know."

"All right. What's your name?"

"Jolene Tilman. You live around here?"

"Naah. I live just outside of Ocean Pines. We'll get together next Saturday or Sunday."

"Bob's not overloaded with compassion for people," Joe Tucker told Jolene the next morning at breakfast. "He's not going to do anything wrong; too much pride for that. But he looks out for himself, and anybody else, male or female, can catch as catch can." She suspected that he'd rushed to breakfast early in order to warn her about Bob, for he hadn't buttoned the cuffs of his red shirt.

His stern expression gave her the willies, but only momentarily. If Bob would take her to Baltimore a few times, maybe she could find a job there instead of in Salisbury. She had money from the funds her mother left her and from the sale of the house, but she didn't intend to spend a penny more of it than was absolutely necessary.

"So what was your reason for not coming to church this morning?" Gregory asked her as soon as he drove away from the boarding house that Sunday afternoon.

He listened to her tale of Arnetha's comment and Louvenia's speculations about her with barely any interest. But when she added, "I couldn't appreciate a church service with those two women amening and shouting all around me," his head snapped around, and she thought he braked abruptly.

His stare held anything but the warmth and compassion she had associated with him. Indeed, it seemed hostile. "I hope you're kidding," he said.

Realizing that she had dropped a few notches in his estimation, she hastened to redeem herself by playing upon his sympathy. "I hope I'm going to see you on my birthday, since you're my only good friend."

He rubbed his chin slowly and, she didn't doubt, thoughtfully. "Your birthday is when?"

"Wednesday."

He didn't respond until after he'd parked in the parking lot
of a roadside movie house on the outskirts of Ocean City, got out
of the car and opened the door for her. He stood beside the car,
inches from her, staring down into her face until her nerves seemed
to stand on end. After what seemed like ages, with his fingers
raking over his tight curls, he said," Would you like to go out to
dinner?"

She caught herself a split second before she said, *I'm paying for
my supper at the boarding house.* "Thanks. I . . . uh . . . I'd like that."

He didn't respond. Somewhere, she'd made a mistake, for he
had little to say then or on the drive back from Ocean City, and
he didn't suggest that they swim as she had hoped he would.

"I'd like to get home early. PBS is showing a story on Muddy
Waters tonight."

"I wish I could see it," she said. "I can't imagine the folks at
the boarding house letting me watch that in the lounge."

He parked, went around to the passenger side and opened
the door for her. "They probably won't. Well, I've received several calls requesting references for you, so you'll soon be working, and you can put a television in your room."

When she walked into her room, two thoughts plagued her:
Gregory hadn't offered to give her a television for her birthday,
and he didn't kiss her on the cheek as he'd previously done.

At supper that night, she wanted to ask Joe Tucker, her seat
mate, what he thought of Louvenia, but decided against it and
was glad she did when the two of them began to carry on a conversation across from her. She wondered if any of the other
boarders felt as lonely as she, an outsider who the others ignored. In the far corner, Richard Peterson, who joined the group
after she did, carried on what appeared to be an amiable conversation with Fannie. Everybody talked and smiled with someone.
Everybody but her. How she wished she could understand the
emptiness, the constant ache inside of her! On Wednesday, she'd
be thirty-six, and nothing interesting had ever happened to her.

Gazing up at the two white-globed chandeliers that shone bright above the green and white and red and white checkered tablecloths that gave the room its hominess, she saw them as remnants of the gas-light era, anachronisms well suited to Fannie's house laws and restrictions. Bob didn't think she belonged there, and he was probably right, but she needed a family, and the boarders were the closest approximation to one that she had.

Gregory arrived at six-thirty that Wednesday evening, dressed in a business suit much like the one he had worn to church, and she was glad she'd worn her good black dress with the ruffled collar. But if he noticed how she looked, he didn't comment on it. He didn't bring flowers, either, but maybe men didn't do that in Ocean Pines and Pike Hill. She'd have to ask Fannie.

When they walked into the restaurant, she stopped and stared at her surroundings. She had never been in that kind of place. Soft lights, candles on the tables, white tablecloths and napkins and three or four long-stemmed glasses beside each plate. She couldn't believe what she saw. A man led them to a table, and she gasped when she saw the beautiful vase of tea roses.

"Are they for us? I mean can we keep them?"

"They're for you," Gregory said. "I hope you like them."

She didn't think she ought to tell him that no one had ever given her flowers. "They're beautiful. I definitely like them a lot. Thanks, Gregory."

"My pleasure."

She watched him carefully so that she wouldn't make a mistake. With three forks, two knives and two spoons facing her, she felt lost, almost as if she were the butt of a joke. He didn't talk much, but she didn't notice that until they were leaving the restaurant.

"You've been awfully quiet tonight. Don't you feel well?"

"I'm fine." The man who showed them to their table handed her a small shopping bag into which he or someone else had put the tea roses. Gregory gave the man a bill. "Dinner was delightful. Thank you."

"Who's that man? Is he the owner?"

"He's the maitre d'."

"Oh."

He disappointed her when he didn't ask if she wanted to go anywhere else. It would have been a good time for him to start her on the dance lessons he'd promised to give her, and she said as much.

"Isn't there any place around here where people dance?"

His right shoulder flexed in a quick shrug. "Probably, but this isn't the night for it." He said hardly anything on the way back to Pike Hill, and let the jazz voice of Billie Holiday erase the silence.

"I had a good time," she told him when they reached the boarding house. "It's the best birthday I ever had."

"Is that so? I'm glad you're happy."

He walked her to the front door, but didn't go in. "I'll see you Saturday afternoon."

She waited for him to kiss her, but he only half-smiled, winked, and left. She didn't know what to make of it. She did know that she'd lost some ground, that he could be a useful friend—already had been, in fact—and that she had better find a way to straighten things out.

"This is the third time I called. I didn't think there was anything to do in Pike Hill but swim. Where were you? This is Bob."

She looked around to see whether anyone was in earshot. "A friend took me out for my birthday."

"Yeah? Congratulations. I'll be over Saturday morning around eleven, and we'll go over to Baltimore and see what's happening. Okay?"

Excitement coursed through her. She had a feeling that Bob Tucker lived by his own rules. "Great. What'll I wear?"

"What? Uh . . . whatever you want to. We're not going to a grand ball."

They were nearly halfway to Baltimore that Saturday when she remembered that she hadn't called Gregory to tell him that she couldn't see him that afternoon. *Oh, well. He's not much interested now anyway. And Bob is a lot more to my taste.*

But she would find that she lacked the sophistication to keep up with Bob Tucker, for he was constantly coaching her. None-theless, she wanted entrée into his world of beautiful women, bars, and jazz.

"What do you want? Beer or a cocktail?"

"I . . . uh . . . I don't drink."

"You don't . . . is this some kind of joke?"

"No. My mama wouldn't have it in the house, so I never learned how."

"Want to learn now?"

She shook her head. "I'd rather not. Maybe next time."

"You're all right, babe," he said, as the evening grew late. "Fannie's gonna blow a gasket if you walk in there at two o'clock Sunday morning." He took a few sips of beer, let his gaze travel slowly over her, not hiding his appreciation for what he saw.

"Tell you what. You spend the night with me at my place."

She nearly choked. "I'd better not do that tonight, Bob. Fannie may put me out, and I need the boarding house."

"I got a feeling that this is something else you never learned how to do. What a waste! Am I right? You never stayed out all night with a man?"

Feeling as she did when her mama found her diary and read it, she squeezed her eyes tight and prayed that she wouldn't cry. She found the strength to nod, but in the depth of her shame, she couldn't utter a word.

He put the beer bottle on the bar and stood. "Stop beating hell out of yourself, babe. It's no problem. There's always an-other woman."

When she got inside the boarding house, she sneaked up the stairs as quietly as she could, but when she opened her door it creaked as if its hinges had rusted, a sound she hadn't previ-ously heard. She opened her cell phone, saw that she had four messages and closed it without checking, for she knew Gregory had called her.

"Well, if he had been warmer the last two times we were to-gether, maybe I wouldn't have forgotten to call him," she said to herself. *You shouldn't have made a date with Bob knowing you had one with another man,* her conscience nagged. She shrugged, un-dressed and crawled into bed as her watch confirmed that it was one-thirty, later than she had ever been out of the house in her life. She set the clock alarm to seven-thirty. If she went to church, maybe Gregory would forgive her.

It did not surprise Gregory that Jolene went to church that Sunday morning, for he knew she would be seeking ways to make amends. He didn't care what excuse she gave. If Miss Fannie didn't know where Jolene went or with whom, that meant Jolene had deliberately stood him up. Lately, he had developed misgivings about her, but he had been willing to trust her until she proved unworthy of it. He'd never cared for women who expected gifts from men, and she had sorely tested him when she hinted that she'd like to have a television. Giving her a cell phone had sent her the wrong signal.

His anger at having been stood up, wasting his Saturday afternoon, had already abated, and he was glad, because he had been furious enough to insult her. His passion for her had tempered, and as far as he was concerned, her behavior the previous afternoon had served as a wakeup call. He'd been traveling too fast. She was still in him, but he didn't have to do anything about it.

As soon as the service ended, he left church by a side door, walked around to the front and waited. She came out of the front door and he walked directly up to her.

"Where were you yesterday at one o'clock?" She didn't have a car, so someone must have taken her somewhere, someone whose company she preferred to his. She gaped at him, and he knew he'd caught her off guard.

"Hi. I . . . I meant to call you, but—"

He cut her off. "I don't care about that. Where were you? Miss Fannie couldn't imagine your whereabouts."

"Are you going to fall out with me about it?"

"Definitely not. That would be a further waste of my mental energy. See you around." He dashed across M. L. King Jr. Avenue to Delaware Heights where he'd parked his car, got into it, and headed home. One woman was able to trick him because he was an idealist. If another one duped him, it would be proof that he was a fool. He was not a fool.

Chapter Three

Judd adjusted the pillow that separated him from the straw bottom of the white rocking chair on Fannie's side porch, leaned back, and let the salty breeze sweep over him as he rocked. Richard didn't think he had ever seen a man more at peace with all that was around him. He asked himself why Judd radiated contentment, while he himself was beset with agitation. Finding no answer, he put the question to Judd.

"Old people don't expect anything of themselves, and nobody expects them to do anything but waste away. If one of us starts being useful, there's hell to pay, and we're accused of taking jobs from the young people who have families to support. Never mind that we have to eat, and nobody's prepared to give us anything." What was he supposed to say to that? He hadn't given the matter any thought.

"Oh yes," Judd went on. "You want to know why you can't relax and live off your bank account. Well, it's because people expect a man your age to work, and you think that way, too. Find something to do."

"I want to do something worthwhile, and I don't mean manual labor, either," said Richard.

Judd rocked slowly as if to savor every minute of the rhythm he created. "I hope you don't think I didn't already know that. Richard: your pride was the first thing I saw when I looked at you. If you'd like, I'll introduce you to the high school principal.

He'll give you something to do, and you'd be an inspiration to the students."

Richard didn't see himself volunteering at a high school, but it would probably beat the boredom he had to tolerate. "Why not? It might prove interesting."

"Y'all want some sweetened ice tea?"

At the sound of Marilyn's voice, Richard stifled a groan. "I try not to consume too much caffeine. I've had my quota. Thanks."

"How about you, Judd? Next time, I'll bring Richard some herbal tea. I blend great herbal teas."

"Don't mind if I do," Judd said and accepted the glass of tea that Marilyn handed him.

Marilyn's face lit up with a smile intended for Richard alone, and left them, letting her left hand trail casually across Richard's shoulder. As he had suspected, the woman was both aggressive and brazen in her pursuit of a man. In the past, when a woman expressed an interest in him, he had merely considered it his due and, if he liked what she offered, he took it with no thought of a lasting relationship. With that one heart-shattering exception. Judd's laugh startled him.

"I won't ask what you're thinking," Richard said to the man who was becoming his friend.

"You may as well have it out with her," Judd said. "She's gonna plague you till you either insult her or take her to bed and make a mess of it."

"If I insult her, she'll probably serve brains for supper every night for a week, and if I make love with her and louse it up, she'll broadcast it and ruin my reputation. I'll have to think about this."

Judd turned his chair to face the ocean and the wind, settled back and eyed him with what Richard knew was compassion. "Try not to hurt her feelings. A little gentleness goes a long way with women. If you scorn a woman, you've made a life-long enemy."

Richard hadn't spent much time worrying about how women responded to him; he had usually gotten what he wanted with a smile, a few words of flattery, and a stroke here and there. And he never worried about the effect on a woman of his subsequent disinterest. When he left, he was gone.

"Tomorrow morning, I'll take you to meet the principal. The school's right across the park on State Street and Delaware."

From his peripheral vision, he saw Marilyn approaching with what he was willing to swear was a glass of herbal tea. "I grow herbs in my own garden," she told him. "This is mint, and there is not a bit of caffeine in it."

A burglar caught climbing out of a window wouldn't have been more afraid of captivity than he was at that moment. "I was just leaving," Richard told her, realizing that the words didn't make sense. What he wanted to do was pitch the glass across the lawn.

She glanced at him from the corner of her eye and bathed her bottom lip with her tongue. "You have a minute for this, don't you?" she asked him. "Anything I give you will make you feel good."

"I'm not going to test that." He thought he'd said it under his breath, but the expression on her face told him that she heard it. "Did you hear what I said to her?" he asked Judd after Marilyn left.

"Of course I did. You don't think you whispered it, do you? But you needn't worry; that wasn't strong enough to make her back off. Truth is, I've never known her to change course."

Jolene had alienated Gregory, so now she had neither a particular focus nor a friend with whom to spend her time. "So what?" Jolene said to herself, as she thought about it. It was no skin off her teeth if he'd decided to ignore her. She spent her time wandering along the beach which, she had discovered, held many facets. She walked in the town park, and when she didn't feel up to pretending she was happy being alone, she stayed in her room.

If only one of the six entrepreneurs to whom she had applied for a job would telephone her! That morning, after sitting beside the swimming pool for an hour, afraid to jump into it, she despaired, put her long blue skirt over her bathing suit and headed home. As she stepped up on the porch, she collided with Richard.

"Sorry," he said. "I was sitting around there on the shady side with Judd. I hope I didn't hurt you. Are you all right?"

She refused his help, picked herself up and walked around him toward the front door, but he grasped her arm, startling her.

"I said, are you all right?"

"I'm fine, Mr. Peterson. Would you please let go of my arm?"

He reminded her of a red-combed cock with his plumes raised and ready for a fight. "Yes, indeed," he hissed. "Bubbling with friendliness, aren't you? I'd like to know what you're trying to prove."

She slapped both hands on her hips—something mama said a woman shouldn't do—and glared at him. "I could ask you the same question. You're not the only peacock in the yard. Excuse me."

She dashed up the stairs to dress and got the twelve-thirty bus to Salisbury for her appointment with the hairdresser. "You're right on time, as usual," the hairdresser exclaimed when Jolene walked in. "Have a seat, and I'll be with you in ten minutes." Knowing that the ten minutes might stretch into forty-five, Jolene sat down and slumped in the chair. She could just as well have gotten the one o'clock bus.

"Did you see in *The Maryland Journal* today where Callie Smith got married last Saturday?" one woman asked another.

"Did I ever! Can you beat that? We all thought poor Callie was gonna die an old maid."

"Well, not quite," another woman chimed in. "Callie ain't been no maid in thirty-five years. How old you think Callie is? Fifty?"

"Pretty close to it," Mabel, the hairdresser, said. "And she can wear the hem of her skirts up to her behind and get that weave with the hair hanging down her back, but when she gets in bed with that man, he gon' know the difference between twenty-five and fifty."

"You telling me?" the woman holding the newspaper said.

"He already know the difference," another said, "but I guess it didn't bother him none. He married her."

"What he look like?" one asked

"Well, from this picture, he ain't no Prince Charming, and he sure could use some hair. Course, hair ain't what makes it swing it the sack."

"You telling me?"

With her head half-bowed, Jolene's gaze scanned the room. Every woman there, except her, had an opinion about Callie Smith, whoever she was. She walked over to the magazine rack, not for something to read—she seldom read anything—but for a means of appearing engrossed in something other than the conversation. Her eyes nearly doubled in size at the sight of a book, the cover of which showed a nearly nude blonde in the arms of a swashbuckling pirate. She glanced around, saw that no one looked her way, picked up the book and went back to her chair.

With no interest in reading the book, she skimmed the first few pages without knowing what she saw. "Good Lord!" she breathed and nearly sprang from her chair when her gaze captured a description of a lovers' kiss with the man's tongue deep in the woman's mouth. She slammed the book face down on the chair next to her. But when she realized that none of the women paid her any attention, she picked up the book, made a note of its author and title and replaced it on the chair face down.

"How far is the nearest bookstore?" She asked Mabel as she was about to leave the beauty parlor.

"Walk down to Easter Street, turn left, cross two streets, and it's in that block."

Jolene thanked her and hurried to the bookstore. "You have this book?" she asked a clerk, and was assured that the store carried that and several other books by that author. Jolene left the store with seven romance novels by an author known for her sizzling sex scenes.

"It's a good thing you're getting off at the end of the line," the bus driver said to Jolene, "otherwise you'd have missed your stop." She got off the bus, her face afire, thanks to her newly acquired knowledge of what goes on between a man and a woman. She rushed up the stairs to her room, closed the door and, without opening a window or turning on the air conditioning to temper the ninety-eight degree heat, Jolene flopped down in a chair with the book she'd been reading on the bus. By the time Fannie banged on Jolene's door to remind her that she was late for supper, Jolene was well on the way to acquiring a sexual education.

For the first time, she took an interest in her supper companions, wondering if they did or had done the things she had been reading about. Somehow she didn't think Louvenia's pursed and wrinkled lips belonged to a woman who had frolicked in bed with a man, but Barbara Sanders, who clerked at the local movie house and whose skirt hems brushed her knees, was definitely suspect. Did Percy Lucas, a truck driver about fifty-five years old or so, wear his pants tight and walk with a swagger because he could make women scream in bed? And was that the reason why Ronald Barnes, the fishnet maker, always winked at her? Was he telling her something?"

She finished her dessert as quickly as she could, though she barely tasted it, said good-night and rushed back up to her room and to her reading. As she opened the book, furor blazed up in her. Emma Tilman hadn't told her one thing about sex, only ranted against men, turning her daughter into a eunuchoid, a sexually deficient woman. A woman without even the urge to have sex, who didn't know what it was or what it was supposed to mean.

"You must have wanted it at least once," she said aloud as if her mother were there with her, "or you wouldn't have had me. I'm entitled, and I'm not passing up anything that's supposed to be this great."

At nine-thirty the next morning, Richard walked with Judd up the steps of Pike Hill High School. "You sure we aren't too early?" he asked Judd.

"I was a businessman for over fifty years, and I know that when I want to see somebody important, I should make an appointment."

If he had paid attention to Judd's navy blue suit, white shirt and red tie, he'd have spared himself that reprimand. "I stand corrected, sir," he said.

"And well you should."

They passed security and were escorted to the office of the assistant principal, who informed them that the principal was in Annapolis at a meeting. "It's good to see you, Mr. Walker, she said. "I was planning to call you about taking some of our honor students on another expedition next fall. I think the last one you offered was our most popular project ever."

"Thank you, Ms. Marin. Mr. Peterson here is a citizen of the world, used to be an ambassador and executive-director of an important nongovernmental organization and all that. He's looking for something to keep him busy, and I told him that you could use a volunteer of his class."

She didn't look him in the eye, and when he let her know that he appreciated her good looks, the blood heated her face. His antenna shot up. *Better not get on the wrong side of this woman*, his inner sense warned.

Quickly, Richard cloaked himself in his most professional demeanor, banishing the womanizer he'd once been and leaving her to wonder if she had imagined his signal. "I'd be happy to run a career guidance clinic for you, or to give your seniors a series of workshops on international relations as a possible career. However you think I could best be of help."

She followed his lead, and if she reacted to him, she hid it. "Would it be an imposition to ask if you would do both?"

"None whatever. I'm glad to help."

Her aplomb apparently restored, she leaned back in her chair, signaling that she was in command of the meeting. "It's too late for career guidance this year, because school closes in a couple of weeks, but we could schedule the clinic for the beginning of the next term. We've needed this from someone who knows what isn't in the text books, who has experienced success in his chosen field, and knows what kind of information our children need. Mr. Walker, you can't know what a favor you've done us by introducing us to Mr. Peterson."

"He's a good man, and that's what we need around here. Well, we'd better be going. You can reach us over at the boarding house," said Judd.

She glanced at Richard as if to ask, "You too?" And he'd have given anything to know whether she wanted the information for personal or for business purposes. "Thank you so much, Mr. Peterson," she said. "I look forward to working with you."

He extended his hand, and her reluctance to take it did not

escape him. "I'm glad to have met you, Ms. Marin, or is it Dr. Marin?"

"Dr. Marin," she said and refused to let her gaze connect with his.

"Let's stop over here in the park for a spell," Judd said as they left the school. "I love to sit here among the flowers and shrubs. My Enid loved flowers, and she kept our garden and our home filled with them. By the way, what kind of message were you sending Miss Marin? For a minute there, I thought you were hitting on her."

Richard stretched his long legs out in front of him, picked up a short stick and threw it into a bush. "I was only reacting to the look she gave me, but when I caught myself doing it, I nipped it in the bud. I'm not going to start something with a white woman in this tiny Southern town. She didn't look *that* good."

Judd rubbed his chin a few times and then leaned forward. "I just figured out something about you, Richard. You're a player. A natural born player. How'd you manage to go so far in life without getting into trouble? I mean serious trouble?"

"Damned if I know. Luck. Maybe. But as I told you before: that's behind me."

Judd nodded his head. "Maybe."

There was a time, as recently as six months earlier, that when a woman showed as much interest in him, and especially extemporaneously, as Dr. Marin did, his libido heated up, and he didn't rest until he got her. With one exception, getting the woman had neither taxed his imagination nor his energy. That exception was Estelle Mitchell. He had thought that his interest in her was of no greater moment than what he'd experienced for any of the dozen or so other women he'd slept with and forgotten. But Miss Mitchell had let him know that she required substance in a relationship and found it in the person of John Lucas, a man he had dismissed as unworthy of consideration as his competition. Too late, he discovered that the man had won Estelle's heart.

He pulled himself out of his reminiscence, back from the past that still pained and depressed him. He meant to get a handle on it, and he'd start by making himself busy and keeping his penis in his pants.

"I see you don't believe me," he said to Judd, "but somehow I don't have an urge to convince you. Is there a library here in Pike Hill?" He had to do something while he waited for school to open, and writing his memoirs hadn't yet engaged his interest sufficiently to make him knuckle down and do it.

"Library's on M. L. King Jr. Avenue, facing the Baptist church."

"Thanks." He opened his cell phone and called Fannie. "I won't be in for lunch today."

To his disgust, the library had only one old and outmoded computer. He'd have to buy his own, although he didn't want to encumber himself with possessions for he didn't know how long he would remain in Pike Hill.

"That library doesn't even have a modern computer," he told Fannie at dinner.

"Well, tell 'em they need one, and help 'em get it," she said, as if it could be done with little more than the snap of his fingers. "Mr. Barnes is going to be leaving us, so if you know a good person for his room, please tell 'em about Thank the Lord Boarding House. 'Course, I'm not worried. The Lord always looks after me."

"My circle of friends is very small, Fannie."

"Yeah, but it would be a lot bigger if you'd quit looking down your nose at people. Judd and I are the only people you ever talk with in this house, and you been here going on two months. Doesn't that tell you anything? Look at poor Jolene over there. She doesn't even know how to relate to people. Talk to her sometime."

He sipped the espresso coffee that he suspected Marilyn had made just for him, and tried to figure out the best way to rid Fannie of that idea. "She went out with Joe Tucker's brother, which means she knows how to relate to the kind of man who interests her."

Fannie gaped at him, her coffee cup suspended between the table and her mouth. "She *what*?" He repeated it. "Well, I'll be . . . that explains a few things. Another woman who doesn't know the difference between a strong wind and a little breeze."

Richard didn't see the tragedy of it if, indeed, there was one. "No point in worrying about it. If a man's got the music that makes a woman dance, she'll move to his beat. Period. Common sense has nothing to do with it."

Fannie rolled her eyes toward the ceiling. "Haven't you paid any attention to Jolene? She doesn't even know that people dance. She's got every mark of a sheltered, over-protected woman. Well, I did my best."

"Nothing's going to happen to her as long as she stays here," he said. "Nothing good and nothing bad. And while she's marking time, she'll probably learn something about life."

Fannie reached over and patted his hand. "Right. And I hope you have the same good fortune."

He stared at her. How could she say that to him, a man of the world? "Are you insulting me?"

When he tried to extract his hand from hers, she held on to it. "No, I'm not, Richard. I'm trying to tell you that, for all your accomplishments, until you open yourself to people and give yourself to them, you won't understand life any better than Jolene does."

Half-standing and half-sitting now, he glared at her but, unfazed, she smiled, though the smile came slowly. "Okay. That's my last lecture." She got up, as if to leave the table, and bumped into Marilyn, the cook.

"How'd you like your espresso tonight?" Marilyn asked Richard, ignoring Fannie. "You're a man of taste, and I know you're used to having things just right." She patted his shoulder and then slid an arm across it. "Y'all have a nice, pleasant evening. You hear?"

He watched Marilyn swish out of the dining room toward the kitchen, then glanced back at Fannie. "What does she want from me?"

Fannie's eyebrows shot up, and she appeared to stifle a laugh. "If I thought that was a serious question, I'd answer it. But I will say this: When Marilyn decides she wants something, she goes after it like a wolf after fresh meat. So you watch out."

He threw up his hands. "Can't you say something to her? Call her off?"

A grin spread over her face. "Wouldn't do a bit of good. *Whatever Lola wants, Lola gets.* Put a new lock on your door."

When he closed his bedroom door that night, he secured it with a chair. As hot as he suspected Marilyn would be, he definitely was not going *there*.

Fannie couldn't wait for the service to end that Sunday morning. Her mind hadn't been on the sermon, but on what could have happened between Jolene and Gregory. He had been incensed at her place the Saturday afternoon when Jolene stood him up. She didn't meddle in the affairs of her houseguests and prided herself in that fact, but she was always happy to help if she could. And Jolene had been acting strangely lately, walking around with her head in a paperback book and her mouth covered with rouge.

"You looking fine this morning, Mr. Hicks. Didn't Rev. preach this morning! Hallelujah."

"How are you, Miss Fannie? Yes. He was up to his usual high standards."

She could see that he didn't plan to ask her about Jolene, and she didn't know how to bring up the subject, so she stalled. "Supposed to be a scorcher today, Mr. Hicks. I guess everybody will be heading for the beach. Jolene told me once that she can't swim."

"That so? Well, have a blessed day. Good-bye."

She felt like a fool. He knew she was fishing for information about their relationship, and he didn't intend to discuss it. Well, she was going to ask Jolene. She'd done the woman a favor, and she deserved an explanation.

When she got home, she found Jolene sitting on a side porch with her face buried in a paperback book. "Rev. sure did preach this morning, Jolene. You should have heard him. What you reading?"

Jolene closed the book and dropped it in her tote bag. "A novel. I was just going inside away from this heat."

"Spent a few minutes with Mr. Hicks at church, and I'm a little disappointed that he didn't ask about you. Have you spoken with him since that Saturday he came here and you'd forgotten you had a date with him? Surely he isn't still mad about that. The Bible says forgive and forget."

"That's easier said than done. By the way, I'm going to Salisbury Monday morning to check on a job. It sounds like something I can do."

"Well, I gave you a good reference."

"Thanks. I appreciate that."

"Not a peep out of her either. Some men don't hold still for two-timing, and looks like that's what she did," Fannie murmured to herself as Jolene hurried up the stairs to her room.

"Four hundred and twenty-five a week is all I'm paying for somebody who never held a job," the man said to Jolene. "It's good pay. If your work's satisfactory, you should get a raise in about six months."

What choice did she have? She hadn't heard from any of her other applications. "Do I get paid for overtime?"

"Yeah. But you have to do something about your hair and the way you look. This is a beauty spa, and the women who work here have to look great. I'll give you a hair cut and style, and one of the operators will give you a facial and a make-up job. That's free." His gaze swept over her. "You wear a size fourteen?"

She nodded, though she wore anything from twelve to sixteen depending on how much of a bargain it was. He opened what looked like a storage closet and handed her a uniform. "Women operators wear pink uniforms, and the men wear pink shirts and black pants. You ready to go to work?"

"Yes, sir." He took her to the front of the shop. "You answer the phone real cheerful so people will want to come in here. You work the cash register, and you keep the operators' accounts straight. I'll spend today working with you as soon as we fix up your hair and your face. I don't want to catch you reading. The gal who had this job couldn't do her work for reading books."

"Don't worry, sir. I'll do my job."

Three hours later, Jolene hardly recognized herself, although she attributed the change she saw to the pink uniform. She didn't have one bright color in her closet, and maybe she should buy something pink.

Joe Tucker's long sharp whistle when Jolene sat down beside him at dinner got the attention of everyone in the dining room. "If I didn't know it was you, I'd swear I was seeing things," he said. "You sure do look great." After determining the reason for Joe's exclamation, the other boarders returned to their food and their conversations.

Jolene thanked Joe for the compliment, though her heart wasn't in it. After the hottest lovemaking she had read about so far, Blake Edmond Hunter had nonetheless walked away from Melinda Rodgers, and she just couldn't see how he would do such a thing. The way Melinda had made him feel, you'd think he'd keep himself glued to her. In her disappointment, she had been tempted to toss *Scarlet Woman* into the wastebasket without finishing it. For the first time in her memory she had released a string of expletives, and she'd aimed them at the author of that book.

She caught the seven-thirty bus to Salisbury the next morning and finished *Scarlet Woman* during the trip, greatly relieved that Blake went back to Melinda and made love to her again. She read the love scene over and over until she finally substituted herself for Melinda. She would have to buy some more books, but at six dollars each and at the speed with which she consumed them, she had to find a second-hand bookstore or a library that carried them. She didn't feel so alone, now that she had the books.

"Hmmm. This place is looking up," said a deep male voice that sounded as if it were but a few inches from her ear.

She glanced up to find a young, handsome man cataloging her assets, something she hadn't previously observed. However, she pretended not to understand that he was making a pass at her. "Did you want to make an appointment with one of our operators?" She asked him.

"Hardly. I've got a load of stuff on the truck from Kemi Laboratories and Pink. You want to sign for it?"

She wasn't certain that she had the authority to sign for anything, and she told him as much. "Trust me, babe, anything you got's good in my book."

"We're talking about my signature."

"How about going to a movie with me one night? Where do you live?"

"Over in Pike Hill."

"In that case, let's make it Saturday. We can see a five-thirty show, eat something, and get you home before midnight. What do you say?"

"What's your name?"

"Jim Riggs. What's yours?" He turned over a receipt and prepared to write. "And what's your address in Pike Hill?"

"Jolene. Number eighteen, Ocean Road."

He winked at her. "See you Saturday at four," and she watched him walk through the shop in search of the owner. Tight jeans covered what seemed to her like an exquisite behind, and he strode like the heroes in the novels she'd come to love.

As she boarded the bus to go home, she watched the couples who waited in line and those who were already seated. Did they do the things those people did in her books? She wished she could ask the woman in the red dress who snuggled so close to the man beside her. Age apparently didn't make a difference, she decided, watching one aged couple holding hands. *I'm missing all this. Lord, I wish mama was alive and I could tell her what she did to me. I'm not over the hill yet, and I'm going to get some of what's due me.*

Meanwhile Richard decided to take Fannie's advice and try to have modern computers placed in the library, for he suspected that the schools were short of them if, indeed, they had any. After calling in favors from friends in Washington and New York, he got a promise of six modern desk-top PCs.

"I'm taking your advice," he told Fannie at supper that night. "In a week, we'll have those computers. Now, we'll have to find somebody to teach these kids how to use them."

"I'll ask Mr. Hicks if he can help. He—"

"We got baked Alaska tonight, Richard, and you get yours first."

He glanced up to see Marilyn holding a flaming white mounded cake-like dessert with raspberries strung around its sides. At the buzz of murmurs from the other boarders, Marilyn hastened to reassure them. "Everybody's getting one, so don't get your backs up."

Before he could respond, Fannie practically growled her disapproval. "Where's mine? Richard is not the only person sitting at this table."

Marilyn's face bloomed into a broad smile. "No, but he's the only one wearing pants." She grinned down at Richard. "Taste it. I knocked myself out making it."

He didn't want to encourage her, but he loved baked Alaska, so he tasted a forkful. Heaven. "First class," he said in what he regarded as an understatement.

"I know it. Nobody beats me making this." She stroked his back before rushing to the kitchen.

"I sure hope you put a new lock on your door," Fannie said, her annoyance at Marilyn evident in her tone and demeanor.

"I forgot it, but there are other means. Fannie, this stuff is to die for."

"I know it. Problem is she also knows it."

"Where's the fire?" Judd asked Richard when he hurried out of the dining room without drinking the espresso that Marilyn had begun serving for Richard's benefit.

"I believe in heading off trouble."

"You mean Marilyn? I wish you luck. A couple of men finally left here because she wouldn't leave them alone."

"We'll see. I'd love to beat you at blackjack, but not tonight. Let's meet for breakfast around eight." He had begun to enjoy his morning talks with Judd, aware that a liking for the old man had begun to steal up on him like a wind out of nowhere.

Minutes after he stepped into his room, he heard a light tap on his door. With his fists locked to his hip bones, he told himself to ignore it, but upon reflection, he figured that Marilyn hadn't finished after supper clean-up. So, the second, louder knock drew him to the door.

He opened it. "I knew you wouldn't want to pass up your espresso," Marilyn said, brushing past him into his bedroom, "since you know I make it 'specially for you. I'll take care of you. You know that." She put the coffee, a napkin and a bar of chocolate on his night table and smiled in anticipation of a gesture of appreciation from him.

He leaned against the wall beside the open door, his arms folded and his ankles crossed. He didn't have to be a gentleman about it, and if she made a move, he'd have it out with her. If he was going to fall off the wagon, so to speak, he'd go after a woman less in a position to beleaguer him constantly.

"Members of the opposite sex are not allowed in guest bedrooms, Marilyn. You know it's against house rules."

"Those rules aren't intended for me, you know." She sauntered over to him, and he raised both hands, palms out.

"If I had wanted coffee, I would have remained in the dining room until you or Rodger brought it."

"Aw, come on. You know you want it."

If he had ever heard a double entendre, that was it. "Do I look like the kind of man who's incapable of going after a woman he wants? Do I?"

"No, but here in the house with all these people, you're just shy."

"Shy, hell! I like to choose my own poison, and I'm damned good at it. I'd like you to leave."

Her long mascaraed lashes closed over her eyes as she looked down and kicked at the carpet. "You're joking."

"Joking? Do you see me laughing? Let's not let this turn ugly, Marilyn. This was a mistake. If you got the impression that I'd welcome any level of intimacy with you, I'm sorry. I'm not here for that."

She cocked her head and looked up at him, her expression unreadable. "You're not gay, are you?"

His laugh came out harsh and unfriendly. "My sex partners have been females aged thirteen to sixty-four, black, white, Latino, blondes, brunettes, redheads, tall, short and in between, skinny and fat. Anything else you want to know about them? When I want a woman, she does not have to chase me. Understand?"

"You won't tell anybody about this." She raised her head. "Will you?"

He lifted his left shoulder in a careless shrug. "Not unless we have another, similar encounter." He pointed to his night table. "Would you take that with you?" She took up the tray and walked out without meeting his gaze.

Richard walked over to the window and looked out on the moon-light shrouded bay. He needed someone, but not Marilyn. Someone who could make him forget Estelle. In the distance he saw a fisherman's boat silhouetted in the night and shook himself vigorously as if to unshackle himself from the chains of unrequited love, to sail free as that boat sailed over the waves. He was making progress; only a short six months earlier, he would have emptied himself into Marilyn without a single qualm and let her deal with it. For many respectable men, refusing to tomcat wouldn't be an achievement, but for him, it spelled progress. If he could do something *for* someone, as Fannie had suggested, maybe that would make up for some of the wrongs he'd done. He turned away from the window, got ready for bed and wrestled with himself and his libido. He hadn't set out to alter his lifestyle, but in trying to change his attitude toward and behavior with women and in choosing to eschew superficiality and to contribute unselfishly to the community, he had done precisely that. Only God knew what he could expect.

He joined Judd for breakfast the next morning, expecting Marilyn to give him a cold shoulder. However, her smile beamed as brightly for him as ever, although she didn't put her arm around his shoulder or touch him as she had recently made a habit of doing.

"I saw her sneaking up the stairs last night right after supper," Judd said when Marilyn left their table, "but from the look of things this morning, she didn't score any points."

"I'm a resolute man, though I concede that if it had been Halle Berry, I wouldn't be boasting this morning about the strength of my resolve."

"Looks as if she backed off . . . at least for now."

He looked at Judd and grinned. "She works here, so it would be easy to indict her for sexual harassment."

What passed for laughter rumbled out of Judd's throat.

"What judge would believe you? People look at you and see a player, just like Marilyn does."

"Players have rights. I'm getting some computers for the library, and Fannie says she knows a man who'll teach the local kids who don't already know how to use them. Maybe I'll start a computer club or something like that."

Judd extended his hand for a shake. "Now, you're doing something important for the people around here. You won't be the big shot you used to be, maybe, but you'll make more friends than you dreamed of. I'm proud of ya, son."

Richard stopped eating and pushed the plate of waffles and sausage aside. "That's the first time I have ever heard those words." When Judd frowned, he added, "I wasn't the child who tried to please his parents. I was too selfish for that."

"But that was then."

"Yeah. I'm on a different course now."

Jolene, too, was on a different course. She met Jim at the door of the boardinghouse and realized that she had forgotten how he looked. Not bad, she thought. "Where are we going?" she asked him after he kissed her left cheek.

"Salisbury. I thought we'd see *Hurricane*, unless you'd rather see a different movie. It's old, but I hear it's pretty good. What do you say?"

She hadn't seen it but, in any case, she didn't care which movie she saw because she knew nothing of screen actors and actresses. She hadn't kept up with theatrical news, so the names of most stars meant nothing to her. Shaken by the sight of violence and blood, she snuggled close to her date and held her breath until forced to expel it.

"Want to go for something to eat?" Jim asked her. "You'll never get back to your place in time to eat supper there."

"You're right, and my landlady can't stand the thought of anybody coming to the table late."

"Do you like Chinese food?"

Embarrassed to tell him that she had never eaten in a Chinese restaurant or tasted Chinese food, she said in as offhand a manner as she could affect. "Who doesn't?" She hadn't lied, but she hadn't exposed herself, either.

"You really do like Chinese food, don't you?" he asked her later as they ate in the first Chinese restaurant she'd ever entered.

"It's good. I love these flavors."

"I'd been hoping they had a better kitchen," he said, and she knew he realized that she either hadn't eaten much Chinese food, or had poor taste.

Outside the restaurant, he faced her and put both his hands on her shoulders. "It's early. Come by my place, why don't you? I'll take you home when you're ready to go."

She turned her back to him and looked into the distant darkness. He was a tall man, well over six feet, strong and nice-looking. Maybe he would introduce her to the way the women felt in her books. She thought of them as her books, because they were so precious to her. Her flesh quivered when his big hands stroked her back, warming her through her blouse. She closed her eyes, remembering how Melinda felt when Blake's lips covered her nipple.

"Come on," he whispered, "if you want to go."

"If it isn't too far," she said, camouflaging her eagerness to receive what, according to her books, he wanted to give her.

"It's not far. About ten minutes by car. Coming?"

Why did he ask her a second time? Couldn't he see that she wanted to go with him? If he asked her one more time, she'd find the bus to Pike Hill, get on it and go home. "How far is your car?"

"Across the street." He took her hand and didn't release it until he seated her in the passenger seat of the car.

He fastened their seat belts and a few minutes later, stopped in front of a four-story apartment house, a corner building on a quiet, clean street. When she remarked that he lived in a nice neighborhood, he replied, "Think so?" She didn't know what to make of that. They entered a small, reasonably tidy apartment on the third floor at the front of the building.

"Have a seat," he said. "I'll get us something to drink."

"I don't drink," she said.

"How about half a glass of white wine to toast our friendship?"

She wished she was sophisticated and at ease with men, so she could lean back and cross her legs the way the women did in the books she read. "Relax," he said. "I'm not going to do anything you don't want me to do. Whenever you say the word, I'll take you home." Why was he leaving it to her? Then she remembered that the men in her books always made certain that the women wanted them, and she relaxed a little.

He left the living room and returned with two glasses of white wine. He clicked her glass and said, "Here's to us."

Here's to mama, she said to herself, *If she could just see me now*! She put the glass to her lips.

After a few sips, it seemed as if warm smoke swirled around in the pit of her belly and began working its way toward her vagina. She crossed her legs so that she could better enjoy the glorious new feeling.

Jim took the glass from her fingers, leaned over and pressed his lips to hers. Then he gazed at her. "Open your mouth for me."

Oh, Lord. He was going to put his tongue in her mouth. With her right hand, she gripped his shoulder for support and parted her lips. His tongue plowed into her, and he held the back of her head while it danced in and out of her mouth. *Just like Blake did to Melinda.* She opened her mouth wider, and his fingers fumbled at the buttons on her blouse. Anxious for more, she unbuttoned it for him, and he took it off her and tossed it into a chair.

"Ooh. Oh, Lord," she screamed, as he sucked her right nipple into his mouth and massaged her other breast. Suddenly, he stopped. "Wh . . . What is it?" She asked.

"Let's go in here." Within a minute, he rid her of her clothing. "Hmm. Nice," he said, picked her up and put her on the bed.

She didn't look at him while he undressed. She couldn't. She had never seen a man naked. He got in bed and began to fondle and kiss her. She waited to feel something, but didn't until he began suckling her and his fingers found their way past her belly to the lips of her vagina.

"Open your legs," he said, and she did, eager now for what would come.

He was on top of her now with one hand beneath her hip. "Take me in."

She didn't know what he meant, and when she didn't respond, she suddenly felt the pressure of his penis, big and thick against her, and stiffened. "Relax. You'll adjust to me in a minute."

"Ow!" She screamed, as he tore into her. She had never felt such pain. Tears streamed down her face.

"What the hell!" He stopped and looked down at her. "Are you telling me this is your first time? My Lord, woman! Are you out of your mind?"

"Please," she said.

"Please what?"

"I needed to do this."

"I wish you'd told me." He wiped her face with a corner of the sheet, bent to her breast and suckled her first gently and then vigorously.

"It's all right," she said, but he didn't answer. After a while he began to move in a frenzied rhythm the way she imagined the men in her books did, but all she felt was the pressure of that large organ pushing into her. At last he stopped and pulled out of her.

"I've never been so shocked in my life," he said later, lying beside her. "Let's dress. It's getting late, and I have to take you home."

As they drove back to Pike Hill, he said very little, and she wondered if he was mad at her for some reason. Shouldn't she be mad at him? He was supposed to make the earth move and volcanoes erupt, wasn't he? But, except when he was sucking her breasts, all she'd felt was a deathly pain.

He parked in front of Thank the Lord Boarding House and cut the motor. "Why did you do this, Jolene? I want to know why a good-looking woman your age would throw away her virginity on a stranger, a man she doesn't know a damned thing about. You haven't asked me one question about myself. You don't know whether I impregnated you. I can't believe you did this."

Fear streaked through her. She'd die if her next period didn't come. "Did you?"

He turned and looked straight at her. "Hell no, I didn't. I'm not crazy if you are. I pulled out. Look, I gotta be going. I know you feel badly, and I'm sorry, but I sure wish this hadn't happened. I wasn't even serious when I asked you to go home with me."

"Then why did you ask me?"

"The answer to that question tells me a lot about a woman."

"Are we going to see each other again?"

He shook his head. "Only when I deliver something to the shop. This was too much for me."

He got out, went around to the passenger's door and opened it. "I'll walk you to your front door."

She raised her head and laid back her shoulders. "Don't bother. You were just as big a mistake for me as I was for you. Good-bye."

"I didn't say—"

She waved a hand in dismissal. "Whatever!"

Upstairs in her room later, she showered, crawled into bed and sought solace in her copy of *Scarlet Woman*. Maybe if she read a couple of chapters before she went to sleep, she would forget that Jim what's-his-name existed. She reread once more the sizzling scene in which Blake introduced Melinda to the mysteries of lovemaking, adoring and cherishing her. Tears blurred her vision, and she closed the book. Dejected. Jim hadn't cherished her, and he'd made it clear that he didn't care to see her again.

A sadness seeped into her, draining her of hope and of the expectation that she would ever know the joy with a man that other women knew. Suddenly, she brushed away a tear and sat up straight. Surely, the author of her books wouldn't write those wonderful things if they weren't true. Jim hadn't done right by her. She wouldn't give up.

In her loneliness and desperation to have what other women experienced with their men, Jolene did not see her own role in the fiasco attending her abortive liaison with Jim, for she didn't know the role that love, affection, and tenderness played in the enjoyment of sex. She fell asleep plotting another sexual romp. According to her books, men loved sex and needed it frequently, so getting one should be a cinch.

Chapter Four

Richard met Gregory Hicks in the librarian's office and shook hands with him, glad to see a young professional man. "Fannie told me you'd teach the computer classes, and I'm grateful for your help. I'm beginning to see how much our people need a leg up."

"Glad to do it. These teenagers should be able to do something with a computer other than surf and play games. What do you have in mind?"

Richard outlined his suggestions for classes with use of the six computers installed at one end of the library's reading room. "I'd be happy if the kids learned more than surfing. This is their opportunity to get experience building web sites, writing simple programs, word processing, and other useful things. I've blocked all so-called adult sites."

"I can teach site building and basic programming," Gregory said, "but this is a public library, so I don't think we can restrict the program to youths. Adults also need the service."

"I suppose you're right. "

"Yes," Tyler Griffon, the librarian said. "I had no idea so many people would want these services. Adults are registering in droves."

"Great," Richard said, pleased with the results of the first truly unselfish thing he'd ever done. "I couldn't be happier."

"I expected more men to sign up," Gregory said to Richard the first Tuesday evening on which they held the adult classes.

"Yeah. Me, too."

"Would you please come over here and check my margins?" a woman asked Richard, allowing her breast to press firmly against his arm.

Stunned by her blatancy, he uttered the first word that came to him. "Excuse me, uh . . . Miss."

"No problem whatever," she replied. "No problem at all. It was my pleasure."

He spun around and headed for the front door where he leaned against the wall and prayed for equanimity. He hadn't felt the enticing pressure of a warm, sweet nipple in months, and he stood there taking deep breaths and trying to reclaim his poise while his mouth watered.

"Thank you so much for all you're doing for our community, Mr. Peterson," a high pitched female voice said. Slowly and reluctantly, he looked around, and his gaze landed on a tall, willowy and well-dressed woman of about forty-five. "I was wondering if you'd come to dinner Saturday evening. My reputation as a cook is considerable."

He couldn't ask her how many guests she would have, and he didn't care to be the only invitee. He decided to be on the safe side. "I hate to forego a big party at the home of a gracious hostess and miss an opportunity to meet the town's important people, but it looks—"

She interrupted him. "My dear, you don't think I'd share you with a houseful of half-sober people, do you?"

Whoever said Southern women were sweet, shrinking violets didn't know which side was up. Sweet, maybe, but if the ones he'd met were a good sample, steely was more like it.

"I'll be away."

She smiled the smile of a lottery winner. "Next Saturday, then. I love dinners for two on a Saturday evening. They're so romantic."

The tightness in his chest slipped down to his belly. He'd never seen the woman before in his entire life, and he was damned if he'd let her crowd him. "I can't say I agree with you, ma'am. I . . . uh promised the good Lord never to participate in another one, and that's one promise I wouldn't dare break. If you'll excuse me . . ." He headed back inside.

He wasn't sure, but he thought she bared her teeth after she locked her knuckles to her hips. *Women!* He'd always delighted in their predatory antics. But where the hell had he been and what had he been thinking? Wasting his life on games.

"Oh, there you are," a petite blonde exclaimed. "I've been looking every place for you. Do you give private lessons? I can't make the evening classes."

He looked steadily at her, his patience rapidly expiring. "Classes in what?"

Her smile exposed not one dimple but two. "Uh . . . computer."

"Sorry. That's not what I teach."

All of a sudden, his annoyance gave way to laughter. The lion had finally gotten his fill. He went into the men's room where he encountered Gregory. "Man, how do you handle these women?"

A knowing grin spread over Gregory's face. "I don't have to. They leave me alone."

"But they tried, didn't they?"

"Oh, yes. All you have to do is invite them to Wednesday night prayer meeting. Unless it's one who doesn't know what that is, you're safe."

He shook his head from side to side. "Thanks. Give me a big city any day." *Prayer meeting. He couldn't even say the words.*

Richard didn't know when he had been as exhausted from anything that could be described as work. The responsibilities of an ambassador and, later, as an executive-director hadn't once pushed him to a mental sweat, not to speak of a physical one. He got back to the boardinghouse at about ten-fifteen, saw Judd in the lounge and joined him. A few minutes later, Jolene came into the lounge and got a soft drink from the machine, waved at them and left.

"I wonder if she realizes that she resembles Fannie," Judd said.

"Does she? I hadn't noticed."

"What have you noticed about *anybody* who lives in this house?"

Richard stretched out his legs and crossed his ankles. "I've noticed your sharp tongue but I ignore it, because your age gives you license to be overbearing."

A half-smile played around Judd's lips, lips slightly shriveled from age. "You and Miss Tilman have something in common, and from where I sit, it isn't laudable. She walks around here with her face in a book so she doesn't have to look at the rest of us, and you strut around here with your nose in the air for the same reason."

Richard couldn't help being amused. When Judd got on a roll, his thoughts became words, and if you didn't want to hear them, you'd best leave. "Aw, come on Judd," he said. "I don't try to ignore you."

"Course you don't, but I'm the only one, 'less it's Fannie."

"I'm too tired to argue with you. You know, it's been years since the last time I was tired. I could use a good long swim."

"Doesn't pay to swim out there at night, but I'll join you for one in the morning."

Richard stood. "Works for me. I'll be down here at seven ready to go."

He told Judd good night, and as he walked through the foyer, he saw Jolene's back and stopped. She leaned against the wall beside the dining room door talking with Percy Lucas, the truck driver. He let them have the privacy they seemed to want—since they elected to talk there rather than in the lounge—and headed up the stairs.

"I can't give you a ride in my rig," Percy Lucas was telling Jolene. "It's against company rules." Percy must surely be between fifty and sixty, she figured, not too good looking, and old enough to appreciate a woman as young as she.

Thinking that if she smiled, he'd give in, she forced a smile, and pressed her right hand to his chest. "But just for a short ride. I've never been in a big eighteen-wheel truck." She put a pout in her voice and on her face.

"Look, babe. You're cute and all that, but not enough to make me put my head through a noose. If a man my age loses his job, he ain't gonna get another one. Pussy just ain't that good, babe."

"Who said anything about—"

He interrupted her. "I tell it like it is, and that's what you're leading up to. I was here when you came here months ago, and you just noticed me. You been acting strange ever since you started walking around here with your eyes in some book."

"Now, Percy, that's not fair. You've got it all wrong. I don't have anybody to talk to, so I read. And I always noticed you, but you didn't expect me to walk up to you and tell you I thought you were nice, you know, start up a conversation, did you?"

He shifted from one foot to the other. "Well, I guess not. When can we go out? I'm off Sunday through Tuesday."

Maybe she was making a mistake, but he looked like a man of experience, and since he was older, she surmised, he'd be grateful for a younger woman's attention.

Somehow, she didn't anticipate the Sunday afternoon date with Percy with the same enthusiasm she had invested in Bob and Jim. Nevertheless, she put on her little gray and white seersucker suit and headed for the parking lot beside General Hospital three blocks south of the boardinghouse, where she had agreed to wait for him. When she passed Rhone Street, she could see the Assawoman Bay and the powerful turbulence of the Atlantic Ocean, and her thoughts drifted to Gregory Hicks and the one time he gave her swimming lessons. Maybe she shouldn't have stood him up for Bob Tucker, but Bob had excited her in a way that she didn't understand. A crazy, itchy kind of way.

When she turned into Bay Avenue, she saw the red Hyundai at the entrance to the parking lot. Percy reached over, opened the door, and she got in and fastened her seat belt. She couldn't help comparing him unfavorably with Gregory, who had always fastened her seat belt. And he'd never failed to get out of his car, walk around to the passenger's door and open it for her, too.

Percy handed her a pair of dark glasses. "Hi, babe. Put these on so people won't recognize you. All anybody around here ever does is gossip."

"Thanks for being on time, Percy. I didn't want to stand out here in the hot sun and get a sun stroke."

"I always look out for my women, babe."

He drove to the outskirts of Ocean Pines, turned off the highway and parked in front of a modest, two-story private house.

"Don't say nothing to nobody, babe. Just walk straight up the stairs."

A queasiness settled in her belly as she walked into the house. With the center stairs facing the door, she had no difficulty following Percy's instruction. At the top of the stairs, her guess as to what he intended became a certainty. She didn't like it, but consoled herself with the thought that he probably had plans to make their tryst memorable. After all, he'd said she was attractive. With that and her youth, you'd think he'd do everything he could to please her.

He followed her up the stairs, opened a door, took her by the hand and walked into a very small bedroom.

"This is a nice clean place, so you don't have nothing to worry about," he said, kicked off his shoes and began pulling off his clothes. She dropped herself into a chair and stared at him. Even with her limited experience, she knew this wasn't right.

He pulled off his boxer shorts, walked around to the other side of the bed, got in it and pulled the covers up to his neck. "Come on, babe. What you waiting for? I'm paying by the hour."

She dropped her pocketbook on the floor beside her chair and braced her hands on her knees. "I don't feel right about this, Percy. In fact, I don't feel a thing. This isn't how I expected the afternoon would go."

He sat up in bed, dropping the covers and exposing his paunch. "What are you talking about? You wanna go spending a lot of money in bars and restaurants pretending what ain't real, when all the while this is where you plan to end up? Come on, woman and get in this bed."

"I'm sorry. I guess prostitutes can do that, but I can't."

"Well, if it's a kiss you want, come over here and I'll give it to you."

She shivered as if a cold draft had blown over her. Wouldn't anybody ever understand how she felt? "What I want now is to go home. I'll pay for the room, but I'm not getting into that bed with you. I need somebody to care about me, cherish me and make me feel loved, and you don't know what that is." She tried to hold back the tears that streaked down her cheeks, but the sounds of her sobbing soon filled the little room.

"What are you crying about? Hell, woman, I should have known better than to get mixed up with you. The room's thirty-five dollars."

She heard his feet hit the floor, and when she looked up a few minutes later, he stood before her. Dressed. "What did you think I was? You were the one making up to me and giving me the come on. Don't tell me you just wanted to hold hands; a man don't get no charge out of *that*." She only glared at him, too humiliated and too angry to respond.

"Don't you breathe this to a soul. You hear?" he went on, and held out his hand. "It's thirty-five dollars. Let's go." She opened her pocketbook, counted out the money, and handed it to him.

He counted it, folded the bills and put them in his pocket. "And I mean don't you tell nobody. I'd be the laughingstock of the boardinghouse."

"Don't worry. I wouldn't want anybody to know, either."

Twenty minutes later in the hospital's parking lot, he parked and let her get out of the car. "I'll see you at supper," he said in a voice approximating a growl.

She didn't answer, merely turned away and headed with leaden steps up Ocean Road to the boardinghouse. Her shoes made prints in the softened asphalt when she crossed to the other side of the street where trees would shade her from the searing sunshine. She wiped perspiration from her hairline and stained her once-white handkerchief with the bronze face powder that caked on her skin. At the corner of Rhone and Ocean Road, she leaned against the lamppost, exhausted from the heat and from her travail with Percy, and waited for the light to change. If only she could tell somebody how she felt. So alone, and with no one to care whether she lived or died.

What makes you think you deserve a friend? She stopped short. Where did that idea come from?

* * *

"Pretty hot out there, isn't it?" Judd asked Jolene when she entered the boardinghouse. "You look like you mighty near wilted."

"It's hot, all right." She started past him toward the stairs.

"You can cool off just as well down here," he said. "I was just about to treat m'self to a nice cold bottle of ginger ale. Can I get one for you?" He stood between her and the stairs, all but challenging her to walk around him.

"Thanks, but I'm beat."

He stepped back and let her pass. "A man who lives alone, dies alone."

She stopped midway up the stairs, as pictures of the seven people at her mother's burial floated back to her. Emma Tilman had lived alone, died with only her daughter present, and had been on speaking terms with only two of the people who stood at her burial. She turned and walked back down the stairs.

"I'll have a ginger ale, but I won't be much company."

He walked over to the soft drink dispenser, tall and sprightly for all his eighty-four years. She took a seat in the lounge, although she wished she was in her room.

Judd opened one of the bottles, got a paper cup and poured her a drink. "Sometimes, you don't need talk, just company. I've been sitting here watching the tennis matches over in Ocean Pines and wondering if I was ever that young."

"Tennis in this heat?" she asked. "It must be over a hundred degrees out there. I could hardly make it back here to the house." She slapped her hand over her mouth, fearing that he would ask where she'd been, but her comment brought a different kind of response from him.

"Live your life while you're young enough to enjoy it, Jolene. I hope you don't mind my calling you Jolene. When you get old, all you can do is watch other people live."

"But I've seen you swimming in the bay, Mr. Walker."

"And thank God I can still do it. Been swimming since I was three, so it comes natural."

She drank the remainder of the soft drink and rose to leave. "Thanks for the drink, Mr. Walker." She paused. "And for the company."

"It was my pleasure. We live here in this boardinghouse, because we don't want to be alone. And that applies to all of us."

It was nice talking with him, she admitted to herself, and while she sat with him, she hadn't felt lonely. She stepped into her room and was closing the door when she heard Fannie's voice.

"Philip! What a surprise!" Philip? Did Fannie have a man? She threw off her jacket and skirt and headed for the shower.

"Jolene. Jolene," Fannie called, knocking on Jolene's door as she did so. "Reverend Coles is here, and he's asking to see you." She opened the door. "Come on in, Fannie. You're his sister, aren't you? He said you are, but I forgot about it, I guess because I didn't see a resemblance."

"That's what everybody says. Philip looks just like our mother, and I look like our father. Put on something and come downstairs."

She slipped on a pink linen shirt-dress and went with Fannie to the lounge where Philip Coles sat talking with Judd and Richard. He rose and walked to meet them. Looking at him not as a preacher, but as a man, she saw a handsome, sleepy-eyed man who reminded her of the men in her books. She had never noticed that his smooth brown skin, towering physique, and chiseled features set him apart from most men. Even at the age of sixty or so, Philip Coles could give Richard Peterson a run for his money. She wondered why he had never married.

"How are you, Sara Jolene? You look wonderful, like a new person. I knew you would thrive here."

"I'm fine, Reverend Coles. And I'm Jolene now. I dropped the Sara. I . . . uh . . . I'm working as a receptionist in Salisbury." She wanted to laugh and to dance when she said it, for Philip Coles knew that she'd had no experience at holding down a job and taking care of herself financially. She smiled and her chest felt as if it expanded. "I'm doing just fine."

"Yes, I can see that," he said, "and you can't know how happy that makes me."

She glanced at Richard Peterson and shrank back. His gaze was a laser piercing her and making her transparent before his eyes. What did he know? He didn't blink, and she had to look away, but not before Judd Walker examined the expression on

Richard's face. He had caught her at something, but what and with whom?

"I'm glad you came, Reverend Coles," she said. "Good-bye." She didn't care what they thought. She had to get out of there. Richard Peterson had seen her with either Jim, Bob, or Percy. She ran up the stairs to her room, shut the door and bolted it. Lord, please don't let him tell Reverend Coles. And Judd. Don't let him tell Judd. She didn't know how she would face them at supper.

She sought solace in one of her books, but the magic didn't work, and it was the old Sara Jolene who trudged down the stairs that night, walked into the dining room and took her assigned seat without looking left or right or saying a word to anyone. She got up to leave the table and saw that Philip Coles had faced her across the room during the entire meal. But if she had looked in his direction, her gaze would have landed on Percy Lucas, and she preferred never to see him again, so she had focused on her plate.

"Join us in the lounge?" Fannie asked her. She shook her head and was the recipient of Fannie's glare of disapproval.

"Maybe later," she said, and didn't stop walking until she was in her room with the door closed. Sitting alone on the side of her bed, she asked herself why she couldn't chitchat with people the way the other residents in the house did with ease. And what had she wanted from Percy? Would it have been better, as he said, if he'd dressed it up with flowers and a meal at a nice restaurant? And if he had, would his stripping, getting into bed and telling her to "come on" have disgusted her anyway? Was the way men treated the women in her books a fairy tale, lies that made the women who read them miserable? She wished she knew.

She got up and began preparing for bed. "I'm going to find the answer to that if it takes the rest of my life," she vowed. "I want what's coming to me."

"What was that all about?" Judd asked Richard later, as they sat alone in the lounge.

"You mean Miss Tilman? I dunno. You would have thought she'd be happy to see the pastor of her mother's church."

"Oh, that? I was talking about the way you were studying her, first during supper and then in the lounge here. You made her cringe. I saw it with m' own two eyes, and there was no lust in it. Did you catch her at something?"

"I never talk about a thing unless I'm sure of my ground, Judd."

"Or unless you figure it's something you should keep your mouth shut about. Well, I respect a man who keeps his own counsel."

"Sure you don't want to go with me to the library tomorrow evening?"

"For what? To sit around watching people learn how to use a computer? Anybody who's not making a contribution is in the way. Besides, I spend enough time watching other people live."

Richard patted Judd's shoulder. "You're a tough one, friend."

As he scaled the stairs two steps at a time, he realized that he enjoyed the old man's company, that he had begun to regard him as a friend, and he had never thought that of any man. He didn't have men friends, as much for the judgment of other men as for his own reasons. He had always preferred the company of women and saw men as competitors, obstacles to be pushed from his path by whatever means he chose.

He entered the dining room at a quarter of seven the following morning, intent upon forcing Jolene Tilman either to ignore him or to talk with him, since he knew they would be the only two eating at that time. He read Cooper's *The Future Has a Past* until the kitchen door swung open promptly at seven and the odor of fresh perking coffee wafted into the room teasing his nostrils with images of the food to come.

Simultaneously, Jolene walked into the dining room. "Good morning," he said. "We're the only ones here. Will you join me?"

He'd never seen a deer caught in the glare of head lights, but from her reaction he could imagine what it was like. He had no doubt then that she had fled the lounge the previous evening because she thought he would confront her about something.

"I'm running a seminar on uses of the computer," he hastened to say, "and I was wondering if you'd be interested."

She stopped walking, toward her assigned seat, turned and came back to him. "I have to use the computer at my job, and so far, I can't get the hang of it. I can type in the records, but that's all." She sat down, and he relaxed, aware that he had thrown her the perfect hook.

"Adult classes are from eight to ten Tuesday and Thursday nights at the library on M. L. King Jr. Avenue next to the Town Hall."

"I ought to be able to make that, since I can finish supper by a quarter of eight, provided Marilyn will serve me my dessert separately."

"I'm sure she will." He intended to skip dessert rather than give the woman an opportunity to resume making passes at him.

"How're you making out here? Adjusting to a town this size isn't easy," he said, fishing for something that would draw her into conversation.

"It's no worse than Hagerstown," she said, keeping her gaze on the biscuits that Rodger placed before them. "I know as many people here as I did there."

"But you grew up there, didn't you?"

"Yeah, but that doesn't have anything to do with not knowing people. You've been here almost as long as I have, and you don't know any of the people who live here accept Judd and maybe Fannie. Where'd you grow up?"

So she knew how to turn the screw. "New York City."

"How are y'all, this morning," Lila Mae Henry, the fourth grade teacher, said, taking her assigned seat. I sure don't welcome this heat today. Friday was the last day of school, and I thank the Lord."

There went his opportunity to find out what Jolene Tilman was up to. "What are you doing for the summer?" he asked Lila Mae.

"I got a job as a cashier at Wall-Mart, and you don't know how happy I am that I can keep my room here. If I'd gone home to Virginia, Fannie would put someone else in my room in a minute. And you can't blame her; she has bills to pay."

"Did she get any one to take Ronald Barnes's room?" he asked, his curiosity about it almost nonexistent.

"Somebody said she was negotiating with a woman in Ocean City, or maybe Ocean Pines. I forget which."

"Have a good day," he said, mostly to Jolene, as he rose to leave the table. "Hope to see you at the seminar tomorrow night. We have an excellent computer science teacher."

"Who's that?" Lila Mae asked. "Could be someone I know."

"Gregory Hicks. He's with the telephone company in Ocean Pines."

When Jolene's fork clattered to the table and her eyes rounded to double in size, he knew he wouldn't see her at the computer classes. The fact that Hicks would be teaching the classes gave her a solid jolt. He was certain of it. Who besides Percy, Bob Tucker and, now, Gregory Hicks had she been involved with?

"When did you say you came to Ocean Pines?" he asked, looking directly at Jolene.

"March."

He nodded. A lot of traffic in three short months. She didn't look the type, but what you saw wasn't necessarily what you got. He went to the lounge for the morning edition of *The Maryland Journal*. He didn't care what Jolene Tilman did, but he hated the thought of her entrapping an unsuspecting, unsophisticated, and lonely man like Percy Lucas. He had exploited women, many of them, but he could say that, with that one glaring exception, he had always let the woman take the lead. If she wanted a player, he accommodated her. If she got more than she bargained for, he never regarded that as his problem. And from the looks of Percy the previous evening at supper, he'd swear Jolene did a job on him.

Hell! Who am I to accuse her? Remembering how Jolene had folded into herself, he shrugged. *They might have messed up each other's heads.*

"There you are, Miss," he heard Fannie exclaim. "Reverend Coles was extremely disappointed that you didn't seem pleased to see him, especially when he came mostly to find out how you were getting along after your mother's death. You hardly spoke to him." Fannie had her good points, but her sanctimoniousness grated on him. He closed his door.

Jolene's hands went to her hips. It didn't take much to exasperate her with Fannie. "He didn't pay much attention to me all those years when my mama treated me as if I were her personal slave, so how was I to know he'd suddenly started worrying about my well-being? I'm not a mind reader."

Fannie looked toward the ceiling. "Lord, give me strength. He was probably trying to guide your mother."

"No he wasn't. For six years, she was bedridden, unable to go out of the house. Except to bring communion every three months, he didn't go into her house until I sent for him a couple of weeks before she died. I don't know what he wants from me."

"Philip is a good man, a man of God, and you be careful how you speak of him."

"Yes, ma'am. Excuse me, but I have to leave now or I'll miss my bus to Salisbury."

She reached the bus stop as the driver was closing the door. "Come on. Get in. You know I don't wait for anybody. I have to keep my schedule."

She thanked him, paid her fare, and sat down to read her book. "What are you always reading?" he asked, and she realized that he watched her through the rear view mirror."

"A book. No point in wasting a good hour when I could be reading."

"I'd like to know what's in those books that keeps your nose stuck to them like a fly to flypaper. I'm beginning to wonder if I'm losing my touch."

Losing his touch? She closed the book and focused on him. A big guy. Over six feet tall, she surmised—although she had only seen him standing once—lean and muscular. And young! He couldn't be a day older than she. Hmmm, she'd have to pay more attention to him.

Vida Boney, a hairdresser at the shop in which she worked, asked Jolene, "Want to stop by, meet my family, and have a cup of coffee or tea before you go home? It's walking distance from here."

Jolene thought for a minute. Vida was always nice to her. If she went, maybe they could become friends, and she would have someone with whom to talk and ask questions about the things she read in her books. Yet she hesitated.

"I take my dinner where I live, and the landlady won't like it if I'm late."

"Tell her you were with a friend and forgot the time. At least, stay for a few minutes. I promise to get you back to the bus stop in time."

Friend? Did Vida regard her as a friend? She didn't see how that was possible. Still . . . Okay. I'll stop by for a few minutes."

Vida's three-year-old twin daughters greeted Jolene with laughs and giggles, took her hand, and led her to their private sanctum, where they insisted that she play with their toys and games and read to them from their books. She'd had no experience with small children and was impressed that they seemed captivated with her. When she remembered to look at her watch, she saw that she had less than twenty minutes to get to the bus stop.

"I'll come back again," she assured the twins who were loathe to see her leave. She ran most of the way and reached the bus as the driver was about to close the door.

"What're you up to?" the bus driver asked her. "Lately, you come close to missing me every evening. You were late this morning, too."

So he'd been watching her! "You knew I'd be here," she said and took the front seat across from him. "What're *you* up to?" Too bad you couldn't tell by looking at a man whether he would be affectionate and treat you as if you were the most precious person on earth. She'd had sex with Jim and hadn't felt anything. She hadn't wanted to do anything with Bob, because she feared he would tell his brother, Joe, and Percy made her feel like trash. Gregory hadn't bothered to bring up the subject.

"What's your name?" she asked the bus driver.

"Harper Masterson. He glanced toward her, a grin displaying his even white teeth. "Any particular reason why you wanted to know?"

"It's easier to talk to a person if you know his or her name."

"Don't you plan to tell me yours, or is this some kind of game?"

She told him her name and added, "And you keep it to yourself."

His chuckle surprised her, because she had meant that he shouldn't yell out her name when she boarded or left the bus. "Are you on the lam or something? You sure don't look the type. People say the river that runs silent runs deep, and I bet that applies to you." He pulled up to a stop, opened the door and let two women board. "What do you do on Sundays? That's my day off."

This time, she was going to let the man worry a little bit. She folded her arms and leaned back, her mind spinning with ways to inveigle him into getting involved with her. "I know what I'll do," she said to herself, "and I'll test it tomorrow morning." To him, she said, "I go to church in the mornings, but you know the Baptists; mornings last till two in the afternoon."

"You playing hard to get? You must do something after church, so what about doing it with me?"

"Let me get to know you first. Then we'll see."

He brought the bus to a stop at a red light, turned and looked at her. "I've got the patience of Job, baby, and when I decide I want something, I get it."

Remembering her decision moments earlier to let him work for what he got from her, she quelled the excitement that raced through her. "I'm planning to go to school evenings, so I won't have a lot of free time."

The light changed, and he drove on. "That's got nothing to do with how you spend your Sunday afternoons. Don't try to dangle me, Jolene. I don't dance to anybody's tune but my own. If you're not interested, say so right now. It definitely won't cause a tidal wave." He reached Bay Avenue in Pike Hill and brought the bus to a halt. "Last stop," he called out to the four remaining passengers.

"I'll see you in the morning," she said, rushing to get off the bus.

"And be on time, because I'm not allowed to wait one minute. By then you should be ready to answer my question, though I've found that when a woman doesn't come right out and say no, she's eventually going to say yes. See you in the morning."

The next morning Jolene stepped on the bus three minutes before the scheduled departure time. "Hi. I see I'm the first one on this morning." She opened her pocketbook to look for the fare.

"Yeah. Couldn't wait to see me." His grin made it impossible for her to know whether he intended it as a joke.

"I . . . uh . . . I think I left my billfold home." She looked at her watch and allowed an expression of panic to settle on her face. "I haven't got a penny."

"All right. Sit right over there." He pointed to the seat she occupied the previous evening. "And you had definitely better be on time this evening, unless you want to walk from Salisbury to Pike Hill."

She sat down. That had been much easier than she had imagined. She had the money for her fare, but she needed to know whether he cared about her. "I don't know how to thank you. My boss is not an understanding person."

The engine roared into action, and he drove off. "Forget it," he said. "You'd do the same for me." She kept a solemn face. This one would be easy. He was already planning to let her ride home free.

"We're getting a new boarder," Fannie sang out to Richard and Judd as they left the breakfast table. "Thank the Lord, and she's an upstanding, church-going, law abiding citizen."

"I hope she's not sanctimonious," Richard said under his breath. "One of them in this place is more than enough."

"Could be worse," Judd said. "Better that than one of these young floozies."

Richard stared at Judd. "A what?"

"I guess that's what you young people call a femme fatale, a woman who's always drawing attention to her breasts and behind. Heck, if they're worth looking at, a woman doesn't have to wave a flag; I'll see 'em." They sat facing each other in their favorite chairs in the lounge and, as if summoned by mental telepathy, Rodger appeared with coffee for two.

Richard stretched out his long legs, relaxed and aware of it. "I was hoping the time would come when the sight of high breasts and a well sloped behind wouldn't start my libido roaring."

The gurgles in Judd's throat spilled out of him in the form of laughter. "You've got a lot to learn, son. It never stops. Your half-hearted libido tells you to go after something, and then Johnny-one-note down there tells you *don't even think it*. Be thankful that, incompetent though Johnny may be, he's still got sense enough to know that and won't start what he can't finish."

"I'm not there yet," Richard said. He saw Fannie post a note on the bulletin board and went over to read it. "Jellyfish in the bay this morning, so it isn't a good idea to swim unless you don't mind those stings."

"When is the new boarder coming?" he asked Fannie.

"She should be here any minute." In that case, he would remain in the lounge with Judd and see what she was like.

About twenty minutes later, Rodger walked into the foyer, rested three suitcases by the door and literally strutted into the lounge followed by a woman who Richard assumed to be the new boarder. He stood as the woman approached. She had an infectious smile, and he watched her intently, captivated.

"You must be the new boarder," he heard Judd say. "M' name's Judd Walker and this here is Richard Peterson. We both live here."

"Happy to meet you," Richard said, arousing himself from his momentary stupor. He told himself that it wasn't her looks, but her persona, her commanding presence that reminded him of Estelle.

"I'm glad to meet both of you. I'm Francine Spaldwood, and I just had quite a scare when an eighteen-wheeler nearly ran me off the highway."

"Let me get you a cold drink," Judd said. "I don't drive any longer, but I remember how nervous driving can make you." He went to the soft drink dispenser and got a bottle of ginger ale. Judd thought colas ruined your teeth and didn't believe in drinking them.

"Have a seat, Ms. Spaldwood," Richard heard himself say. He had expected someone like the women who lived in the house, not a fashionable, career type who was both good looking and self-confident.

"Thank you."

She sat down, crossed her knees and leaned back, sipping the cold drink and as comfortable as if she'd lived there for years. *This woman knows her way around*, he said to himself. *I'll bet she gives all of us a surprise.*

"Thanks for the drink and the company," she said after a few minutes. "I want to see my room and unpack. I hope I have a good view."

"You have a wonderful view, ma'am," Rodger said, picked up her bags and headed up the stairs with her.

"So that's the new boarder. Ought to liven things up around here," Judd said. "She's really something to look at, but I see you're aware of that."

He hated it when he let others divine his private reactions and especially his responses to women. "Yeah. She's good looking, all right, and she's also a no-nonsense person. Pity the poor bloke who hits on her thinking she's just another pretty dame."

"I noticed she got your attention."

Richard jerked his left shoulder in a quick, dismissive shrug. "Oh, I knew she was there. I appreciate an occasional reminder that women are the greatest source of pleasure on the Lord's good earth. But man, not at breakfast every morning."

Judd's laughter carried a cynical ring. "I have a feeling that you're not ready for this one. She'll be good for you, though. It's time you got your nose out of the air and settled down here with the rest of us."

Among the crowd in which he'd traveled all of his professional life, his behavior was more or less standard for a man in his position, but these people probably saw him as standoffish and smug. "Look, Judd, I'm not arrogant."

"Not quite as much as you were when you came here, but you still need to loosen up some."

Richard changed the subject. He had yet to influence Judd's opinion about anything. "What do you think of Percy Lucas?"

"Percy? Humph! A weak man with practically nothing going for him."

"I used to think of such men as weak and feckless," Richard said, "but for some reason, I pity Lucas."

Leaning forward with his hands bracing his knees, Judd shook his head as if perplexed. Then, he sat back in his chair and closed his eyes. "Maybe you feel sorry for him because you have everything that he doesn't have. You may yet develop into a humanitarian. I wonder what Jolene saw in him."

"*Jolene?*" So his guess had been right. "Something happen between Percy and Jolene?"

Judd ran his fingers through his few remaining strands of hair. "The way I figure it, Percy's problem is that nothing happened. But you never can tell."

The picture of Jolene standing a foot from Percy and making up to him floated through Richard's mind's eye. He didn't want to develop a hard crust about women who left men hanging, for his bad luck with Estelle was his own doing. He knew that his empathy for Percy sprang from his own experience with the pain of rejection. He had to work at dispelling that pain, ridding himself of his constant loneliness and finding another focus before his need for Estelle became an affliction.

Chapter Five

"Everybody, this is our new boarder, Francine Spaldwood, who arrived this morning," Fannie announced at supper. "Introduce yourselves, beginning with Judd at table one. It would be nice if we all gathered in the lounge after supper to make Francine feel welcome."

"Like in high school," Jolene murmured.

"Won't hurt none," Joe Tucker said, surprising her, for she hadn't thought he heard her.

With no means of avoiding it, Jolene spent twenty minutes in the lounge, said goodnight, and rushed up the stairs to iron a pink blouse for the next day and to finish reading *Obsession*. To her mind, Francine was okay but, with her stunning looks, every man in the house would probably be after her. She didn't think a woman who looked like Francine Spaldwood would make friends with another female. A tall woman with flawless ebony skin, rich brown almond-shaped eyes, thin facial features, and a curvaceous body. Her full breasts jutted out from beneath her lavender-colored T-shirt, and her slacks looked as if she'd been poured into them. Jolene sucked her teeth, disgusted with Joe and Percy who ogled Francine like starving men eyeing a choice steak. Nobody had to tell her that the boarding house was about to change.

The next morning, Jolene ran a full two blocks to avoid missing the bus and hopped on out of breath. "I like you in pink,"

Harper Masterson told her when she boarded, covering the fare box with his hand. "In fact, I like you, period. What'll we do Sunday?"

She appeared to think about it, although she had already made up her mind that the date would cost him a movie and a dinner in a good restaurant. "I want to see that new Will Smith movie, and ever since I came here I wanted to eat at Ocean Grove." He raised one eyebrow at her preference for the most expensive restaurant within a twenty-mile radius of Ocean City and pulled away from the curb. "My pleasure. Don't be late this afternoon. You hear?"

He could bet she wouldn't, not when he'd indicated that he'd let her ride free of charge. "I'll catch the six o'clock," she said. "My girlfriend wants me to keep her two children for an hour while she runs a few errands."

He nodded. "See you at six."

That afternoon, she went directly from work to Vida's apartment, where the three-year-old twins tested her patience until they learned that she wouldn't yield to them. "Come over here and sit beside me. I'm going to read to you," she announced after she got them to settle down, and they sat quietly and starry-eyed while she read the story of *Little Bo Peep*.

"How'd you do that?" Vida wanted to know when she arrived at fourteen minutes to six, her face red and her ample bosom heaving as if running had robbed her of her breath. On her first visit to the beauty parlor, Jolene had thought that Vida and the three other operators were white, but had learned subsequently, that her boss preferred African-American women who had large breasts, full hips, and who could pass for white. She couldn't pass for white, but she wasn't dark dark, and she met his other criteria.

She didn't feel nice, so she didn't smile. "How'd I do it?" she asked, her anger almost suffocating her. "By letting them know who's the adult and who's the child," she flung over her shoulder as she raced out of the house to the bus stop. She stepped on board, and Harper closed the door and drove off.

"You sure you were with a girlfriend?"

"I was keeping her kids, and she promised to be home at five-thirty," Jolene said between her teeth, showing her vexation at Vida.

"Don't promise to help her out Sunday."

"I won't." He asked her again where she'd like to go for dinner. "The Ocean Grove restaurant in Ocean Pines," she answered, repeating what she told him that morning. She thought he grimaced, but she wasn't sure. And why should he? If a man liked a woman, he also liked to please her. Didn't he?

"I had a nice time," she told him when he brought her home Sunday night. "Maybe next time, we can go to some nice places in Ocean City. Good night."

She turned to leave, but he grabbed her shoulders and pressed his mouth to hers, startling her and exciting her with the force of his kiss. "See you in the morning," he said, in guttural a tone that she couldn't fathom, unsure whether she had annoyed him or pleased him.

Wednesday evening, she missed her bus and her supper when Vida didn't get home until six-thirty. "I missed my bus and my supper, Vida. Now, I'll have to wait for the eight o'clock bus and buy my supper because I missed the one I already paid for."

"I'm sorry, but I couldn't help it."

Jolene stared at her for a minute when she realized that was all the explanation she'd get. It occurred to her that Vida might think herself superior, but she dismissed the thought. After purchasing fried catfish, hush puppies, and cole slaw at a fast-food shop, she boarded the eight o'clock bus and ate her dinner during the ride home. Thank God, she had her fare. At the boarding house, she slipped up the stairs to her room unnoticed, or so she thought.

Minutes later, she opened her door in response to Fannie's knock. "You're supposed to call if you're skipping a meal. I waited fifteen minutes for you."

"I missed my bus."

"You could still have called. You have a cell phone, don't you?"

Jolene braced her hands on her hips and looked at Fannie. "I'm sorry, and I'm tired. I'd appreciate it if you'd excuse me."

Fannie's tone softened, and she spoke without the stridency evident in her earlier words. "Just don't make it a habit. If you break your routine and don't tell anybody, we'll think you're in trouble somewhere."

"Yes, ma'am." She watched Fannie leave, dropped herself to the edge of her bed, folded her arms, pressed them to her middle and rocked herself.

Memories of her mama's tongue lashings lapped at her as waves lap at the shore. Ugly, hate-filled reminders of a time she longed to forget. *If she does it again, I'm going to tell her off.* Why didn't anybody understand her loneliness, how she longed to have someone care for her? She got ready for bed, opened her latest treasure, *Obsession*, crawled in, and began to read.

After an hour, she closed the book. *I wish I knew why Prince, a ne'er-do-well who isn't worth two cents, excites and thrills me and I feel nothing for Magnus, who's strong, loving, protective, and as sexy as Prince.* She put the book into the drawer of her night table, turned out the light and tried to sleep, but she couldn't help comparing Prince to Bob Tucker and Magnus to Gregory Hicks. *I wonder if something's wrong with me. I want a man like Gregory and Magnus, but the Princes and Bobs excite and attract me.*

"What happened to you?" Harper asked when she boarded the bus Friday morning. She told him, and his facial expression changed to one of disgust. She was sure of it. "If you want to let other people run your life, go to it."

"But she's my friend, and I couldn't leave the children alone."

"Think she didn't know that?" he replied and didn't speak again until they reached her stop.

"You coming Sunday?" she asked.

"Didn't I say I would?"

"Then can we go to one of those amusement parks before we see a movie and go to dinner?"

"Whatever you want, babe."

* * *

Before the week's end, Jolene realized that she had misread Francine Spaldwood. The men who lived at Thank the Lord Boarding House treated her with the kind of respect reserved for nuns, and all but Judd and Richard gave her a wide berth.

"You staying long?" Judd asked Francine as he and Richard sat with her in the lounge Thursday evening after supper.

"As long as my job holds out. I work in Ocean Pines."

"Doing what?" Richard wanted to know. She had a manner that suggested she was accustomed to wielding authority.

"I work for the state in the Department of Internal Affairs. Nothing special. Just nine to five drudgery."

He didn't believe the last part, but he didn't share his thoughts. She was too intelligent, too well informed to content herself with a job that bored her. "I hope you'll be happy here with us." He realized he meant it, and that surprised him, for ordinarily he concerned himself with other peoples' well being only in the most abstract and impersonal sense.

She sat forward, and her demeanor held a peculiar urgency as if life depended on his response to whatever she was about to ask. "How do you spend your days, Richard?"

"Writing his memoirs and talking to me," Judd said, "and he's giving free seminars at the local library and at the high school."

Why did Judd find it necessary to defend him, Richard wondered, for the man's tone and words showed his testiness.

"That's it, more or less," he said to Francine and changed the subject. "If you haven't explored Pike Hill, would you care to walk around with me after supper and before dark?"

She didn't hesitate. "I'd like that. All I know of this town is the route to Ocean Pines."

A straight shooter who didn't beat around the bush. He'd known only one other woman of that type: Estelle Mitchell.

Harper Masterson rang the doorbell before Jolene could get down to the front door and wait there for him. She knew he'd made a point of doing it, for he remarked on their last date that she apparently didn't want him to meet her landlady or any of the other boarders. He took her to the amusement park, a movie starring Samuel L. Jackson, and to dinner at the restaurant of her choice—the Lobster Pot in Snow Hill, the most expensive seafood restaurant in the region outside of Ocean City. When they were about to leave the restaurant, she took his hand and led him to the souvenir shop near the door.

"I've always wondered how they get ships into these bottles," she said. "They're fascinating. I love to look at them."

"It's an art. Look, it's getting late. We've been to an amusement park, seen a movie, been to two museums, and had a long dinner. Let's go. I need to stop by my place."

He hadn't mentioned sex, so she had begun to think he wanted to do things for her because, as he said at first, she was beautiful and had plenty of everything in the right places. But just in case, she unbuttoned the top button of her pink linen shirt-dress,

"Okay." She didn't look at him. He'd spent a hundred dollars for dinner alone, so he deserved whatever he wanted. *Oh, no. Not that!* It occurred to her at once that Melinda didn't have sex with Blake the first time he wanted it. *Besides, if I wait till the next time he wants it, I may get that bottle with the ship in it.*

Harper parked in front of the building in which he lived, cut the motor and said, "Coming?" His question reminded her of something, but she wasn't quite sure what.

Inside his small, neat apartment, she didn't get a chance to see her surroundings before he put one hand on her buttocks, the other at the back of her head and fastened her body to his.

"Mmm . . . wait a—"

"I've waited as long as I'm going to. Open up to me. I want you here and now."

The hard length of him pressed against her belly, and excitement shot through her, sending blood hot and fast to her vagina. Visions of herself exploding in orgasm while he pounded into her had her twisting and rubbing against him in a frenzy to experience the pleasure of which she had read in her books. Recklessly, she unbuttoned her dress and exposed her high, rounded breasts.

"My Lord, I never dreamed you were so hot," he said and sucked her right nipple into his warm mouth. When, acting out her fantasies, her hand grabbed his penis and squeezed it, his groans matched her loud cries. He slipped her dress to the floor, ripped off her bikini panties, sat her in a chair, got on his knees and plowed his tongue into her. She howled as he worked at her. Unable to bear it longer, she twisted her hips and squeezed her nipple, locked her ankles across his back, and screamed as she burst into orgasm. He dragged her off the chair and on to the zebra rug that covered a part of the floor.

"Don't make me pregnant," she pleaded.

"No way, baby." He slipped on a condom and drove himself into her. Immediately the pumping and squeezing resumed and she raised her body to him with such force that she nearly threw the two-hundred-pound man off her. He gripped her hips and accelerated his pace. It seemed to her that a thousand strange images darted before her, her nerve endings burned, and she thought she'd die if whatever he built inside of her wouldn't let itself loose. At last, he held her still and rode her mercilessly as her hips ceased to slither over the zebra rug.

"Oh, Lord," she screamed and sank into a vortex of oblivion. He sucked a nipple into his mouth, pumped hard a few more times, and collapsed into her arms.

Several minutes passed before he raised his head, looked down at her and said, "You came so hard. I never knew a woman to come that hard."

Shocked by what she believed to be an inadequacy, she apologized. "I'm sorry if I disappointed you. I . . . uh . . . haven't had much experience."

He stared at her in what was clearly disbelief. "You sure as hell don't need any lessons, baby." He left her, went to the bathroom and returned fully dressed.

Embarrassed because, hoping for more of what she had just experienced, she had remained as he left her, she looked around for her dress, but didn't see it. "May I please have a towel?" He threw her a towel and left the room while she dressed.

"When am . . . are we going to see each other again?" she asked as he walked with her to the front door of the boarding house.

"We'll see."

Oh Lord, she'd made a big mistake. She should have told him to take her home. Fear streaked through her. He couldn't drop her after making her feel like that. "What do you mean?" she asked him.

He put his hands in his trouser pockets and kicked at the wooden floor of the porch. "I was liking you a whole lot, but you don't have any real feelings for a man. You're just after what you can get."

Cringing, she stepped away from him. "How can you—"

He continued as if she hadn't attempted to speak. "You were getting to a place deep inside of me, but if I hang out with you, I'll be broke before I know it. I don't like women who're only out for what they can get from a man. I'm a bus driver, and you know it. I spent over two hundred dollars on this date, and that's twenty percent of what I made last week. On top of that, you wanted a hundred and fifty dollar model ship. Last Sunday, you also wanted to go to museums, a movie and have dinner at the most expensive restaurant you'd heard about. I'm looking for a woman to build my life with. Be seeing you."

She didn't bother to wipe the tears that bathed her face, but ran into the house and up the stairs to her room. At last she had found a man who could do the things the men in her books did, and she'd mishandled the relationship. She didn't know what to do or how to do it. She had never had a girlfriend, never talked with any girl or woman about boys and men and had no idea how you got a man to love you and care for you. All she had were her books, and those women were so perfect, they were educated and knew so much. She wasn't like them and couldn't be. She had thought that Harper cared for her, but he hadn't.

"I'm not going to cry," she told herself. "Maybe I won't have anything else to do with men." She washed her face, put on her pajamas, went to the window and gazed out at the quiet, deserted night. "It must be my fault. All these women I see with men couldn't be crazy. But what am I doing wrong?" Dispirited, she closed the curtain and, in doing so, banished the night and let her own gloom envelope her. Needing comfort, she reached for her book, but put it aside. Nothing the men in those books did matched what Harper did to her and how he made her feel. For the first time in months, she didn't take one of her books to bed.

The following morning, Monday, she arrived at the bus stop early, counted out the exact fare and boarded as soon as the bus arrived. She dropped two dollars and fifty cents into the slot and headed toward the back of the bus before she realized that Harper wasn't sitting in the driver's seat. Maybe he'd asked for another route. A twinge of pain settled in the region of her heart when she recalled his lecture prior to his parting words: "Be seeing you."

He didn't have to quit his route just to get away from me. If he doesn't want me, I sure don't want him. Why hadn't she told him that instead of running away, ashamed?

Fear streaked through her when her boss met her at the door, for she was certain that he intended to fire her or, at least give her a tongue lashing, although she couldn't imagine what for.

"I'm putting fifty dollars more in your pay envelope every week, Jolene. You're doing okay."

Stunned, for he hadn't complimented her on her work or even suggested that he was satisfied, her weak expression of appreciation caused him to gape. "If you don't need the raise, I can put the money in the bank for my kid. Ask any of these operators whether I ever volunteered to give them a raise."

"Oh, no, sir. I'm so surprised, I didn't know what to say. I'm grateful for it. I sure am."

His expression had the air of a man who appreciated himself. "That's better."

"Can you help me for an hour after work today?" Vida asked Jolene while they sat in the back of the shop eating their lunch. "I swear I'll be home at five-thirty sharp. I'm sorry about last time."

Harper probably wouldn't be driving the six o'clock bus, and even if he was, it wouldn't matter. She had nothing planned. "All right, but if you're not there at five-thirty, I'm leaving."

Vida's stare had a hint of hostility, but Jolene didn't back down. She wanted Vida for a friend, but she didn't want Fannie to make her leave the boardinghouse. "Last time, I didn't get home till nine o'clock, and I had to listen to my landlady dress me down for missing supper. The cost of supper's included in my rent, but I had to buy another supper 'cause you came home later than you said."

"I'll be there on time, Jolene. Just please help me out this afternoon."

"All right. But I'm leaving there at five-thirty."

She enjoyed Vida's twins and looked forward to being with them, but she sensed that it would be unwise to let Vida know it. At five twenty-five, she had an attack of anxiety. If she didn't get to supper on time, she'd have an argument with Fannie and probably have to leave the most peaceful life she had ever known. But did she dare leave the twins alone? The two little brown faces looked up to her with brilliant smiles and sparkling eyes waiting for her to read more of *Puss 'n Boots.*

"I can't do it," she said to herself. "I'd die if anything happened to them. From now on, Vida can pay her sitter to stay here until she comes home from wherever she goes after work. She doesn't bring packages home, so she isn't shopping, as she said she was."

At ten minutes to six, she telephoned Fannie, and asked her to have Marilyn save her some supper. "I can't help it," she said. "If you're up when I get there, I'll tell you all about it."

To her surprise, Fannie agreed. "We don't usually do that, but you seem distressed, so I'll put something away for you."

"Sorry," Vida said when she rushed in.

Angry beyond words, Jolene walked past her without speaking. Her mood hadn't changed when she boarded the bus for her trip home, and not until the driver said, "What put that scowl on you face, sistah?" did she look at him. The voice did not belong to Harper Masterson.

"I think you drove me to Salisbury this morning," she said.

"I did indeed."

Did that mean Harper didn't work that day? It wasn't his day off, she mused. "Where's the man who usually drives this route?"

He closed the door and headed for Pike Hill. "You mean Harper? He got in an accident last night on one of those back roads between Ocean Pines and Pike Hill. Got banged up pretty bad. I expect he'll be out for a good while." She wouldn't have been more stunned if he'd shot her. She opened her mouth to say she was sorry, but no words came.

The driver glanced up at her. "Was he your old man?"

She didn't dare tell the truth. "N . . . no. But we talked a lot. I'm . . . uh . . . If you go to see him, tell him I'm sorry." And she was. About everything. She trudged to the back of the bus and sat down. She hadn't caused Harper's accident, but guilt pervaded her. She had the presence of mind to tell the driver good night when she got off the bus. As she turned off Bay Avenue into Ocean Road, looking neither right nor left, she grabbed her chest. "Oh!" she exclaimed, before remembering that the ghostly figure before her could only be her own shadow. She walked faster, nearly tripping over a crack in the sidewalk, until she reached the boardinghouse. Once on the porch, she leaned against the house to catch her breath.

Almost immediately, Fannie opened the door. "Come on in. You seem washed out. I hope you don't mind eating your supper in the kitchen. I don't want the others to see you and think I make exceptions."

She wondered what Fannie's moment of largess would cost her, but she was so glad for it that she smiled her appreciation and told herself not to be cynical. "The kitchen's fine. Thanks."

Jolene followed Fannie into Marilyn's pristine sanctuary, a kitchen furnished with polished stainless steel shelving, refrigerator, freezer, sinks and stoves, hanging copper cookware, all set off with brick walls and floor. She'd never seen such a kitchen.

"This is beautiful."

"Cost me a fortune, but it's worth it. If Marilyn can't have the best working conditions, she won't stay. Let's sit over here at this little table," Fannie said, bringing a tray of food for Jolene and a cup of coffee for herself. "What happened to you?"

She told Fannie about her relationship with Vida and added, "My mother never let me have friends. Never. I was always alone, and I still don't have any friends. Vida's the only one at the shop who talked to me. I wanted her to be my friend, but she upset me today. I told her I wouldn't get my supper if I missed the six o'clock bus, and she walked in the house five minutes before six. If I had left those little children alone in that apartment,

I could have been jailed for it, and she knew it. It's the third time she's let me down, promising to be home by five-thirty and not getting there till it's almost six o'clock."

Jolene stroked the back of her neck trying to rub away the tension. She thought for a second. "Each time Vida asked me to baby-sit, she said she had to buy something for the children, but each time she came home without a shopping bag. Empty-handed. She's not shopping. So, what is she doing? Why does she need me to baby-sit every day all of a sudden?"

Fannie sipped coffee and tapped the table with the fingers of her left hand. "She's using you. You want her for a friend, and she knows it, so she's taking advantage of you. The woman's not shopping; she's probably seeing a man. You should put a stop to this right now. She isn't behaving as a true friend, and you shouldn't accept that kind of behavior from anybody."

"I just wanted to help her."

"No. You wanted a friend, and you did things for her that you thought would make her like you. You convinced yourself that she needed you. She doesn't. Jolene, look straight at me. The richest person in the world can't buy friendship or love. You can buy people's company, but when the money's gone, the people go with it."

"But I—"

"What does she offer you other than a chance to play with her children? You don't need playmates."

"I thought . . . I don't know. I guess I'm not good at making friends with women or men."

Jolene lowered her gaze to avoid seeing the pity in Fannie's eyes. "Honey, your mother was an unhappy woman who hated men and distrusted women, and she really did a job on you. Stop letting her attitudes weigh you down, girl."

Fannie was right in that Emma Tilman was a bitter, hate-filled woman, but she had never associated herself with it, hadn't realized that she had assimilated her mama's attitudes.

Burdened by Fannie's admonishments, Jolene stood to end the conversation. "Yes ma'am. Thanks for saving my supper."

"Are you going to baby-sit for that woman tomorrow?"

"No, indeed. She can find somebody else. Not me."

Jolene tried to force herself to tell Fannie good night and go to her room, but her conscience flailed her, and she stood rooted to the spot. *How do you think Harper felt when he realized you used him? Is that why he had the accident? And what about Gregory? Did you treat him right?"* In her mind, she denied both, but she didn't believe in her innocence.

She looked steadily at Fannie. "If a man asks you for a date, does that mean he cares for you?"

Fannie's lower lip dropped. "It means you interest him. Whether he learns to care for you depends on a lot of things including how you act, what you say and how you say it, what kind of person you are. He doesn't fall head over heels for you just because you smile at him, wear a size thirty-eight D bra and swing your behind when you walk."

Jolene trudged up the stairs to her room, perplexed and confused. How different was she from other women? *If I had a real friend, somebody my age, we could talk.* She turned on the faucet, tested the water and stepped under the shower. "I want some friends," she said aloud, "but not badly enough to let people walk over me. From now on, I'm gonna be careful."

While Jolene was gaining a better understanding of herself, Richard had begun to think about Francine more often than he deemed wise. "Would you join me for a swim?" he asked her one Saturday morning in mid-September as they left the dining room after breakfast. "I doubt we'll have many more opportunities this summer."

Her hesitation was an unexpected chill, and he fought to shrug it off. He wasn't accustomed to having a woman turn him down for any reason. A smile began to form on his face and, intent upon enticing her, he reached toward her but immediately withdrew his hand. He had to resist the Richard who charmed his way through life, and he didn't want to be that man ever again. He intended to make his way honestly and to deal with a straight deck no matter who the person or what the circumstances, but he knew it wouldn't be easy; a frog is used to croaking, and when night comes, that is what the frog does.

Her smile surprised him, and he was glad he hadn't shown her that womanizing part of him that he considered his worst side. "Give me fifteen minutes, and I'll be right with you. Meet you at the door," she said.

Richard leaned against the wall, gazing up at the stairs and, although he knew she was attractive, he hadn't associated her with the blatant sexiness that her bathing suit and its fish-net coverall revealed. He was about to ask her why she wore that plastic pouch at her hip, its strap crossing her shoulder like a woman's shoulder bag, but thought better of it. She could be one of those people who always carried identification, though somehow he didn't believe it. He could get both of his fists into that pouch with room to spare.

He had always loved the feel of sand between his toes, but not on that hot morning. "Want to go in?" he asked her, peeved that she seemed preoccupied with three men who stood to-gether several yards from the water's edge. The smile that she flashed reminded him of his own shallow charm and the ease with which he had meted it out.

"In a minute," she said. "This is so new to me."

He stared at her. Her behavior seemed to him out of charac-ter, and it perplexed him as to why. Nevertheless, he didn't push her, but repaid her with a smile that didn't reach his eyes or touch his lips.

His fingers dug into his hips. "Three beats one anytime."

But her attention was on the three men. She would have an explanation for it, but he wasn't sure he cared to hear it. He had come to the beach for a swim so, without another word, he headed for the water.

Just my luck, Francine said to herself. *Right down to the pit of my gut, I know he's the one, but what could I do with Richard Peterson standing three feet from me?* From the corner of her eye, she saw Richard dive into a wave. *And I have to cover my tracks from him, too. He's sharp*.

She unzipped the sack at her side, took out a pen and small

pad, made a few notes, replaced the items, zipped up the pouch and plunged into the water.

"You're quite a swimmer," Richard said later, as they sat on a boulder drying themselves in the sun.

She had to be, but he didn't need to know that. "Thanks. It's one of my favorite sports."

He stood. "I'm going back now. If you're interested in going with me . . ."

He didn't finish the thought, but she didn't need more convincing evidence that she had vexed him by paying attention to the three men. "Of course, I'm going back with you," she said as if he had no reason to doubt it. And to put him on the defensive, she added, "Why do you ask?"

His left eyebrow shot up. "You seemed to have other interests, and I'd be the last one to interfere with your fun."

She squashed the smart answer that sat on the tip of her tongue, because she was at fault, and he deserved better. "I thought I knew one of those men. I still think so. Nowadays, bald men grow hair, get transplants and wear wigs, and young men dye their hair or shave it off. Some wear contact lenses to change their eye color. You never know."

"Is it important?"

"I could be wrong," she answered, finessing his question, "but my hunches are usually right. It's getting hot. Ready to go?" He didn't press her for a further explanation as she had known he wouldn't, and she didn't plan to offer more. She didn't like lying, and if she said anything more about it, she would have to lie.

"I enjoyed that swim," she told him after they entered the boardinghouse. "I hope we can do it again."

When he didn't reply, merely smiled and half-bowed, she knew that her response to his question as to whether recognizing the man was important hadn't satisfied him. *Well, it's the best I can do*, she said to herself with a shrug and headed up the stairs to her room. There, she emptied the contents of the pouch into her pocketbook, showered, dressed in white slacks, a lavender T-shirt and white sneakers and took out her cell phone.

"I'm sure it was he," she said, "but my hands were tied."

"Not to worry. Dark clouds don't always bring rain; there'll be another day and another time."

"True," she said and hung up.

Jolene had spent Saturdays alone in her room, except the times when she had her meals, and by Sunday morning restlessness usually got the better of her. When Fannie called her to the telephone a few minutes after breakfast, she raced down the stairs wondering which of the men she knew would telephone her on Sunday morning.

"Hello," she said, nearly out of breath.

"Hi, Jolene. I know you don't usually go to church, and I have an emergency. Could you keep the girls for me this afternoon from one till five? I'll probably be home before five. Can you? It's terribly important, Jolene."

Jolene stared at the phone. *I understand it now*, she said to herself. *You think I'm stupid*. To Vida, she said, "Last time, you knew you'd made me miss my bus, and you didn't even apologize. You didn't ask how I got home, either. Well, Vida, I am never going to baby-sit for you again no matter how many emergencies you have. I wanted us to be friends, but I realize I have a lot to learn. Try one of the other girls in the shop. Sorry." She hung up, and she should have felt good, but she didn't. She went into the lounge where Judd sat watching the US Open tennis men's final.

"Sit down. Sit down," he said. "It'll be over in a few minutes. I don't see how those fellows can play in that heat." She waited with him until one of the players fell to his knees, raised both arms in exaltation, and Judd turned off the television.

"Why don't I get us some ginger ale," he said and headed for the machine before she could respond. He opened a bottle, poured half of it into a cup and handed it to her. "It's nice to have company."

"Do you . . . uh . . . know any books on friendship that I could get from the library?"

"You looking for a text book or something casual?"

"Something casual, I guess."

"Well, a few years ago, sister–friends books were very popular with black women novelists. I read a few of 'em. I could bring you two or three from the library when I go tomorrow night, but you be sure and give 'em back to me. I believe in taking care of library property."

"Sure I will. Thank you for being so nice, Judd."

He laid his head to the side and looked at her. "That's what friends are for, Jolene."

"Yeah, but they take advantage of you."

"Only if you let 'em. Your own sisters and brothers will do that if you permit 'em to walk over you. Your husband will do it, too. The way people treat you is up to you."

"Thanks. All I learned at home was how to clean, scrub, run errands for my mother and my grandmother, cook, and let them make a slave of me. The first thing I ever did all on my own without my mother's interference was arrange for her funeral, and that was a little more than six months ago. It's a wonder I know how to walk straight." She sounded bitter, and she didn't care, for she *was* resentful.

He sipped his ginger ale and rocked back and forth in the Shaker rocking chair. "Hmm. I take it your mother didn't have many friends around."

"She didn't have any. She didn't like men, women or children, and she told me more than once that she wished she'd never seen my father. She died like she lived . . . with nobody near but me."

"Well, I see you're planning a better life for yourself, and that's good. The way to have friends is to be a friend, but that doesn't mean being a footstool for anybody. Friendship is a mutual relationship, and it takes a long time to develop. Treat people the way you want 'em to treat you, and that goes for men as well as women."

Did he know about her and Gregory or her and Harper? "It's hard to know how to act with people."

"No, it isn't. Always do what's right, and you don't have to figure it out."

In spite of the air conditioning, her body began to perspire and she had to resist fanning herself. "I have a few things to do before lunch, so if you'll excuse me . . . I enjoyed talking with you. Maybe we can talk again sometime."

"Sure. That's the great advantage of living in a place like this. We support each other."

Inside her room, she closed the blinds to shut out the sunlight that seemed as blistering as if it were mid-July. "Why did I tell him all that? Maybe he knows I made a play for Percy and then turned him down. Lord, I hope not." She walked to the window, turned and retraced her steps. *I wish I had been nicer to Gregory, but I didn't know. Mama always said women shouldn't trust men, that they were only after what they could get, and that we should do to them before they did to us. Maybe she was wrong. I just don't know.*

Around five that afternoon when the sun had become less intense, she went out of the house and stood by the front steps looking across the park. "If I had a car, I'd get in it and just drive and drive," she said to herself. Without thinking of a destination, she set out down Ocean Road, and when she reached Bay Avenue, she turned toward the beach and continued walking. As she neared the water, she sensed the peacefulness of her surroundings, the quiet broken only by the lapping and sloshing of the distant waves. She sat on a boulder that looked as if it had spent centuries in that spot and wished she'd brought something to read.

The ocean breeze began to cool her skin, the sunrays had disappeared, and she realized that she'd sat there for over an hour.

"It isn't a good idea to be out here alone late in the day and, in any case, I don't suppose you want Fannie to lecture you about being late for supper."

She looked up to see Richard Peterson standing a few feet away. "You're right. The time just slipped away from me. It's so peaceful here that I hate to leave."

"Tourists don't usually come over here, so we have it to ourselves. It's what makes living here worthwhile." He seemed thoughtful. "Look, Miss Tilman. If you're not busy Tuesdays and Thursdays from four-thirty to six-thirty, we could use you at the library. We hold children's computer classes then, and—"

She didn't let him finish it. "I don't know much about computers, Mr. Peterson, only enough for what I have to do at work."

"We have a man to teach the children, but we need someone to help me discipline them."

She could do it, she knew, because her success with Vida's twins was proof of it, but she couldn't face Gregory Hicks again. "I'm so beat from standing on my feet all day that I won't have the energy," she told him. "And besides, I was just thinking that if I stay here much longer, I'll grow old with no purpose in life just like my mother. A bitter, unpleasant old woman. I need to leave Pike Hill."

"Look," he said, falling into step with her as they headed home, "You have to pull yourself out of this."

"If you'd been where I've been, you'd think I'm doing great."

He slowed his steps. "What do you mean?"

"Mr. Peterson, the story of my life is long and dreary. I'm working my way out of it as best I can. Something tells me I'm going to have to reinvent myself, and maybe I should begin that somewhere else."

"I'm anything but an expert on running one's life, but I can tell you that no matter where you go, your misery goes with you. Best thing is to deal with it right here."

She stopped and looked at the man with new eyes and a different level of understanding. "Is that what you're doing?"

He kicked at the sand beneath his feet. "You could say that."

Encouraged, she said, "I hope you at least had a mother who cared about you."

He seemed startled before he said, "She dotes on me. What about your father? Didn't he look out for you?"

She pulled air through her front teeth. "My father? I don't have the slightest idea who he is."

"Good Lord. I *am* terribly sorry." He stopped, evidently disconcerted for having asked her a question that he thought embarrassed her, and she watched, horrified, as his fingers punished his scalp and a frown clouded his face.

All she could think of then was a means of escape. "I'd better hurry, since I have to dress before supper," she said and scampered off, humiliated for having exposed her shortcomings to a man obviously of high status.

For long minutes, Richard remained where she'd left him, bewildered by his own reaction to the disadvantages and, what must have been suffering, of another human being. He had felt for the woman, had for a moment put himself in her place and wondered how he would have fared if he'd suffered as she obviously had.

"This is terrible," he said to himself. "She believes I think badly of her." He walked on to the boardinghouse, more slowly than was his wont, and reached it with barely enough time to wash up and get to his seat in the dining room by seven o'clock.

At supper, he did his best not to let Jolene catch him watching her, but she had become an enigma to him, a puzzle that bothered him. His ability at problem solving was the primary reason why he reached the top in the diplomatic field, and he meant to solve the problem of Jolene. For a start, he wanted to know why she had toyed with Percy Lucas.

"That one's easy," Judd said when Richard broached the matter while they played blackjack later that evening. "Nobody dishes out pain with more skill than those who've been its victims."

"In other words, nobody uses like one who's been used? Right?"

"That's about it," Judd said, "but there's hope for that one, because she'll listen."

Richard glanced to his left to see a small table beside his chair, and looked around as Marilyn approached him with a pot of coffee and a tray of noel cookies.

"You're not about to turn these down," she said. "Judd will tell you how good they are. He loves them."

He stared at her. "Thanks, but in that case, I suggest you put this table beside Judd's chair. I don't care for any cookies."

She fastened her knuckles to her hips and smiled at him. "Richard, nobody turns down my cookies."

He tossed out a joker and smiled triumphantly at his card partner. "I wouldn't either if they didn't come with a price."

She sidled up to him. "Now, Richard, that's not true. I just want to be friendly. That's all."

He looked at Judd. "Friendly, eh? I'm supposed to believe that? Next, she'll pee on my leg and tell me it's raining."

Marilyn stomped off, and Judd leaned back in the rocker and released a guffaw. "Ain't heard nothing that funny in years. You can put that little table over here. Nothing on it will go to waste." He winked at Richard. "I got you to thank for these. They're m' favorites, and she knows it, but you see who she gave them to. The old girl ain't dead yet."

"As far as I'm concerned, she's dead and buried. Pass me a couple of those cookies." He went to the water cooler and got a paper cup. "You use that cup and saucer she brought, Judd. I don't want her to see me with it. You'd have thought she'd bring you a cup and saucer."

Judd savored a cookie and sipped the coffee. "You don't know Marilyn. I told you she's like poverty; you can't get rid of it, and you can't get rid of *her*."

"I look at her as payment for my sins. But if she doesn't back off, I'll change tactics and take everything she offers except what she most wants me to have. And if she acts out, I'll charge her with sexual harassment."

"D . . . don't do that," Judd sputtered. "This is the best kitchen in Pike Hill, and if she went to jail, I'd miss all these good meals. I'd have to testify against you."

Richard laughed in spite of his effort to appear serious. "Now I know that your real friend is your belly." He sobered at once. "Can you believe Jolene Tilman's sitting over there in an animated conversation with Lila Mae Henry. First time I've seen her talk with a woman."

"Same here," Judd said. "Jolene's lonely. Maybe she and Lila Mae can become friends. It would be a blessing."

Chapter Six

Jolene pulled her chair closer to Lila Mae Henry, a short woman who fit perfectly into a size twenty dress. "I wanted to go to college, but my mama said college would be wasted on me. Did you finish?"

"Sure thing, and I got my masters degree, too," Lila Mae said, her eyes sparkling in her attractive, animated face. "You can still go in the evenings. Course, you'd miss the campus fun that full-time students have." Her gaze shifted to the ceiling. "I guess you've passed the age for that kind of foolishness anyway."

Maybe, but she would still like to experience it. She leaned forward, eager to learn about college. "What kind of fun did you have? I thought you just studied in college."

Lila Mae slapped the side of her jaw and rolled her eyes suggesting that the thought was ludicrous. "Girl, go way from here. You kidding? Me and my roommate used to kill a half pint of booze every Saturday night. My dad's a preacher, and he wouldn't even let my sister and me wear lipstick and perfume. Soon as I got to college, I went wild.

"I was popular because I was the drummer in the jazz band." She held both hands up, palms out. "If daddy had known that, he would have jerked me out of Hampton faster than a tornado shoots through flat land. Anyhow, I was slim in those days, and what with playing in the band and being on the speed skating and fencing teams, I had a ball. I quit boozing in my junior year when the dean caught us and I nearly got expelled."

"Gee. I don't drink. My mama didn't allow any alcoholic drinks in the house. She said that only loose women drank."

Lila Mae sucked air through her teeth. "She must have been related to my dad. He was so restrictive that he made every sinful thing appear enticing. Soon as I left home, I did practically everything he told me not to do."

"Didn't you feel guilty?"

"About what? I was young."

Maybe that was the difference, because she was certainly ashamed of the bad things she'd done. "What about boys? Did you . . . uh . . . you know?"

Lila Mae buffed her nails on the sleeve of her blouse. "Yes, indeedy. That, too. And here I am stuck in this place with four men—five if you count Rodger, three of whom don't inspire me to walk in my sleep—and one who wouldn't open his door if I did."

"If Richard opened his door, what would you do?"

Lila Mae's face took on the expression of a purring feline. "I'd crawl in, girl. He can walk around with his head high like he's the president of the United States, but he can't fool me. That man's a stud."

"Richard? He's a gentleman."

Lila Mae's laugh rang throughout the lounge. "Grace and charm are part of being a stud, girl. Don't you know that? I'll bet he can't count the women he's had."

"Francine's his type."

"Women are his type. I'm waiting to see what he's going to do with Marilyn. She's after him like a cat after a mouse."

"He won't go for her."

"If you set food in front of a hungry man, he's not likely to push it aside. Trust me."

Jolene put her hand over her mouth to cut off a yawn. "Don't you like him? He's handsome."

Lila Mae flexed her left shoulder in a quick shrug. "I learned long ago to like who likes me and not to want what I can't get. He wouldn't look twice at me."

Eager for her first lesson in the ways of men, Jolene sought to prolong the conversation. "Why not? You're nice looking."

"Girl, wake up. That man's never been inside of a size twenty and never will, no matter what kind of face is on top of it."

"My mama always said men are only after what they can get."

"I hate to tell you, honey, but your mama had it all wrong. Some guys are wonderful. You have to know how to pick them and what to do with 'em after you get 'em."

"You ever been married?"

Lila Mae frowned, and an expression of sadness swept over her face. "Yeah. And to a great guy, but I messed up, and that was that. I have to do some lesson plans for tomorrow. Nice talking with you."

For a while, Jolene remained as Lila Mae left her, trying to digest the woman's words and to understand her attitudes. Finally, nonplussed, she headed for her room. "I'm not happy with who I am, but I'm not sure I want to be like her."

Up in her room, she stood at the window gazing out past the darkness to the stars that blanketed the night sky and shudders crept threw her body. She folded her arms beneath her breasts for comfort. *I wish I hadn't ruined everything with Gregory. I could help Richard for an hour with the children in the computer classes, and I could go to church with Fannie sometime. I could even walk to the library tomorrow evening with Judd.* She sniffed to a void crying, *If I was just coming to Pike Hill and knew what I know now, I'd do everything differently.*

Jolene overslept the next morning, had to leave the boarding house without breakfast, and hopped on the bus a minute before the driver closed the door. She paid her fare and unable to force herself to take a seat, lingered at the front of the bus. When the driver's radio emitted the haunting strains of "Where Was I?" she turned to go.

"Anything I can do for you, sis?" the driver asked.

She walked back to him. "Have you heard anything from Harper Masterson?"

"I hear he's still slipping in and out of a coma. You sure there's nothing between the two of you?"

"I rode his bus twice a day for three months. Isn't that enough to care about a person?" she said. But did it explain the guilt she felt when she thought of him? Nobody had to tell her that he'd been thinking of her when he wrecked his car.

The driver stopped at a railroad crossing for the approaching train and looked at her. "Hey. Don't bark at me. Go see him for yourself. This bus stops three blocks from Mercy Hospital."

"Thanks. I will."

The morning passed and, at the beauty parlor, Vida ignored Jolene as if she weren't there. "What's with you two?" her boss asked. "I don't want my workers mad at each other. The customers can sense it." She told him the truth. "You should have caught on the first time," he said. "Every gal in this shop is on to Vida. Leave her alone."

"I have, sir, but I feel sorry for her children."

"We all do, but that's no reason to stick your head in the fire."

She remembered Judd's advice and nodded. "I have a lot to learn. I'm thinking about taking some evening classes."

"Yeah? Education is a good thing: Go for it! But text books don't teach you how to deal with people. Experience teaches you that." He patted her shoulder. "You'll do all right."

She didn't know why, but she felt better about herself. *Saturday, I'm going to see Harper and tell him how sorry I am. If I hadn't upset him, maybe he wouldn't have had that accident.*

"Harper, this is Jolene," she whispered, looking down at the man's bandaged head, arms and shoulders that gave him the appearance of a mummy. "Can you hear me?"

"Yes. I hear you."

"I'm sorry about your accident. That . . . and everything else. I didn't act right. Do you need anything?"

"Like what?"

She thought for a minute. What did men use that he might need or enjoy? "I could read to you, bring you some toilet articles, or maybe some food."

A groan escaped him, and she leaned closer. "Something must be wrong with my head," he said. "You don't do things for people. Remember? You have people doing things for you."

She hadn't expected animosity. Indeed, she hadn't anticipated any kind of reaction from him. "I told you I am sorry. I'm sorry about a lot of things, and I'm trying to make amends."

"Well, don't have a guilt trip on my account. The doctor told me this morning that I'll be as good as new. It'll take a couple of months, but I'll get there. Pull that shade down before you go. The sun's shining right in my eyes."

She pulled the shade. "I hope you'll be better soon." He didn't respond. "Bye," she said, but she wasn't sure that he heard her, for he didn't answer.

She met a doctor in the corridor. "Doctor, when did Harper Masterson come out of the coma?"

"A couple of days ago. Surprised all of us. He's out of danger, and from now on he ought to make good progress."

She had to be certain. "So his thinking is clear?"

"Clear as a blue sky."

She thanked him and hurried out of the hospital. It hadn't been pleasant. Harper didn't appreciate her visit, but she was glad she'd gone to see him for she felt less guilty. On the way home, she stopped at a flower stall and bought a bunch of chrysanthemums. She loved flowers, and those yellow and white blooms complemented her room.

She met Judd in the hallway when she entered the boardinghouse and, on an impulse, handed him the flowers. "I hope you like yellow flowers," she told him. "They're my favorites."

His eyes widened, and she could see that she shocked him. "Well. Well, well." His fingers caressed the clear plastic that covered the flowers. "Thank you. I don't know when I've received such a nice present. Do you have a minute for a glass of ginger ale?"

"I'd love it." She tried to make herself tell him about Harper, but couldn't because she didn't want him to think badly of her. Instead, she asked him, "Do you ever feel like you want to leave here?" She had begun to enjoy the ginger ale that he always offered as a king would offer the finest of spirits.

"Nope," he said. "This is my home. After I convinced Louvenia that I wasn't stupid enough to fall into her clutches, I came to love the place."

Her lower lip dropped. "Louvenia? You mean she—?"

"Why not? I don't have any heirs, and she expects to outlive me."

"Well, I'll be . . . ! When I heard her bad-mouthing me to Arnetha Farrell, I figured she was one of those old women who'd led a perfect life and wore a halo to prove it."

Laughter rumbled in his throat. "Louvenia worked over fifty years for one family as a live-in maid. But she did more than cook and keep house, so when the old man died, he left her well-fixed."

Jolene swallowed hard. "She told you that?"

"She brags about it to anybody who'll listen." When Jolene's bottom lip dropped, he added, "No point in being shocked. All the saints are in heaven. The creatures you see around here are all human just like you and me." He looked at his watch. "It's five forty-five. I got to be getting over to the library. See you at supper."

"You know Judd better than I do," Richard said to Fannie at supper that night. He especially liked the Monday suppers because Marilyn had the night off, and the sous-chef always served Italian food. As usual, Fannie didn't wait to hear his point.

"I should. I've known him a lot longer than you have."

"Which proves nothing, Fannie. My point is that he'll be eighty-five in a few days, and I'd like to give him a real party. What I want to know is whether it should be a surprise."

She thought for a minute. "What a wonderful idea. No, I don't think you should surprise him."

"Thanks. One more thing. I'll tell Marilyn what I want and how I want it, and if she shows me she can't follow instructions, I'll hire a caterer and have it somewhere else."

"She'll do as I say."

"I'll believe that when I see it."

"You're fond of Judd, aren't you?"

"Looks that way. He's getting to be the first real friend I ever had."

She stared at him. "You're serious, aren't you?"

He shrugged. "Why shouldn't I be? My life has changed drastically and completely since I've been here."

"I hope you're satisfied."

"Let's just say I'm adjusting. Sometimes I don't know the man who gets out of my bed every morning."

"I'll bet you had a chauffeur."

"Chauffeur? A valet, housekeeper, social secretary, and you name it. As I look back, it's a wonder I didn't step on those people. They were everywhere. I didn't have a damned bit of privacy."

She had stopped eating and stared at him in awe. "And you didn't think about that then?"

He shook his head. "It was laughable. The only thing I lifted was myself and my tennis racket."

"I don't see how anybody could enjoy that," she said, returning to her raspberry sorbet.

"As I think about it, neither do I."

Jolene didn't rush up to her room as she usually did after meals, but headed for the lounge hoping that Judd would go there as usual and that he'd have the books he promised to bring from the library. She started toward him, but Barbara Sanders, a woman of around fifty, who clerked at the local movie house, waylaid her.

"Hi. Feel like a couple of hands of gin rummy?" Barbara asked her.

Surprised by the overture, since the woman had greeted her only with a nod or "Hi" during the six months she'd lived at the boardinghouse, Jolene was at a loss as to how to respond. She didn't play gin rummy, yet she wanted to socialize with the woman. Perhaps they could be friends.

"I'd love to, Barbara, but I've never played gin rummy. Do you know another game we could play?"

"That's the only game I know. I work at the Albemarle Theater down the street about five blocks. Sitting there at that window is the easiest way I know to make a living without doing real work."

"Don't you get bored?"

"I can't afford boredom. If I took another job, I'd have to work, either with my hands, my brain or my back, and neither appeals to me. That job's as close to non-work as I can think of."

"I'm a receptionist/cashier at a beauty parlor, and as much as I have to concentrate on what I'm doing, I still get bored some- times and want to walk off and never go back there. But I stay, because I need a job."

"Tell me about it. The worst thing about living is having to work. I used to think I'd get married, have children and stay home, but keeping house and taking care of kids is more work than farming."

Jolene had an urge to get away from Barbara Sanders. She had discovered that she neither liked nor trusted lazy people, and she certainly didn't want to spend an hour discoursing with one of them about laziness.

She stood and purposefully straightened her skirt to give Barbara the impression that she was not rushing from her com- pany. "I need to speak with Judd. I hope we can continue this another time."

Barbara's face brightened. "Sure. And maybe we can go to the amusement park together sometime."

Remembering Judd's description of friends, Jolene forced a smile. "Or whatever suits us at the time. See you later."

By the time she reached Judd, Richard and Francine had joined him. "I brought your books, and I hope you'll like 'em." He indicated one by a famous writer. "I read this one a couple of years back. It's pretty good."

She thanked him. "I guess I'll go up and get started on them."

"Please join us," Richard said. "We've been discussing the dangers of the ocean."

Her eyebrow shot up. "You can drown in it, and as far as I'm concerned, that's the danger that counts." She caught herself just before she slapped her hand over her mouth. She had devalued something of interest to him, and she wanted to bite her tongue. "I'm sorry. I didn't mean—"

"No need for an apology," Judd said. "Drowning is the worst thing that can happen to anyone, but the ocean harbors a lot of dangers that can make life a living hell."

Percy Lucas passed them, and Richard held out a hand to him. "Say, why don't you pull up a chair and join us?"

Percy looked around, glancing from side to side, as if searching for an exit, and she seized that moment to stand. "You can have this chair, Percy. I was just leaving." Richard's knowing stare nearly unglued her, making her cringe with anxiety, for she knew he'd grabbed his first opportunity to get Percy and her together in order to observe their reaction to each other. She scampered up the stairs as fast as she could, her enjoyment in having socialized with the other boarders dissipated and her self-confidence shaken.

He knows something. But what? She didn't believe Percy had discussed their abortive affair, and that meant Richard saw them together. She would give anything if only she hadn't approached Percy, if she had been more circumspect. She had done it to prove her irresistibility to men, and as balm for the wounds of Jim's rejection. And she had wanted to feel something more than the pain she'd felt with Jim.

Strange, Richard thought. He wondered which of them was the offender, and he suspected Jolene; poor Percy didn't have the self-confidence to take on a woman with Jolene's looks, at least, not voluntarily. Wondering why he cared, he turned his attention to Percy.

"Making any long trips before the winter sets in?" he asked him for want of a better topic. He reasoned that if he asked the man to sit down, he ought to try to converse with him.

"I'm gonna be hauling oranges and grapefruit till after Thanksgiving. Right now, my rig's full of pecans and southern yams. If y'all don't mind, I think I'll turn in. I drove thirteen straight hours, and I gotta get started early in the morning."

"Have a good evening." He admitted to himself that he was glad to see Percy go. A duller creature hadn't been diapered.

"How'd the computer classes go this afternoon?" Judd asked

Richard. "I went down there to check out some books for Jolene, but I didn't have time to look around."

"Great. We may have to move those classes to the high school. We had sixty kids. The library can't handle all those kids."

"Maybe what's needed is a community center," Francine said, "but that would cost a few million dollars."

"Yeah. I think I'll speak with Dr. Marin. This may prove to be more successful than I had hoped."

Francine appeared thoughtful. "I still think we should work at getting a community center."

Had he heard her correctly? "Did you say 'we'?"

"I did indeed. It's a worthy cause, and I think we ought to go for it."

He noticed that Judd leaned back in his rocker, looked from Francine to him and nodded his head. It surprised him that Judd didn't offer an opinion.

"If I can help in any way, let me know," Francine told him. "You'll need clearance by the authorities, and I can manage that for you."

Richard faced her then, moved by her willingness to work for the success of a project so dear to his heart as the children's computer learning program. He reached for her hand and held it. "Thank you. You can't imagine how much your offer means to me."

She didn't move her hand, and he resisted tightening his grip. *I want this woman, but I'm not sure what I'm willing to invest or how far I'm willing to go in order to get her. She knows I'm here, and she responds to me as a man, but do I want her because I feel something for her or simply because I haven't had her?*

She separated her hand from his and he wondered what expression she saw on his face. "I'm going to say goodnight, gentlemen. If you're up early, I'll see you at breakfast."

He wanted to walk with her as far as his room, but the presence of Judd and the other boarders was sufficient to chain him to the chair. From the corner of his eye, he saw Marilyn standing in the doorway looking in his direction. What a mess, he thought. She wants me, and I want Francine.

"I hope you're not planning to toy with Francine," Judd said. "It wouldn't be proper . . . or wise."

"I've already learned not to take a woman like Francine for granted, and I neither need nor want such a lesson twice. The price is too high."

Judd's boney fingers tapped the table beside his chair. "But a minute ago you were willing to test the waters. I saw that, and she did too."

"Hell, man. I didn't realize I was so transparent. Six months ago, that wouldn't have happened. I'm, slipping."

"Which means you're losing your phoniness. And a good thing it is, too. Your feelings were plain as day on your face."

"That's too bad, because I'm not sure what my feelings are." He couldn't help grinning as he rubbed his chin with his forefinger and thumb. "So you two know more about it than I do."

"Humph. You're not fooling me."

"Listen, friend, I'm planning a party for you on your birthday, so don't make any other plans."

Judd sat forward. "You're what?"

"You heard me. Eighty-five is an important number of years for a person to have lived, and I'm throwing a party for you. All you have to do is be there."

"Well, I declare. I've never had a birthday party. You're a fine man, and I thank you. Well, whatta you know. Isn't this something!"

Judd was agreeable to the idea of a birthday party; now all he had to do was tackle Marilyn and get her cooperation without losing his temper or his independence. He excused himself and headed toward the door where Marilyn stood. Best to get it over with.

She would have lied if she said it came as a complete surprise, but the intensity of what he communicated to her knocked her off balance. In her mind's eye, Francine could still see the expression on Richard's face, and dizzying currents of need danced through her. *I'd better get my act together*, she said to herself. *I didn't come here to be sidetracked by a man's bedroom eyes and mesmerizing charm. I've got a job to do.*

Francine went to the dining room earlier than usual, as much to avoid meeting Richard as to make a time-consuming business stop en route to her office in Ocean Pines. Jolene was alone in the dining room, so Francine saw no choice but to join her.

"Good morning, Jolene. I'm rushing this morning, so please don't think I'm rude if I don't talk."

"I'm in a hurry, too. If I miss my bus, I'll be an hour late for work."

They left the house together. "I'm parked down the street," she told Jolene. "You and I haven't had a chance to get acquainted. If you'd like, maybe we could go bowling one night. Ocean Pines has some nice bowling alleys."

"I'd love it. If you don't mind bowling with a beginner, just let me know when. I'm usually free after dinner."

"All right. Have a great day."

"You, too."

Francine headed for Spring Creek, a few miles north of Ocean Pines, parked at an all-night eatery, felt around in the bottom of her pocketbook, jumped out of the car and went inside.

"Coffee, please. As black as you can make it." Francine spoke louder than was her habit, but that didn't perturb Mike, the counter cook.

"Sure thing. I'm just mixing flapjacks. You want some?" She swung off the counter stool, went over to the jukebox and dropped two quarters in the machine. As she walked back to the counter and her black coffee, her gaze swept the room.

"I think I'll skip the calories this morning, Mike. Been gaining in the wrong places." She took a few sips of coffee. "Kinda chilly this morning. Looks as if we'll have an early fall."

"Don't count on it. Birds all over the place." She pushed the coffee cup to Mike. "See you next time." Code language. Her detour had been a waste of time.

She got into her sleek white Cougar, started the engine and within minutes brought the car to rest in the parking lot of her office building. Mike was one of the best, and their successes read like Tiger Woods's record at the PGA major events of golf. But six months of hard work at that job had netted them nothing.

"Maybe I'm going about this all wrong. Maybe I need a decoy."

"The boss wants to see you, Francine," a male co-worker said before she had a chance to sit down.

"Thanks." She grabbed a writing pad and strode up the concrete stairs to the second floor. "You wanted to see me, sir?"

"Yeah. The mayor and the city council are gunning for my head. We've been on this job for almost six months. Any progress?"

"None to speak of. I'm doing my best. If you want headquarters to put someone else on it . . ." She let the suggestion hang.

"I don't, and you know it, because you're the best we've got."

"I'm thinking of getting a decoy."

"Theoretically sound, but dangerous. I don't support it."

"Okay." She lifted her shoulder in a slow shrug. "I'll stay with it."

He twirled a pencil. "Drop by from time to time and let me know how you're doing." She promised that she would, but his disapproval of the best idea she'd had in weeks made her spirit sag.

I won't solve it by sitting in this office, she told herself, got into her car and drove to an amusement park. Almost immediately, her antenna shot up, and she stopped, took out her cell phone and recorded what she saw. At home that evening, she looked at the pictures she took with her cellular phone.

"Hmm. Wonder who he is. I don't believe he's the person I'm looking for." What she needed was a tip.

She didn't want to make a habit of sitting with Richard and Judd after dinner every evening—although she would have enjoyed chatting with Judd alone—because she didn't want to drift into an affair with Richard. And nothing would be easier than to allow her libido and his sexy masculine persona to trap her. So after supper that evening, she waylaid Jolene and walked with her to the lounge. She suspected that, given the chance, Jolene would be good company—at least for an hour.

She fished around for a conversation opener. "Do you work here in Pike Hill, Jolene?"

"I work in Salisbury. It's the first job I ever had, other than taking care of my sick mother and grandmother. I've been a receptionist at the beauty parlor for three months, and I already got a raise."

"Congratulations." Very soon, she knew the story of Jolene's life from birth until her arrival at the boardinghouse and, for a woman who a few weeks earlier uttered the time of day only grudgingly, she wondered at the change in Jolene.

"We need to do a little work with you," she told Jolene. "Unfortunately, your mother closed her eyes to a lot of truths and misled you."

"I sure don't know much about men, Francine. Looks like I make a wrong move with every man I meet."

"You've been operating with your mother's attitudes. Get rid of them."

Jolene's gaze shifted to the floor. "Do you mind if I ask whether you're married?"

"I'm a widow now, but I was a happy wife. If my husband so much as smiled or winked at me, it was as if the heavens opened up and the angels sang."

"Gee. That's the way it is in the romance novels I read, but my mama said men just use women, getting what they want out of them and . . . Ever since she died and I've . . . uh, been on my own, I've . . . ." How could she say it without indicting herself?

Francine sat forward, aware that Jolene was about to release a bombshell. "You've been what?"

"I've been using them in every way that I could."

Francine didn't want to believe what she heard. "And you've been killing your chances to develop a meaningful relationship. Men are human beings. They feel, hurt, ache, and love the same as we do. You'll meet good ones and bad ones, honey, but you have to learn the difference."

Jolene traced boards on the parquet floor with her right foot, and Francine wanted to force the woman to look at her. Patience, girl, she counseled herself.

"I . . . uh . . . I've already loused up with somebody who I . . . oh, heck. That's water down the drain."

What could she say to that? She sensed that Jolene was warming up to her when Jolene changed the subject and said, "I'm sorry you lost your husband, Francine. That must have been a blow to you. You know, when I first saw you, I thought there was something sad about you, but I didn't follow it up; I'm just beginning to think about other people."

Francine didn't want to sink back into that loneliness, so she forced a smile. "It's been eighteen months. I've learned to thank God that, for five years, I had greater happiness than some people have during their lifetime. I'd better get up to my room and make a few calls before it gets too late." She stopped to say good night to Judd and Richard. "How's the game?"

"I'm winning as usual," Judd said without taking his gaze from the cards in his hand. "Richard's giving me a birthday party Saturday. That's m'birthday. You coming?"

"If that's the invitation I'm getting, yes. I wouldn't miss it."

Richard looked up at her with what appeared to be a reprimand in his eyes. "I completed the arrangements today. Tomorrow, you will all find an invitation under your door."

Her eyes widened. "Oh my! Did I do bad?"

"We missed your company tonight," Judd said, and she knew that he had deliberately doused the flame of their rising conflict.

Judd's eyes had witnessed a lot in their day, and she didn't doubt that he'd seen more in her and in Richard than either of them had seen in each other. She climbed the stairs with the unwanted weight of an attraction to Richard bearing on her. She had come to Pike Hill to locate a smuggler of illegal aliens, a man who always lived and operated around open waters, and she didn't need to have her wits clogged by the numbing effects of passion.

Marilyn moved from the doorway as he approached, and Richard knew she did that so as to have more privacy with him.

"How'd you like the cheese soufflé tonight? I knew you would appreciate it if nobody else did."

"Up to your usual high standard. I'm planning a birthday party for Judd on Saturday night, and I'd like you to prepare the food. I have a menu, and I want you to follow it to the letter."

A smile crawled over her face, and he'd never seen anyone, not even a sexually sated woman, with a more exultant expression of satisfaction. "Honey, that's right down my alley. I'll fix you a party that'll make their eyes pop out. Just tell me how much I can spend, and I'll do the rest."

He didn't blink. "I said I'll give you a menu, and I want you to follow it. If you can't do that, I'll hire a caterer from Ocean City."

Her hands went to her hips, and her glare held no semblance of sexuality. "No caterer you hire is gonna cook in my kitchen."

His gaze bore into her. "In a battle of wills, Marilyn, if you tie up with me, you will lose. I appreciate that you're a first class cook, but I want what I want the way I want it, and that's what I'm used to getting. It's my menu or a caterer. Is five hundred dollars adequate compensation for the extra work?"

She drooped against the wall, rubbing and twisting her fingers and, for the first time since he'd known her, stripped of her aplomb.

"Five hundred did you say?" She let out a long sigh. "Bring the menu to breakfast in the morning. I'll need to order whatever we don't have, so I'll need to speak to Fannie."

"She's already cleared it. The party will start at seven, replacing supper. Give me your grocery list, and I'll shop for you in Ocean City or Ocean Pines." She nodded, visibly subdued, and he hoped she wouldn't give him any more trouble.

He needed help choosing favors for his guests and, considering Fannie's lack of imagination in decorating the house and her choice of table linens, he didn't think she would be of much help. He didn't want to ask Francine either. Something had happened between the two of them; she didn't want it, and he didn't trust that or any other attraction so long as Estelle Mitchell

owned his heart. Moreover, he didn't think Francine would accept the paltry affair that was all he could offer her. Yet, he wanted
her, and he had a feeling that his newly found self-discipline and
honor in regard to women was about to be tested.

Lila Mae had no taste and, of the female boarders, that left
Louvenia and Arnetha. Out of the question. Deliberately, he joined
Jolene for breakfast and related to her his problem. To his amazement, her face lit up. "Balloons. We can fill 'em with helium, tie
bunches of them to long ribbons, attach them to sandbags, and
put clusters in the lounge and dining room. The more the better.
How about a color scheme matching the balloons and table
linens? And we can get party hats—" Flabbergasted, he stared at
her. Speechless. Her enthusiasm seemed to wane. "You think
that's too much?"

"I think it's perfect. Wonderful. I had no idea what to do. Can
we manage this by Saturday?"

"I saw a party store in Salisbury near where I work. I can call
you from there today while I'm on my lunch hour. What's your
cell phone number?"

He gave it to her, and she told him to expect a call around
twelve-thirty. She hurried off to work, and Judd soon joined him.

"She's a perfect example of what improper nurturing can do
to a person," Judd said after Richard related his conversation
with Jolene. "A grown woman over thirty with breast milk still
on her lips."

"Come on, Judd. You really believe she's that naïve?"

"She didn't get a chance to be a normal teenager, so of course,
she's naïve," Judd said. "That girl's matured more in the six or
seven months she's been here than in her previous thirty-some
years."

Richard sat back in his chair and allowed a long breath to
leave him. "Makes me appreciate my parents more and more."

Judd nodded his thanks to Rodger when the man refilled his
coffee cup. "Me, too. Good thing is that she realizes she's handi-
capped."

"Man, that girl is smart. Think what she could have been if
she'd had the opportunity."

"Yeah," Judd said. "Six months ago, she was so drawn into

herself, like a turtle hiding his head, that you wouldn't have been able to figure out whether she was smart or stupid. One thing's certain; something happened to make her open up."

"Right. I won't be around much today. See you this evening."

He hadn't expected to see Francine in Ocean Pines, although he knew she worked there, and he stumbled when he saw her get out of the driver's side of a car that had police lights and megaphones attached to its roof.

"What a surprise! I was about to look for a place to eat lunch. Do you have time to join me?" When she seemed taken aback, he added, "I only have time for a short one, but if you're busy—" He let it hang.

She pointed across the street. "I was about to eat in that restaurant over there. The food's pretty good, but it might not be to your cultivated taste."

His right eyebrow shot up. "For a good part of my life, curried goat with rice and peas was my most frequent meal. My mother eventually learned to cook other things, thank goodness." He fell into step with her and, a minute later, nearly knocked her down moving her from the path of an on-coming car as they attempted to cross the street.

"Oops." She said as they stood pressed together chest to chest. "That was close. You are very disconcerting. I never start across the street without looking both ways."

Anxious to move the hardened tips of her breasts out of contact with his chest, he turned her to one side and, in response as, she raised an eyebrow, he said, "I probably saved your life, Francine, and that makes me responsible for you."

"I'm not going there, Richard."

He opened the restaurant door, stood aside, and allowed her to enter. "Refusing to entertain the idea does not, repeat does not, refute its veracity."

She ignored him. "I'll have the shrimp Scampi," she told the waitress, when they'd seated themselves.

"I'll have the same, along with rice and the chef's salad."

Silence enveloped them while they waited for their food, and he was tempted to see how long she would allow it to prevail. After two or three minutes, he realized that she didn't feel obliged to talk.

"You're neither shy nor skittish," he said. "Is it possible that you just don't want me to know who you are?"

"Let's say, I've never had an impulse to satisfy other peoples' curiosity about me."

It was a cop out, and she knew it. "I'm not 'other people' as you put it, and we both know it. If you don't want us to be any closer than we are, so be it. Right now, I'm not sure how free I am to enter into a meaningful relationship, but I do want to get to know you."

She stopped eating, put her fork down and frowned. "Not free? Are you married?"

He rippled his long fingers over the white table cloth, idly, as if he didn't know he was doing it. "No, and I never have been, but when I realized that I wanted marriage, it was too late. Much too late."

"So you were a player who destroyed his chance and lost out to another man?"

"Not quite, but close enough. I had more integrity than a player. In any case, those days are behind me."

"Do you still love her?" He thought he detected apprehension in her voice.

"It's been a year since I opened a newspaper and saw an announcement of her marriage, and I still think of her. There's been no one since."

"I'm sorry, Richard. I've been a widow for eighteen months, and I haven't formed any kind of liaison either."

"Were you happy . . . in your marriage, I mean?" It was too personal a question, but he had to know.

"Oh, yes. In every respect."

"It must have been a terrible blow." He hurt for her, and the realization that he had rarely before known such empathy for any one made him uneasy.

"It was, but I'm grateful for what I had."

A remarkable woman. The ringing of his cellular phone intruded upon his thoughts. "Excuse the disturbance, please," he said. "I'm expecting this call."

"Hello . . . Great. Ask him if they will deliver it Friday, and we need a helium tank, too. You did? Super. Let me speak with him." He gave the man his credit card number. "Good, I'll expect it Friday morning. Listen, Jolene, pick out everything. Oh. Silver and blue will work fine, then. Twenty people. Right. Thanks a million."

He hung up and couldn't help laughing as Francine gaped at him in astonishment. "Did you say Jolene? *Our* Jolene?" she asked.

"She surprised me, too. I was in a quandary, mentioned the party to her at breakfast, and she was full of ideas. I think her mother impeded her maturity with her negative attitudes.

"To say the least. That woman did a hatchet job on her daughter."

He didn't want to talk about Jolene; it was Francine who interested him. "Is there a reason why I shouldn't know you were driving a squad car?" He could see that she expected that or a similar question.

"I don't broadcast it, because wide knowledge of it might hinder success in what I'm doing right now."

"Nobody will learn it from me."

She leaned toward him. "Thanks. I was looking for someone that day on the beach."

"And you thought you recognized him?" She nodded, speared a shrimp with her fork and put it into her mouth. "He's been in that area, and he hangs around the ocean and the bay."

"What does he look like?"

"About five-eight, slim, could be Latin, Native American, African American or a middle easterner."

That reminded him of someone, and he put on his thinking cap. "Fits the guy who moved out of our boarding house a few days before you came. I think he had your room."

She stopped chewing. "Did he have a slight limp, so slight you'd hardly notice it?"

He stared at her, mostly because her question stunned him. "I noticed it because it was pronounced whenever he walked *down* the stairs."

She reached for his hand and held it. "Richard, please don't mention this to anyone, not even to Judd. I've been on this case for six months, and this is the first clue I've had that I'm on his trail. The man's a smuggler. I work for the Treasury Department, but while I'm on this case, I'm a police lieutenant."

"My lips are sealed. I would never betray you. If there's anything I learned as a diplomat, it's how to keep my mouth shut."

A frown spread over her face. "You're a diplomat?" She folded her arms and rested her back against the booth. "Why am I not shocked? That explains your persona."

He held up both hands, palms out. "I *was* for nearly thirteen years, but that's in the past. I walked away from it, and I'm not sorry. By the way, do you have children?"

"Uh—no. Why? Would it matter?"

"Not to me," he said. "If it did, would that bother you?"

Her laugh wrapped around him like a blanket of warm chocolate fudge. "You could grow on me, Richard Peterson."

He showed her a sober face. "I like fast and permanent results. Where should I spread the fertilizer?"

She looked him straight in the eye. "Wherever you think it would be most productive."

She could be a smart aleck, too, he noted, and he was not amused. "Don't play with me, Francine. I'm serious, and you know it."

"And you think I'm not? I have to get back to work. Let's go."

What could he say to that? This woman knew who she was and would issue a challenge as easily as she would accept one. Excitement coursed through him. He wanted to know her in every way that a man could know a woman. But she would never accept half a loaf, and as long as he saw Estelle Mitchell whenever he closed his eyes, he couldn't give more.

He took her hand, dropped some bills on the table and they left the restaurant. "My bill was eleven dollars," she told him.

He gazed steadily at her. "It was the least expensive date I've had in twenty years, but I enjoyed it far more than most, so please let me pay."

She stopped walking. "Don't tell me you're always so serious. By the way, what was the name of that man who had my room just prior to my arriving at the boarding house?"

He didn't remember. "I'll ask Fannie at supper tonight. If you ask her, she'll be curious as to why."

"You're right. Thanks. I'll see you this evening."

He walked with her to the squad car, leaned down and kissed her cheek. She gazed up at him, wide eyed. "Damn," he said to himself. "Let me get the hell away from here."

Chapter Seven

Richard bought a case each of Pinot Grigio wine, ginger ale, Coca-Cola, Pilsner beer, and other party essentials and stored it all in the trunk of Dan's taxi. He had developed a fondness for Dan, the cabbie who had brought him to Pike Hill, and used his services whenever possible. Next, he tackled Marilyn's grocery list and, by three o'clock in the afternoon, had finished shopping. Dan helped him carry the grocery bags into the house, and Marilyn rewarded the cabbie with a bag of warm buttermilk biscuits. Richard waited in the lounge for Jolene and was relieved when she arrived before five-thirty.

"How do we do these balloons?" he asked her. She showed him, but suggested that they wait until Saturday morning to decorate. She assured him that it wouldn't take long and suggested that they begin immediately after breakfast.

"Do you like what I bought?"

"Absolutely, and especially the colors. Silver and blue is a dignified combination that suits an older person."

"I hope you don't mind that I added candles for the tables."

"I'm glad you did. I hadn't remembered, and Marilyn's making him a chocolate cake. I hope it all goes well." It amazed him that he had more anxiety about Judd's party than about some of the big and important international conferences over which he had presided.

"It will be very special," she said, and added with an expression of awe, "Imagine doing all this for somebody you didn't know existed eight months ago. Until I came here, I wouldn't have believed anybody would do such a thing. I'll be down at seven in the morning, and we can start on the balloons after breakfast."

"Thanks. I will definitely need your help." He mused over her words, marveling at their similarities to each other. Because of the treatment she'd received from her mother and the influence of her mother's attitudes, she had had to learn late in life to care for others just as he had. He wasn't very religious, but he suspected that Providence had a hand in bringing both of them to Thank the Lord Boarding House.

By noon Saturday, Jolene, Fannie and he had made two dozen clusters of balloons that stood like trees of varying heights, suspended by silver and blue ribbons from the silver-colored sandbags that anchored them.

Fannie stored them in the pantry. "We'll decorate after lunch," she told them. "I'm so excited. Richard, the Lord is definitely going to bless you and Jolene for making the old man feel so special."

Richard cocked an eyebrow. "Fannie, I never think of Judd as an old man. He beats me at cards just about every evening and swims along with me at least twice a week."

"Yep," she said. "He's blessed, all right."

Jolene put on a yellow crêpe sheath that ended in a flounce at the knee and the first three-inch heeled patent leather shoes she had ever worn, combed down her hair, and ran downstairs to the dining room. She found Judd in conversation with Joe Tucker and joined them.

"You sure do look pretty in this dress, Jolene," Joe told her. "If I was twenty years younger, I'd stake a claim. Judd looks pretty snappy in his suit, too." The more she saw of Joe, the more she liked him as a sturdy, decent and self-respecting man, and she was grateful that in her foolish days, she had not tried any antics with him.

"I'm the guest of honor," Judd said to them with a wink, "so

I didn't have the nerve to come in here looking like a box-car bum. I never been so touched in m' life."

Across the room, Richard stood in a corner near the pantry talking with two men who had their backs to Jolene. Rodger circulated among the boarders with a tray containing glasses of wine, soft drinks, beer, and hot hors d'oeuvres. The beer, which Fannie did not ordinarily permit in the house, was her concession to the occasion.

"This is the first party I ever attended," Jolene said, mostly to herself. "Lord, I sure have missed a lot."

"Supper's ready," Fannie said. "Everybody have a seat. My brother, Reverend Coles, is with us, and he'll say the grace."

The minister turned around and, his gaze fell on her, so she rushed over to him, forgetting her behavior during his previous visit. But as she extended her hand to greet Philip Coles, a familiar voice reached her ears.

"Hello, Jolene."

She looked into the face of Gregory Hicks, and nearly lost her balance. "Hello, Gregory. How are you?"

"I'm surprised that you remember me."

She couldn't believe he'd said that. "Of course I remember you."

Both of his eyebrows shot up, and she said, "I've wanted to talk with you, but I haven't been able to get up the courage. A lot of things have happened to me since I last saw you, and I understand myself and people much better than I did."

"Why are you telling me this?" he asked, obviously unmoved.

"Because I'm sorry for the way I behaved. I had a lot to learn, and I still do. I'd give anything if I could change your opinion of me, but I know I can't . . . See you." Without waiting for his reaction, she left him and walked across the lounge to the dining room to her usual place. Then she realized she hadn't said one word to Philip Coles.

She was about to take her usual seat when her gaze captured the table that Fannie had added to accommodate Philip and Gregory and found them both looking at her. She waved at Philip and relaxed when he acknowledged it with a smile.

After Philip said grace, Richard stood and raised his glass of wine. "Tonight, we're celebrating Judd Walker's eighty-fifth birthday. Judd has done what my father tried, but didn't succeed in doing." He paused, grinned, and said, "You don't have to know what that is," and was rewarded with a ripple of laughter.

"I see Rodger standing at the kitchen door anxious to begin serving the meal, so I won't test your patience or his. When I decided to give Judd a party, I didn't have a clue as to what was involved. Jolene came to my rescue. The decorations are her idea and choice, and she and Fannie helped me set them up. I gave Marilyn a menu and she sent me on a shopping trip. All in all, I've never enjoyed anything as much as I've enjoyed this. Judd, my friend, you deserve the best."

Judd stood. "I want to thank m' family for making this one of the happiest days of m'life. It's the first birthday party I ever had, and I'm loving it. I thank m'friend Richard for brightening m' life. Let's eat."

When Rodger set bowls of oyster chowder before them, Joe Tucker rubbed his hands together as if he were washing them. "Jolene, my friend, I wouldn't have missed this for the world. We all know Richard is 'class,' but you surprised me. The decorations are great. We could be in a five-star hotel. You have changed a lot, right in front of our eyes."

"I'm learning, Joe. This is the first party I've ever been to."

"What?"

"I don't want to spoil the party for you. Sometime, if you're interested, I'll tell you what it's like to be your mother's slave."

His sharp whistle split the air, and everyone in the dining room looked their way. His silence told her that she had either shocked or scandalized him. After a few minutes, he said, "That fellow over there with Richard is looking at you. You know him?"

"He's Gregory Hicks, and he goes to Fannie's church. I went out with him a few times, but I messed up. Joe, I didn't know anything about men or anything else when I came here. He's a very nice man." She marveled at her ability to discuss personal things with a man she knew only as her seatmate at supper. *I have come a long way*, she said to herself.

"He likes you," Joe said.

"Maybe, but he won't do anything about it. Like I said, I ruined things with him."

The seven course meal ended with crème Courvoisier and espresso coffee, which Marilyn herself served, to a round of applause.

Joe turned in his chair and faced Jolene fully. "You say you don't know much about men. Well, I guess you don't. I don't know what you did to him, but that man over there is interested in more than the dress you got on."

Jolene smiled and patted Joe's arm. "Thanks. You've done wonders for my ego tonight, Joe." When she saw Fannie introduce Francine to Gregory, she knew that Gregory still hadn't settled on a girl. *He'll have to come to me; I've made a dunce of myself over a man for the last time.*

She headed toward Judd to congratulate him but, seeing the crowd around him, gave up the idea. Feeling a tap on her arm, she turned to face Philip Coles. "I've been trying to get a moment to speak with you. You're finally blooming," he said, "and it looks as if you have a talent for decorating. My, my. You look wonderful, too. I can't tell you how proud of you I am."

In that moment of pride, she could feel her shoulders go back, for only Philip Coles knew what she'd overcome, indeed what she was still climbing over. "You think I'll make it?"

He nodded vigorously. "Oh, yes. Indeed, I don't see how you can fail. The difference since I was last here is phenomenal."

"Well, sir, there's been a lot of pain to go with it. Mama didn't give me one positive thing to help me; I'm finding that practically everything she crammed into my head about people was untrue. And especially about men. Why did she hate men so much? Do you know she refused even to tell me who my father is? And that was the least she owed me."

Immediately, she wished she hadn't spoken so candidly, for the blood heated his face and neck, and he stammered his sympathy. "What's d-d-done is done, Jolene. I'm glad you've found a home here."

He seemed anxious to leave her, so she did her best to put him at ease. "I'm glad you're here for the party, Reverend Coles. Having an outside guest makes it special." Her gaze caught Judd,

Gregory, and Richard looking at her and Philip Coles, and she hoped they didn't think she was involved with the minister in any way.

To make sure that they didn't, she excused herself, walked over to Judd and hugged him. "Happy birthday, Judd. Now you know who's special around here."

"I always knowed it. I'm twenty years older than Louvenia over there, and the next most important person is the cook."

"For heaven's sake, don't let Marilyn know you're more special here than she is; she might downgrade the meals," Richard said.

"Humph," Judd snorted. "No way. She's too vain."

"Would you like to dance?" Gregory asked Jolene. "That music is too good to waste."

"I never learned how," she said, unwilling to make an excuse or to give him the impression that she didn't want to dance with him. "I'm just learning how to walk in high heels." She had intended to draw a laugh, but the solemn faces before her were proof that they knew she told the truth and empathized with her.

Evidently not to be outdone, Gregory said, "Even if you knew how, I doubt you'd be able to dance in those shoes. I don't see how women walk in them. Let's find a glass of wine."

"Something strange going on here," Judd said to Richard when they were alone, "and I'm not about to say what I'm thinking."

"Yeah. I was thinking something like that a minute ago, and I've thought it before." He also feared what he'd start if he articulated his thoughts. "The women are all looking great for you tonight, Judd," he said, changing the subject. "Strut your stuff, man."

"I got a lot to thank you for, Richard." He fingered the few stubs of beard that had begun to emerge on his chin. "Say, I haven't seen Francine anywhere around here for the last half hour."

"Maybe she went to her room."

"It ain't like her to hide. The gal loves being around people,"

Judd said. "Excuse me." He went to the house telephone, which was, in effect, an intercom, and dialed the number for Francine's room. No answer. "Where could she be at nine o'clock Saturday night?" he asked Richard minutes later.

"Maybe she has a date," Richard said, although he didn't believe it. It crossed his thoughts that Francine may have received a tip as to the whereabouts of Ronald Barnes, and he worked hard at slowing down his suddenly accelerated breathing.

"I wouldn't worry too much, Richard. Francine strikes me as a woman more than able to look after herself."

So he hadn't managed to hide his anxiety from the shrewd old man. "She'll miss the finale," Richard said, pretending not to have caught the implications of Judd's words. He looked around at his fellow boarders who talked among themselves and realized that Jolene and Francine were the only ones other than Judd who had spoken to him to thank him for the party.

A few minutes later, Fannie dimmed the lights and Marilyn and Rodger entered the room with a big chocolate cake lit with eighty-five candles, and Rodger lent his baritone voice to the words and tune of "Happy Birthday to you." As Judd cut the cake, Richard was certain that he saw Francine's red dress flash up the stairs, and he knew he'd been right when she returned to the party without the gray fishnet stockings she'd worn earlier and which he had admired on her long shapely legs.

"Just in time for cake," he said when she walked up to him wearing an expression of innocence. But he wasn't fooled, for the heaving of her chest meant either excitement or that she had been running. He suspected both.

"Thanks. I love chocolate."

He maneuvered her into a corner. "Any luck?"

She shook her head. "He's slick as a fish right out of water, but I'll get him."

"What happened to those great stockings you were wearing earlier? I liked them."

Her left eyebrow shot up. "You don't think I'd risk snagging my fifteen dollar stockings, do you? It only took me a second to get them off."

He laughed, as much from relief and from the humor of a police officer removing her stockings before going after a criminal. "You're a perfect example of a feminine woman doing a man's job and up to the task."

"You definitely know how to make a woman feel good."

"I can do a hell of a lot better than that." Seeing that they were alone, he leaned down and kissed the side of her mouth. "But I warn you that if you give me a chance to show you, you won't soon forget it. I'm a thorough man, and nothing pleases me more than to satisfy a woman." Her lower lip dropped, her eyes blinked rapidly, and she backed away. He hadn't meant to discombobulate her; he'd looked down at the alluring, feminine bundle so close to him and said exactly what was on his mind. He was in no mood to apologize.

She stared up at him, her face flushed. "How did you get from stockings to sex? I remember your telling me that you aren't ready for a relationship, so why are you—"

He interrupted her. "You might say my self-control slipped a fraction. Let's go over there and get some ice cream and cake."

They walked to the dining room table where Marilyn held court, savoring the plaudits of the boarders who surrounded her, giving her the admiration she craved.

"You outdid yourself tonight, Marilyn," Richard said. "My hat's off to you."

Her half smile and lowered head, surprised him. He wouldn't have thought her capable of diffidence. "I mean it," he added. "The Waldorf Astoria couldn't have produced better fare than you created. You're a master chef."

"You don't know what that means to me coming from you, Richard. I did my level best, and I'm so glad you're pleased."

He resisted patting her on the shoulder, accepted the home-made ice cream, the best he'd ever had, and a slice of chocolate cake and looked at Francine. "You can eat all that without worrying about gaining weight?"

"No, but opportunity doesn't knock often, and this stuff is to die for. I'll run an extra time around the block. You don't seem worried about inflating your flat middle."

"If anybody had told me a year ago that I'd have this conversation with a woman, I wouldn't have believed it. I never got on a really personal level with women." He paused as the knowledge struck him. "Not even with—"

"And yet, you loved her. I don't understand that, and I think you're in for a stunning surprise, Richard."

"What do you mean?"

"When you finally fall in love, you will know that you have never truly loved before. Loves comes with intimacy. True intimacy."

"If it's more devastating than what I've already experienced, I want no part of it."

Her wink took him back a bit. "Then, resist kissing the side of my mouth. I might take a shine to you and, trust me, friend, I go after what I want."

He straightened up from his slouch against the wall and stared down at her. "You and I have the same attitude toward challenges, so let's pretend this conversation never took place. I don't gamble and I don't accept dares. Before I issue a challenge, I know how I am going to deal with the response. I value your friendship, Francine. Let's stop this one-upmanship."

"You're right, Richard. It's a substitute for a deeper intimacy, and whether we know it or not, we're fanning the fire."

He couldn't help grinning. "Oh, I know that, but the idea of treating you like a baby sister boggles my mind." When he looked around, he saw Gregory and Jolene seemingly in deep conversation in the hallway beside the stairs. "How do those two strike you?" He nodded in the other couple's direction.

"I think they're picking up where they left off last winter. He must be the one she told me about. Claimed she ruined what could have been a good relationship."

Francine couldn't have been closer to the truth. "Could we spend some time together tomorrow afternoon?" Gregory was asking Jolene about that time. "I've never been satisfied with the way we split up. You should have been more considerate, and I should have refused to do anything I didn't want to do. Why did you stand me up?"

"You were the first man I ever went anywhere with, and I

didn't have the slightest notion how to treat a man. I was loaded down with my mother's prejudices."

"I understand that. Can we be together tomorrow afternoon after church?"

She had promised herself that she would visit Harper, and she didn't intend to change her plan; he was in the hospital because of her self-centeredness. "Maybe. I have to visit a friend at the hospital first."

"A man or a woman?"

"A man, but I won't stay more than ten or fifteen minutes, if that long. He may not want to see me." When Gregory raised an eyebrow, she added, "You're not the only person I've mistreated."

"May I drive you to the hospital and wait while you visit your friend?"

"Uh . . . all right. I'd like that."

Jolene walked into Harper's hospital room at three-fifteen Sunday afternoon carrying a basket of grapes, strawberries, apples, dates, and tangerines, fruits she knew the hospital wouldn't serve. He sat beside the window in a wheelchair looking out at the gardens now bare of flowers and foliage.

"Hello, Harper." He swung the wheelchair around with such energy that she knew he recognized her voice.

"To what do I owe this . . . this visit?"

She put the basket of fruit on the table beside his bed and walked over to him. "Regardless of what you think of me, I'm not all bad, Harper." When he winced, she added quickly, "Please give me ten minutes. That's all I'm asking. And listen carefully to every word I say. It won't undo a thing, but you will understand." He motioned toward the only chair in the room. She closed his door and sat down. Ten minutes later, he knew the story of her life up to that minute with nothing significant omitted. He gazed out of the window, motionless as if hypnotized.

"Why couldn't you have told me what your life was like instead of pretending to be sophisticated? Woman, I fell in love with you, and you hurt me. You will never know how I hurt. I made love with you to get even, but you were so loving and so giving. Not even a prostitute gives the way you did. After that, I never wanted to see you again. I was afraid I might make a complete fool of myself over you. I don't remember taking Beaver Road on the drive home. I'm told they had to cut through the wreckage of my car in order to get me out of it."

"I won't say that I'm sorry, because you know I am. What does the doctor say?"

"That I'll be as good as ever, but the therapy is pure hell. Still, I'm blessed to be alive." He was silent for a moment, and she stood to leave. "Thank you for coming and for bringing the fruit. You think you and Gregory will get back together?"

"I really don't know whether he can accept the truth when I finally tell him all that I just told you, including about you."

"You don't have to tell him all that, just the essence of it. Trust me, he won't want to know." She offered to shake hands, but he reached up for a hug. She made it brief, for she no longer teased or played with men.

"I'll be back," she said. "Thanks for being so kind."

When she got back to Gregory's car, he reached across the passenger's seat and opened the door for her, locked her seatbelt and started moving away from the curb. "What would you like to do?"

"I'm leaving that up to you," she said. "Maybe I'll get an understanding of what you like. Before, we only did what I suggested."

"How was the visit?"

"Better than I had hoped for. At least we can be friends."

"You feel like explaining that?"

"I will, but I'm going to start at the beginning and tell you everything about myself. He, that is, the friend I visited today, said I shouldn't do that, but I want a clean slate, and if you can't handle it, I'll understand. To begin with, my mother hated men, and she did everything she could to make me as wretched a woman as she was."

"You told me some of that."

"Right, but a lot has happened since then, and I'm not going to spare myself. Let's go some place that's not public."

"The only place I can think of that's not public is my apartment. You want to go *there*?"

"Definitely not. How about a place where we can just drink coffee?"

He stopped at a small roadside coffee house near Ocean Pines. "I hope this is all right."

Her hands shook so badly that she put them in her lap, and when she began to talk, the chattering of her teeth made her words barely understandable.

"If this makes you so nervous, let's forget it, Jolene."

"No. I've thought of you every day for weeks, and I want a chance with you. But I want it honestly, because you know who I am and still want me."

He ordered coffee for them, and while she spoke, beginning with her mother's funeral—almost in whispers at first—she sipped her coffee cold without realizing she tasted it. By the time she finished the story of her life, tears streamed down her face, though she was unaware of that until Gregory's handkerchief wiped them away.

"You don't have to comment, Gregory. I'll know how you feel about this by the way you act."

"How do you feel about Harper Masterson?"

"Sympathy, I think. I know I'm grateful to him that because of what he suffered, I finally took a good look at myself, and I hated what I saw. I know I'm responsible for his accident, and that is very difficult to live with."

"But you don't love him."

"That's the awful part, Gregory; I never once thought I did."

"If I had known you were so naïve, not the sophisticate you made yourself out to be, we wouldn't be having this conversation. Come on. I want to show you something." He glanced down at her feet. "Thank goodness you're wearing comfortable shoes. I don't see how anyone could walk in those things you had on last night."

She wanted to scream with laughter, to jump and shout. So far, he hadn't said one censorial word about the awful things she'd told him. She knew he might later, but at least he planned to let them enjoy the afternoon. "Where is this place?" she asked him as he drove down to the water's edge on the outskirts of Ocean Pines.

He parked, went around and opened her door. Pointing to a low, one-story building, he said, "That used to be a marina, but it hasn't been used as one for a couple of years. I bought it three months ago, and I've started my business making sails for small ships. I also mend them, and so far, most of my business is in mending, but I recently got a nice order to make sails for a racing boat."

"Congratulations, Gregory. I'm so happy for you. I remember your telling me you wanted to do this. So you left the telephone company?"

"Full time, yes. I have consultant's status with the company and I give them four or five hours a week, but as my business picks up, I'll have to drop that. I forgot to ask how your job is working out."

"I got a raise, and I didn't have to ask for it. I'm proud of that."

They walked through his sails factory, and she could see his pride in the first venture that he could call his own, as he showed her the sailcloth, ropes, and other materials that he used. By the time they left the building, they walked hand-in-hand, and she felt that if she breathed normally, he would realize it and drop her hand. She knew she wasn't out of the woods with him, but maybe she had a chance.

I don't deserve it, Lord, but if you give me a chance to show my appreciation for what I trampled on and lost, I'll cherish it and make good use of it. I promise.

He drove her home, talking amiably as they went, and she forced herself not to ask him how he felt about the things she told him and whether they would see each other again. At the boardinghouse, he kissed her cheek.

"Thank you for this afternoon, Jolene. I'll call you." He started down the steps, turned and walked back to her. "I meant to ask how you happen to know Philip Coles."

Flushed with relief that his question demanded nothing more than the simple truth, she said, "He's pastor of the church my mother attended, and he recommended that I move here.

You heard Fannie say he's her brother." When his eyebrows lifted sharply, she added. "Fannie said she looks like their father, and he looks like their mother."

He studied her for a second, causing her to wonder what he was looking for. His right shoulder flexed in a shrug. "It happens. We'll speak this week."

From inside the door, she watched him stride to his car. At least he's whistling a lighthearted tune, she thought. Maybe she wouldn't see him again, and although it would hurt, she could accept it. Neither he nor Harper deserved her treatment of them, and by telling them, she had gained a sense of freedom, of relief from the burden of her past.

"The way to get along with people is to treat 'em the way you want 'em to treat you," Judd had said. She would try to do that but, remembering her experience with Vida, she resolved also to watch her back. With half an hour before supper time, she dashed up the stairs to her room to freshen up and met Francine at the landing.

"You looked super in that red dress last night, Francine," she said.

"Thanks. Not one bit better than you did in that yellow flounce and those spike heels. You were turning heads, girl. See you later."

Jolene washed her face and hands, repaired her makeup, reached for her comb and stopped. She had just chatted with Francine the way the women in the beauty parlor talked with each other, and they had spoken as equals. She shook her head in wonder. Sophisticated Francine had paid her a compliment. She knew she had changed, that she had grown as a person since coming to Thank the Lord Boarding House, and she recognized in herself a new self-confidence. When and how had it happened?

At supper, she took her usual place between Joe Tucker and Louvenia Monroe and greeted each of them. A little of Louvenia went a long way with her, but as usual, she smiled and kept the thought to herself. Fannie said grace, and Rodger served them chestnut soup that Marilyn had laced with a goodly amount of sherry.

"Richard, why don't you sit over here with us for a change?" Arnetha called to him from her table. "Percy doesn't get in till tomorrow morning, and we could use another man at this table." Silence greeted her suggestion, for Fannie had established a rule that boarders should always take their assigned seats.

"Oh, come on, Richard," Arnetha, a retired nurse's aide, insisted. "Ain't gonna hurt you to bend a little."

"Aw, leave him alone, Arnetha," Louvenia said. "Let the man eat."

"Yeah, leave him alone," Jolene chimed in. "Some lower class might rub off on him, and we don't want that, do we?"

"You didn't have to say that, Jolene," Joe Tucker said beneath his breath. "After all the nice things he said of you last night. You wouldn't want him to say anything like that about you, would you?"

She stopped eating and glanced across the room to find Richard staring at her. "Joe, I didn't mean to . . . I didn't think. I was just joining in with the talk. I mean—"

"He's a good fellow," Joe said, "even if he does stay pretty much to himself. After what he did for Judd, he's okay in my book."

Oh, dear. I forgot my resolution to treat people like I want to be treated. "Joe, I'm ashamed of myself. Richard's been nice to me. I . . ." She lost her taste for the meal, although some of the items were her favorites, shoved her plate aside and asked her table mates to excuse her. But how could she leave the dining room without apologizing to Richard? Both Fannie and Richard watched her as she approached their table.

"Richard, I just realized that what I said a minute ago wasn't nice. I'm ashamed of myself, and especially when you've been so nice to me. I hope you'll forgive me."

"It's never good to be clever at another person's expense," Fannie said. "I was surprised."

"I wanted to feel like I belong, so I talked without thinking, and I wish I'd kept my mouth shut the way I used to. Richard, I . . . you deserved better from me."

"It's all right, Jolene. Don't sweat it."

He didn't look her in the eye, and that was so unlike him. She had hurt him. "It isn't all right, Richard, and I'm so sorry. Please excuse me, Fannie. I'm going to my room."

Richard didn't join Judd and Francine in the lounge after supper. Jolene's comment had enforced what he'd come to realize the night before. He stood at his bedroom window staring out at the blackness of the night accentuated by the vast expanse of the bay and ocean in the distance. The boardinghouse had begun to feel like home, he enjoyed his volunteer work at the library and the high school, and the feeling that he belonged to no one and no place, which had plagued him for years, troubled him less frequently. But perhaps he'd been fooling himself.

When he heard a knock on his door, he moved away from the window and went to open the door. He hoped Marilyn wouldn't provoke him into insulting her.

"Francine! What—?"

"I know it's against the rules for me to come here, Richard, but I couldn't help it. She didn't mean to hurt you, and she's in her room crying about it. She just didn't think."

"You came here to fix it up for Jolene?"

"Yes. No. I couldn't stand knowing how you're feeling right now."

"Last night, I gave a very elegant party for Judd and everyone here enjoyed it, but the only people in this house who thanked me, other than Judd and Fannie, were you and Jolene. Tonight, Jolene made an unfortunate remark about me, and several people snickered. They don't care about me."

She stepped into the room and gripped his arm. "Don't say that. They just haven't figured out how to reach you. How could they not care about you?"

It seemed that the emptiness inside of him broadened into a deep hole, an aching void. He grabbed her shoulders. "You. What about you, Francine? Do you care about me?"

"Yes. Of course, I—"

"I don't want to hear that. I need you. Do you hear me? I need you."

"Oh, Lord." It slid out of her in the form of a groan and, recognizing it for what it was, he lifted her into his room, kicked the door shut, and plunged his tongue into the warm and welcoming space between her parted lips. Shivers shot through him when her arms went around his neck and tightened as the hard tips of her breasts pressed against his chest telling him that she also needed him. For the first time in his life, he trembled in a woman's arms.

"Francine. Oh, Francine, I want you in my bed. I want to lose myself in you."

Clearly shaken, she broke the kiss and stepped away from him, her breath coming in short, rapid pants. "In all my life, I've only made love with one man. He loved me, and I loved him. You need me and want me, but you don't love me. I can't do it." When he reached for her, she put a finger to his lips. "I'm not old-fashioned, but I won't be an item in your collection, Richard, no matter how badly I want you. And let me tell you, I want you." She reached up, kissed his cheek, strolled from the room and left him gaping in her wake.

He stood there, rooted to the floor, poleaxed, wondering what had hit him. Footsteps on the stairs brought him back to himself, and he managed to close his door, wiping the sweat that poured from his temples as he did so. What I need, he told himself, is a good run. He put on a sweat suit and sneakers, slipped unnoticed down the stairs and out on to Ocean Road. He welcomed the cold wind bruising his face, and raced into it. At the corner of Ocean Road and Rhone, one block from the boardinghouse, he turned toward the beach.

The more energy he used, the more he enjoyed the punishment to his body, the body that threatened to enslave him to a woman, something he swore would never happen. Estelle had brought him to his knees, but no other woman would be able to claim that. He was through with using women, but he was not averse to a relationship with a woman who understood that he was taking care of his needs and she was taking care of hers.

As he neared the water, he became aware of several human figures near the water's edge, and he slowed down. In the distance, he saw a light. It was dim, but unmistakable. Remembering Francine's mission, he turned, raced back to the boarding house and found her in the lounge, talking with Judd.

He greeted Judd as casually as he could. "Francine, I need to talk with you. It's urgent."

"I'll be with you in a minute."

"Oh, now," Judd said. "Go on, Francine. I'm not one to stand in the way of romance."

"You're way off, Judd," she said, then looked at him. "Can't it wait?"

Annoyed that she would put him off in Judd's presence, he replied. "Of course it can wait, and you will be very sorry if it does." He spun around and headed for the stairs, but she caught him before he reached the landing.

"What's so urgent?"

"By now, probably nothing. I jogged down to the beach and caught your boys in action."

"What? Where?"

"At the end of Rhone Street. A boat with a faint light stood some distance from shore, and at least three men were waiting for it."

"Excuse me." She dashed toward her room, and he didn't doubt her intention to call authorities.

"You're probably too late," he said when she came back to him.

"I'm sure of it. Those guys move quickly. Still, my men will be there in minutes. You were right, I *am* sorry I didn't give you a chance to tell me right away, but I'm carrying a heavy weight and I didn't have the option of running it off." She looked up at him. "Thank you for helping me, Richard."

"You'd do the same for me." Richard went into his room and closed the door. The run might have been good for his health, but it did nothing for his emotions. He took a shower and prepared for a long night. He knew he had mistreated a lot of women, had gladly followed wherever his "devil libido" had led him, but that was behind him; he was a changed man, and he wanted to know when the hell he would stop paying for his past.

* * *

Lord, I'm lost, Francine said to herself after she left Richard. *Falling for this man is probably the dumbest thing I ever did*. She went to her room, closed the door and dialed her captain. Richard was honest, personable and masculine to the core. But he was too handsome and too charming. How was a woman to know when a man had seduced her and when she loved him for his worth as a person, loved him enough to share her body with him?

I'm too old to be so confused. A forty-seven-year-old woman should be too smart to allow a man to hoodwink her. With a sigh, she sank on to the bed, unmindful of its delicate, tissue-taffeta lavender cover. No point in trying to fool herself, she'd fallen for Richard as much for what she saw in him as a man as for his male magnetism. *It's a good thing that man doesn't know he affects me the way a torch affects dry grass*.

"Hello? What did you get?"

"We caught one woman because she's too old to run away," her captain said. "We don't know how many were on that boat. They landed and scattered before we got there, and that little boat was a ghost ship. The smugglers had disappeared, too. Damn, Francine. We were so close."

"You think we can get any tips from that old woman?"

"Naah. She doesn't even know she's in custody. Stay with it."

"Will do." She hung up. The captain would give her points for that effort, but the praise really belonged to Richard. She couldn't dwell on how that could be fixed, however, for the more time she spent thinking of Richard Peterson, the more he would mean to her. She vowed to leave Pike Hill as soon as she put Ronald Barnes in handcuffs.

After a night of wrestling with the sheets, Richard dragged himself out of bed, brushed his teeth, washed his face, dressed, and moseyed down to the dining room, hoping to be able to eat his breakfast alone. It was not to be. Minutes after he sat down, Judd joined him.

"From the looks of you, I'd say you don't want company," Judd said, "so I'll just sit here. You don't have to talk. I got used to eating m' breakfast with you, and I like it that way."

In spite of himself, Richard couldn't help laughing. "Enjoy your breakfast, Judd. I'm aware that I can't get around you."

Rodger brought the coffee and, after cooling it with his breath, Judd took a few sips. "Francine is a nice girl. Intelligent, too. I wish the two of you would work out whatever's bothering you and accept the fact that you're going to be lovers."

Richard stopped chewing his raspberry pancake, placed his fork on his plate and looked at Judd. "Where'd you get that idea?"

"From you and Francine. She came in the lounge looking and acting like a hen tripping over hot asphalt, and you go jogging after ten o'clock. I may be old, but I still got sense."

Richard sighed in resignation. "All right, but there's nothing to it."

Judd pulled air through his front teeth and rolled his eyes. "You hope." He looked toward the door. "Come on over here and eat with us, Jolene. My, but you look nice and fresh this morning."

"Thanks. It's not because I slept well." She looked at Richard. "Mind if I eat here?" To his amazement, she reached for his hand, took it and held it. "I'd give anything if I could take back that stupid remark, Richard. Do you think you'll be able to forgive me?"

His first reaction was to suggest that she let him eat in peace, but when he looked at her, he saw pain reflected in her eyes. He remembered her having once alluded to experiencing more than her share of unhappiness and misery, and he accepted that she didn't want to cause him to suffer as she had. The thought softened his attitude toward her.

"I know you didn't want to make me uncomfortable," he said. "You weren't thinking."

"No, I definitely wasn't, and maybe that's the problem. All my life, I've thought only of myself, how to get out of my misery and then, how to get even or how to get what I want. I'm just learning to feel for other people and to care about them."

He nearly choked on the pancake, for he, too, was a recent repentant, and he only hoped she didn't have as much to atone for as he did. Or, at least, that the pill she had to swallow would be less bitter. "We all have to start somewhere, Jolene," he said. "You've made a lot of progress since I've known you, and you're to be commended."

"Yes, siree," Judd said. "You're doing just fine. By the way, how'd you happen to know Reverend Coles?"

"He was the pastor of my mother's church in Hagerstown, Maryland. I didn't see much of him, though, because I never went anywhere during mama's illness, which lasted almost seven years, and he came to see her only every three months to bring communion. In fact, in those days, I seldom saw anybody. Reverend Coles suggested that I close up the old house, sell it, move here, and start over.

"You know, I've decided to enroll in that Lifelong Learning Program at Catawba College in Salisbury, and maybe I can volunteer at the library one evening a week."

Richard stared at her. When he asked her months earlier to help during the computer classes, she refused. "That would certainly make our work easier. How about Tuesday?"

"Fine. I'd better hurry, or I'll miss my bus."

"You're doing the right thing, Jolene," Judd said. "I'm proud of you."

"Yes," Richard said. "Congratulations. You will always be proud that you did it."

"Thanks. See you this evening."

"I thought I understood women," Richard said to Judd after Jolene left, "but she is a colossal enigma."

"If you understand women, my friend, you deserve a medal. Jolene likes Gregory Hicks. Enigma solved."

Jolene tightened the scarf around her neck as she hurried down Ocean Road to Bay Avenue where she boarded the bus each morning. With the trees totally bare, the wind whipped in from the ocean unrestrained, drawing tears from her eyes. The bus drove up simultaneously with her arrival there and, grateful for the warmth it offered, she jumped in and greeted the driver.

"Did you ever go to see Masterson?" the driver asked her. She told him that she had visited Harper twice. "Yeah? Well, since you two are friends and nothing else, according to you, suppose you and me take in a movie one night?"

She hesitated. Here was a good looking, strong man, and she didn't really have anyone who cared about her. Maybe if . . . She stared down at him, while he gazed up at her expectantly, as if he knew she wouldn't resist him, that she was available and waiting for him to make a move. His gaze went to her breasts, their outline visible beneath her coat, and her nipples tightened and she could feel a warm flush in her vagina. Why not?

"Whatever I do, I do it thoroughly," he said. "No woman has ever complained that I don't know how to give her the ride of her life. What do you say?"

No pretense about friendship or even that he liked her. Hadn't she been down that road before and walked off it empty and ashamed? And hadn't she promised herself never to do it again? She could feel her bottom lip begin to curl. "No thanks. I'm seeing someone."

"I can definitely believe that, babe, cause you really smoking."

She didn't answer but took a seat in the back, proud that she had sense enough not to be a convenience for a man just because he showed an interest in her, proud that hearing a man say she looked nice did not inflate her ego.

As soon as she walked into the beauty parlor, Vida rushed to her with a frantic expression on her face and grabbed her arm. "Jolene! Jolene, I'm so glad you got here before any customers came in so we can talk. Could you ask to get off an hour early and stay at my place till I get home? The nanny has to leave today at three-thirty."

Jolene stared at the woman, hardly able to believe she had heard her correctly. "Why can't you take an hour off?"

"Please, Jolene. I want to go to the Bahamas in January, and I'll need all of my vacation time."

Heading for the dressing room to change into her uniform, Jolene threw over her shoulder, "Like I won't need my vacation time? Take a shorter vacation, and when people befriend you, remember not to abuse them."

"What was that about?" her boss asked. "I told you once

you're better off leaving Vida alone. If you stick your hand into a patch of poison ivy and it swells up and starts itching, you gonna keep doing it?"

She smiled a smile that came from her heart. "No, indeed, sir. I've learned a lot since I came here. Vida can't ring my bell anymore, because I won't let her."

"Way to go. You doing good, and if you continue to do this well, I can maybe take some time off and leave you to manage the shop. Business has picked up a lot since you've been answering the phone and making the appointments. What I needed was a good receptionist. You got a head on your shoulders."

"Are you serious? You'd leave me in charge of this place while you go off somewhere?"

"Yeah. You'll get another fifty bucks in your envelope Saturday."

"What? I . . . thank you. Thank you, sir."

She walked to the cash register thinking how different her life was now from what it was the day she began working in the beauty parlor. Her mama said she wasn't worth a cent. *Well, mama, that's one more thing you misled me about. Who knows what I might have become if you hadn't bathed me in your misery?* She dusted the counter, the computer/cash register, and the vase that held the artificial calla lilies.

I think I would be happy now if only Gregory would call as he promised. But if he doesn't, I'll have to live with it. It won't kill me. At least I have a clear conscience. Well, almost. I ought to try and put things right with Percy Lucas. He acts as if what happened between him and me took all the air out of him.

When she left work that afternoon, she stopped at a florist shop and ordered some roses for delivery to Harper Masterson. Doing that gave her a good feeling, elevating her mood, and she headed for the bus stop with light, spirited steps. As she hopped on the bus, her cell phone rang.

"Hello, Jolene. This is Gregory."

Chapter Eight

Richard hunched his shoulders against the wind that howled from the Atlantic and, with Judd walking upright beside him as if unmindful of the cold, headed down M. L. King Jr. Avenue toward Rhone Street. "Too bad we can't drop these computer classes until spring," he said to Judd. "I know it sounds chicken, but I do not like this weather."

"It only lasts two or three months, and think how good it is living here the rest of the year."

"I'm glad the library is close to the boardinghouse."

"Everything in this town's close to the boardinghouse. Trouble with you isn't the cold weather. You're in the dumps, and you gotta get yourself out of it. What's the problem?"

"I'm not in the dumps, Judd. I'm discovering that life can throw a hammerlock on you with no warning, and I have to deal with it. I also have to figure out what to do about the boarders' attitude toward me. When I came here, I didn't give a damn what any of them thought of me, but I see how they are with each other, almost like brothers and sisters and . . . well—"

"Everybody wants to be liked, son. Trouble is you thought they should look up to you. They probably did, but you're getting to know them, and you want them to care."

"Judd, do you know that Francine and Jolene are the only people, other than you and Fannie, who said anything to me about the party I gave for you? All the rest acted as if a party like that was their bloody due. Did any of them congratulate you on your birthday?"

"Joe Tucker did. I guess they figured singing 'Happy Birthday' to me covered it. Worrying about that hasn't crossed m'mind, and shouldn't bother you, either. They're humble people. You did that for me. Do something for them, and maybe they'll see you in a different light. Did you invite any of them to come to the adult computer classes?"

"No, but I will. Good idea."

It had been twenty years since his status was a matter of concern to him. Once he had set his sights for a career in international politics, he shot arrow-straight to the top. And now, he had no status that meant anything to his fellow boarders. After supper that night, he created a notice on his computer, printed it out, gave it to Fannie and asked her to put it on the bulletin board.

"Sure," she said. "This is wonderful." She read the notice: FREE INSTRUCTION IN TENNIS, SURFING, DARTS, CROQUET, BRIDGE. "Richard, honey, you'd better do this in groups of three or four. Otherwise you won't have a scrap of time for yourself. Of course, I doubt any of them have a clue as to what croquet is."

"Anybody sixty or sixty-five years old ought to appreciate a game that doesn't involve using a lot of energy."

"Right. I'll read this out at supper tomorrow evening. Uh . . . Richard. I appreciate what you're doing. You're improving the quality of life for my boarders, but you may find that some of them won't appreciate it. They will appreciate you, but they may not like some of these activities."

"As long as some of them enjoy it," he told her, as a tightness settled in his belly. If no one accepted his offer, it wouldn't kill him.

"I want to learn how to play bridge," Jolene said when Fannie finished reading the notice. "I can't swim, so it wouldn't make sense for me to take up surfing." Titters of laughter followed her admission that she couldn't swim.

"What can you teach me that doesn't involve sitting down?" Joe Tucker asked him. "That's all I do when I'm not on the construction site."

He'd known somehow that Joe Tucker would accept his offer.

"Tennis and darts. I have a feeling you'd love darts," he told the man. "And all of you are welcome to take the adult computer classes we're running at the library from four-thirty to six-thirty Mondays and Wednesdays.

"You can teach me how to throw those darts, too," Judd said. "I played tennis when I was twenty, and it got to my legs even then."

"I'll play tennis with you sometime," Francine said, but he knew without being told that she didn't mean it, that she offered because she thought the other boarders expected it of her.

In the end, it was clear to him that his offer would change nothing. Later as he sipped espresso coffee and played blackjack with Judd, he had an urge to be alone, to relapse into the self-centered behavior that he'd told himself was in the past.

"I think I'll turn in, Judd."

"Why doesn't that surprise me? What ails you's got nothing to do with the attitude of these people toward you, and you know it. You want her, but you can't have her on your terms. And you should be thankful for that. Maybe she can bring new meaning to your life. If she proved to be just another notch in your belt, pretty soon you wouldn't want to be around her, certainly not on the same floor in a house this size. You turned over a new leaf, and you're not a player any longer. Remember?"

"Judd, I've accepted more lecturing from you than I have or would from my father. What man wouldn't want Francine? She's beautiful."

"It ain't her looks that's got you tied up. It's her."

"Point taken. Now, cut me some slack, will you?"

"All right. But get used to a little deprivation; it's good for you."

Richard leaned back in his chair and let the laughter roll out of him, and he felt better, cleansed, as it were, because of it. *A little deprivation*? Hell, he hadn't had a woman since he left Geneva, Switzerland, eight months earlier. He had missed the sex, but he was proud that he had freed himself of the compulsion to charm and bed every woman who let him know she was available, proud that he had rid himself of the false persona, the automatic chicanery.

"What's so funny?"

He brushed his chin with the fingers of his left hand and looked at the cards in his right hand. "Funny? Not one single thing. Play your hand."

"You're getting so good at blackjack that I think I ought to introduce you to pinochle. Of course, we'd need at least a third person."

"Teach Francine. That is, if she doesn't already know."

"Not a bad idea. I may have to show you two how to have a real friendship, one that will withstand the effect of your libidos."

Richard knew that Judd meant well, but he didn't want to think about Francine. It was about all he'd done for the past twenty-four hours. "You just may have to do that. But for now, change the subject, will you?"

When Judd's eyelids seemed heavy and he began to play with less enthusiasm, Richard told him good night and started up the stairs. "Uh, you got a minute, Richard?"

He turned to face Joe Tucker. "It's a good thing you're doing for us, but this gang would rather play pinochle, whist, or blackjack or shoot pool than do the things you offered to teach them. These people think croquet is something you fry."

He looked at the man who spent three to four days a week as a construction worker and yet volunteered to help Fannie whenever she needed a handyman. "You're probably right, but I have to teach what I know."

"I'm not working this Friday, so if you're around, I'll be glad to get a lesson in dart throwing."

"Okay. I'll bring a dart board and some darts home tomorrow. I love the game, and I'll enjoy having someone to play with. You think we can get Percy interested?"

Joe flexed his shoulder in a shrug. "I dunno. Percy's been acting strange ever since summer, as if he doesn't have any confidence in himself."

So he wasn't the only one who noticed the change in Percy, although he was probably the only one of the boarders other than Percy who had a clue as to why. "If we can get him to play darts with us, that ought to change."

"Maybe. I wouldn't bet on it. Still, I'll ask him if you want me to. Let's start this Friday."

He agreed and continued up the stairs to his room. He felt better, and he didn't understand why. The object of his discontent hadn't said anything to him all day, except to offer to play tennis with him in the presence of the other boarders. Yet, he had a sense of peace, the same feeling that had pervaded him when the computers he'd managed to obtain arrived at the local library. He heard the sound of footsteps made by high-heeled shoes, and his breath lodged in his throat, but when they continued past his door, he let out a long harsh breath and stopped himself seconds before his fist slammed into the wall.

Jolene made her way up the stairs to her room, glad that at last she could stop smiling. All evening, she had faked joviality and warmth, when she had wanted to crawl into bed, tuck herself in a fetal position and bawl. Gregory had called because he said he would, but he hadn't said anything that would allow her to believe they would be friends again. Didn't men want truthfulness and honesty from women? It was just her bad luck that she'd been forced to talk with him while riding the bus and her conversation wasn't private. He didn't say he would call again, nor did he suggest that she call him.

It's my fault. Still, I had to tell him the truth, because I don't want to live a lie. I want him to like me as I am; if he can't, I'm glad I know it now. I care for him, but I'll get over it. I have to. And I'm going to help Richard with the children in that class. I promised, and I'm not going to let Gregory's attitude get in the way. She lifted her gaze to the ceiling and, in a prayerful tone asked aloud, "Isn't there one person anywhere who can love me? Really love me?"

At breakfast the following morning, she joined Judd and Richard without waiting for an invitation. "I'll be at the library at five-fifteen, Richard," she told him. "Believe me, as soon as those kids get used to me, you will not have any disciplinary problems."

"I'm glad to hear it. They get rather rowdy sometimes. Once or twice, I've wanted to smack them."

She raised an eyebrow. "Really? I don't think that's permitted."

"It isn't, but that didn't stop me from wanting to do it. If you think you can make them orderly without committing a crime, more power to you."

The following afternoon, Jolene walked into the children's computer class and looked around. She didn't see how anyone could learn in that atmosphere. She saw a ruler on a table, picked it up, walked to the front of the room and slapped the ruler vigorously against the desk.

"Be quiet, all of you," she said. "Sit down, and give me your attention. The first one to speak without permission will go home at once and will not be allowed to come back." The silence was immediate and complete. "I'm Miss Tilman, and I do not tolerate misbehavior. I am here to maintain order during this class. If you cannot be quiet and pay attention during the class, your parents will have to pay for private lessons, because you are not going to disrupt this class. Misbehave once, and you are out."

She glanced toward the door and saw Richard and Gregory standing there with their mouths slightly ajar. "Your teachers are here," she said, "so show them how well you can behave. I'll be in the back of the room, and I'll be looking at every one of you."

Within minutes, she realized that she should have brought along a notebook and pencil, for those children were learning what she needed to know. *Next Tuesday I'll be one of the students and, if it isn't too late, I'm going to register for the adult courses. I must have been out of my mind to pass up an opportunity like this. What about Gregory? What will it be like seeing him three nights every week and being just another one of his students? I'm not a baby*, she told herself. *I'll deal with it.*

At the end of the class she stood at the door as the children filed out of the room. "Goodnight," she said to them.

"Goodnight, Miss Tilman, see you next week."

Richard approached her, his face wreathed in smiles. "This is the best class we've had. You were wonderful."

"It was amazing," Gregory said. "And they didn't seem to resent you."

She tried not to show her pleasure in receiving their compliments. "Children expect two things from us: love and discipline. They accept that the two go together, and they will put you to the test. I just let them know that they are the children and I am the adult. I rule." She laughed, although mostly from nervousness, for Gregory had trained his piercing gaze on her, and she couldn't fathom its meaning.

"How do you know this?" Gregory asked her.

With her head tilted to the side, she took a good look at him. Tall and handsome with eyes that could make a woman want to drown in them. *Remember, girl, you're not pumping up any man's ego. So straighten up*, she told herself. To Gregory she said, "I was once a child, and I know what worked and didn't work with me. I got more discipline than I needed, but I wouldn't have minded that if there'd been even a modicum of love to go along with it." She switched her gaze to Richard. "Where's Judd?"

"He's in the reading room working on his plans for the spring camping trip he gives for high school senior honor students every year."

It seemed as if everyone she admired was doing something for the community. *I really have been on the wrong track*, she told herself. "Richard, hadn't we better start home? It's twenty-five minutes to seven, and Fannie will trip for sure if three of us are late for supper."

"Absolutely."

"I can drop you over there," Gregory said, and Richard accepted the offer before she could turn it down.

She walked past Gregory without speaking and went to the reading room. "Come on, Judd. It's almost time for supper. Gregory offered to take us home, and Richard accepted before I could say no."

"Why would you say no? M' legs will appreciate the ride."

If she had told him the truth, that it was because of her pride, he would have lectured to her about it, so she didn't answer him. No doubt the three men expected her to sit beside Gregory in the front seat, but she reached the car first, opened the door and sat in the back. When the three men stared first at her and then at each other, she sought to soften her action: "I defer to you, Judd."

"Are you sure that's what you did?" Richard whispered to her as Gregory pulled away from the curb.

Why should she lie? "No, but it sounded good."

Three weeks after making his offer to teach recreational activities to the boarders at Thank the Lord Boarding House, Richard admitted to himself and to Judd that what he offered held no interest for his fellow boarders. Only Joe Tucker and Jolene had taken advantage of his generosity. Francine didn't need tennis lessons; she had played since early childhood. "They aren't interested in me," he told Judd at breakfast one morning, "and I have decided that I don't give a damn."

"You do, or you wouldn't mention it. Why don't you and I go fishing over on Isle of Wright Bay? It's just a few miles from here, and it has some of the best striped bass anywhere. Or we can go down to Assawoman Bay and see if we can get a few crabs, but I'd rather fish."

"Let's fish. Won't it be cold?"

"Yeah, but the fish will bite. If it was summer, we'd go at daybreak, but around eight will be fine. We can call Dan, the cabbie, and—"

"I'll rent a car, and we can do as we please."

The minute he said it, he realized that he was settling into a friendship with Judd, a meaningful and deepening relationship that he'd never had with anyone, man or woman. And how strange that it should occur not with a man his age or who had known the world as he had but with a working-class man senior to his father. A man whose formal education had ended with a high school diploma, but whose knowledge often surpassed what one would expect of learned individuals, and who possessed an enormous capacity for friendship and caring.

As he rose to leave the table, he patted Judd's frail shoulder. "I'm glad I know you."

Judd stopped eating and gazed at Richard. "What brought that on?"

"If I didn't have you for company, I would probably have left here long before now. Can we go fishing tomorrow?"

"We can, and if we catch enough, Marilyn will cook them for us."

Richard imagined that his face showed his distaste for the idea that popped into his head. "Who'll clean them? Not me."

"Rodger. The man loves fish."

"They're not biting today," a fisherman told them the next morning as they drove up to the bay. "Been out here two hours and didn't get so much as a jerk on my line."

Seeing the disappointment on Judd's face, Richard said, "We're going to fish. Let's go over to Ocean Pines. Gregory's shop is right there at the water's edge, so he'll know where we can get a boat."

By noon, they had a dozen striped bass, plus catfish and pike. "These fish practically jumped into the boat. I have a feeling that nobody's been fishing here for a while," Judd said.

They offered Gregory some of their catch. "I'm not one for cleaning fish," he said, "but if you two are willing, I can fry up a batch of the catfish that I bought from the fishmonger, bake some cornbread, and whip up a salad, and we can lunch here in the shop. I have soft drinks, tea, coffee, milk and water."

"Sounds good to me," Judd said. "Richard, you got your cell phone with you? If we don't tell Fannie we won't be in for lunch, she'll preach us a sermon."

"I told her not to expect us. Plenty of good food between here and there."

Halfway through the meal, Judd wiped his mouth on the red paper napkin and looked straight at Gregory. "I've reached the age, Gregory, where I say what I think, and if I need an answer, I go to the source. I don't gossip about anybody's business, and I don't lie about anybody." Richard wondered what was coming, and Judd didn't keep him waiting.

"Jolene. She's not m' daughter, but I feel like a father to her. She's a girl who's known nothing but tragedy and ugliness, and she's just easing out of that shell she used to live in. She's never mentioned you to me, but I'm certain you're very important to her. Do you think things are going to work out between the two of you?"

Gregory placed his knife and fork on the edge of his plate
and looked his questioner in the eye. "I don't know, Judd. When
she first came to Pike Hill, I thought so, and I wanted that, but so
much water has flowed under the bridge, so to speak, that I'm
no longer sure. I can't say no, because there's much about her
that attracts me, and I don't know how she feels about me. So I
can't say yes, either."

"Fair enough. As long as you're straight with her—"

"Bet on it."

"Gregory's a good man," Judd told Richard on the drive back
to Pike Hill. "I suspect Jolene took a wrong turn somewhere."

"I think she probably took more than one wrong turn, but
something happened to shake her up, and she's showing remarkable maturity for somebody who was still wet behind the
ears less than a year ago. I'm realizing that I like her."

"Me, too. I think a lot of her. I wish there was some way I
could . . . well, never mind."

Richard slowed down to take a sharp curve. "Something happened between her and Percy that took the starch out of the man.
I'm sure of it. He's a pitiable caricature of his old self."

"I thought I was the only person who suspected that. I've a
mind to speak to her about it, but I'm scared that if I do, she'll
cave back into herself."

"I know," Richard said. "I was hoping he'd play darts with
Joe and me, but when Joe asked him to join us, he refused."

At the boardinghouse, Richard followed Judd to the kitchen
to find Marilyn. "Richard and I caught a lot of striped bass, some
pike and catfish. How about a good fish fry for supper?"

She looked at her watch. "I was going to have roast pork, but
nothing beats fish right out of the water. Roast pork can wait till
tomorrow. I'll tell Rodger to get to work on 'em." She looked at
Richard with a lowered gaze and a half smile. "Which ones did
you catch? I want to be sure and eat one of those."

Damned if flirting wasn't as much a part of her as her skin.
The woman couldn't resist doing it. He'd have to stop getting
angry with her and learn to ignore it. "I don't know one fish
from the other until I taste it. Seems there's something different
about catfish, but I don't know what that is."

"And here I was all primed to eat something of yours."

"Give her a bar of chocolate," Judd said. "Thanks for cooking the fish, Marilyn. I'm beginning to feel as if you're discriminating against me."

She nearly glared at him when she said, "What do you mean?" so he knew she understood his comment.

"Let's see, there was Henry Gray who left because you drove him half crazy. Ronald Barnes, Joe Tucker, and Percy Lucas managed to cool you off, and I thought Richard had done the same, but apparently not. You shouldn't cheapen yourself by making a play for every man who lives here. You're too fine a woman."

"I don't do that," she said. "Can I help it if everybody misunderstands me?" Richard watched her demeanor sag, a proud bird whose wings had been cut. Mortified.

"Happens to all of us," he said and wondered why he felt the need to soothe her.

"If you're going to the lounge," she said, "I'll send Rodger with coffee and some of the pineapple-upside-down cake we had for lunch."

Judd thanked her, and they went to the lounge to wait for Marilyn's effort to redeem herself in the only way that she knew, by serving impeccable food.

"You felt sorry for her," Judd said. "There's something about this place that changes people. Six months ago, you would have spoken harshly to her. I see you're thinking more about other people and less about yourself, and it's a good thing."

"She was more hurt than embarrassed. Anyway, I've stopped disliking her."

Rodger arrived with cake and coffee. "I see you brought a mess of good fish. I'll get to 'em right away. Nothing makes me happier than a good Southern fish fry, some good old hush puppies and some collard greens stewed down with some smoked ham hocks. I tell you, I can taste it right now."

"I know what you mean," Judd said. "Thanks for cleaning them."

"My pleasure."

"Feel like a stroll along the beach this afternoon, Judd?"

"Naah. I've breathed enough cold salt air for one day. You go on and enjoy yourself."

He didn't feel like working on his memoirs. Facing who he'd been for most of his life had become increasingly painful with each chapter he wrote. He'd stopped writing at the point where Lindsay Elliott fell out of bed reaching for him and begging him to spend the rest of the night with her. She had been a sexual carnivore, exhausting him with her need for orgasms. To begin with, he'd had no interest in her as a person, but the beautiful breasts she'd all but exposed to him and her invitation to have his way with her when and as he pleased fitted his usual pattern; it was easier to take what was offered than to risk his reputation as a distinguished diplomat and seduce a woman. She had offered, and he took until he'd had a surfeit of her. But now, he hated that era of his life to the extent that he was unable to write truthfully about it.

He put on a black leather jacket and headed for the beach. He saw Francine at once, disguised as a clam fisherman. Did she think she would apprehend a smuggler at three o'clock in the afternoon? He strolled along until he came to a huge irregularly-shaped boulder and sat on the side away from the bay but where he had a clear view of Francine. The wind stormed in to shore bringing a blast of cold and salty air from the ocean beyond. He knew she had to be cold, and he wanted badly to put his jacket around her, for in her disguise, she was thinly dressed.

At about five o'clock, as winter darkness encroached, she took her bucket and shovel and trudged toward Rhone Street. He didn't intercept her, fearing that he might destroy her cover. He remained on the beach for another ten minutes until he figured she'd left the area, but as he reached Rhone Street and Ocean Road, he met three men, and one of them walked with a slight limp. He didn't doubt that that man was Ronald Barnes. He took out his cell phone to call Francine and realized he didn't know her cell phone number. Furthermore, he doubted that she had gone to the boardinghouse dressed in that manner.

"I can't call the police, because this is a secret operation, and I'm not supposed to know about it. Well, hell!" He jogged home and waited in the lounge to intercept her when she came in. Why the hell did he have to fall for a woman who, at any minute, could be killed by a bunch of thugs? Exasperated, he popped his knuckles for the first time in fifteen years when he became a first-level ambassador and was advised that knuckle popping was unbecoming to his status. A policewoman. A mental picture of his former associates' faces upon learning that he wanted a policewoman made him laugh.

"We're phonies, every last one of us."

At about six-thirty, he heard her quick steps in the hallway and dashed out of the lounge. "Can I have a private word with you, Francine? It won't take but a second." A look of apprehension flashed across her face, and he knew that his visage mirrored his concern.

"What is it, Richard?"

"Ten minutes after you left the beach this afternoon, Barnes and two other men arrived. I wanted to call you, but I don't know your cell phone number, and I couldn't call the police without breaching your confidence." He grasped her arm. "Please don't go back down there. It's too dangerous. You can't handle three men, and I don't want anything to happen to you."

She inhaled a long deep breath and let it out slowly. "You recognized me?" He nodded. "I got a tip, and now I realize it was meant to get me out of the way. According to the information I was given, those men were supposed to meet there between three and four. I stayed until five fifteen, and they arrived around five-thirty."

"The person who gave you that tip is a worm. Is he or she in your department?"

"Absolutely. But not for long. I'd better get—"

"Please, Francine, don't go back out there now. Call the police, but don't go. I couldn't bear it if anything happened to you."

"That's the nicest thing you've ever said to me. I have to do my job, Richard."

"Then take me with you. I'm as good a shot as you'll find anywhere."

She lifted an eyebrow. "That would be against the law, but thanks. How'd you learn to shoot so well and why?"

"Skeet shooting. I'm also an Olympian."

"Hmm. Why doesn't that surprise me? I'd better hurry. See you at supper."

He held her arm, unwilling to countenance her going back to the beach alone. "Does that mean you are not going back to the beach tonight?"

"I'm not going back, but I have to alert my captain so that he can take the necessary measures. Thank you for caring." She dashed up the stairs and left him standing there.

Now what? She was a professional, and he respected that, but knowing she could be in danger and unable to circumvent it went against his grain. He went back into the lounge and challenged Judd to a game of blackjack.

"So you aiming to take it out on me, are you?" Judd said. "You'd be better off throwing darts with Joe Tucker."

"Aw, come on, Judd. It isn't that bad."

"It is so. It takes a tough man to love a woman like Francine. My wife was like her: soft and sweet, but strong and independent. She could change a tire quicker than I could, and she wasn't afraid of anything. I never felt threatened by it. She loved me, and she was as soft as a ball of cotton in my arms. Francine will be like that; she'll love you, but you'll never be able to tell her what to do."

He knew that, and he had to decide whether he could handle it. As things were going, the choice was being taken from him. He would support her in whatever she decided to do, but he was damned if he wanted a life in which fear drained the blood out of his body every time his woman left him. He picked up the hand of cards that Judd dealt him and looked at them.

"I should have been paying closer attention to you, Judd. I suspect you're not above cheating me."

"No, I'm not, but as long as there's no money on the table, you can depend on m'honesty."

Richard looked at his watch. "This hand's useless. I'm going to wash up before dinner. I'll bet you've got blackjack."

Judd spread out his cards. "A joker and the ace of spades. See you later."

* * *

Jolene walked into Harper's hospital room that Friday evening with a bunch of pink roses and a pint of butter pecan ice cream. She didn't know how to get his attention, for he sat in his wheelchair facing the window precisely as he had when she last visited him. She supposed he knew that she had a strong sense of guilt about him, and that she wanted him to know she was sorry and wished him well.

"Hi, Harper. I hope you don't mind a little company for ten or fifteen minutes."

He turned the wheelchair around to face the door. "Well, hi. I'd begun to think that after all you told me last time you were here, you weren't coming back. Come on in. They took my neck brace off yesterday. See?"

She wanted to ask him if he had any visitors other than herself, but didn't. Such a handsome man as Harper would have girlfriends. She sat in the one chair in his room, and he rolled his wheelchair to face her.

"Thanks for the flowers, and thanks for the others that you sent. They lasted a long time." His gaze seemed to penetrate her, but she didn't mind, for it bore no hostility. "You're nice to come here to see me, Jolene. We didn't part on good terms that night. I was hurt and angry and self-righteous and . . . I drove like a maniac. I also wasn't nice the first time you came to see me, and I'm sorry about that."

"I know, Harper, and it was all my fault."

"How's it your fault? I'm a grown man. Nobody made me drive like that on a road I'd never been on before. I knew better."

But she didn't feel absolved. "Like I said, I didn't know how to treat people, but I'm learning. I'm still worried about . . . you know . . . I told you about the man who lives in the boarding house. His personality has changed. It's as if he tries to shrivel up, as if he'd like to crawl into a hole and hide. He doesn't talk to anyone, only eats his supper and goes to his room. I'd give anything if I could undo what I did, but I just couldn't participate in that. He's still mortified, and I don't know how to help him."

Harper shook his head as if perplexed. "That's a tough one.

One of the worst things that can happen to a man is to get that kind of proof that a woman doesn't want him. You're probably the first woman to tell him that he didn't have any technique. Sounds to me as if he's been seeing ladies of the evening."

"The change in him is becoming obvious to all the boarders. I wish I could do something."

"Well, if you can get him alone, tell him you hope he hasn't told anybody about that incident, that you're still embarrassed, and that you appreciate the fact that he was such a gentleman about it, or something like that. He was, you know. Some men would have forced you."

She nearly laughed when she remembered what actually outraged Percy. "Maybe it was wasting his money that got to him at first. I offered to pay for the room, and he accepted that, but when he parked to let me out about a block from the boarding-house, he seemed near tears and ordered me not to tell anyone about it. I assured him that I didn't want anyone to know, either. I'll do as you suggest."

Her gaze fell on the bag in her hand. "Good grief, I forgot to give you this butter pecan ice cream."

He reached for it. "I'll take it. The last thing I'll get in here will be ice cream." She handed him the ice cream, a paper napkin and a plastic spoon. "I'd better be going. My landlady gets bent out of shape if any of us comes to supper late. She's got more rules than a third grade teacher, but they make the boarding-house a really nice place to live." As she stood to leave, a tall, stately woman who she figured to be about sixty or sixty-five walked into the room.

"Hi, Mom. This is Jolene Tilman. Jolene, this is my mom, Louise Masterson."

"How are you, Mrs. Masterson? I would have known you were Harper's mother, if no one had told me. What a striking resemblance! I'm glad to meet you."

"I'm glad to meet you, and I'm really happy to see that Harper has company. I live in Hyattsville, and I can't get here every day."

Jolene edged toward the door. "I'll see you again, Harper. Good-bye, Mrs. Masterson."

"Thanks for the flowers, and especially for this great ice cream. Bye."

I can't visit him too often, she told herself. *I remember how he said he felt about me, and I don't want to cause any more problems than I already have.* She hurried to the bus stop, and when she boarded, she dropped her money in the slot, said "Good afternoon," to the driver, and made her way to the back of the bus.

I'm not getting friendly with any more men. If you say, "Hi" to a man, he thinks you want to go out with him, and if you're not friendly, he thinks you're stuck up. I guess I would have learned all that if I had ever been a teenager. She looked skyward. "Mama, you did a real job on me. You took away my youth, and I'm just learning what I should have known when I was sixteen. You got a lot to answer for."

Jolene rushed into the boardinghouse at twenty minutes to seven and headed to her room to freshen up. She met Percy Lucas on the stairs and stopped, prepared to speak to him in the way Harper suggested, but when Percy saw her, he turned and went back up the stairs and on to his room.

Shaking her head, perplexed, Jolene said aloud, "I've got to do something about that man, but what?"

She looked up to see Francine walking toward her. "What's wrong? Is something bothering you?" Francine asked her.

"Something is, but I have to work it out myself." The warmth of Francine's hand on her shoulder consoled Jolene, and she wanted to ask her help, but the thought of sharing that woeful experience with a woman as worldly as Francine embarrassed her.

"If you need a friend, I'm here. See you at supper."

If she needed a friend? She'd never had a female friend, and after trying to make one of Vida, she wasn't sure that having one was a good thing. Yet, it didn't take a genius to know that gender was the only thing Vida and Francine had in common.

"Maybe we can have some coffee together after supper, Francine," she said and continued to her room.

* * *

After supper, Jolene joined Francine in the lounge, and they sat at a small table beneath a painting of Mary McLeod Bethune. "I always admired this woman," Francine said, pointing to the portrait. "She founded Bethune-Cookman College in Daytona Beach over a hundred years ago, and it exists and thrives today. Gender and race didn't prevent her from making a contribution to her people and from earning a name for herself."

"I wish I could do something like that, Francine. I had so much fun helping Richard and Gregory with the children in the computer class at the library tonight. If I had a college degree, I could do things."

"In four years or less, you can have one. Why not go for it?"

"I was just going to take some courses, but I think I'll register for a degree. There's so much I don't know, and I keep learning by making mistakes, hurting people, and myself."

Francine accepted the cappuccino that Rodger offered, sprinkled it with cinnamon and sugar and took a sip. "Ahh, this is great. Thanks, Rodger." To Jolene, she said, "No matter how many books you read or how many lectures you attend, the only way you're going to learn about life is by living. Oh, the books and lectures help you to reason and to chart your course, but the loyalty of a friend or the kiss of a man who truly loves you are lessons you never forget." Jolene toyed absent-mindedly with the lemon meringue pie, one of her favorite desserts, thinking of Percy and the unpleasant lesson that flirting with him and trying to use him had taught her.

"What's troubling you, Jolene? Can I help?"

"I don't know. What I did was so awful that I'm embarrassed to tell you about it, but I have to find a way to make amends."

"Is there a man involved?"

"Yes. It . . . uh happened about three months after I moved here." With effort, she forced herself to tell Francine about instigating a tryst with Percy Lucas and about the outcome. "I feel as if I've damaged him irreparably. He almost met me on the stairs tonight, and turned and went back to his room. I'm so sorry about the mess I made. He'd never said a word to me or done anything to deserve it."

"You act as if what you did is equivalent to murder; well, it isn't. You had just learned that you have some power over men and you decided to test it. That happens to most girls when they're teenagers. You're a late bloomer. Write him a nice letter telling him how you feel about it, how much you appreciate his gentlemanly behavior, and send him some flowers. He'll be delighted, and he will probably bounce out of his depression, or whatever it is that ails him."

Jolene rubbed her hands together, smiling as she did so. "A letter. Why didn't I think of that? Thanks so much, Francine. Lord, I hope it works, and I hope he likes roses."

"While we're at it, Jolene, there're two sides to this man-woman business. You mustn't flirt if you're not going to follow through and keep your promise, and you never make love with a man on his terms. You do that if and when *you* want to. For me, I have to know that the man loves me. I know that's old-fashioned, but I won't give myself to the care of a man who doesn't think I'm precious to him."

"But suppose you want to and he doesn't love you. Then what?"

Laughter rippled out of Francine. "I deny myself, and I suffer."

Jolene followed Francine's gaze to Richard Peterson. *Ah, so Richard and Francine were at a standoff, because Richard wasn't in love. If I'd had that much sense, I never would have gone to bed with Harper, and he probably wouldn't be in that wheelchair.*

"What if you're in love with him?" she asked Francine, sensing the answer.

"I am, but I'm a disciplined person, and I don't let my vagina make important decisions for me. If the guy doesn't love me, we can be friends, but we definitely won't be in the same bed simultaneously. Period."

"But—"

Francine interrupted her. "It isn't difficult, Jolene. Stand your ground. If you give in, you won't be happy. Men will take what comes easily, but most of them won't value it." She threw up her hands. "My Lord, Jolene, to have a man who loves you and will worship every centimeter of skin on your body and every inch of the inside of you he can reach . . . I get practically unconscious thinking about it. I mean, if that's not heaven on earth, what is?"

Jolene wouldn't have believed that Francine would discuss anything so personal. Both simple and sophisticated, the woman fascinated her. "If you loved him, too," she said. "I'm sure it would be heaven. Thanks for talking with me, Francine. You've taught me more than you can guess. I'm going to write that letter to Percy before I go to bed. Good-night." Her cellular phone rang as she reached the top of the stairs.

Francine had hoped that Jolene would remain with her in the lounge for a while longer. She wasn't ready to go to her room, and if she remained alone at that little table, it would appear that she was deliberately avoiding Richard, since no one avoided Judd. But she wasn't so foolhardy as to think she could sit knee to knee with Richard Peterson and not take a whipping both from her heart and from her libido. She stiffened her shoulders, drained her cup and walked over to the table where Judd was teaching Richard how to play pinochle.

"Glad you decided to visit with your friends," Judd said. "Do you know how to play pinochle?"

"Haven't played it since college," she told him, ignoring his barb.

"Good, I haven't played it since I sold m' business and moved here. It's more fun with three than two or four. Want to join us for a hand? With you playing, Richard will learn faster."

Richard got up and went to get a chair for her, brought it back and waited until she sat down. Then, he took his own seat, looked at her and said, "We can't play tennis until spring. Would you like to learn to skeet shoot?"

In other words, would she spend time alone with him? "Thanks, Richard, but I'd rather not. Sports shooting goes against my politics. I'll hike over one of those nature trails in Ocean Pines with you sometime."

His gaze seemed to penetrate her flesh. "I don't care what we do as long as we do it together."

At her sharp intake of breath, Judd put his cards on the table and said. "I'm getting sleepy. I'll see you in the morning, Richard. Good night, Francine."

"Why did you say that, Richard? You embarrassed him."

"Not by a long shot, I didn't. Judd knows there's something going on between us, and he is also aware that you avoided me this evening. I said that because I figured you didn't plan to be alone with me, and I'm a man known for capitalizing on opportunities, however rare and however small. If you're off this weekend, can we hike as you suggested? I want us to be together."

"You're not ready for a genuine relationship with me, Richard, and I am not going to accept what you offered."

He leaned back in the chair and looked her in the eye. "And what did I offer?"

If he had the guts to ask, she had the guts to tell him. "You offered me sex."

"What's wrong with that?"

She let a shrug enforce her words. "Nothing, if that's what suits you. It's not what I'm about. If you'll excuse me—"

His hand covered hers. "You want a commitment? I can't give it. If I let myself go with you, I'd be a nervous wreck whenever I wasn't looking at you, scared to death that I'd find you in a heap somewhere. Lifeless. I couldn't bear it."

"You care for me, and you don't like the idea. I am who I am, Richard. If and when you come to me with your true feelings bared, I'll welcome you with my arms wide open."

He sucked in his breath, and she knew she'd struck a blow that hurt. "As recently as a year ago, I would have taken you merely because I could and thought nothing of it, but I've put that life-style behind me. I'm straight with you. Why can't you take me for what I am?"

"Eventually, I will, and you will be precisely what I want and need."

He stared at her. "What the devil does that mean?"

She smiled because a glow of happiness flowed through her body. "You'll see. Good-night."

Inside her room, she removed her revolver and cell phone from her purse and placed them on her night table. She wondered how long that red light on her cell phone had been flashing. A check showed three messages from her captain, who wanted her to call him.

"We're holding a man who fits the description of one of those men you saw on the beach. Can you get over here as fast as possible?" he said.

The first call had come in more than an hour earlier. She didn't have to hide her activities from Richard, but after what he'd said earlier, she didn't want him to see her leaving the house at ten-thirty at night. She dressed in a gray sweater, black woolen pants suit, boots, and her storm coat, put her revolver and cell phone back into her pocketbook and prayed that she wouldn't encounter Richard. After mussing up her bed to make it appear that she slept in it, she managed to get out of the house without encountering anyone.

"He's not one of them," she said when she saw the suspect, "at least not one of the three men I saw. Next time, could you please wait until the next morning. If any person in that boarding-house had seen me leaving there at ten-thirty at night, no explanation would convince them that I'm a moral person."

"Sorry, but we had to make a judgment. At least we know he isn't the one."

"I'm staying over here tonight in a motel. The boardinghouse front door will be locked by the time I get back there."

"Say, I *am* sorry," the captain said.

"Sure. From now on, please don't expect me to come out so late unless it's a genuine emergency. Okay?"

"Okay."

Richard walked from one end of his room to the other one and back again several times, pausing occasionally to observe through his window the clear moon and the waves that sloshed and danced seductively beneath it. He plowed his fingers through his hair, punishing his scalp and exacerbating the pain in his head. Where the hell had she gone at almost eleven o'clock at night? And what was she doing? Would she try to handle those thugs alone? He couldn't stand knowing that she was probably in danger and being helpless to protect her.

"If I get my hands on her, I'll shake her. It's too dangerous, and her superiors ought to know that." He slapped his left fist in his right palm. "Of all the women in this world, I have to fall for a police—fall? Who said I'd fallen?" He dropped himself on the side of his bed, leaned forward and, with his forearms on his thighs, clasped his head in his hands.

For most of the night, he listened for her steps on the stairs and in the hallway past his room with no results. At daybreak, he rolled out of the rumpled sheets, dressed and went to the parking lot behind the boardinghouse, didn't see her car and hurried to the beach, his heart in his mouth, as his fear for her well-being rose to frightening proportions. No sign of her, and he didn't know whether to be glad or more miserable. Where was she? If any person had entered that house during the night, he would have known it.

He faced the ocean and let the frigid wind punish him. If she'd been out there, she would have frozen. As he headed back to the house, chills gripped his body, the wind drew tears from his eyes, and he blew his breath upward to warm his face. Hunched over against the elements, he began to run. Maybe she'd come home after he left. He checked the parking lot again. What had happened to her? What if she needed him? He couldn't stand it. She wouldn't stay out all night, unless she was in trouble.

If only he had remembered to get her cell phone number. He telephoned Dan, the taxi driver. "I need a couple of hours of your time, Dan, as soon as you can get here."

"Be there in half an hour, Mr. Peterson."

Back in the house, he paced the floor of the lounge until the dining room opened for breakfast. "I have a couple of errands to do," he told Judd. "I'll see you at supper."

"Where to?" Dan asked him.

"Ocean Pines. Just drive slowly around the center of town. I'm looking for a white 2004 Cougar."

"Yes, sir."

He tried to relax, but knew he wouldn't until he saw her safe and unharmed. When he saw that her car was not parked at the police station, he thought his heart had dropped into his belly.

It was about eight-thirty when he yelled at Dan: "Stop right here." *A motel?* Why the hell was her car parked in front of a motel? His first inclination was to go in and check the register. He stood at the walkway that led to the motel's office and stared ahead catatonic-like, immobilized.

"What is it, Mr. Peterson?" Dan asked him. "What's the matter?"

"Nothing. I've just verified my stupidity. Let's go back to the boardinghouse."

Chapter Nine

That evening after supper, Francine grasped Jolene's hand and walked with her into the lounge. It was an act of desperation, Francine knew, perplexed and hurt as she was by Richard's strange behavior. Not only had he ignored her, but when she did catch his eye, he looked right through her, as it were, unseeing and unfeeling. What had happened to dispel the warmth and caring that he evinced so clearly and so sweetly the previous evening? She didn't want to go to her room, didn't want to sit alone, and pride wouldn't allow her to join Judd and Richard.

"Let's sit over there," she said to Jolene, pointing to a corner where two brown leather armchairs stood with a small table between them. Almost as soon as they sat down, Marilyn arrived to serve them coffee and truffles.

Marilyn treated Francine to a half smile. 'Well, honey, looks like you struck out, too." Francine didn't trust herself to answer.

"Was she talking about you and Richard?" Jolene asked Francine after Marilyn walked away. "Barbara said Marilyn's bitchy."

"Yeah. She was being a smartass, but she can bet I'll never fling myself at Richard Peterson or any other man the way she does."

Jolene patted Francine's hand, tentatively as if uncertain as to the propriety of doing it and of her right to such intimacy. "I hope nothing has happened to . . . to break up you and Richard. He's a really nice man, and I thought he liked you a lot."

Francine wanted to wipe the tears that dripped down her insides, tears that she refused to let fall from her eyes. "Something *has* happened, Jolene. Last night when we spoke, I would have bet my life that he cared for me, and deeply, too. Tonight, he looked at me as if he'd never seen me before. Cold as ice. He's hurt about something, and he ought to tell me."

"Why don't you ask him?"

Francine sipped the cold coffee without tasting it. "I love him, Jolene, but I will never prostrate myself on the altar of love. To do that would only earn a man's contempt."

Jolene stared at her, obviously failing to understand. "But if he loves you—"

Francine interrupted her, already aware of Jolene's deficiency at understanding human emotions . . . "If he doesn't respect me, he can't love me. Besides, I have to respect myself. If I've wronged him, he ought to tell me and give me a chance to explain.

"Love is fragile, Jolene. That's one of the reasons why it's so precious. I could stand on my head and dance naked in the town square, and he would still want to take me to bed, but the same act would make him stop loving me."

Jolene nodded. "You mean a man can want sex with you and not care for you?"

Francine smothered a gasp. "Honey, men do that all the time. Some women also, but I think it's less common among us."

Jolene gave the appearance of one shrinking by inches. "I wish I knew what to do. I like Gregory, and he liked me until I messed up. Still, I wonder if he ever liked me as much as Harper did . . . does . . . I mean . . . I don't know."

"Jolene, when a man loves you, you'd know it if you were blind. And you feel it even if you don't reciprocate it."

"I mistook it for weakness on the man's part, and I exploited it."

"But you're a different person now. You've learned from your mistakes, so stop whipping yourself."

"Whipping myself? I deserve it. Less than a week ago, I came close to making a receptacle of myself again. That's what mama said men use us for. When I thought I was using them, they were using me."

Francine held up her right hand, as if to stop the flow of Jolene's thoughts. "None of that."

"Francine, I get so lonely sometimes for someone who cares about me. Anyone."

Francine placed her cup in its saucer and prepared to terminate the conversation. "Get it into your head that love and sex are not the same thing."

Jolene nodded. "You've been saying that all evening, and I hear you."

They walked toward the doorway of the lounge together and, when they reached the water cooler, Jolene noticed that Francine glanced back toward Richard's table and sucked in her breath. She wanted to console her friend, but she knew that Francine was tough enough to withstand the ravages of unrequited love. *I wish I was like her, and not so stupid about men. It's been two weeks since Gregory called me, and even then, he didn't say much. If she were in my place, Francine wouldn't call him. I won't either.*

The next morning, she stepped on the bus seconds before its departure time. "You're cutting it close, babe," the driver said. "If you weren't such a doll, I'd probably be blocks away from here right now."

"You're not due to leave until eight o'clock."

"What's two minutes? Make it worth my while, and I'll wait for you till the St. Martin River runs backward."

Jolene paused beside him, her heartbeat accelerating and her blood running hotter. She looked down at him and saw the naked lust in his grayish brown eyes. Saw it and identified it. Harper had never looked at her like that. Shocked at the revelation, she told her ego to take a seat and refused to let his comment faze her. Only a few weeks earlier she would have been flattered and, even now, she found it hard to ignore him. Perhaps if she told him what she thought of his comment, he'd stop playing with her.

"You're full of it, Mister. Pick another target, because this one is moving on. All I want from you is a safe ride to and from Salisbury every day. That's all you can do for me." She didn't wait for his response, but headed to the back of the bus, sat down and opened a copy of *Whatever It Takes*. Francine had given it to her at breakfast that morning and said it illustrated the differences between sex and love.

She ate lunch with Vida and another hairdresser, and it occurred to her for the first time that the women who worked in the beauty shop talked only of men and of their personal problems with them. But she didn't feel like sharing her problems and concerns with her co-workers. Vida reported that, the previous Friday, she sued the father of her children for child support, and Gina had a domestic-violence suit pending against her husband. As Jolene journeyed home to Pike Hill that afternoon, she wondered about the wisdom of casting her lot with a man who, it appeared, you didn't know until after you married him or began living with him. Maybe she wasn't too badly off.

Jolene thought of getting off the bus at the stop near the hospital and spending a few minutes with Harper but, fearing that he might regard her as more than a friend, decided against it. As fate would have it, when she rounded the banister to go up the stairs, the Reverend Philip Coles emerged from the lounge hurriedly, bumped into Jolene and sent her sprawling.

"Oh, my! Jolene! I'm terribly sorry. Here let me help you up."

She shook off his hand and pulled herself up. "You must be in a heck of a hurry! Oh! Reverend Coles! I didn't realize it was you."

"Well, yes. I thought I'd drop over and check on Fannie. How are you getting along?"

"The same. I'm fine. This is my home now." Her elbow hurt, but she didn't imagine that telling him would make it feel better. "I have to go up to my room, but I'll be down in a few minutes."

When she came back downstairs and went into the lounge,

where she expected to see the Reverend, she found Judd sitting alone. She accepted his offer of a glass of ginger ale and joined him. They spoke for a few minutes, and she settled into the comfort of Judd's presence.

"Your job still working out all right?" he asked her. She nodded, and told him she'd even had another raise. He leaned back in the rocker and rocked, and she figured he was leading up to something. "Seems like every couple of weeks, the Reverend favors us with his presence. I've been here almost twenty years, and the first nineteen of 'em he came here less than a dozen times, not even twice a year. Lately, he's here every two or three weeks. 'Course I guess that makes Fannie happy."

"Maybe so," she said. "I never saw much of him in Hagerstown, since I didn't have time to go to church."

"Hmm. You seen Gregory lately? Away from the library, I mean."

"No, I haven't, but that's all right, too. He's just one man."

Judd accelerated the rhythm of his rocking. "Atta girl! Now you're thinking with a clear head."

Coles entered the lounge, talking with Fannie and joined Judd and Jolene. She didn't know what to say to the man. They'd never been on a chummy basis, and she wouldn't discuss with a preacher her dilemma about men.

Judd rocked slowly. "What brings you back to us so soon, Rev.?" Judd asked Coles.

Reverend Coles cleared his throat. "Well, you know Fannie is my only living relative, and I also like to look in on Sara Jolene as often as possible. She's a long way from my church's jurisdiction, but I still think of her as my charge."

Somehow, that didn't ring true to her, but Jolene bit her tongue and kept the idea to herself. He'd never paid much attention to her when she was struggling beneath the weight of Emma Tilman's obsessive meanness, and she'd bet her life that he knew about it. The whole town knew about her mother's wrathful nature. Suddenly, she wanted Philip Coles to know that in spite of what she had experienced back in Hagerstown, she had made herself into a person of whom she was proud.

"I'm sorry we're not working with the computer classes, tonight, Judd," she said. "I miss them, but I suppose the children need a few days off during Thanksgiving week."

Philip's eyes gradually returned to their normal size, though he continued to stare at her. Judd seemed to relish explaining Jolene's contribution to the Monday afternoon computer classes at the library, and she certainly enjoyed the minister's reaction.

Later, sitting alone with Judd, Jolene said, "You appeared to be wiping his nose with that bit of information. As if you were giving him his comeuppance. Why? What'd he do to get on the wrong side of you?"

"Just m' instincts getting a little overactive."

After thinking about it for a minute, she dismissed the comment as another of Judd's cryptic remarks. If he wanted to explain it, he would; if he didn't there was no point in asking him. A few minutes before the time for supper, Richard walked into the lounge, though without his usual purposeful gait.

"How're you doing, friend?" Judd asked him in a disinterested sort of way, as if he didn't expect or didn't want an answer.

"Nothing's changed, Judd. How's your back?"

"Better'n an old man should expect. You seen Francine?"

"Naah. Hi, Jolene. How's it going?"

She understood at once that Judd and Richard would not discuss anything of importance to Richard while she sat there, and she wanted to leave them, but didn't for fear of encountering Philip Coles and having to sit with him through supper. Finally, she bade them goodbye and went to her usual place between Joe Tucker and Louvenia Munroe at table two.

"I see we got company," Joe said, nodding his head toward Philip Coles when she sat down. "Wonder why he started coming so often?"

"You mean Reverend Coles? Maybe he's just lonely and likes to be with his sister."

"You mean he doesn't have a wife and children?"

Jolene jerked her right shoulder in a careless shrug. "As far as I know, he never got married."

Joe leaned back in the ladder-back chair and looked at her.

"Maybe he's interested in you. He never showed up so regularly till you came here."

"You're way off. He's known me since I was born. If that was the case, he'd have made a move years ago."

"He's not after Francine, or at least he needn't be, and I don't think Barbara's met him. She only eats breakfast here; she's at the movie theater every night." He took a sip of water. "No point in trying to guess. He's probably just lonely and visiting his sister like you said."

Jolene had begun to enjoy sitting in the lounge after supper and chatting with the other boarders and disliked going to her room instead. So she forced herself to join Judd at his usual place, at the only rocker in the lounge.

"I wonder where Francine is tonight, Judd? I suppose Fannie knows, but if I ask her, she'll think I'm prying in another boarder's affairs. She wasn't happy last night. Do you think she and Richard will make up?"

"Sure they will, as soon as they get over their stubbornness. I wouldn't waste time worrying about those two. What's with you and Gregory?"

She pulled air through her front teeth and rolled her eyes. "I have no idea, and not knowing won't kill me. I didn't appreciate him when I had the chance, and he's unforgiving, I guess." She saw Richard heading their way and moved her chair aside to give him a place.

"Does Marilyn plan a Thanksgiving dinner with a big turkey, pumpkin pie, and all that?" she asked Judd, mainly to be able to include Richard in their conversation.

"Would Marilyn miss a chance to show off?" Richard asked. Suddenly, his head spun around. "I'll see you two later."

Jolene knew without being told that Richard had seen Francine heading up the stairs.

Richard took the steps three at a time, and caught Francine before she reached her room and grasped her by the shoulders. "Just tell me one thing. Where did you sleep night before last?"

She stepped back from him. "Hello, Richard. Why didn't you ask me that last night instead of looking through me as if I were a sheet of plate glass?"

He stared into her eyes. "I was in no frame of mind to ask you *anything*. If you don't want to answer my question, fine. You won't get any more trouble from me." He could see her wavering and knew she was weighing the cost to her of being without him. He held his breath and waited. Waited and prayed.

"I spent night before last at the Assawoman Motel in Ocean Pines." At his gasp, she added, "Shortly after I left you, my boss called and demanded that I come to the precinct and identify a possible smuggler. I went under protest. If I had driven back here to spend the night, I would have had to awaken Fannie around one in the morning, so I spent the night at that motel. If you had ever given me your cell phone number, I would have called you."

He inhaled a deep breath and let it out slowly. Never in his life had he been so relieved. And to think that he had believed her capable of duplicitous behavior! He wanted to take her to him and love her, but he knew she wouldn't appreciate it. He opted for honesty. "I thought all kinds of things. Your car wasn't parked out back, you weren't on the beach, and I knew you weren't in your room. Were you somewhere dead, or were you with another man? I nearly drove myself insane with worry. And then I got angry, but that quickly dissolved into pain. Pure pain."

Her hand stroked the side of his face. "Can't you accept what you feel? If you could . . . if only you would, it would be heaven."

"I'm an honest man, Francine. I've done a lot of things that I regret, but I have never pretended more than I felt or offered more than I knew I could give. I never seduced women, because they were always willing; I accepted what they gave merely because it was there for me. But I no longer take just because it's available. Oh, I'm tempted, but I've put that life behind me. I'm being straight with you because I care for you. You want the whole nine yards, and I don't have it to give."

To his surprise, she smiled. "That's your story *now*." She reached up, kissed his cheek and hurried off to her room. At her door, she turned and said, "Slip your cell phone number under my door. Good night."

As Francine was about to crawl into bed, she suddenly pounded her right fist into her left palm and dropped herself on the side of the bed. *Am I crazy? What on earth have I been thinking? If I make love with him, show him the love, the tenderness, and the passion that I feel for him, he'll be mine. He loves me, and everything he said to me tonight proves it. It's up to me to make him turn that other woman, whoever she is, loose, to show him that he can love another woman. Me.* She turned out the light and fell asleep with a smile on her face.

Although Francine had begun to get her life in order, Jolene's dilemma was only beginning. Philip Coles returned to Thank the Lord Boarding House on Thanksgiving Eve to spend the holiday with his sister.

"My, but you're handy. You're not the person who left Hagerstown last winter. I wonder what Emma would say if she saw you now," he said.

Jolene hadn't seen Philip enter the lounge, which she was decorating for Thanksgiving. On each side of the fireplace, she had placed a horn of plenty from which spilled colorful gourds, apples, pecans, chestnuts, and persimmons. In the act of attaching oak leaves in fall colors to the marble mantelpiece when Philip spoke, she put the leaves aside and turned slowly to face her mother's pastor.

"If you want to know the truth, Reverend Coles, I don't care *what* she would think or what she would say. You, the members of your church, and half of our neighbors, even my teachers, knew how mama treated me, and not one person called her on it. I survived it, and I haven't mourned her for a minute." She eyeballed him, enjoying the sight of his reddened face and relishing the normally articulate man's sudden loss for words.

"I'm sorry you feel this way, Sara Jolene," he said after the lengthy sound of his silence discomfited them both. "A child should honor her parents and certainly should cherish their memory, no matter what," he went on. "The Bible says—"

She tuned him out and returned to her task of decorating. "I guess I ought to thank her for teaching me by negative example how not to be a mother."

He didn't comment on that, although from his facial expression, she thought the words pained him. As if to reinforce her point, she added, "What kind of woman refuses to tell her child who its father is? And don't think I didn't ask her many times."

"Too bad, Sara Jolene. We have to play the hand dealt us. That's life. Please try not to be so bitter."

She stared at him, reflecting on his lame advice. "Well, if you'll excuse me, I have to finish this before supper."

He seemed grateful for the opportunity to leave her. "I guess this isn't the kind of work you can do while talking about serious things. I'll see you at supper," he said and rushed out of the lounge.

I never thought Reverend Coles was a phony, and maybe he isn't, but he certainly acted strange in here a minute ago. Wonder why he's coming here so often. Lord, I sure hope Joe couldn't be right. She whirled around at the sound of footsteps and saw the handsome preacher lean his big frame against the doorjamb.

"I meant to ask you, Sara Jolene, if you've met a nice young man since you've been here."

Jolene laid her head to one side and looked hard at him. "I've met five men and messed up with every one of them. Anything else? Oh yes. My name is not Sara Jolene. It's Jolene."

With his hands out and palms facing her, he said, "Look. I'm sorry. I didn't ask out of curiosity. I'll . . . uh . . . see you at supper."

She put a straw man and two pumpkins in a corner near the fireplace, surveyed her handiwork and swept up the sticks, leaves, and other refuse. Having finished the lounge, she arranged orange and yellow chrysanthemums in vases for the dining room tables, placed yellow candles in Fannie's crystal candleholders and stood back to admire the effect. *Ten months ago, Fannie wouldn't have allowed me to decorate these two rooms, and I wouldn't have had the nerve to attempt it. I may be moving slowly, but at least I'm not standing still.*

She headed for her room and met Judd on the stairs. "Did

Fannie say Thanksgiving supper would be earlier than usual?" she asked him. "I'd like to visit a sick friend tomorrow after-noon."

As usual, Judd's smile gave her a warm and comfortable feel-ing. "What a nice thing to do, visiting a sick friend on Thanks-giving Day. Why don't you ask Marilyn for some goodies to take with you?"

"Would she do that?"

"Sure she will. Marilyn loves to show her authority."

Jolene whirled around, went into the kitchen and spoke with Marilyn. To her amazement, the woman said she would prepare a hot Thanksgiving dinner for Jolene's sick friend.

"Rodger can drive you to the hospital, and it'll still be piping hot when you get there."

"Really? What will Fannie say?"

Marilyn locked her hands to her hips and stared at Jolene. "You planning to tell her? Anyhow, she's the biggest Christian in Pike Hill, so it shouldn't freak her out to do good on Thanks-giving Day. Be in here at noon." Jolene thanked her and raced up the stairs, happy and light hearted.

A few minutes after twelve on Thanksgiving Day, Jolene knocked on Harper's room door.

"Come on in."

"Hi. Gee! You're not in the wheelchair. Wonderful!"

"Hi. I don't use it any more. It's been a while since you were here. I'm glad you came, Jolene."

"I brought you some Thanksgiving dinner. It's what we're having for supper at the boardinghouse, and it's hot. I was afraid you might have been discharged. I mean, I was thinking . . . well, you know what I mean to say."

She wasn't nervous around Harper, so why was she rattling like an empty wagon rolling over the pot holes in Hagerstown's back streets? She rolled the patient's table to the chair in which Harper sat, spread two white napkins on it and set out the food that Marilyn put in Fannie's pretty porcelain dishes.

"This is wonderful, Jolene. A real home-cooked Thanksgiving

dinner. Look at this." He pointed to the different dishes. "Corn chowder, roast turkey with cornbread dressing, gravy, wild rice, asparagus, turnips, relish, pumpkin pie, grapes and coffee." He looked up at her. "My mother has the flu, and she couldn't come today. You're a Godsend. He ate lustily and cleaned the plates. "My goodness. A thermos of real espresso coffee. Man, this is *some* treat. Lean over here and let me kiss you."

Then the scent of his spicy cologne wafted up to her nostrils, a command as it were. She nearly panicked, and her heart began to race like a thoroughbred horse out of control. She tried to catch her breath. "I don't think you'd better do that, Harper."

"O, yes I *had* better do it, and I'll be glad to take the consequences."

Trembling, as fear of she didn't know what streaked through her, she leaned down to brush his lips with hers. But he grasped her head, and for a brief, poignant moment, she stared into his eyes, and the expression in them nearly unglued her. She wanted to back away, but he held on, flicking his tongue back and forth over the seam of her lips until, without due thought to what she did, she opened her mouth for him, as hungry for loving, any loving, as he. He plunged into her, gently at first and then like a starving man testing every centimeter, every crevice of her warm, giving mouth and nourishing himself with the sweetness of her loving.

She savored his masculine taste and sucked him deeper into her mouth, needing all of him. With a groan, he plunged in and out of her, simulating the act of love. When heat settled between her legs, she fought against the rhythmic pulsations that pummeled her vagina, and gripped his shoulder to steady herself.

Shocked at the force of his need and at her own response to him, she backed away. "What have I done? You're going to accuse me of encouraging you, of leading you on. I didn't, Harper. I swear it."

"No, baby. I needed that. Maybe we both needed it."

She glanced at the bed less than three feet away and closed her eyes. She had to get out of there. "I'd . . . uh . . . better go . . . as soon as I can gather up this stuff."

"It's all right, Jolene. Sit down over there and get yourself to-gether. I know you didn't plan this, and neither did I. Please don't let what happened keep us from being friends. Your visits while I've been in this hospital have meant a lot to me."

She packed the basket. "To me, too. I hope your mother is better soon. Uh . . . good-bye, and happy Thanksgiving." She fled from his room, slipped into the elevator seconds before the door closed and let its wall take her weight. Tears streamed down her cheeks as she panted for breath.

What have I done? I know he thinks I'm using him again, but I'm not. I meant to give him a friendly peck on the lips, and then he put his tongue in my mouth and . . . Oh, Lord, am I one of those women who never says no to a man? If he hadn't been in that chair, would I have . . . ? No, I don't do that any more.

She dragged herself out of the hospital and dawdled along Ocean Road unmindful of the bracing and frigid wind, trying to come to terms with what she had experienced with Harper. "But I enjoyed kissing him," she told herself. Then, remembering the explosions in her vagina, she said, "His tongue sure worked its magic. But what should I expect? The only times I've ever had an orgasm, he was inside of me. So it's nothing to worry about."

As she reached the boardinghouse, one thought pounded in her head: How could she feel as she did about Gregory and re-spond that way to Harper?" She inserted her key into the lock, pushed open the door and inhaled the odor of the great feast that teased and taunted her nostrils.

"Oh, I'm just human," she said aloud. "Like Pavlov and his dog, I've learned to respond to Harper." She skipped up the stairs. "It's no big deal. I can unlearn it." She consoled herself with that.

Richard folded a red and gray paisley ascot into his open-collared shirt, slipped on a navy blazer that complimented his light-gray slacks, and bounded down the stairs to the dining room. It was Thanksgiving Day, so he dressed for dinner. If no one else did, he didn't care. Sitting alone at the table he always shared with Fannie, his fingers strummed the yellow tablecloth and he shifted in his chair, crossing and uncrossing his knees as he watched the door, waiting for Francine to walk through it.

After a few minutes, she entered the dining room along with Philip Coles, and something akin to an iron fist clutched at his heart. He had never been jealous of a woman, not even of Estelle, who he hadn't realized he loved until she married someone else. What he felt then was not jealousy, but pain. A laugh that in no way represented his feelings eased out of him, and he raised a hand of greeting to Judd who watched him from a nearby table. Fannie rushed in precisely at five o'clock, joined him at their table and asked everyone to stand for Philip's prayer of Thanksgiving.

"I want y'all to know that our Jolene did the Thanksgiving decorations," Fannie said when Philip finished, "and Judd built the fire in the lounge. Percy brought the maple leaves and branches day before yesterday when he got back from his trip to New England, and Richard bought the horns of plenty that you see in the lounge. Y'all make this house a home, and I thank you. Marilyn is giving us a great meal, thank the Lord, so let's eat."

"How do you manage to keep Marilyn?" Richard asked Fannie, as he savored the best turkey he'd ever tasted.

"I pay her what head chefs in Ocean City get, and I cater to her as much as I can without letting her boss *me*. I tolerate her foolishness, because everybody here is grown up and can take care of themselves. If she gets too far out of hand, one of you puts her in her place."

"What about Percy Lucas?"

"Oh, Marilyn flirts with Percy because he's a man, but she doesn't hit on him. I think she's afraid he'll take her up on it. Now you. She wants you more than she wants money."

He hoped his problems with Marilyn were in the past. "Marilyn and I have reached an understanding. She makes passes and issues invitations, and I ignore them. She expects that."

Fannie rang the bell for Rodger, who appeared at once. "Would you please pass some more dressing and gravy?" To Richard, she said, "How is Marilyn responding to your feelings for Francine?"

His eyes widened, he swallowed too quickly and had to cough several times before he could answer. "I don't know. I also don't know precisely what my feelings for Francine are."

Fannie placed her fork on the side of her plate and pointed her right index finger at him. "Philip used to be a ladies' man. I hope he hasn't decided to go after Francine."

He hadn't considered that. "Why? Is he something of a rake?"

"Let's just say he always seemed to have enough ego and charm to get whatever and whomever he wanted."

A frown gathered on Richard's face, and he moved his head slowly from side to side. "Then why is he a bachelor?"

Fannie stared at Richard. "I won't bother to ask you the same question, but I'll tell you like it is: You're as crazy about Francine as she is about you, so get off your high horse and straighten things out with her. She's a woman who isn't going to accept second best no matter how much she loves you."

Months earlier, he would have resented such an intrusion into his personal affairs, but she ate supper with him every night, and he supposed that gave her a special license.

"It's a long story, Fannie. I've had bridges to cross, but I'm getting there."

"*Good. You don't want to end up like Philip: sixty, single, and sorry.*"

A few chuckles escaped him. "Philip has begun to visit you regularly. What's happened? He hasn't retired from his church, has he?"

Richard thought she seemed pensive for a moment before snapping out of it. "He'll preach as long as he can breathe. Maybe he's lonely, though I don't see how with all those church sisters dying to comfort him. I don't know, but whenever he comes, I'm happy to see him."

No help there. A man had a reason for making such drastic changes in his behavior, and he'd like to know what motivated Philip Coles. It was not Francine. He'd bet anything that it centered on Jolene.

After supper, Richard sat with Judd in the lounge before the fire that crackled and popped out tiny sparks, giving the room the atmosphere of a real home. Presently, Francine walked over to them, and Richard stood, pulled over a chair and waited for her to sit down.

"Welcome back," Judd said to her. "I missed you these past few days when you were sulking at m'friend here.

Francine's bottom lip dropped. "What? I wasn't . . . We had a misunderstanding is all. What a delightful Thanksgiving," she said, changing the subject and looking straight into Richard's eyes. "I'm so glad I found this place."

His heart skipped a beat. Francine hadn't previously flirted with him. Heat flushed the back of his neck and, without thinking, he pushed back from the table. Her gaze didn't waver, and he realized that she was going for the jugular, that she'd played it his way, and now she would call the shots.

"Would you two like some privacy?" Judd asked with a note of merriment in his voice.

Richard's laughter simultaneously with Francine's relieved the tension. "You stay right here," he said to Judd. "I wouldn't like this situation to get out of hand. I think Francine has just declared war."

Judd relaxed in the Shaker rocker and rocked back and forth, his eyes closed and his face angelic. "And a good thing, too. It's high time, 'cause you'll shilly-shally till you're old as I am."

Unmoved by Judd's meddling, Richard went to the cooler for a drink of water, and Francine walked over to him. "How's Judd doing?"

"Fine, as far as I know. Why? Is he ill?"

"No, but his only sister is ailing, and he seemed depressed about it yesterday. She lives in Raleigh, North Carolina, and that's a good distance from here."

He drank the water and dropped the paper cup into the receptacle put there for that purpose. "Thanks for letting me know."

When he returned to the table, he said to Judd, "What do you say I drive you to Raleigh tomorrow to see your sister?"

Judd stopped rocking. "You'd do that? I'd love to see Thelma. She's m'closest living relative, and she's not a bit well."

"I'll rent a car then, and we'll start first thing in the morning. Can you call and say we're coming?"

Judd nodded. "I sure will, and I want you to know that God's gonna bless you, friend."

The next morning, Francine drove them to a car rental agency in Ocean Pines. The gray, snow-capped clouds hung low, and Richard did what he hadn't done since his boyhood days: He gazed up and silently prayed for dry weather.

"Thanks for the lift," he said to Francine and unbuckled his seat belt. But as he reached for the door handle, one of Francine's hands clasped his cheek and the other one touched the back of his head. Surprised, he turned fully to face her and felt the shock of her lips moving over his. "Judd is in the back seat," he warned himself, but her lips parted, and he capitulated and thrust into the sweet warmth of her mouth. She took him, pulling him deeply into her in the rhythmic motions of a woman approaching orgasm, and as hard as he tried to stave it off, he nonetheless rose in a full erection. He broke the kiss.

"Francine! My Lord, Judd is in the back seat."

"He is not," she said as sweetly and as refined as if she hadn't seconds earlier rocked him out of his senses. "He got out of the car as soon as I started to kiss you. Are you angry?"

His head fell back against the seat. "Hell, I don't know what I am. You're asking for trouble."

"Not me. I'm asking for what I want, and what I'll get." Her hand stroked his chest.

"You little imp. I hope you have time to wait here till I get straightened out. Woman, you came up on my blind side, and you're going to pay. Nobody corners me."

Her face shone with the brilliance of her smile. "Pay? Me? Gladly. How much, where and when?" Her satisfied facial expression and its wordless promise sent tremors through him. Francine Spaldwood was beating him at his own game.

He opened the door, glancing back at her as he got out of the car. "Drive carefully; that's what I'm going to do."

He went inside the car rental agency, where Judd sat reading a copy of *The Maryland Journal*. "I was wondering if you two had gotten into a fight," Judd said without shifting his gaze from the paper.

Richard stared down at him. "You're kidding."

"Nope," Judd replied, still looking at the paper. "From the surprise you got, I figured you had either boxed her ears or made love to her, and if you're half the man I think you are, you wouldn't have done that in that car. Anyway, you didn't have time."

Richard leaned against the counter musing over Judd's words until laughter burst out of him, and he laughed until he had to support his belly with both hands.

"'Twasn't that funny," Judd said.

The drive to Raleigh took nearly four hours, and they reached the home of Judd's sister around one o'clock in the afternoon. Judd bounded up the steps to the front door as if he had shed thirty years, his face aglow with smiles. The happiness Richard felt knowing that he was able to give his friend such a priceless gift filled him with the sense that, somehow, he was being redeemed. But Richard couldn't know that before he left Raleigh, North Carolina, he would be a different man, a changed man.

Chapter Ten

Richard watched Judd rush up the stairs, sprightly as a far younger man and seemingly unmindful of his eighty-five years. He sensed that Judd loved his sister, but did love—any kind of love—do that for a person? Alone in the living room, Richard walked over to a window near the fireplace and looked out. Pecans covered the earth beneath two enormous pecan trees. He shook his head in wonder. If the family members didn't want the nuts or didn't need income from them, they could at least give them to a needy person. Musing over the idea, it occurred to him that, as recently as two months earlier, no such thought would have crossed his mind. He marveled at the changes in himself.

"Hi."

At the sound of that soft, feminine purr, he whirled around and stared into the face of temptation. Five feet, eight inches tall; big, almond-shaped brown eyes; a honey complexion; youthful breasts nearly popping out of a tight sweater; and rounded hips in jeans slung so low that he could see the beginning of her pubic hair. He caught himself a second before he would have released a sharp whistle.

"Who're you?" she asked him with all the cockiness of a female aware of her feminine assets and of their effect on a man.

"Richard Peterson. Are you as reckless as I suspect you are?"

he asked her in a tone that was part arrogant and part scornful. He judged her to be about twenty-one or twenty-two.

She shortened the distance between them to about five feet and cocked her head to one side, openly appraising him as a man.

"Like what you see?" he asked, tersely, turned and resumed his inspection of the world beyond the window.

"Sure beats anything I've ever seen in this town," she replied. "How long are you staying?"

Annoyed as he was, he recognized himself in her. A player sure of her shots and unconcerned about what they hit. He commented on her remark. "Beats any *thing* you've seen, huh? Where, other than Raleigh, North Carolina, have you been?"

"Nowhere," she said airily. "Can I . . . uh . . . give you something?"

He thought for a moment that he had swallowed his tongue, and when he recovered from the shock, he said, "You should have more respect for your elders," aware that he was grabbing at any means of shielding himself from her sexual onslaught. However, instead of taking him seriously, she laughed.

"I can take care of myself. Can you?"

He swung around, then, gritting his teeth, and his gazed captured her hardened nipples that strained against the tight sweater. "Oh, I can take care of myself," he said, "and you, too. You like to challenge men, do you? Well, if I take you up on that, you'll never forget it."

She looked him in the eye. "That's what I'm hoping."

"I see you've met Gretchen, m' niece."

Richard looked up to find Judd's gaze locked on him and a quizzical expression on the old man's face. "Yes," he said, hating the sound of wariness in his voice, "we've met."

"Can I tear you loose long enough to take you upstairs to meet m' sister?"

"Sure. That won't be difficult," he replied and immediately regretted putting Gretchen down. Wasn't he partly responsible for her fresh behavior? Hadn't he made the mistake of registering his reaction to her on his face and in his demeanor? Hell, he'd behaved like a stallion on a stud farm for so long, that it had become as native to him as the clothes he wore. He swore harshly beneath his breath.

"How's your sister doing?" he asked Judd as he followed him up the stairs.

"Well, I haven't seen her in a while, but she looks pretty good, and her voice is as strong as ever. Still, I know she's sick."

In the room, a chamber decorated with white furniture and curtains, and heather blue walls, bedding, and carpeting that impressed him as a cheerful place in which to be sick, Judd took his sister's hand. "Josie, this here's m' friend, Ambassador Richard Peterson." He decided that to correct Judd would deprecate him in some way, so he accepted the reference to his *former* status.

"I'm so glad to meet you, sir," she said. "Judd's letters are full of nice things about you. Thanks for bringing him to see me."

"I'm glad we could come. How are you feeling?"

"Pretty good, all things considered. Yesterday, the doctor told me I'd soon be up and that he doesn't expect me to . . . check out for a while yet."

"That's good news," Richard said. "Perhaps the next time we come, you'll be able to show us around your city."

"Not much to see, but I sure will enjoy showing you what's here. Judd, ask Gretchen to come here, please."

"I'll do it," Richard said. He went to the top of the stairs and called her. "Your mother wants you." She didn't answer, and he stood there staring while she took her time, sashaying up the steps like an exotic dancer. At the top of the stairs, she managed to brush his body while looking him in the eye. He'd never seen such a brazen woman, and he had a mind to teach her a lesson.

"You want me, Mama?" she asked, the picture of innocence.

"Honey, would you give Ambassador Peterson and your uncle Judd some lunch? They must be starved after that long drive."

Richard held up his right hand. "Oh, no. We don't want to inconvenience you."

"I baked a North Carolina ham yesterday, and I made some

buttermilk biscuits this morning. We've got string beans, corn and coconut cake. There's plenty," Gretchen added, looking at her mother and not at him.

So she knew that her mother wouldn't approve of her behavior. Hmm. Probably a phony. Suddenly, his bruised nerves heated up. He'd bet a few thousand that she was a virgin. An experienced woman wouldn't feel the need to broadcast her sexuality. Well. Well. He swallowed the liquid that accumulated in his mouth, and closed his eyes, for he remembered the one experience he'd had introducing a woman to her sexual potential. Before it was over, she drove him to the stratosphere, so to speak.

"Until you've eaten North Carolina ham, you haven't tasted ham," Judd said.

Richard observed Judd's eagerness to show him hospitality, even though he expressed it through his sister. "You won't catch me turning down this kind of food," he said. "Of course, I'll stay."

He had to admit that the food was, indeed, first class and that he hadn't eaten better biscuits. "You're an excellent cook," he told Gretchen. "These biscuits are to die for."

"Thanks." Her eyelids fluttered. "I'm good at everything I do."

Judd's fork clattered against his plate. He looked first at his niece and then at him. Now what? She had made her interest in him clear to Judd, who stopped eating and stared at her. But Gretchen continued her game as if Judd was either too old or too stupid to know that she was flirting with Richard. He saw the disappointment and the sadness on the old man's face and was moved by it. In forty-four years, he had made one friend, and he was learning that doing things for a person didn't prove friendship, that loyalty was probably the test. For the past hour, he had been thrashed alternately by the ravages of his libido and by what remained of his habit of accepting what women offered, provided it interested him and had no strings. He looked at Judd, who seemed shrouded in sadness, and decided to put an end to it.

"How old are you?" he asked Gretchen, and he could see that she was taken aback.

"Uh . . . twenty-two."

"I'm exactly twice your age and old enough to be your father. You've been flaunting your breasts and your behind at me ever since I've been here. I'm tired of it, and I'd appreciate it if you'd stop it right now."

She gasped. "How can you say that?"

"I'm a man of the world, Gretchen, and when it comes to women, I haven't misunderstood one in years. And trust me; I've had a slew of 'em. No point in being offended. I didn't get mad when you deliberately brushed against me at the top of the stairs." He changed the subject. "Judd, if I told Marilyn how good these biscuits are, she'd never forgive me."

He hardly believed the change in Judd's demeanor. Had Judd really thought he would take his friend's niece to bed for the sport of it? "You're too smart to tell Marilyn that," Judd said and turned his attention to his niece. "You just learned a lesson and, if you got any sense, you won't have to learn it again. You thought I didn't know what was going on, didn't you? I was on to you from the time I came down here to ask Ambassador Peterson to come meet m' sister. Try that on some men, and they'll make you deliver whether you want to or not."

"I'm sorry, Uncle Judd."

"You should be. You got any lemonade or sweetened iced tea?"

She brought a pitcher of each and, to Richard's surprise, she rejoined them at the table. "What's it like where you live, Uncle Judd?"

Judd sipped the iced tea with relish, the pleasure of it mirrored on his face. "Water everywhere. Perfect in summer, and just cold enough in winter. All in all, it's a lot like paradise."

With a long sigh, she leaned back in her chair, a person without purpose. Richard looked at Gretchen, *twenty-two years old, bored with her life, and ripe for trouble. If she thought he was going to provide excitement for her, she could forget it.*

"We ought to get started pretty soon," Judd said. "Fannie will kick up a storm if the two of us are late for supper."

"Right," he replied, though the prospect didn't worry him. "I'll run up and say good-bye to your sister."

Judd drained his glass of its remaining iced tea. "I'll go with you."

"I don't think we'll make it home for supper," Judd said about two hours later. "We're just getting to Northampton."

"You're right, and this looks like a good place to stop," Richard said as they approached an inn, a large white brick structure with red shutters at its windows, smoke billowing from its chimney, and an elegant facade that faced the ocean. "Let's see what this place is offering."

"Nice place," he said to Judd when he returned to the rented Chevrolet. "What do you say we spend the night here? I'll call Fannie and let her know. It's on me."

"I can't let you pay for m' room," Judd said. "Pretty soon, you'll be broke, and I'll have to take care of you."

"I already paid in advance," he told Judd. "Come on."

After an excellent supper of fish right out of the bay, he sat in the lounge sipping coffee and thinking over the day. A day in which he'd done something that he would always look back on with pride. He hadn't let his friend down, and he had turned his back on what every molecule of his body screamed for—sex with a luscious female naïve enough to give him carte blanche.

"I got a lot to thank you for," Judd said, bringing him out of his reverie.

"What's that?"

"You could have had Gretchen if you wanted to, and for a while there, I thought you would because she was getting to you. You'll never know what a relief I felt when you put her in her place. She loves to toy with men; I've seen her at it since she was twelve or thirteen. She's a tease, and I hope you taught her a lesson."

Richard rubbed the back of his neck with his left hand. "For once, I did the right thing."

Judd rubbed the stubble on his chin. "Yeah, and you haven't

always done that, have you? When you dance with the devil, son, you gotta pay the tab, and I suspect you owe him."

Richard leaned back in his chair and closed his eyes. "And how! I'm no saint, and you know it. If she hadn't been your niece, I'd probably be in her right now, good intentions be damned. It's been a year since I touched a woman." He sat forward and looked straight at Judd. "You know, something happened to me. You could say it was an epiphany of sorts. I felt cleansed after I straightened her out. For the first time in my memory, I did the right thing with a woman at a time when . . . when my needs said do the opposite."

The fire crackled, and sparks shot up the old fashioned chimney, but it was more than the fire that warmed Richard Peterson. For the first time in his life, he had a friend with whom he could talk, a friend with whom he needn't bother to posture or pretend. He leaned back again, clasped his hands behind his head and spoke softly.

"You know, Judd, I don't believe there are many men my age who can regret as many deeds and as many experiences as I do. I was self-centered from childhood, demanding things that my parents couldn't afford. As I look back, I realize they made so many sacrifices for me, denied the fulfillment of their own needs for my sake and with no thanks from me.

"I've mistreated more women than I've been gracious to. Oh, I didn't abuse them physically, slander or betray them, but I took what they offered—knowing that I had beguiled them with charm, manners, and my appearance—and then I left them to deal with it as best they could. I'm speaking of dozens of women, Judd. Married, single, young, old, white, black, any color or nationality. I made love to them efficiently, flawlessly, felt nothing but physical release, and went on my way.

"When I was nineteen, I fathered a child with a girl I loved and wanted to marry." Judd's eyebrows shot up, but he said nothing. "But she had her own agenda," Richard continued, squeezed his eyes tight and said, "and she aborted it. I felt that for many years."

"Is that what keeps you from committing to Francine?"

"No. I got over that some years ago. But I met a woman in my circle, well placed, and her status about equal to mine, and she was no pushover. I thought she was playing hard to get, but as it turned out, she wasn't. She was elegant and well aware of who she was. There was a guy around her, but I discounted him as of no importance. Certainly no competition for me, an ambassador.

"I meant to have her as one of my trophies, nothing more. When I'd about given up, she let me make love with her, and I fell in love, but she didn't. More proof that I didn't understand her. She let me down gently, and about six month later, she married another man. Not a night passes when I don't think about her."

"How long ago did all this take place?"

"I last saw her three years ago. I reached the pinnacle. I had everything. I went from life in a four-story walk-up apartment in Bedford-Stuyvesant, Brooklyn, to executive-director of an important nongovernmental international agency in which my personal office was bigger than the apartment in which I grew up. The world was my oyster, and I walked away from it."

Judd's creased brow showed how perplexed he was. "Why, for goodness sake?"

"I had paid too dearly, stepped on too many people on my way up. I couldn't enjoy it. I began to see my shallowness and that of my colleagues. I couldn't stand it. I wanted out. Forty-three years old, and I didn't have a person I could call friend, didn't even know I needed one." His sigh seemed to pour out of him like water streaming from a jug. "When I realized that I cared deeply for you, I was shocked. It was a strange new feeling. I don't know how it came about, but I'm thankful."

Judd sipped what was left of his cold coffee, thoughtfully, as if he wanted his next words to have strong import. "You've painted a dark picture of yourself, Richard Peterson. Now, I'd like you to tell me some of the good things you've done."

"What do you . . . Oh, I suppose there've been a few."

"But the ones that stay on your mind are the ones you're not proud of. Whatever you did that you're not proud of, let it loose. Let all of it go, including that woman."

"Judd, I can't forget her. It's as if she's my jail sentence."

Judd cocked his head to one side and looked Richard in the eye, his expression stern. "You want it to be your jail sentence. Don't enjoy your punishment so much. Go to see her, talk with her, and get rid of that thing that's bedeviling you. Then you can get on with your life."

"But, she's married. I can't do that."

"You can so, and it'll be the best discipline you ever had. When you face her, you may find you've been overestimating your feelings for her."

"Suppose I find that I care more for her than I thought I did. What if seeing her exacerbates an already intolerable situation?"

Judd threw up both hands as if losing patience. "It can't happen. If it could, you wouldn't feel the way you do about Francine. You haven't taken Francine to bed, because you won't lie to her and treat her the way you treated all those women you didn't care about. Doesn't that tell you anything?"

Richard got up, walked to the fireplace, stood there for a few minutes, and then went back to his chair and sat down. "I promised myself I wouldn't call or contact Estelle in any way, that I'd respect the fact that she's married."

"Normally, I'd agree, but your passion for that woman has been your bedmate for so long you think you can't sleep without it. I see what's going on between you and Francine, and I say you don't love any other woman."

"How can you be so sure?"

"'Cause I've lived a long time. I know when I'm looking at lust and when I'm looking at love between two people who are perfect for each other."

"Wish I could be that certain," Richard said and blew out a long breath. He had exposed himself to Judd, a man he'd known a mere eight months, in a way that he'd never revealed himself to another human being. He spoke to the man in soft tones. "You don't think less of me after what I just told you?"

Judd furrowed his brow. "Me? Not a bit, and why should I? I'm only concerned with who and what you are now, m'best friend, the fellow who gave me—an old man—m'first birthday party, who opened a new world to a lot of people in Pike Hill. Sixty adults and well-nigh seventy-five kids will have computer skills because of your efforts. You're a fine man."

He hoped his eyes communicated his feeling at that moment, for Judd's words touched him deeply. "Thank you," he said. "You don't know what hearing you say that means to me."

Richard and Judd arrived in Ocean Pines around eleven o'clock the next morning and returned the rental car. After wondering what he could do to placate Fannie, Richard bought a bushel and a half of crabs, called Dan, the taxi driver, and he and Judd got to the Thank the Lord Boarding House in time for lunch. Fannie met them at the door.

"I don't like my boarders to stay out all night, but at least you called so I wouldn't worry."

Instead of responding, Richard pointed to the sack of crabs. "We thought you'd like to have these. The crabber had just pulled them out of the sound."

The reprimand forgotten, her eyes widened, and a smile brightened her face. "Oh, thank you. Thank you! Lord, I do love these crabs. We'll have them for supper." She dashed off in the direction of the kitchen.

Richard gazed at Judd. "How do you like that? I knew she'd lecture to us, and I also knew that those crabs would cool her off."

"Yes, siree," Judd said, scratching his head. "There's more than one way to seduce a woman."

After a day of acting for the first time as manager of the beauty parlor in her boss' absence and dealing with the consequent hostility of her coworkers, Jolene stepped off the bus and rushed up Ocean Road, her eyes burning from the wind's assault. Getting a second promotion should have made her happy, and in a way, it had, but she didn't seem able to shed the weight of Gregory's indifference or to forgive herself for having caused

it. Maybe if she hadn't told him all those things about herself . . .
No. She wanted a clean slate, and she'd done the right thing. "I'll
get over it," she told herself.

With the icy wind slamming into her, it seemed to her that
the short, three-block walk took far longer than usual. When she
finally reached the Thank The Lord Boarding House, she fumbled in her pocketbook for the door key, but couldn't find it.
After a minute or so, the door opened, and she stared into
Richard's face.

"Thanks. My fingers are so numb I couldn't feel the door
key."

"No problem," he said. "Glad I was down here."

She started up the stairs, turned and walked back. "Richard . . .
you . . . uh . . . got a minute?"

"Sure. Let's go in there." He pointed to the lounge.

She sat across from him and tried to figure out how to begin.
"I've never known a man like you," she began without planning
to say that. "You're so perfect, Richard, so you must know a lot
of people."

He stiffened, and she suspected he thought she intended to
ask him for something. "Richard, how do you make friends, and
how do you know when somebody is your friend?"

He stared at her until, embarrassed, she rose to leave. "Please
don't go. I'm the last person you should ask that question,
Jolene. I have no idea. Judd is the only friend I ever had."

It was her turn to stare. "What? You're joking. You're so
handsome and so . . . so polished that anybody would want to
be your friend."

His laughter held no mirth. "Jolene, what a person looks like
hasn't a thing to do with friendship. The way I see it, friends are
people who're there for you when you have nothing to give
them. What's the problem?"

She hadn't thought he'd tell her anything so personal as his
not having friends. She reached toward him, but quickly withdrew her hand. "Richard, my life is a mess. I had a chance to
start life here without my mother riding my back, free to live like
other people, to make friends so I wouldn't be so lonely, and to

find someone who would care for me. I never had anyone who loved me, starting with my mother, a mean, bitter woman who wouldn't even tell me who fathered me."

He didn't seem to react to her statement and she remembered that she had already told him about her mother.

"You've made remarkable progress here, Jolene, and you should take pride in that."

"Richard, whatever I know about life now, I should have known when I was sixteen. I'm almost thirty-six."

She looked him in the eye and took a deep breath. "I've met several nice men since I've been here, and I've messed up with every one of them."

"What do you mean?" He wasn't sure that he wanted to serve as a confessor for Jolene or anybody else, but he remembered his relief after spilling his guts to Judd, and he softened his tone to give her courage. "Sometimes it helps to talk about it."

"I thought all men wanted from women was sex, that they used them and left them to handle the result as best they could. That's what my mama said, and she said it all the time. I think she hated men. When I came here, I'd never gone anywhere with a man; all I knew about them was what my mama said.

He leaned toward her. "You didn't date any of your school mates?"

She shook her head. "Gregory Hicks was my first date. He liked me, and it gave me a . . ." she looked for the word . . . "a superior feeling, so I used him, asking him to take me to expensive places, maneuvering him into buying me a cell phone, writing me a job reference, and things like that. Then, I stood him up for Bob Tucker. I see my mistake now, but he's apparently not much interested. Oh, heck, I might as well tell you all of it." And she did, including the insensible loss of her virginity. He whistled sharply at that.

"I didn't know it was important until Jim was so shocked and disgusted. Mama had never mentioned it to me."

"My Lord!"

She plodded on. " Harper told me I didn't have feelings for a man, that I was only out for what I could get. I caused him to have that accident, and the first time I went to the hospital to see him, he told me that he'd fallen in love with me, but he didn't want any part of me." She sat forward. "Richard, I don't mourn my mother."

"Wait a minute! You can't blame this on your mother. You could read, and you could have talked with other people. You could also have observed relationships between the men and women you met. You're the one who charted your misdeeds. A thirty-five year-old woman is responsible for herself and for everything she does, so stop blaming your mother. You wanted revenge against her, your unknown father, or maybe against life, and you took it out on men because you'd been taught that men are the source of all problems."

She pushed back the tears that threatened to embarrass her. "Maybe you're right, but I was so immersed in my newly found freedom, that I didn't consider the effect of what I was doing. Francine told me that men have feelings, that they love, hurt and suffer just like we women do. She said a man's tenderness is a precious thing. Richard, I had never heard words like those."

"That caused you to change?"

"No. I was already looking hard at myself, thanks to Harper's accident, experiences at my job, and living here. You, Judd, and Francine have taught me what I should have known twenty years earlier."

Hearing the agony in her voice and seeing the pain etched on her face tugged at his heart. He knew nothing of women's sufferings, had become inured to the effect on them of his callousness. In Jolene, he saw himself as he had been when he strode through life stepping on women as if they were weeds.

Francine would love and cherish him, but he wanted Estelle. Jolene wanted Gregory Hicks, but Harper Masterson nearly gave his life for love of her. Jolene had the power to straighten out her life and, he realized with a start, he could do the same with his own life. He leaned forward and capped his knees with the palms of his hand.

"I'm not used to giving personal advice, but I think you're pining for the wrong man. And you ought to straighten things out with Percy. I knew something had happened between the two of you, and I can see why he was devastated. It took the starch out of him."

"I know. I wrote him a letter, but I haven't given it to him yet."

"A letter? Talk to him. Face him. If you don't, he'll continue to avoid you."

"Thanks, I'll try to find an opportunity."

"If you're interested in doing the right thing, Jolene, you'll *make* an opportunity."

"I will. Thanks for talking to me and listening to me. I hope you don't think I'm a bad person."

"Why should I? Your slate's as clean as mine. I'd be the last person to judge you."

She rose to leave him, and he stood. To his astonishment, she reached up and kissed his cheek. "See you at supper." She did it impulsively, he knew, but the feeling it gave him of belonging, of rapport with a kindred soul would remain with him for a long time.

She started toward the stairs, stopped and turned back. "Francine is in love with you, Richard. Are you going to try to fix things up with her?"

That she would ask him such a personal question startled him at first. Then he smiled. Hadn't they just shared intimacies such as only friends would do? "Right now, she's my number-one priority. Thanks for telling me that."

Judd would be coming down soon, so he hurried to his room for a few minutes to himself before dinner. He didn't feel like sharing his feelings with his friend. He had a decision to make, an important one, and he didn't want to be influenced by anyone's logic but his own. He stared out of his bedroom window at the darkness that fell so early on November evenings, the waves that lashed on the sound barely visible. As he stood there, a full moon seemed to rise out of the ocean beyond, casting its light upon the waves that danced and undulated beneath it like a woman grasping at sexual relief.

A knock on his door brought an end to his ruminations. "Yes?" he opened the door and gazed down into Fannie's face.

"I wondered if you were all right, Richard. You've never been late for a meal, and I wondered if anything was wrong. Is everything okay?"

He could hardly believe the tender solicitousness in her voice. She was not exercising authority or attempting to control his behavior as he might once have thought. She cared, and the idea stunned him. As quickly as he could, he retrieved his aplomb.

"I'm sorry, Fannie, but I've been wrestling with . . . something that's terribly important to me, and I let the time slip by. I'll try not to let it happen again."

She continued to look at him very much in the way that a mother examines a child. "I've never done this unless one of my boarders was sick, but if you won't feel comfortable eating in the dining room, I'll bring your dinner up to you. You seem a bit ill at ease."

He forced a half smile. "You'll never know how much I appreciate your thoughtfulness, but I'll go down with you."

She patted him on the shoulder, and he realized that was the first time she had touched him. "I'm glad. If I can do anything, you'll let me know, won't you?"

"I certainly will," he said, and he meant it. When they reached the bottom step, he voiced the decision at which he arrived while descending the stairs with her. "I'll be away for a few days beginning this weekend, but I ought to be back here by Wednesday."

After supper, he sat with Judd and Francine in the lounge, exchanging banalities, for his mind wasn't on the conversation. Finally, he said, "I have to be in New York the first of the week, but I should be back here by Wednesday. You two behave yourselves."

He glanced at Judd who nodded his approval. "When you get to be my age, nothing for you to do *but* behave."

"When will you leave?" Francine asked him.

"Sunday morning."

"I spent the day getting m'annual medical checkup," Judd said, "and I'm worn out. See you in the morning."

Francine accepted a cup of cappuccino from Rodger and took a few sips. "Is this a business trip?"

He tapped the table with the fingers of his right hand. "You could say that."

She lowered her gaze, and he knew that she had guessed correctly that he intended to see a woman. "When did you decide to go?"

"While I was walking down the stairs on my way to supper. Francine, it's important that I do this. I have to know where I'm going. Do you understand?"

"Not really."

"I need to put my house in order."

She toyed with the fingers of his right hand, concentrating on them as if seeing a Rembrandt for the first time. After a few minutes, she looked up and focused her gaze on his face. "You have my blessing."

On Saturday afternoon, Jolene sat in her room reading one of the books on personal development that Judd brought her from the library. She was realizing that any information she needed could be found in a book and that Richard was right in saying she shouldn't have been ignorant about the facts of life because she could read. She hadn't bothered to tell him that if her mother thought she was reading, she would find something for her to do, that she had no life of her own. She had hardly begun the chapter on manners when her cell phone rang. Thinking that it was probably her boss, she was tempted not to answer.

"Hello," she said, letting the tenor of her voice tell the caller that she was being disturbed.

"Hello, Jolene. This is Gregory. How are you?"

She managed to get her breath back. "Hi. It's nice to hear from you, Gregory. I'd begun to think you weren't planning to call me again."

"Uh . . . no such thing. I had some issues to work through."

She told herself that it was his call, and that she should wait to find out what he wanted but, in her eagerness to resume a relationship with him, she eased his way with small talk. "It's pretty cold outside. I didn't expect this so early in the winter."

"I hope you don't think it's too cold to take in a movie with me this afternoon."

Her antenna went up. The women in the beauty parlor claimed that if a man invited you out during the week or for an afternoon date, he didn't think much of you. "I'm busy this afternoon," she said, "but we could see a movie this evening."

"I was thinking we could see a movie this afternoon and then have dinner someplace."

She wanted to kick herself. Hadn't she learned that conniving to get something from men could backfire? She could offer to change her plans, but she remembered that she broke a date with him in order to go out with Bob Tucker. "Maybe tomorrow, Gregory, provided you're not busy."

"Well, I usually prefer dates for Saturday, because I have to get to work early Monday mornings, but . . . all right. Why don't I come by for you about two tomorrow afternoon?"

"Fine. I'll be looking forward to seeing you."

After she hung up, she replayed the conversation in her mind. "Something's wrong, here," she said aloud. "Wonder what it is."

When she walked into the dining room that Sunday morning, Richard sat at his usual table, and an overnight bag leaned against the wall beside it. "Mind if I join you?" she asked him.

"Not at all. Judd will probably be down here in a minute, so pull up that chair over there."

"You going somewhere?" When he told her his travel plans, she said, "Gosh, I hope you don't decide to stay up there. I'm so used to you, it wouldn't seem like home here without you."

He stopped eating. "Jolene, that is the nicest thing you ever said to me. I've also begun to regard this place as my home, and I think that's because this really is a family."

"It is, I guess. We're a bunch of misfits, but we get along better than some blood relatives. Would you believe Gregory called me for a date? I'm seeing him today."

"Have a good time, but take a good look at the situation and try not to pretend what isn't real."

"Meaning?"

"If you don't feel it, don't act it. You know what I'm saying?"

"Good morning, Rodger. Scrambled eggs, sage-sausage, pop-overs, coffee, and orange juice, please." She turned to Richard. "I think so. After I talked with him, I felt something wasn't right, but I'll give it a shot."

"Here's Judd," he said. "How are you this morning, friend?"

"I'm m'usual self for this time of day. Too bad it's not sum-mer. I could use a good, bracing swim."

She waited until Richard finished eating and stood to leave. "I think I heard the doorbell."

Richard looked at his watch. "That's Dan. Right on time. Wish me luck."

"You don't need luck," Judd said. "You need a clear head. Safe trip."

"I'll walk you to the door," Jolene said, but when they en-tered the hallway, she saw Francine leaning against the banister rubbing her eyes. "I got up to tell you good-bye," she said to Richard.

The situation appeared awkward to Jolene, so she said, "Why don't you kiss him good-bye, Francine, and let him go. His taxi is here."

Richard thanked her with his eyes and drew Francine into his arms. To give them privacy, Jolene went back into the dining room and sat with Judd.

"I thought you were telling Richard good-bye." Did she de-tect a note of censorship in his voice?

"I've done a lot of dumb things since I've been here, Judd, but flinging myself at Richard Peterson is not one of them. Richard is busy kissing Francine."

Judd drained his coffee cup. "That sure is a relief." She didn't know what part of her statement he referred to, but it didn't mat-ter. Judd was their judge-penitent, though she knew he didn't aspire to the role. But he was the one person all of them could count on for the unbridled truth.

Once, she would have awaited two o'clock and Gregory Hicks in a state of anxiety, and she couldn't understand the calmness with which she dressed, saw that she had half an hour to spare, and went down to the lounge in the hope of finding Judd there.

He sat alone watching the Ravens wallop another team. "Who's winning?" she asked him.

"The Ravens, but that ain't nothing to crow about. They're playing the worst team in the league. My, but you look nice! Who's the lucky fellow?"

"I'm going to the movies with Gregory."

He locked his fingers together, pressed them to his diaphragm and leaned back. "Now there's a fine young fellow. All the same, you watch your step."

She tried to assimilate the meaning of his cryptic advice. "I'm only going to the movies and maybe to dinner with him, Judd."

"If you're eating out, don't forget to call Fannie before supper time."

"I won't," she said. The doorbell rang, and she leaned over and kissed his forehead before strolling to the door. "Hi. Won't you come in while I get my coat?"

Gregory's eyebrows shot up, and she realized he hadn't expected that, possibly because she either met him on the porch or at the door when they dated previously.

"Thanks. I'll wait here," he said and stepped inside. If he noticed her blue suit, he didn't mention it, but there was still time. He drove to a movie house in Ocean Pines, explaining, "I remember you liked to get away from Pike Hill. This place is nice, and the popcorn's good." He parked in the parking lot across the street from the movie house, and she was relieved when he walked around to her side of the car and opened the door. Maybe having told him all the terrible things she'd done didn't cause him to change his mind about her.

For ninety minutes, they munched on popcorn and held hands. She didn't see much of the movie, and that didn't much matter, because she'd already seen *The Philadelphia Story* twice. As she watched it, she wondered why he hadn't asked her if she wanted to see it. After the movie, he drove them through Ocean Pines, stopped at a roadside restaurant and parked in back of it.

At least it will be warm inside, she thought, wondering why

he said so little, and why she seemed so dissatisfied, when she had waited months to be with him again. "It's beautiful," she told him as they entered. His sharp glance signaled his awareness of the sound of relief in her voice, but she couldn't help it. Not even her one date with Bob Tucker had been so strange.

"Surely, you don't think I'd take you to any other kind of restaurant," he said, and though the contours of his face changed and his teeth gleamed, the result couldn't be called a smile. She ordered a pork chop dinner, not because she wanted it, but because it was the cheapest entrée on the menu.

"How's your business coming along?" she asked him.

"Real good. I don't remember tell . . . I hadn't started my business when we used to see each other. How'd you know about it?"

"Judd was bragging about you."

"That's nice of him. How's your job going? You still at the beauty parlor?"

"Yes, and I've had three raises. Whenever the boss is away, I'm the manager." Both of his eyebrows shot up. "I'm going to learn as much as I can about that business, and I might open one myself if I decide to stay in this part of Maryland."

His interest heightened. "Why wouldn't you stay? You can make a good living here, especially in the beauty business. Tourists crowd in here from April to October, and you know the sisters and their hair."

What was it about that topic that made him warm up and talk? Well, the pork chop wasn't as good as the ones Marilyn cooked, but it wasn't bad, so he could talk or not. She put a smile on her face and let herself enjoy the meal.

"Would you like a glass of wine?"

She gaped at him. "I don't drink, and I didn't think you did."

He seemed disappointed, though she couldn't imagine why. "It rounds out a good meal." When he glanced at his watch, she did the same and saw that it was only a quarter of six.

"Would you like to see my shop?" he asked her.

"I would, indeed. I'd love to see how you make sails. I always thought they were so beautiful billowing in the wind. Is it far from here?"

"No. It's right in town, down at the water's edge. I bought the place a few months back. It suited me perfectly."

It wasn't the shack she thought it would be, but a sturdy structure that gleamed with a fresh coat of pale blue paint, the windows and door trimmed in white. She imagined that he painted it himself, and he agreed that he did.

"I save however I can," he said. "Come on in."

The room she entered could have been any store with the merchant's wares and talents neatly and attractively displayed. He walked through the store. "I work back here." He pushed open an adjoining door, took her hand and walked into what was clearly his private quarters. "I cook in my work room, but I sleep and entertain in here." She gazed around, taking it all in, the long and roomy sofa that she figured became his bed at night, the big leather chairs, the oriental carpet, wide-screen flat television, the furnishings of an elegant living room.

She whirled around and looked at him. "You live here. This is your home."

"Why, yes. I didn't see the point in owning this and paying the high rent that apartments in this town demand."

"It's great. Congratulations. I didn't know you were taking me to your home. I'd like to go now, if you don't mind."

"Why? We . . . uh . . . haven't had a chance to renew our friendship. Sit down over here, and I'll make us some coffee."

"I'm surprised you're not offering me wine."

He walked up to her, big, strong and handsome, and wrapped her in his arms. "Kiss me, baby."

She moved her face from the path of his oncoming mouth. "I'm surprised at you, Gregory. I looked at you as a man among men, a perfect gentleman. But you aren't. I want to go home right now."

"Look, you've been around," he sneered. "So why not me? At least I won't mistreat you."

"You're mistreating me now. I don't feel anything for you, Gregory. Not a single thing. You could be one of those poles in your office back there. I haven't felt right about this since you called me yesterday, and now, I know what it was that I sensed. You were too calculating. I know, because that's how I was until

I caused Harper to have that accident, and until Francine, Judd and Richard, taught me some sense. Everybody thinks you're so great, and I did too, but honey, you ain't worth pig droppings."

He grabbed her shoulders. "How dare you say something like that to me!"

"It didn't cost me any more nerve than it cost you to do what you did. And don't think this will make me fold up. No, sir. I'll be at class tomorrow evening on time."

She rushed through the store, out of the shop and on to the street, walked a block, saw the car rental store and went inside. "I need a taxi to Pike Hill," she told the man, whose gaze suggested that he would gladly take the job. "I can call Dan for you. He'll go anywhere so long as you pay him," the clerk said.

She thanked the man and prayed that Gregory wouldn't walk into that store until she was in Dan's taxi. Dan arrived almost at once, and as she walked out of the store with him, Gregory drove up, got out, and rushed to her.

"I don't need you, Gregory, and I'm not going anywhere with you. If you don't leave me alone, I'll call the police on this cell phone you gave me." She got into Dan's taxi and left him standing there. As soon as she was inside her room, she wrote a check for seventeen dollars and eighty cents, the cost of the dinner and movie, and put it in an envelope. At eight-thirty when she knew Judd would be in the lounge, she went downstairs and gave him the envelope on which she had written Gregory's name.

"Would you give him this tomorrow evening, please?"

Judd looked at the envelope in his hand. "Any reason why you can't give it to him?"

"I won't be speaking to him," she said. "Thanks."

"I see. You mad with him, or with yourself?"

She started to sit down, but changed her mind. From now on, she planned to keep her sins to herself. Nobody was perfect, including Gregory Hicks. "Let's say I've finally grown up."

Judd rubbed the little hairs that had begun to surface on his chin. "I'm glad to hear it, and I'll be more than glad to deliver this letter."

She told Judd and the others gathered there good night and went to her room. To her amazement, she neither cried nor

wanted to, but busied herself laying out the clothes she would
wear to work the next day. Later, as she prepared for bed, she remembered Richard's words that she was pining for the wrong
man, and wondered whether he was aware that Gregory didn't
respect her. He had, once, she knew, but in her desire to be honest with him thereafter, she'd made the mistake of telling him
how she had behaved with men, and he probably wondered
why he shouldn't have her too. *It would never happen. Not as long
as she breathed.*

When her cell phone rang, she knew that Gregory was the
caller, and she was tempted not to answer. *But I've invested a lot
in that man, and I owe it to myself to have the last word.* "Hello,
Gregory."

"How did you know I was the person calling you?"

"I knew."

"I wanted to know whether you got there safely and to tell
you that I'm sorry the evening ended as it did."

"No hard feelings, Gregory. I made the mistake of being honest with you and giving you a choice. You made one. You did
your thing, and I did mine. That's all there is to it. Good night."
She didn't wait for his reply, because no matter what it was, it
would not have made a difference.

She got to the bus stop the next morning minutes before the
bus arrived. "I see you're early," the driver said. "Couldn't wait
to see me, huh?"

Her immediate reaction was one of annoyance, but when she
looked at the man, he held up both hands, palms out. "You can't
blame me for trying. You said `no,' and I understand that word.
Okay? I hear Harper Masterson's scheduled to leave the hospital
one day this week. Man, that's a miracle. Doctors gave him a
thirty percent chance to survive, and they say he's walking
around."

Gregory and memories of her date with him had pushed
most other thoughts from her mind, and she realized she hadn't
thought about Harper. "I'm glad he's going to be all right," she
told the driver. "He's a very nice man."

"So I hear, and you said that before." She dropped her money
in the box, and he pulled away from the curb. "You have to go

after what you want in this life, girl. That's the only way you'll get it." She looked around, but didn't see another passenger to whom he might be talking, walked on to the rear of the bus and sat down. If Harper would be as good as new, and if she could manage to speak with Percy, maybe she could get rid of her guilt, or at least some of it, and stop worrying about all the wrong she'd done.

Chapter Eleven

Richard entered the revolving door of the United Nations Secretariat Building, and looked around. He had remembered to bring along his diplomat's badge and flashed it to the guard who stood at the door.

"May I help you, sir?"

"Thanks," Richard said as casually as he could, "but I need to step over there and look at a phone directory."

"Certainly, sir."

He found her phone number and office location at once and, as he had expected, Estelle Mitchell had moved a step higher. After copying the information, he headed for the second floor where he knew he would find telephones and comfortable seating.

"Ms. Mitchell's office. How may I help you?"

"Good morning," he said to the familiar voice. "This is Richard Peterson, and I'd like to see Ms. Mitchell for about fifteen minutes. I'm only in New York for the day."

"Uh . . . How are you, Mr. Peterson. This is Ms. Mitchell's secretary. I'll speak with her. Hold on."

He thanked her and held his breath, as it occurred to him for the first time that Estelle might refuse to see him. This had been his world, where being seen at all the right places and in the right company meant everything to a man's career. He smiled inwardly as he watched a woman grasp at another's coat sleeve begging, "You will call, won't you Dr. Ammil?" Dr. Ammil nodded and rushed on without having verbally committed herself. Self-importance was another commodity in abundance there, and he had certainly possessed his share of it.

"Hello Mr. Peterson. Sorry to keep you waiting. Ms. Mitchell said she can see you at eleven-thirty this morning. Should I put you down?"

"Absolutely, and thanks. I'm in your debt."

He had about two hours to throw away, but he didn't mind. If he hadn't gotten his request in early, the trip would probably have been a waste of time, not to speak of emotion. In earlier days, he would have passed the time in the North Delegates Lounge, seeing, being seen, and consuming a Scotch mist, something he no longer drank. He walked through the Security Council Chamber, now empty, its staid presence proclaiming its importance in world affairs. Eleven-twenty-six. He headed for the high-rise elevator.

"Well, if it isn't Richard Peterson. Where've you been hiding, man?" He recognized the Jamaican ambassador and shook his hand. "When I heard you'd quit one of the biggest posts in the international community, I didn't believe it. You look ten years younger."

Small talk. Something else that he didn't miss. "I haven't regretted it for a second."

"What are you doing these days?"

"I live in a tiny town a stone's throw from the Atlantic Ocean, and . . . Sorry, I get off here. Good to see you." Thank God. Just in time to avoid the kind of banalities that he hadn't engaged in since he left Geneva. He wondered at his lack of anxiety or of any feeling of excitement as he approached Estelle Mitchell's office.

"Mr. Peterson! How are you? It's been a long time." The lovely secretary's smile registered with him as sincere, and he remembered that he had regarded her as honest and straightforward. He extended his hand, and she rose to shake hands with him.

"I'll tell Ms. Mitchell you're here."

Minutes later, Estelle's office door opened, and she walked

through it, more elegant and more beautiful than ever, her face wreathed in smiles. "Richard, how nice to see you!" He took the hand she offered, shook it and, to his surprise, the earth didn't move. Indeed, considering the complete lack of emotional undertow the handshake caused him, he could have been shaking hands with a stranger. "My, but you look wonderful," she said. "Leah told me you'd dropped ten years, and she's right. Come on in."

"You look well, too," he said. "Very well, indeed. Congratulations on your new status."

"Thanks. What brings you to New York? I was stunned when I learned that you'd turned down the offer of a five-year contract and walked away from one of the most coveted posts in international civil service. Are you content with your decision?"

"Absolutely. I've learned how to be a real person. That's one of the reasons why I'm here." He decided to be honest. "I needed to slay some ghosts, and that's what I'm doing."

Her smile vanished. "Are you making any progress?"

He didn't hesitate, simply went with his gut feelings. "I'm doing nicely, far better than I would have thought. When I read of your marriage, it was as if the air had been sucked out of me with a vacuum, and I became something of an emotional cripple." Her face crumpled into a worried frown, and he held up his hand to signal a halt to the direction of her thoughts. "I'm in great shape now, and your agreeing to talk with me for a few minutes has done wonders."

She leaned back in her chair. "You don't know how glad I am to hear this. Are you planning to live here in New York, or will you return to Geneva?"

"My home is in Pike Hill, Maryland, right on the Atlantic Ocean, and I'm very happy there. I left the service and Geneva because I thought I saw the person I'd become, and I didn't like it. That was only the beginning."

He stood, satisfied that he'd done the right thing in facing her and his demon. "Thank you for these few minutes. I'm happy that life is treating you well, and I hope it continues that way."

She got up, walked toward the door, turned and smiled. "I'm glad you came, Richard. When we last saw each other, we didn't part on the happiest of terms, and we can both remember this parting with satisfaction. I see a difference in you. Not many men or women have the courage to do what you did."

He stood there looking down at her, letting his gaze sweep over her. Then he smiled a smile that came from his heart. "You've done exceedingly well. This is a man's world, and you've made it and still retained your femininity. It's admirable," he told her, and he smiled because that was all he felt for her, admiration.

She held out her hand for a cordial good-bye. "Thanks. I wish you good luck."

He shook her hand, unmoved by the physical contact. "Thanks. I certainly wish you the same."

"I appreciate the appointment, Leah," he said to Estelle Mitchell's secretary. "You're as gracious as ever."

"Thanks. All the best to you, Ambassador Peterson."

Minutes later, he was in a taxi on the way to his hotel. With any luck, he could be back in Pike Hill in time for supper. As the taxi sped up Third Avenue, he dialed the airline on his cell phone and booked a two o'clock flight. At the hotel, he paid the driver. "Wait for me. I'm going to LaGuardia Airport. I'll be back in ten minutes."

He got off the plane in Ocean Pines at five-forty and phoned Dan for a ride to Pike Hill. *Gosh, I'd better tell Fannie to expect me for supper.*

"That certainly didn't take long," Judd said when Richard dropped his overnight bag by the door and walked into the lounge.

"No point in staying longer. I did what I had to do and came home."

Judd turned off the television. "You satisfied with the way things went? Or you planning to let me worry every minute you were gone and then come back and not tell me a blasted thing."

"Of course not. She's as beautiful, elegant, and intelligent as ever, and I didn't feel a thing. Not a single spark."

"Well I'll be danged if I didn't tell you so."

"We had a gracious, civilized meeting in her office and wished each other well. Period. I never felt so good in my life."

"Yes siree," Judd said. "This is a fine day."

He looked at Judd and couldn't help grinning. "Think you can substitute a glass of wine or sherry for that ginger ale you love so much? I feel like celebrating."

"I don't mind if I do. Haven't had a glass of sherry in years."

"We can go down to the Inn after supper. No chance Fannie would have any spirits here."

Richard's gaze settled on the fire that crackled in the fireplace, warm and welcoming. "Tell you what. Let's have a glass of wine. It's too cold and too windy for a stroll down Ocean Road." He looked at his watch. "I'd better get up to my room and change before supper."

"Yeah," Judd said. "You don't want everybody to think you're being uppity, and you sure don't want Francine to walk in here and see you chatting with me when you haven't even told her you were back."

He patted Judd's shoulder. "Right. I'd trust you to mind my business any day. You're good at it. See you shortly."

"*You* haven't been doing such a good job of it, though I admit you're improving all of a sudden."

"Better late than never," he replied, enjoying the intimacy that comes with friendship.

He bounded up the stairs, and as he reached the hallway, Jolene closed her room door. "Hi, Richard, I thought you were coming back Wednesday. Is everything all right?"

"Couldn't be better. I finished my business, so I came home. How are things with you?"

She seemed thoughtful, nodding her head. "Good for you. I turned a corner, and I think it's for the best."

"Glad to hear it," he said. "We can talk after supper. See you then." Whistling the Toreador's song from the opera, *Carmen*, he dropped his bag beside the door, inserted his key and walked into the place he called home. He went at once to the window, pushed aside the curtain and looked out as if to reacquaint himself with the view of the sound and the ocean that he'd come to love. Not the clear green water of the Caribbean Sea, the Lido beach outside Rome, Italy, the banks of the Seine in Paris or the majestic Mount Blanc that he often saw from his office windows in Geneva ever gave him the peace he found in the Atlantic's frolicking waves.

Good heavens, he thought, I haven't whistled in years, a lot of years, but it felt good to let go. He had twenty minutes, time for a shower. If he was lucky, he'd see Francine before the watching eyes of their supper companions inhibited his greeting. "My Lord, I'm bursting at the seams," he said to himself. "Down boy!"

He was on his way down the stairs when the front door opened, and a gust of wind chilled his body, still warm from the shower. His instincts told him to wait, and he stopped midway on the stairs. He heard her pointed heels tapping quickly in the hall floor, and then he saw her. She stopped and stared at him, speechless.

She had never looked so vibrant or so beautiful. Surely the sun was shining on her. He opened his arms, and she raced up the stairs and launched herself into them. "Is it all right, now?" she whispered. "You're back so early. Tell me it's all right."

He locked her to his body. "It's all right, sweetheart. Things couldn't be better." It wasn't the time for what he wanted and needed. He kissed her hair and the side of her face. "Hurry, or you'll be late for supper."

When Richard entered the dining room feeling as if he walked on air, Judd's face shone with delight, and he wondered how and when he had become transparent, at least to his friend.

"You're back early," Fannie exclaimed. "I sure hope that means things went well with you up there."

"Exceedingly well. Thanks." He looked around and lowered his voice to a whisper. "Where's Percy?"

"He's on a run down to Florida. Ought to be back tomorrow. Poor Percy; he's gotten to be the saddest person I ever saw."

Francine entered the dining room followed by Barbara, and Fannie stood. "We're all here. Let us bow our heads and thank the Lord." She said the grace, Rodger placed generous portions of spiced shrimp before them, and a hush fell over the room. "When they don't talk," Fannie said, "they're enjoying the food."

He glanced toward Francine, saw that her gaze was upon

him and smiled. At least he hoped he smiled, for he felt like splitting his face with a grin. He didn't think he'd ever been so happy, not even when he was elected executive-director of the IBNDA.

"You're in a great mood tonight," Fannie said. "Anybody would think you just won a divorce."

For a woman who never went near the water, Fannie could beat anybody he knew fishing. "Right church; wrong pew. I've never been married," he said, and hoped that took care of her curiosity.

Just as he was beginning to think the evening couldn't be more perfect, Marilyn emerged from the kitchen, walked over to him and put a dish of crème Courvoisier in front of him. "I made it 'specially for you," she said, rubbing his back, "and you'll get your espresso later."

"Thanks," he said, "but I make it a habit not to mislead women, Marilyn, so I'm letting you know right now that I'm spoken for. I appreciate the dessert, though."

"Well, I'm not spoken for," Fannie fumed, "and the next time you bring something to this table, be sure you bring it for *both* of us."

"I keep forgetting," Marilyn said.

"I'll bet you do," Fannie retaliated. "If I had male equipment, you'd remember."

"Wouldn't be able to forget it," Marilyn said, with her head high as she flounced toward the kitchen in a huff.

After supper, Richard asked Fannie to excuse him and rushed to speak with Francine. "This is one time I'm sorry I don't have a car. We could go to one of the lounges in Ocean Pines and talk in private," he told her.

"We can drive my car, but first I think you ought to ask Judd to excuse you. He's so used to having your company after supper that—"

"Yours, too. Get your coat." He walked over to Judd. "Francine and I are going for a ride so we can talk."

"Do a good job of it, friend. Opportunity usually knocks only once. Was I right that you're over that New York lady? Estelle, I believe you said."

"Yes. We had a pleasant talk, and I got back here as fast as I could."

"I wish you luck with Francine. She's a tough one, but she's worth every bit of the feeling you invest in her. Have a good time."

They walked hand-in-hand to her car. "Would you like to drive?" she asked him.

"I don't mind." She tuned to an easy-listening radio station, rested her head against his shoulder and waited for whatever he wanted to say. "Let's just listen to the music. When we talk, I want to look at you."

He parked in front of the Bridle and Saddle Lounge. "Does this place suit you?" he asked Francine.

"It's perfect, especially since the tourist season is over. It will be almost empty."

"What would you like?" he asked her after they took a booth in a far corner.

"A piña colada."

"I'll take the same without the rum," he told the waitress.

"Did you see her?" Francine asked, letting him know that how he felt about Estelle had been uppermost in her thoughts.

"Yes, I saw her in her office this morning for about fifteen minutes. Neither of us needed more time. We talked, wished each other well and meant it, and we parted on good terms."

She knitted her brows. "But I had the impression that you cared deeply for her, that you might still love her. I thought your feeling for her was what prevented the two of us from developing a meaningful relationship."

"And that impression had merit. Until this morning, I hadn't seen her for several years, not since I learned that she married and, until recently, I believed that I still loved her. When my feelings for you became so strong, I was less certain about Estelle, and I wanted the freedom to . . . to let what I felt for you have sway."

The waitress brought their drinks and a large bowl of trail mix, and he lifted his glass to Francine. "Here's to a long, happy relationship."

She nodded, sipped the drink and began stroking the back of his hand, almost absentmindedly, as if her thoughts were elsewhere. "And you could settle that within yourself in fifteen minutes?"

"Less than that. The minute I saw her, I knew. Oh, she's still a knockout, but after longing for her all that time, mind you, I was with her, and I didn't have the least urge to touch her. We shook hands, and I felt nothing." He ran his hands over his hair. "Francine, I'm talking about a woman who once rocked me clear out of my mind. Who knows how it would have been if I . . . if I hadn't developed this feeling for you."

"So you were lovers."

"Once. It sunk me, but the earth didn't move for her. I suspect that helped her to realize she was in love with another man."

"Is she happy?"

"I didn't ask her. My response to her, my evaluation of my feelings for her wasn't contingent upon that, but she appeared to be very happy, and I'm glad about that."

Francine sipped her drink slowly, contemplatively. Then she raised her head, and her gaze bore into him. "Can there be anything between you and me, Richard? I want to know now. I'm in deep enough as it is."

He leaned back in the booth, and took her hand in his. "You've given me some anxious, painful moments and cost me one entirely sleepless night when I didn't know whether you were in trouble or not, alive or dead. I thought I'd go crazy. I'd rather you had most any profession other than that of undercover cop, because I fear for you whenever I'm not looking at you. But fate or providence . . ." he let a grin slide over his face . . . "has taken the matter out of my hands. I love you, and I want you, badge and all."

Her hand grabbed her chest, and she gaped at him. "You *what*?"

"Francine, if you love me, I want us to see if we can make a go of it."

She seemed addled. "I do love you. I'm certain of that. What will we do?"

The sudden thudding of his heart startled him, his breathing accelerated, and he grasped both of her hands. He didn't know if he could speak. What had he done to deserve such happiness? "Francine. Sweetheart," he managed to say. How could he tell her what he felt?

"How will the folks at the boardinghouse react to us?" she asked him, but that was the least of his concerns.

He slipped his arm around her and tightened it. "For the time being, we'll have to be circumspect, and Fannie will have to change places with you in the dining room."

She snuggled up to him to the extent allowable in that cherished watering hole of the Maryland Blue Bloods. "I hope I don't have to break Marilyn's arm," she said with a brilliant smile lighting up her face.

He needed to hold her and love her, and he could see trouble ahead. Until now, he hadn't minded the rules that Fannie stipulated as if they were equivalent to the four Gospels, but he would need Herculean willpower to stay out of Francine's bed while she slept three doors from his room. "Let's go home," he said, stood and held out his hand.

She drained her glass and took his hand. "I never prayed so hard as I did when you were in New York. You didn't say you'd be seeing a woman, but I knew it, and I knew why. I'm so thankful that it's over."

"So am I."

He assisted her into the car, went around to the driver's side, got in, closed the door and turned to her. She was his woman now, locked in his arms with his tongue deep in her mouth, and he intended to see that she never wanted another man. Now that he had stopped trying to control his feelings for her, what he felt in his heart nearly overwhelmed him.

He broke the kiss, and she gazed at him, puzzled. "I'd rather not have an accident on the way home," he told her. "And I think we'd better plan a weekend some place, and soon." As he held her, he had a sensation of not belonging to himself, of seeming to float into space, a part of the universe. Lord, he loved her!

"I love the feeling of your arms around me, strong, like an ancient fortress," she said. "How about Miami next weekend?"

A woman who wasn't coy, but honest and forthright about her feelings was to be prized. He hugged her, rejoicing in the treasure he held in his arms. "Great. I'll meet you in Ocean Pines when you get off work Friday." He put the key in the ignition and headed for Pike Hill and Thank the Lord Boarding House.

The next morning, Jolene raced down the stairs prepared to gobble up her food and get to the bus within thirty-five minutes. If only she hadn't overslept, but after a nightmare awakened her, she hadn't been able to get back to sleep until nearly dawn. She sat at the table with Judd and Richard, comfortable with the notion that they would welcome her.

"Ask Rodger to wrap up your breakfast," Judd said, "and you can eat it on the bus. No point in making yourself sick."

She looked at Rodger. "Would it be too much to ask?"

Rodger smiled, as he always did when one of the boarders asked a favor of him. That smile and his willingness guaranteed him many presents at Christmas. "Give me ten minutes, Miss," he said.

Jolene thanked him and looked at Richard. "Maybe it's too personal, but I would like to know if everything's all right with you and Francine. I wouldn't like her to be . . . well, hurt."

When he stopped eating, she thought she might have annoyed him, but he winked at her. "I'm pretty certain that she's happy, Jolene. Thanks for your concern."

Maybe she had changed, but so had Richard. "That's wonderful," she said with a feeling of true joy. Rodger handed her a box and a thermos, and she thanked him. "See you both this evening. Bye." She floated down Ocean Road, singing "God Didn't Make Little Green Apples," a pop song she learned from a schoolmate and the only one she knew. If it hadn't been for Judd's thoughtfulness, she'd have missed the bus, for the driver revved the engine as soon as she stepped on it. *I guess that's what love is*, she thought as she dropped coins into the box. *Caring about a person's well being. If so, that means I care about Judd, Richard, Francine, Joe, and Fannie.* She laughed to herself. *Imagine me caring about Fannie.*

"Good morning," she sang to the driver, still in heightened spirits.

"And good morning to you. From the way you sound, I guess you heard."

She looked down at him with what she supposed was a quizzical expression. "Heard what?"

"I dropped by to see Masterson yesterday after work, and he told me he's going home day after tomorrow."

"Really? That's good news." She headed for the back of the bus where she could eat in peace.

"He told me to tell you to come to see him before he leaves there," the driver called to her.

"He did? Thanks." She kept walking.

"When you start managing my new shop," her boss said that morning, "I'll raise you to seven hundred a week. You're doing all right. Just be careful, and don't let people like Vida walk all over you. She's a user."

She gave him a hard look. "You're really going to give me that job?"

"I said I would, didn't I? We'll open the first of the year."

"Thanks," she said, feeling weak in the knees. "I'll do my best."

"I know that. You'll do all right," he told her, and it was high praise coming from him.

She left work that afternoon thinking of her future, confident that she would always be able to take care of herself. She hadn't spent a penny of her inheritance since she went to work at the beauty parlor. Richard was right, she admitted. She alone was responsible for herself and everything that happened to her. She could read and reason, so she couldn't blame Emma Tilman for anything but being a lousy, unfeeling parent and for not telling her who fathered her.

Deciding that she should visit Harper to see whether he needed anything, she got off the bus at Crane Street and, on an impulse, bought a pint of butter-pecan ice cream and, with the December wind at her back, hurried to the hospital. At his door, she hesitated before knocking, remembering when, in her nightmare the previous night, she walked through a door and dropped into space. She knocked.

"Come in." He leaned against the wall beside the window, and his voice was strong and steady.

"Hi. Gee, I forgot you were so tall."

He turned toward the door and, when he saw her, a light flashed in his eyes—nice eyes, she realized—as a grin spread across his face. He started walking toward her. "Jolene!" he exclaimed, his joy almost palpable. "I'm so glad you came. Did Jack tell you what I said?" He leaned down and kissed her cheek.

"He told me you were going home tomorrow," she said backing away from the heat of his nearness. "What did he tell you? That guy doesn't even know my name, and until you called him Jack, I didn't know his." She didn't want Harper to think she got on familiar terms with every man who drove the bus between Pike Hill and Salisbury.

"He didn't have to know your name; he described you perfectly."

Better not ask what Jack said. She didn't want Harper to think the man interested her. She didn't ask herself why she wanted Harper to think well of her, but she admitted to herself that she was off his blacklist and she wanted to stay off. She changed the subject.

"I brought you some ice cream."

"Gee, thanks. I haven't had anything good since you brought me that dinner Thanksgiving Day. Have a seat." He opened the ice cream and took the spoon from the bag.

"Won't that spoil your supper? You won't be hungry."

"No way can you spoil hospital food." He stuck the spoon in the ice cream, pulled the heaping spoonful out with the relish of one removing a dart from the bull's-eye, and savored it. "You still seeing that guy in Ocean Pines?"

She hadn't expected that question, and a frown creased her forehead. "Uh . . . he did something I didn't like, and I don't plan to see him again. My boss promoted me. He's opening another shop the first of January, and I'll be the manager."

He savored several spoonsfull of ice cream. "That's great,

Jolene. Congratulations. You know, you're not a bit like the Jolene who rode my bus every day, and I really like the change."

"Thanks, my friends at the boardinghouse are telling me I changed, too."

"I can imagine. So what happened between you and that guy? I want to know if he still means anything to you."

Hadn't her experiences with Gregory taught her not to tell a man everything? Still, it paid to be honest, and Harper was only a friend. "Well, I told him as much about myself as . . . as you said I should. He cooled off for a couple of weeks, and then he attempted to get me in a compromising position, I mean he . . . he didn't give me a choice. He . . . just assumed . . . Oh heck, I walked out on him, and the next day I sent him the price of the movie and dinner."

He sat as still as the night, and he seemed to have stopped breathing. "Have you talked with him since?"

"He called that night, but I told him what I thought of him and hung up. I think more of myself now, Harper."

"Right on. You gave the guy what he deserved." He handed her a piece of paper. "That's my address and phone number. I know where you live, but I don't have your phone number."

She gave him the boardinghouse phone number. "I'm going to return this cell phone to Gregory. I can afford one myself." She put the paper he gave her into her pocketbook, looked up at him, and he shifted his gaze, but not before she saw mirrored in his eyes such affection and feeling as she had never seen before.

She jumped up, nearly knocking over the chair in which she sat. "I'd better go. I don't want to be late for supper."

He placed the container of ice cream on the floor and stood. "Thanks for coming and for this treat. I love ice cream. You made my day." He walked with her to the door. "When I get back to work, I may not be driving a bus, and even if I do I probably won't have the same route, and I want to see you again. I don't mean while I'm driving a bus; I mean socially, man to woman."

Her heart seemed to tumble down to her belly. "After all the trouble I caused you, I didn't think—"

His arms went around her, his tongue flicked across the seam of her lips, and she opened to him and took him in.

"You must feel something for me," he said after releasing her, "or you wouldn't tremble in my arms. I'll call you when I get home." He stared down into her face, and she stared back at him. Poleaxed. Reeling from the shock of what she felt while he kissed her.

She had to get away. "I'll . . . uh . . . bye." With a hand on his chest, she pushed herself from him, rushed down the corridor to the exit and fled down the stairs, forgetting about the elevator or the sign-out notice at the nurses' station. She left the hospital in a trot, almost running until, breathless, she leaned against a lamppost, gasping. Winter darkness had set in, and the clear moon shining above made the night seem colder and her world lonelier. For the first time in months—since Harper made love to her and then told her why he didn't want to see her again—she felt like crying.

Maybe she was one of those women who lost her common sense whenever she was near a man. No. That wasn't true, because she stood her ground with Percy and Gregory and hadn't let them treat her as if she were a nobody. If only she understood men. If only she'd had a father to teach her those things!

She walked on to the bus stop and, when the bus arrived, she gave thanks that Jack was not its driver. When Jolene reached the boardinghouse, she didn't stop in the lounge but hastened upstairs to freshen up and get a grip on her nerves. She was midway up when Percy started down the stairs as if in a hurry. He saw her and stopped, then turned in retreat, but she rushed forward and grabbed his arm.

"What you want with me? Turn me loose," he said.

"Please. I've been trying for weeks to thank you, but you won't give me a chance."

He stared at her. "Thank me. For what?"

"For being so kind to me, Percy. I did a terrible thing. A lot of men would have forced me to . . . you know, but you were such a gentleman, and I appreciate it from the bottom of my heart."

"I didn't look at it that way," he said, his voice low and tremulous. "I figured you'd be laughing at me."

"Oh, no." She rested her right hand on his arm. "I'm grateful, and I thank you so much for not telling anybody here about it."

He moved his head from side to side, seemingly perplexed. "You can bet I didn't tell anybody about that, and I'm glad you didn't. Maybe we can forget about it."

"Thanks. I don't do things like that any more, Percy. When I came here, I'd never had a date with a man in my entire life."

He stared at her. "What do you take me for?"

She told him of her life with her mother and grandmother and her ignorance of the world beyond Emma Tilman's house. "I've learned a lot since I've been here."

"You lucky you still living. Well, thanks for talking to me. I tell you, I feel a whole lot better about it knowing that I didn't do nothing bad. I'll see you down at supper."

Inside her room, she closed the door and leaned against it. "That's taken care of, thank the Lord, but tomorrow after work, I have to go to the library and face Gregory, a man who has no re-spect for me." The thought tempered her relief at having restored Percy's self-esteem, which she did at the expense of the truth. However, she promised herself that she would take that com-puter training course and help keep the children orderly during their computer training, Gregory Hicks notwithstanding. She washed her hands, replaced her woolen sweater with a long-sleeved red blouse, combed her hair, and headed for the dining room.

At the bottom of the stairs, she bumped into the Reverend Philip Coles and, caught off guard, she articulated her reaction to seeing him. "Are you here again, for goodness sake?"

He seemed to shrink, obviously taken aback, but she felt no remorse for her ungracious remark. "Well, it *has* been several weeks since I was here."

"How are things, Reverend?"

At the sound of Richard's voice, Jolene whirled around and looked up into his censoring eyes. At least, she thought he cen-sored her. If she had heard him coming down the stairs behind her, she wouldn't have made such an incautious comment to Philip Coles. After all, she had the reverend to thank for her pre-sent state of well-being.

"Uh . . . hi, Richard."

"Hi, how's it going?" he said and continued to the dining room.

She had known Philip Coles all of her life, or at least as long as she could remember, and she had never felt hostile toward him, mostly, she supposed, because she accepted her fate and never considered his failure to help ease her plight. Looking back, it seemed to her that he abandoned his role as her mother's spiritual leader.

She took her seat between Joe and Louvenia, and greeted them with more cheer than she felt. Philip Coles said the grace, and she made herself bow her head while he did it.

"You seem down," Joe said, "and that's a pity 'cause you look real nice and fresh like you just came in out of the wind."

"It's cold tonight," she said and in an effort to be friendly added, "I got a raise today, and after the first of the year, I'll be managing one of my boss' beauty parlors."

"That's wonderful, Jolene. You oughta be jumping straight up and down. I never saw a person change as much as you have since you came here, and it's all been for the good, too."

She liked Joe, but she'd never found a way to tell him that, and she didn't want him to think she was coming on to him. "I wish I'd had you for a big brother," she told him and watched his face crease into a smile.

"That would've been great. I never had any sisters. I . . ." He lowered his voice. "Did I hear Percy ask Judd if he'd like to have some tangerines when he came back from Florida Saturday? I hope he's coming out of that cocoon he's been living in."

She glanced toward Percy and saw that Judd had locked his gaze on her. "He can only guess," she said to herself. To Joe, she said, "I wonder where Francine is tonight."

Jolene was tempted to go to her room after dinner, but she knew Fannie would take her to task for ignoring Philip Coles. However, to her surprise and satisfaction, he did not approach her but sat with Judd and Richard.

"What a night!" she said to Joe when Percy walked into the lounge and took a seat.

"Yeah. I'd give anything to know what's come over Percy all of a sudden. He's like his old self."

* * *

Richard looked at his watch. So this was what his life would be like, wondering and worrying about Francine whenever he wasn't looking at her. She'd said she had to go to Ocean City and would be late getting home, and he couldn't call her because the ringing phone might alert someone to her presence. He sighed and accepted Rodger's offer of a cup of espresso.

"You know, this is an odd coincidence," Judd said to Richard and Philip, "they're not a bit of kin, but they sure do look a lot alike."

"Who're you talking about?" Richard asked him, as if he didn't know.

"Fannie and Jolene. I noticed it when Jolene first came here, but with both of them wearing red tonight, they could be mother and daughter."

"Well, I can assure you that Jolene's mother is dead," Philip said, "because I officiated at her funeral."

"That's right," Judd said. "I believe Jolene did tell me that you were her mother's pastor. What do you know of her father? Jolene said her mother never told her who he was, and I think that's the least a person should know. Don't you?"

"In most cases, I'd say, yes. From what I can tell from casual conversations with her, Jolene seems to be making wonderful progress. She's developed into a charming woman." He didn't look at Judd while he spoke, and neither that nor what appeared to be an attempt to change the subject was lost on Richard.

"You're right," Richard said. "She's blooming in spite of the wreck she was when she came here. I can't imagine that none of Jolene's teachers, the members of your church or even *you* didn't call her mother down about the way she treated Jolene. She came here knowing less about life than the average fifteen-year-old girl, and she paid for it."

"And she paid a lot," Judd said. "Seeing what she's done with herself since she came here and the talent she's got, it's difficult to imagine what she could have amounted to if her life had been different. Somebody's got a lot to answer for."

"Yes," Philip intoned, "but we shouldn't speak unkindly of the dead."

Judd stared into the man's face. "The dead? I never said a word about the dead."

"Would you like more coffee?" Rodger asked.

The man looks as if he was drowning and someone threw him a lifeline, Richard said to himself.

"No, thank you," Philip said. "Coffee keeps me awake. Well, if you gentlemen will excuse me, I'll have a chat with Fannie before I turn in."

"Where does he sleep?" Richard asked Judd after Philip left them.

"In Fannie's sitting room, no doubt. That man's a hypocrite. What are you thinking?"

"Something very similar. If you don't mind, I think I'll take a short walk."

Judd locked his hands behind his head and rocked. "Stop worrying about Francine. She can take care of herself, and if she told you where she'd be, that ought to satisfy you."

He couldn't tell Judd why he worried about Francine, because he wouldn't dare expose her even to his friend. He ran up the stairs, got a coat and headed outside into the bracing wind. *She told me she was going to Ocean City, but I have to make sure she's not down here on that beach by herself tracking Ronald Barnes.* He tightened his coat collar when he turned off Ocean Road and started up Rhone Street. Seeing the elongated figure in front of him, he turned and looked back, then walked on when he realized that it was his own shadow. In the bright moonlit night, he saw the Milky Way. What a scene, he mused as he wiped the wind-induced tears from his eyes. White foam at the tips of the waves sprang out like flashes of light in darkness. Standing alone on the beach, he spread his legs to anchor himself against the force of the wind and stood transfixed while stars shot through the heavens and clouds raced over the moon, momentarily subduing it, but never fully obscuring it. He didn't know how long he stood there, dazzled by nature's gymnastics.

The cold began to seep into his body, and with reluctance he started home, thankful that he hadn't found Francine risking her life on that beach and wondering what life with her would be like, but exhilarated by the salty air and the night's brilliance. As he entered the boardinghouse, Francine stepped from the lounge into the hallway.

"Richard! Judd told me you'd gone for a walk. In this weather?"

For an answer, he lifted her and twirled her around. "You're going to drive me loco," he said, locked her body to his and lowered his head. As far as he was concerned, anybody who wanted to could watch; his joy at having her unharmed, with him, and in his arms was so great that he didn't care about convention.

"Hmm. The times are changing," Fannie said, misquoting Pete Seeger.

"Not to worry," Francine replied. "We'll keep it between the lines."

"Humph. Doesn't look like it, but you make sure that our senior ladies, Miss Louvenia and Miss Arnetha, don't give me a hard time about what this house is coming to. I remember how it was with me and my dear husband, God rest his soul. Too bad I couldn't get something going between Jolene and Gregory Hicks. He's such a fine man."

Richard draped his right arm across Francine's shoulder. "Fannie, these things work themselves out. Jolene will do just fine. She's a very gifted, very attractive woman; in fact, she looks a lot like you."

Fannie patted her hair. "You think so? In my younger days, I didn't doff my cap to no woman."

Well, well, he said to himself. *When you lift the lid, there's no telling what you'll find.* To Fannie, he said, "You don't have to do it now, either."

Her smile eclipsed her whole face. "Oh, you go way from here, Richard Peterson. I do declare!" She rushed off, her color bright and her spirits high.

"She surprised me. I thought she'd start spouting one of her rules," Richard said to Francine.

"I did, too, and if we took it any further, I expect she would. Did you find a place for us to stay in Miami?"

"I did, indeed, and the plane tickets are upstairs in my room. I couldn't possibly overlook a thing like that."

* * *

Jolene greeted Richard and Francine, when she emerged from the lounge on her way to her room. "Hi, you two."

"We didn't get a chance to talk," Richard said, "but I want to hear about that corner you turned. Perhaps we can speak tomorrow at breakfast."

"I'll get down here a little earlier," she told him. *Maybe she should explain to Richard her rudeness to Philip Coles, but somehow she didn't feel compelled to do it. The more she learned about people, the lower her estimation of the preacher became.*

Chapter Twelve

On her lunch hour the next day, Jolene bought a cell phone, and when she went to the library after work, she asked Richard to program it for her, explaining that she hadn't had time to study the manual.

"Did you lose the one you had?"

"No. Gregory gave me that one when I first came to Pike Hill, and I'm giving it back to him tonight."

Richard looked hard at her, but she was neither embarrassed nor inclined to protect Gregory. "Because he presumed too much, and it's my way of straightening him out. I bought my own phone."

"An angle of the corner you turned?"

She nodded. "Harper wants us to be friends. He leaves the hospital today, and he wants us to see each other."

"How do you feel about that?"

"Like . . . maybe I'll finally have a normal relationship with a man. He's—"

"Are you attracted to him?"

"Uh . . . the last two times I've been with him, things have been . . . he just sort of swept me away. Richard, he's the one man I ever felt anything with, and he's always been respectful, even when he told me he didn't want any part of me."

"You told me." He handed her the cell phone. "Do you remember my saying you were pining for the wrong man?"

"Yes, but—"

"Open your eyes, Jolene. When a man cares for a woman, and if she's available, he's not likely to hide it. Will you be at the children's class?"

"Of course."

She stood at the door while the children filed in, addressing them by name and patting their shoulders, letting them know she was their friend as well as their disciplinarian.

"You're doing a great job with these children," Gregory said to her at the end of the class. "You make teaching them easy."

Thank God, she didn't need his compliments or his approval. "I respect them, and they know that," she said, looking him in the eye. "Every human being deserves respect. Good night." She left him standing there, and went to the reading room to find Judd. How sweet it was!

Before she could reach Judd, she felt the weight of Richard's hand on her shoulder. "Gregory said he'd drive us home. Is that all right with you?"

"Rough as that wind is? Sure. And thanks, Richard." She had done it. She had faced Gregory Hicks with her head high and her shoulders straight. "From now on, nobody's dragging me down," she said to herself. "Not even *me*."

That resolve prevented her from rushing to her room after supper and telephoning Harper on her new cell phone. Instead, she joined Judd, Francine, and Richard for coffee and the chocolate fudge that Marilyn had announced would be served after supper. She didn't talk but sat quietly and observed the interplay between Francine and Richard in an effort to learn how a woman behaved with a man.

They just act . . . normal-like, she said to herself. *Natural, like they've always been together*.

"Jolene," Fannie called. "Telephone."

She told herself not to run. Maybe it wasn't Harper, but her boss. She remembered that her boss never called her at home and knocked over a chair in her haste to get to the telephone, which hung in the hall across from the lounge. She didn't want him to know how excited she was, how impatiently she'd waited for his call, so she took a second to catch her breath and slow down her heart beat. "Hello. This is Jolene."

"Hi. This is Harper. I'm home, and I ought to have my car by the weekend. Will you go to a movie with me?"

She hadn't expected that. So much activity days after his release from the hospital didn't make sense to Jolene, and she indicated as much. "The weekend? Aren't you pushing it?"

"No. My doctor said the sooner I get back to a normal life the better."

Maybe her ship had come in, and she would have a normal life with another person. "Harper, I'd love to see a movie with you." They talked for a while, and then she said, "I bought my phone today, and I enjoyed giving Gregory's back to him." She gave Harper the number. "You can call me on my cell phone now."

"I will. I'm glad you did that, Jolene, and I'm glad we're going to be friends."

If the course of Jolene's life had begun to run more smoothly—thanks to her determination to mend her ways, to give to others, and to be less concerned for what she received—Richard was about to fall from his newly-found paradise and out of his state of grace. He answered his cellular phone shortly before noon that Saturday, and the sound of Francine's voice soothed his ears and warmed his heart.

"How'd you like to go to a showing of paintings by African-American artists? It's in a gallery in Ocean Pines, and the three-ninety-five entry fee is on me."

Laughter rumbled out of him, and he fell across his bed, relaxed and happy. "We'll fight about who pays later. What time?" She told him. "Okay. Meet you downstairs in twenty minutes."

He could barely control his feet. Maybe he would fly. In his life, he had never before had that sense of completeness, of total well-being, had never felt so suffused with joy as when he walked out of Thank the Lord Boarding House that morning with Francine's hand wrapped in his. And for the first time, he knew that what he felt was mutual. He was in love, and he had a

woman who cared for *him*—not for his status and looks—and
wanted him to know it. Not even the crisp Albemarle breeze
could chill him, warmed as he was by her loving presence. He
smiled down at her.

A tall, elegant woman jumped out of a white Mercedes sedan
and rushed up the walk toward them. "Richard," she called,
suddenly running to him as if he were alone. "Darling, I've
spent the past two years trying to find you. I know I said it was
just a momentary weakness of mine, but after what we shared, I
could never sleep with my husband again." The woman stopped
talking and looked at Francine. He tried to remember who she
was, what, if anything, had happened between them, and where
he had known her. Francine's hand slid out of his, and he had a
sudden sensation of drowning.

"I'm sorry, madam, but I don't recall meeting you."

"Please," she begged. "I've given up everything for you.
Everything."

"But I don't know who you are, and I'm sorry that you came
here . . . for nothing. I have never deliberately seduced a woman,
so if anything did happen between us, you engineered it with no
strings attached."

He stepped back from her when she grabbed his sleeve. "I
know, but I fell in love with you. It was at that conference in
Nairobi, Kenya. Don't you remember?"

He remembered the conference, but he couldn't recall ever
having seen her before. "I'm sorry, Fran . . ." He looked around,
but Francine was nowhere to be seen.

"What are you trying to do to me?" he asked the woman.
"Do you want to ruin my life?"

Her face crumpled into a palette of despair, and tears rolled
down her cheeks. "That's what you did to mine. I . . . I know I
asked for it, but . . . C . . . can't we talk?"

He shook his head. "I'm sorry if you're disappointed and
upset, but I'd appreciate it if you would leave. Right now."

She persisted. "I can't. Not after all the time, energy and
money I've spent looking for you. Not after I left my husband
for you. The Jamaican ambassador gave me my first clue as to
where you were. Please, can't we talk?"

He was probably guilty, because he didn't remember most of the women he'd taken to bed. He did know, though, that he hadn't given her a reason to expect anything of him, for he'd never tricked a woman; that hadn't been necessary.

He forced himself to speak gently. "I have bedded more women than the average man will meet, but I have never seduced one or given one a reason to believe she was more to me than a moment mutually shared. I'm in love with that woman who was with me, and you've probably screwed that up. So, we're even. Good-bye." She didn't move. "Lady, please don't force me to have you arrested for harassment."

He watched as she turned, walked to the car with wooden steps and got in the backseat. *We've probably been cursed with the same disease: she with the idea that her money could buy anything she wanted, including me; and me with the notion that my status and physical attributes could get me whatever and whoever I wanted. We've both had our day of reckoning. He shook his head. But for me, it's the second time around.*

The rising wind gathered leaves, sticks and other debris and flung them around his ankles, while the cold air seeped into his body, replacing the warmth that—minutes earlier—had suffused and uplifted him. He went to his room, closed the door and fell across the bed. From heaven to hell in less than a minute. He put his cell phone on the little table beside his bed with no intention of using it to call Francine. When she left him, judging him without giving him a hearing, she told him what he needed to know. And what could he say? He'd never given a moment's thought to the effect that his practiced, precision lovemaking had on a woman beyond her multiple orgasms that made him feel like a giant of a man. He had thought losing Estelle was his punishment. *But if he lost Francine . . .*

At one o'clock that afternoon, two-and-a-half hours later, Richard forced himself to get up and go to the dining room. He hurt as he'd never hurt before, but he could not allow himself to sink into the bowels of despair as he had done when he read of Estelle's marriage.

"What you so somber about?" Judd asked Richard when he joined his friend at the table for lunch. "First, Francine flew past me looking like somebody had just stolen her birthright. Never saw a woman so angry. And now you mope in here like you're about to face the executioner. What is—"

"Knock it off, Judd. I'm . . . Look, I'm sorry. Just when I had the world by the tail . . . Oh, hell! What's the use?"

Judd's boney arm rested on his shoulders in what he recognized as a gesture of comfort. "Can you talk about it, son?"

Judd cared deeply for him and wanted the best for him, but he didn't want . . . A long breath swept out of him. "Judd, I thought I'd paid for my days as a player, but it looks as if I've just begun." He told Judd about the woman whose uninvited passion drove Francine from him. "I don't remember the woman, but I've had so many that I can't say she lied. Now, Francine will walk. She will, and I'm in love with her."

"Talk to her."

"How? She walked off without asking me whether what the woman said was true and whether she was justified in tracking me down. What kind of loyalty is that?"

"Slow down. You've got no reason to be self-righteous. If you want her, you gotta work for her. No woman wants another one to claim her man." Judd rubbed his chin and let a grin flash across his whiskered face. "I hope that woman wasn't too good-looking."

Richard smothered a whistle. "Man, she was a knockout!"

"That's a pity."

"I was gonna give you a crab salad for lunch," Marilyn said to Richard, as she stood at the table smiling at her own cleverness. "But I noticed you looked the picture of gloom when you walked in here, so I made you a crab soufflé. Everybody else gets salad."

He was too far down in the dumps to reject her kindness. "Do I have to share it with Judd?"

She patted the back of her hair and lowered her lashes. "His is in the oven."

"Well, thank you for remembering that I'm alive," Judd said.

She swished off, patting the old man's shoulder as she went. "Don't worry. I know there're still red coals in your bones, Judd. I just don't know how much trouble it would be to fan the flames."

Richard's eyebrows shot up above widened eyes, but Judd let out an enormous belly laugh. "I hate to let her know I think she's funny," Judd said. "Before long, she'll be clowning on cue."

Fannie joined them and stared at Richard's plate. " I thought we were having crab salad for lunch today. Before you know it, I'll be working for Marilyn. That woman does as she pleases."

Richard placed a hand lightly on Fannie's arm. "Please don't give her hell about this. She was being fresh as usual, but this stuff is so good that I'm glad to suffer her foolishness . . . for now, that is."

He looked up as Marilyn placed an individual dish of crab soufflé before Judd and glanced at Fannie for her reaction. "I thought I planned crab salad for lunch," Fannie said.

"They didn't look like they wanted salad," Marilyn said. "Your salad is coming right up."

"Would you like some of my soufflé?" Judd asked Fannie after Marilyn left the table.

Fannie's pursed lips and puffed cheeks were answer enough, but she looked at her tablemates, frowned and said, "I wouldn't taste it to save her life. By the way, Richard, one of the town councilmen told me he wants to put your name up for mayor of Pike Hill." Richard stopped eating and stared at her, but she held up her right hand, palm out. "Hear me out. He said you'd done more for this town in the short while you've been here than anybody has in the last quarter of a century. He said that, because of your example, people are volunteering to do things that used to cost Pike Hill plenty. He couldn't believe you've got kids sitting still to learn the computer at five o'clock in the afternoon. You think about what he wants you to do."

He didn't want to hear it. In his present mood, he had a mind to leave Pike Hill. But where would he go? Pike Hill was home, the place where he'd finally found himself. "I don't know, Fannie. I've always stayed clear of partisan politics."

"Nothing but Democrats here," Judd said, "so you'll still be clear of it."

"I am not going to walk around this town begging people to vote for me. I think this habit of adults kissing babies and leaving their germs on them is scandalous, and I refuse to say a thing merely because it's politically correct."

Judd scraped the soufflé dish for the last morsel of crab soufflé and locked his gaze on Richard. "It hasn't been *that* long since you were an ambassador. I thought all you fellows did was lie with a straight face and drink martini cocktails."

Richard leaned back and looked Fannie in the eye. "That's behind me. I might consider it, if it's a part-time job. I'm not giving up our tutoring classes, and after Christmas, I want to start a career-guidance workshop for high school juniors and seniors. It would be good if we could get visiting experts in different fields to talk with them. I've been working on that, and—"

Fannie interrupted him. "And you'd make the perfect mayor."

The booted footsteps of Percy Lucas entering the dining room drew their attention to the man who they had thought was somewhere around Charleston, South Carolina, en route home. "I thought you were due in tonight or tomorrow morning," Fannie said.

"I was, but we're supposed to get a bad hurricane, and they say it will tear up things from Florida to Maine, so I put my foot on that pedal and hightailed it back here as fast as I could. I haven't slept in thirty-six hours. Any lunch?"

"I'll get you something," Fannie said and went to the kitchen.

"It will do you good to have a steady job," Judd told Richard.

"I know. That's why I'm considering it, but damned if I want to come home tired every night."

"Pshaw. You wouldn't get tired if you spent the day visiting every citizen in this town. Ever been in a hurricane?" Richard shook his head. "Well I have, and being this close to the ocean during one can make you pray."

He answered his cell phone. "Hello. Peterson speaking. *What?*" He stood up. "What a surprise! This is wonderful." He walked out of the dining room to the hallway and leaned against the wall beside the house telephone. "You'll love it here. No, it won't be any problem. I have a very large room facing the ocean, and I'll ask my landlady to put a single bed in there for you. It's been a long while since we spent any time together. Me?

Something's different about me? What do you mean? Right. We can talk about it when you get here." He hung up, went back into the dining room and took his seat.

"That sounded like good news, so I don't suppose it was one of your faceless lovers on her way here to finish off your relationship with Francine. Was it?"

"Hate to disappoint you, friend, but that was my dad."

He hadn't spent any quality time with his father over the last twelve or thirteen years, mostly because he hadn't valued the minutes they had together. As he'd bathed in his status and his rising fame, he'd forgotten that, while he floundered in his teenage years, his father had propped him up, constantly sacrificing his own well-being for his son's goals.

He recalled those days to Judd adding, "He deserves better than I've given him."

Judd patted Richard's hand. "I suspect most of us could have said that at one time or another. You gonna introduce him to Francine?"

"If she'll let me. I'll speak to Fannie about a bed for him. See you at supper." He trudged up the stairs and knocked on Francine's door.

Jolene raced out of her room and barely missed plowing into Richard as she rounded the corner to speed down the stairs. "Oh, I'm sorry."

"Which one of them are you going to meet?" he asked in a teasing tone.

"Harper. I don't know what's going on with me, but I think Gregory is out of my system. I have a feeling that what he did straightened me out."

"He was never in your system, Jolene. He's an attractive prospect for a woman, so he might have been in your head but, from what you've told me, he was never in your heart. Have a good time."

She skipped on down the stairs and, as her feet touched the bottom step, the doorbell rang. Fannie reached the door first and opened it.

"Good afternoon. Is Miss Tilman here?"

"Uh . . . why . . . yes. Come in. Who should I say is calling for her?"

Jolene rushed to them. "Hi, Harper. This is my landlady, Mrs. Fannie Johnson. Fannie, this is Harper Masterson."

Harper stared from one to the other. "How do you do, ma'am? I'm glad to meet you."

"And I sure am glad to meet you," Fannie said. "Jolene, you bring him to supper one night, you hear?" She looked at Harper. "We've got the best kitchen anywhere around here, so you come see us."

"I will, if he'll come," said Jolene.

Harper eased an arm around Jolene's waist and half turned toward the door. "I hope to see you again soon, ma'am."

Jolene looked up at the big man beside her and thought that she had never been so happy. He wore a brown tweed overcoat, brown leather gloves, and a green paisley scarf, and she could see that he wore a tie. However, it surprised her that what he wore didn't matter, that she would have been happy with him if he'd worn a leather jacket and a baseball cap.

"Anything special you want to see?" he asked her.

"You pick something. I don't really care what we see."

He stopped in the process of opening the passenger's door for her. "Are you serious?"

"Yeah. I just want us to be together."

He grabbed both of her shoulders and stared into her face. "Are you handing me a line? Don't mess with me, Jolene. I was getting the impression that you were different from what you were when you used to ride my bus, that you were a tender, caring woman, and that you had stopped being manipulative."

Stunned, and aware that he was capable of walking off and leaving her right there, she opted for the truth. "I've been on high all day waiting for you to ring that doorbell. I hardly slept last night. I don't want to manipulate you, Harper. I just want to be with you. If you don't believe me, I'm going back in the house."

His cold lips bruised hers, but his groan warmed her heart and she opened to him and pulled his tongue into her mouth. As quickly as he started it, he stopped. "That's the first time I ever kissed a woman in public, but I'd have done it if we'd been standing on the White House steps. Have you seen, *Swept Away*?" She shook her head. "Come on. Let's go."

During the movie, they held hands, and from time to time, he squeezed her fingers. She wished the frames of their seats didn't separate them, and that she could be closer to him. "Maybe I'd better ask Richard and Judd about this," she said to herself, for her feelings seemed to be getting ahead of her mind.

They left the theater holding hands, and it seemed to her so natural, but how good a judge of character, of men was she? "Would you like to have supper with me at the boardinghouse tomorrow night, or we could do it Monday. But I work Monday, and I'll hardly have time to wash my hands after I get home."

"Tomorrow, if you like. What does she charge?"

Why was he asking her that, and how much proof did he need? "I pay my room and board bill monthly, and as my guest, you pay nothing. It's on me."

"But—"

"You coming or not? You can't pay to eat in my home. Harper, what do I have to do to prove to you that I learned my lesson, that I am no longer struggling under the yoke of my mother's prejudices?"

He took his time answering. They walked nearly half a block before he said, "I don't believe anybody can understand how hurt I was that night. I'd never been in love before, and I knew I loved you, but all I could see was that you were the wrong woman for me. I made love to you for the hell of it and . . . almost lost my mind. You were so perfect for me; I had never touched a woman who made me feel as you did. Can you blame me for being wary, for feeling that this second chance with you is too good to be true?"

Her shoulders slumped, and she expelled a long breath. "No, I can't blame you, and I don't. I'd give anything if I'd been different. It took your accident to shake me up. Then, Francine and Richard opened my eyes, talking to me about life and how people relate, telling me things I should have known when I was sixteen. Judd taught me about friendship, and he did it just by the way he acts. I'm glad I found that place, 'cause only the Lord knows what kind of person I'd be now if I hadn't."

They reached his car, and when they were both inside with the doors closed and locked, he asked her, "How do you feel about me?"

"I'm scared to say, but you mean a lot to me, more than . . . than anybody else ever has. At least I think so."

Her shivers when he eased her into his arms were out of her control. She wrapped her arms around him, and held him while he kissed her eyes, lips and cheeks until she could taste her own tears.

"Why are you crying?"

"Because I can't undo all those stupid things I did when I first came here, and I'd g . . . give anything if I could."

His arms tightened around her. "All right. Let's both of us put that in the past. I don't dwell on it, and neither should you. Let's see what we have going for us."

She nodded. If only he meant it. On the way back to Pike Hill, he stopped at a drive-in fast food shop and bought them grilled barbecued shrimp kebobs, French-fries, and coffee.

"Is any man at that boardinghouse going to be jealous because you brought me to supper?" he asked as they ate in the car with Aretha Franklin's "Chain, Chain, Chain" in the background.

His question surprised her. "No, indeed. I told you about Percy, but I straightened things out with him not so long ago, and we're on speaking terms now. I cleaned up my act."

"I wasn't talking about him. Who is this Richard fellow?"

"He's Francine's guy. Wait'll you meet him."

He cleared his throat. "Something tells me that boardinghouse has an unusual cast of characters."

"You can say that again."

With a heavy heart and fear cramping his gut, Richard knocked on Francine's door and waited. He knew she hadn't left the house, so he knocked again. After what seemed like hours, but was only a few minutes, she opened the door.

"Francine, I have two things to say. I believe I deserve a hearing about what happened this morning, and I want my father to meet you when he comes here next week. Will you step out of the room and talk with me?"

"That's three things," she said, and his heart leaped in his chest, for if she could joke or tease, she would be amenable to reason. "I don't want to talk about anything standing out here, but tell me this . . . you really didn't remember her?"

He crossed his heart. "So help me God, I don't remember ever having seen her. I also know that I probably did it."

She stared at him for a long while, and he waited for the hatchet to fall. Then, she looked at her watch. "If we sit at one of those side tables for two down in the lounge, no one will join us. I'll meet you there in five minutes."

And not a hint as to how she would react to what he had to tell her. When he got down there, she had chosen a table against the wall, far away from where they usually sat with Judd. He nodded to Judd as he entered the lounge.

Francine didn't soften what she had to say with preliminaries. "I'm in deep with you, Richard, but I can walk away, and I can stay away. So please start at the beginning and don't leave anything out. I'm not judging you; I just want to decide fairly if I want to cast my lot with you."

"Fair enough," he began. "The man you're looking at would hardly be recognizable to the man I was less than eighteen months ago." He left out nothing of what he remembered from his nineteenth birthday to the day he decided to leave Geneva and the diplomatic world.

"The fact that a woman chose to abort my child rather than marry me, even though I was only nineteen does not explain the life I've led. When Estelle rejected me, and that was before she married, I realized for the first time how it felt to be pushed aside. And until this morning, I didn't realize the effect that a casual one-night stand could have on a woman."

She rubbed her right hand across her brow as if clearing her head. "Do you remember any of them?"

"Of course. After it was over, one told me she had a husband, and I didn't repeat the act, because I was disgusted. She became a pal . . . of sorts. These women—mostly chic professionals with no home life—were out for a thrill, looking for something different, and I suspect now that they played the field."

She leaned forward and looked him in the eye. "You changed your life drastically, giving up a stunning career because you didn't like what you had become or the people you dealt with, and that's a credit to you. You know, when I walked out of this house with you this morning, I was certain that I wanted you to be my husband." He sat forward, fighting the tentacles of fear that gripped him. "Maybe I still do," she went on. "I don't know, but I need to digest all this." Her face creased into a frown. "I'm not sure I would have the guts to look at myself as you did and then walk away from what you left. I admire you for it."

He wanted to say thanks, but he couldn't get his breath. She hadn't condemned him, and she hadn't said it was over between them. That meant he had a chance. He took her hand, and she allowed him to hold it. "If I should lose you, I'm not sure I could bear it."

"Did you need the variety?" Her voice had a distant, wary quality, and he realized that what concerned her most was his ability to be faithful to one woman. That hadn't occurred to him, and suddenly he understood how she interpreted what he'd told her.

"Francine, I've been completely celibate since I walked out of my office in Geneva all those months ago. Celibacy hasn't bothered me too much until now, and that's because of what I feel for you and want to experience with you. As long as I felt that I was in love with another woman, I didn't let myself get as close to you as my body wanted to. I have personal standards, and they have strengthened with the years. Are you listening to me?" She nodded, but he knew he wasn't out of the woods.

He didn't like the unshed tears that glistened in her eyes, but he could only reach out and caress her cheek. And she allowed him that privilege, too. Maybe he should content himself with whatever she could give, but he wasn't used to taking tidbits. He nearly laughed at himself. He wasn't used to being deeply in love, either.

"When is your father coming?"

"Day after tomorrow."

"I'll make sure I get home early."

He had hardly settled in his room to write when his cell phone rang. "Richard, this is Jolene. Can you please spare me a couple of minutes?"

"Sure I can. What's up?"

"I told you about Harper Masterson, the man who got in the accident after I—"

He interrupted her. "I remember all that. Is there a problem with him?"

"I don't know, Richard. I think the problem's with me. Is a woman supposed to let a man know she's half-crazy about him? It's like I'm in a new world. I never dreamed that being with somebody who cares a lot for me—he does, 'cause I can feel it—could make me ditsy. I can't sleep, and I almost went nuts waiting for him to get here today to take me to a movie. Is this normal, Richard?"

"Does he love you?"

"He does, Richard. I know he does."

"Then, I say, go for it. You're falling in love. Let him know how you feel, but don't forget to be your own woman. Never look up to a man. Admire him if he's admirable, but as an equal. I think he's a lucky fellow. When will we meet him?"

"Tomorrow. He's coming to supper with me."

" I'll look forward to it." She thanked him and hung up.

He heard the front door close and wondered who'd come in or gone out. More curious than he normally was about the activities of others, he put his writing pad aside and went downstairs to find Judd in the lounge talking with Philip Coles.

"Good afternoon, Reverend," he said. "Did you come in a minute ago?"

"Why yes, I'm thinking about buying a place down here for my retirement years. I'll be seventy in ten years, and it'll take me at least that long to pay for a house. Fannie's my only living relative, so I'd like to be near her."

Judd rocked and sipped his ginger ale. "Would you care for

some ginger ale, Reverend?" Fannie swished into the lounge before Philip could answer and stopped short.

"Philip! I didn't know you'd come." She rushed over and
hugged her brother. "I'll tell Marilyn to set a place for you at
supper."

Hmm. So Philip had a key to the house. Richard got a container
of raspberry ice cream from the machine, ate it there to be socia-
ble and went back to his room. *Why did Philip have to give them a
reason for coming to see Fannie so soon after his last visit? Oh, what
the hell,* he thought. *Francine was more than enough to keep his mind
active. What Philip did was his own business.*

On Sunday morning, Jolene went down to breakfast early
and found Judd and Richard eating the elaborate breakfast that
Marilyn always served on Sundays. She joined them. "Have you
had a chance to speak with the Reverend Coles?" Judd asked
her. "He said he's planning to settle in Pikes Hill when he re-
tires."

Jolene sucked air through her teeth, looked toward the ceiling and rolled her eyes. "I don't know, Judd, but the more I see
of that man, the more he distresses my nerves. There's something about him—I don't know what—that brings out the worst
in me."

"So I noticed," Judd said, "but he doesn't seem like a bad fellow."

She ignored that. "See y'all this evening," she said and dashed
up the stairs to dress for church.

Harper arrived promptly at a quarter of seven that evening
and when she saw him, she was glad she'd chosen a pretty red
dress with a flounced skirt. When she took his coat, she had to
stifle a gasp. This was a good-looking man.

"Hmmm. You look so nice," she said, referring to his oxford
gray suit, white shirt, and gray and yellow striped tie.

"And you look beautiful," he said, handing her a bunch of
red roses. She thanked him, though she didn't know where she
got the breath to do it, took his hand and led him to the lounge.

She knew that all eyes were trained on them, and she had never been so proud. She introduced him first to Judd and Richard.

"Where's Francine?" she asked Richard. "Is she coming down?"

"I expect so." His wink signaled his approval of Harper, and when she looked at Judd, he said. "Pull up a chair, Harper, and join our little circle. I'm glad to see you."

"And I'm glad to be here," Harper said. "Jolene talks about all of you with such fondness, that I couldn't wait to meet you. This is—" Fannie entered the lounge, and he stared from Fannie, who also wore red, to Jolene and rubbed his chin. "Hmmm."

"What is it?" Jolene asked him.

"Just a thought."

She didn't miss the quick exchange of glances between Judd and Richard. Francine walked in, devastatingly attractive in a royal blue velvet suit, and Jolene rushed to greet her. "Come on over. I want you to meet my boyfriend."

Richard and Harper stood as they approached the table. "Francine, this is Harper Masterson." They shook hands, and Richard got a chair for Francine and placed it beside his own.

"Well, Harper," Judd said, "we're Jolene's only family. I'm the oldest person here, old enough, you might say, to be rude with impunity, so I can ask if you have good intentions where our Jolene is concerned?"

Harper stretched out his long legs, folded his arms, looked at Judd and winked. A grin played around his lips for a bit, and then he said, "Judd, somehow I knew you had a streak of deviltry. Good. It keeps a person from being boring. You can tell the world that I'm in love with Jolene and that I will always behave honorably with her."

Judd rocked in the boardinghouse's only Shaker rocker. "Don't surprise me none; you got the bearing of a real man."

Harper looked at Richard and grinned. "If I don't pass muster with you, I'm out of luck."

"I think you're both lucky," Richard said, but it seemed to Jolene that Harper's mind had wandered , that he hadn't heard what Richard said.

Fannie rested a hand on Jolene's shoulder. "It's good to see you again, Mr. Masterson. We'll eat as soon as I introduce our guest and Reverend Coles says the grace."

Harper's frown was that of one thoroughly perplexed, but he said, "Thank you. I appreciate your hospitality." He took Jolene's hand and followed Fannie into the dining room.

Chapter Thirteen

Judd stood and gazed up at Richard. "So I'm not stupid. Harper is downright suspicious, and I suspect he'll mention it to Jolene before he leaves her tonight."

"Yeah. My thoughts exactly. What do you think of him so far?"

"Looks solid to me. I think she's done well for herself."

He slid his arm around Francine's waist and began walking to the adjoining room.

"So do I, believe me, she's come a long way. I'm glad for her."

"I am, too," Francine said. "This man is thinking marriage. Maybe not next week, but that's the way he's headed."

He watched as Jolene introduced Harper to each of the boarders, including Percy Lucas, who spoke cordially to Jolene's friend. In the lounge after supper, when Jolene and Francine left to repair their lipstick, Harper leaned back in his chair and looked directly at Judd.

"Is either of you able to tell me why Mrs. Johnson and Jolene look like mother and daughter?"

Richard looked at Philip and got the reaction that he expected. "If you'll excuse me," Philip said, "I have to call a couple of parishioners. They aren't well, and I want to have a few words with them."

Richard's lower lip dropped when Judd grabbed Philip's arm, restraining him. "That can wait. I've been wondering the same thing ever since Jolene came here. You've known Jolene ever since she was born, but you don't know who her father is. She doesn't know, and her mother refused to tell her. "

Harper sat forward, his brow deeply furrowed and his body tense, like that of a hunter crowding his prey. "Is Fannie Johnson Jolene's real mother?" When Philip seemed to relax at that question, Richard narrowed his eyes.

"I can tell you that Jolene's mother is dead," Philip assured them. "I knew her when she was carrying Jolene, and I performed the baptismal ceremony. Fannie has no children."

Judd raised his head slowly, and Richard had never seen such an expression of disgust, almost hatred, on his friend's face, for Judd was a man who preached goodness, grace, and kindness. "I know you don't have any brothers, because you said yesterday afternoon that Fannie was your only relative. Why did you let Jolene's mother treat her as if she wasn't human, and why haven't you told Jolene that you're her father?"

At the loud gasp, they all looked up to see Jolene and Francine standing there. Philip remained mute, tacitly admitting Judd's accusation, while the three men stared at him.

"Say something," Jolene said, in a voice that was abnormally low, tight, and harsh. "Why don't you say something?"

Harper jumped up, ran to her, and wrapped her in his arms. "It's all right, sweetheart. Don't cry, honey. You made it without him, and you don't need him. Please don't cry." His hands stroked her back and her shoulders, as her tears became sobs.

Fannie ran over to the group. "What's the matter? What's wrong with Jolene?"

"Nothing, really, when you get right down to it," Judd said. "She just found out that Philip here is her father."

Richard lunged forward and caught Fannie just before she collapsed. "I knew there was something fishy about the Reverend's sudden rash of visits," Joe Tucker said to Louvenia with whom he had observed the scene from a nearby table. "Jolene deserved better than that from him." Richard wondered who else had heard it.

Louvenia shrugged and rolled her eyes. "At least she's got his genes, and she can thank him for her good looks, 'cause that is one good-looking man."

Joe stared at Louvenia. "Oh, hell, woman. You always get everything ass backwards." He walked over to Richard. "I'll help you take Fannie upstairs to her room."

"Thanks," Richard said and looked at Francine. "I think it would look better if you came with us."

"Of course," she said. "I wasn't thinking. This whole scene is horrifying. What an awful experience for Jolene."

"Yeah," Joe said as they plodded up the stairs carrying Fannie. "But if Judd hadn't challenged the Reverend, he never would have admitted it, and Jolene would never have known who her old man was. Tell you the truth; I think he ought to be horsewhipped."

"What happened?" Fannie said when she regained consciousness as they put her on her bed.

Francine recounted as much of it as she knew. "He didn't deny it, Fannie."

"Well, of late, I'd been more and more suspicious about that. Before Jolene came here, I saw Philip maybe three times a year. At first I thought he wanted her for himself, but I didn't see any evidence of it, and then it came to me one day that she looked just like me and just like my father. And then I thought that, if Philip was her father, he'd have told her, and I saw no evidence of that, either. So I decided it was a strange coincidence. She must be terribly upset."

"She is," Francine said, "and if you'll excuse me, I'll go see what I can do to help her." She left and took Richard and Joe with her.

At the bottom of the stairs, Richard looked at Joe. "I thought I'd screwed up my life, but the Reverend is a humdinger."

"Yeah, man," Joe said. "He obviously cares about her, which is why he's here so often, but the brother's a coward. A real dilly of a coward. He preached at her mother's funeral and didn't put his arms around his daughter and say, your mother's gone, but you still have me, your father. That dude couldn't preach to me."

"Nor me." He returned to the lounge and walked over to Judd, who sat alone watching television, the commotion having emptied the lounge. "Where's Jolene?"

"Harper took her with him. He said they'd be back in about

an hour, that he thought she'd be better if he got her away from the Reverend. He's a good man. I like him."

"So do I." Richard sat down and leaned back. "He's a tough man, too, and he'll take good care of her."

"Where's Francine"

"She went to the kitchen to ask Rodger for some coffee. Marilyn's gone home."

"How're you two getting on? I can see you're still together, but—"

"I have hope that we'll make it. She has to wade through the minute details of what I told you, and that may take a while. I'm not patient, but I have no choice."

Richard sucked in his breath as Francine glided toward them, her hips swaying gently as if to the rhythm of cool jazz. "You should hear those kitchen windows rattling. The wind must be at least forty miles an hour," she said, put cups of coffee in front of them and looked at Richard. "Is your window closed?"

"Yes, it is, but the hurricane isn't due here for another day or so. I'd better check my corner window, though." He stood and, impulsively, leaned down and quickly kissed her mouth. He didn't look at her, because he didn't want to know her reaction, but as he walked away, he heard Judd say, "You two need more of that and less of whatever else it is that you've been doing to each other, 'cause it ain't working."

He checked the window, and found that it was closed, but more important, he saw in the distance what seemed like flashlights in the vicinity of the beach. If he told her, she'd go out there, exposing herself to that strong, cold wind, but if he didn't tell her, wouldn't he be guilty of disloyalty? He turned and ran back down the stairs.

"Francine, may I see you for a minute?" he called to her from the door of the lounge. As she stood within inches of him, her voluptuous lips so close and her teasing breasts within the reach of his fingers, he nearly faltered. "I saw what looked like flashlights on the beach. Call your boss, but please don't go out there alone." By the time he finished the sentence she was halfway up the stairs. He wanted to follow her, but what could he do? He couldn't go with her, and he couldn't force her to stay home.

Five minutes later, she raced down the stairs wearing pants and a hooded storm coat.

"Don't worry, I'm not going all the way there, and my boss will meet me." She reached up, patted his left cheek and was out of the door before he could clear his head sufficiently to ask if he could go with her.

"I'd like to know what that was about," Judd said when he went back to the table, "but nobody's gonna tell me. Why didn't you go with her?"

"I'd tell you, friend, but I can't betray her confidence. I'll say this much: She's an admirable woman."

"Oh, I know that" Judd said. "This has been some night. What kind of conversation do you think Fannie's having with Philip right now? I'll bet she's hotter than an iron poker in a bed of red coals. I imagine you got your niece with you, one of your two blood relatives on the face of the earth, and you don't even know it."

"That's rough. I'd been thinking about the effect this has on Jolene, but you're right. Fannie must be undone."

As they spoke, Harper and Jolene walked in and sat with them. Richard could see that Harper had managed to calm Jolene, and he hoped she'd be able to get over her animosity to Philip, and that she'd give him a chance to have his say.

"You had a shock," Judd said to Jolene, "but you got Harper here to help you through it. If I were you, I'd let Philip say his piece. Then, if you want to, you can say yours."

"She shouldn't be disrespectful to him," Harper said. "Anyway, she doesn't need him. She's got me for as long as we live, if that's what she wants." Jolene looked up at Harper, causing Richard to wonder if Francine would ever look at him that way again.

"I only want to know why he didn't tell me," Jolene said. "The last time he was here, I complained to him about my mama refusing to tell me who my father was."

Harper slung his arm across Jolene's shoulder. "That's all right, sweetheart. Don't stress yourself disliking him. The man will need you before you need him. I'd better go. That wind is picking up rapidly."

"I'll see you to the door," Jolene said. "Good night Judd, Richard. See you at breakfast."

Richard looked at his watch. Twenty-five minutes. *Lord, please don't let her get out of her car unless her boss is there.* He went to the cooler for water that he didn't drink, walked to the front door, and made himself go back and sit down.

"Take it easy," Judd said. "She'll be back."

At midnight, Richard was still in the lounge, alone, when the door opened. He rushed to meet Francine, grabbed her and folded her into his arms. "Thank God you're here and you're safe. Did you get him?"

"No, but we caught one of his cohorts, a man who claims to know every move Ronald Barnes makes. I can't thank you enough for telling me you saw those lights. I know what it cost you, because you knew what I'd do."

Drained of both energy and emotion, he put an arm around her waist. "Come on. Let's go upstairs."

At her room door, Francine looked up at Richard for a long time, and he waited. Silently. Finally, she repeated what she said earlier, "You didn't have to do that," hugged him, squeezed him to her body and opened her door. "See you in the morning."

He hadn't expected that she would give in easily, but she hadn't made him sweat, either. She was honest and sincere in her relationships, and if he got her, it would be more than he deserved.

"I'm going to try to get back home—when had he begun to think of the boardinghouse as home?—before my dad comes," Richard told Judd the next morning, leaving the breakfast table a few minutes after Francine went to work. I have to go down to the courthouse and fill out some forms for my mayoral candidacy."

"You mean you're not meeting your father?"

"Meet him? How can I? He doesn't own a watch, doesn't believe in schedules and hates regimentation. Said he'll be here today, and he will."

Judd seemed perplexed, and he didn't blame the man. A lot of people thought his father odd.

"What if he gets lost?"

Richard zipped up his leather jacket, tied a scarf around his neck and let a grin slide over his lips. "My dad get lost? Judd, he could find his way to the Khyber Pass without a map. See you later."

Jolene plodded down the stairs for breakfast, wishing she were somewhere else. She didn't want to encounter Philip Coles. Why hadn't she guessed, and why hadn't her resemblance to Fannie rung a bell? "How's it going this morning?" she asked Judd, who'd already begun to eat.

"Same as usual. How are *you*?"

"I called in sick this morning. First time I have done that. I didn't feel like smiling and being cheerful all day, and since I'm off, I'll do some Christmas shopping. Want me to get something for you?"

Judd stopped eating. "Hold on. You're babbling, and that means you're nervous. I'm the same Judd, and you got no need to hide your feelings and your problems from me." He paused. "Good morning, Philip. Come over and join us. No point in sitting by yourself. We're family."

To her amazement, Philip Coles got up, came to their table and asked her, "Mind if I sit here, Jolene?"

Time was when she'd have told him what she thought of him, but Harper had begged her not to be rude to her father. "No. I don't mind."

He sat with them, and Rodger brought Philip's breakfast of fruit, Belgian waffles, sausage, and coffee. He ate silently for a few minutes and then stopped. "Jolene, I didn't have proof that I was your father until two weeks before Emma died. I asked her right after you were born, and she swore there'd been other men. I accepted that because I wanted to, but I knew even then that she had never been with another man. I made her admit it when I brought her that last communion. Oh, I'm guilty. I knew it all those years, because you looked just like Fannie and my father."

She felt no compassion as she gazed at him. "Why didn't you marry her?"

"Emma broke it off before I knew she was pregnant, and then she began to live like a hermit with that mother of hers. When you were born, I got a shock, because I hadn't known she was pregnant. I thought she'd stopped coming to church because she was angry with me. And she became as mean as a rattlesnake. I stopped caring for her. When she did admit it, she made me swear not to tell you. I didn't have to take that oath, but it was an easy way out for me. I . . . I hope you will forgive me."

"It's gonna take a lot for you to forgive yourself," Judd said, "'cause the first time you saw Jolene, you knew she was yours. How's Fannie taking this?"

"She was furious with me at first, but she seemed to get used to the idea and told me how proud of Jolene she is, and how happy she is to have a niece and an heir. Jolene, that man who was with you last night is first class. Solid as a rock."

"I know. Harper's wonderful, and to think I almost loused up with him." She answered her cell phone. "Hi. I called in sick, but I'm fine. I was on my way to being depressed, but I'm getting over that. Reverend Coles? He's eating breakfast with Judd and me. I'm going shopping. You will? Wonderful. I'll be ready in an hour. Bye." She hung up. "That was Harper. I have to dress. See you later."

She was supposed to feel something, wasn't she? Shouldn't she feel some natural kinship for her father? Well, she didn't, and maybe she never would. She loved Harper and Judd and Richard and Francine and Fannie. For now, that was enough.

Richard got home late that afternoon after having been fingerprinted, photographed, questioned, and interviewed and after submitting to a physical examination. He had also filed papers, espoused his political philosophy, and articulated his plans and dreams for Pike Hill. And he had begun to wish no one had suggested that he run for mayor. Where was the running? He didn't have an opponent. "We'll have posters and petitions out by noon tomorrow," the councilman had told him. "You're a celebrity around here; most any newcomer is. You're a shoo-in."

He paused at the entrance to the lounge. Every boarder except Francine, Jolene, Barbara, Lila Mae Henry—the fourth grade teacher—and himself crowded around his father, and he had never heard such laughter in Fannie Johnson's earthly haven.

"I see you're at it again, Dad," he said and rushed to embrace his father.

"Richard, honey, you got real roots. See if you can get your daddy to stay with us for a while," Louvenia said, her eyes gleaming.

"Yeah," Arnetha agreed. "He's real folks."

Richard stared at the two women who hadn't spoken a hundred words to him in the ten months he'd lived there with them. And he was ready to keel over when Percy Lucas sidled up to him and said, "Richard, would you and your father care to go with me down to Bakerside? We could pick up some nice crabs, and your father would see how the crabbers work. It's real interesting."

Since when did Percy Lucas know how to pronounce his name? He caught himself before his lower jaw dropped. "I'd like that a lot, Percy, and I'm sure my dad would, too. I can't thank you enough." Percy looked suitably pleased, and Richard looked around him, aghast, for there was Marilyn stroking his father's arm and holding a dish of her homemade ice cream inches from his father's mouth.

Harland Peterson had conquered the Thank the Lord Boarding House. Richard observed his father closely and realized that he looked like Percy and Joe and Judd, that he drank the ginger ale—no doubt provided by Judd—straight from the bottle, and that no one would have confused him with an ambassador.

His father raised himself to his full six feet three inches and hugged Richard. "Glad to see you've settled down with some real human beings. I take it you've finished with that cocktail crowd. I never felt comfortable with that bunch. Judd tells me you're like a son to him. I may get jealous."

"Better watch 'em. They're like Mutt and Jeff," Louvenia said, her comment reflecting her age.

Richard didn't know what to say to all the camaraderie directed at him. He thought of the schemes he'd tried in order to get his fellow boarders to like and accept him, with no luck. Yet, his father managed it merely by being himself. Harland Peterson was one of them, so they accepted him and therefore also his son.

Percy, of all people, came to his defense. "Now y'all stop teasing Richard."

"How long have you been here?" Richard asked his father.

Harland leaned back in his chair and stretched his suspenders, running his thumbs up and down them. "Got here just in time to eat that fantastic food Marilyn served for lunch." He winked at Richard. "Pardon. I mean dinner."

And just long enough to charm your subjects, Richard thought with a grin, although he failed to associate his own ability to charm women effortlessly with the trait he observed in his father. To his knowledge, Harland Peterson had been a woodsman, an amateur boxer, truck driver, and taxi driver. His father would probably say that he'd also been a bum in most European countries and that, since his retirement six years earlier, he had tramped through a good part of the world. He was a people person, and the bigger the crowd around him, the happier he appeared to be. That was one trait he didn't get from his father for, although he'd mastered it while in international circles, he had little tolerance for small talk with strangers.

Arriving from school, Lila Mae Henry burst into the lounge. "Y'all see that weather out there? Those clouds are almost jet black, and the wind is so strong I could hardly control my car. Looks like that hurricane is finally coming."

"In that case, we'd better board up the windows," Harland said. "Any hardware stores around here?"

Harland purchased supplies, and as the men boarded up the windows, he let them see his skill with saw, hammer, and nails. "Your father is a wonderful man," Fannie told Richard. "If he wants to have a beer, it's all right with me."

He stared at her listlessly, for his thoughts were not on his father, Fannie or the house. He needed to know where Francine was and what she was doing. The windows rattled, and it seemed at times as if the entire house shook. He watched Judge Judy with Judd, his father, and Joe Tucker, but if his life had depended on it, he couldn't have described one case. When his cell phone rang, he jumped up, ran to the hall and answered it.

"Peterson speaking."

"This is Francine. Grab Joe, Percy, or Rodger and come to that big rock on the beach. Put on your storm coat and hurry. *Now!*"

He didn't have time to explain, so he grabbed his father. "Come with me, Dad. I need you for something." Five minutes later, they headed for the beach in his father's rented car. He explained the situation. "Do whatever she tells you to do."

"Sure. What's she to you?"

"Everything. If my luck holds out, she'll be your daughter-in-law."

"All right. I'm with you all the way."

Richard parked half a block from the beach. "This wind is really something," he said as they plodded along, pitting their strength against the wind's brutal force. "I've never been in this kind of storm—Stop." He thought he saw her sitting on the sand beside the huge boulder. He resisted calling her, but he knew she didn't see him.

"What's that?" his father asked. "Could that be some men pulling a boat to shore? Do you see Francine?"

"Shh. Over there beside that big rock. Let's see if we can get there without those men seeing us. They crawled to within a few feet of her. "Francine, this is Richard."

"Thank God. Stay down low. There're three of them. Who's with you?"

"My Dad."

"Not to worry, Francine," said Harland. "I spent a few years as a heavyweight amateur boxer, and I can still put it down. Quiet. Here they come."

Richard trained his eyes for the man with the limp, Ronald Barnes, the ringleader and the one Francine had to take. Suddenly he heard the snap of a gun, and Francine stood up.

"Treasury Department Officer. Freeze or I shoot."

He had never been really scared before, but he could hear his teeth chattering. All three of the men lunged toward Francine, and he heard the gun as one man fell backward. He grabbed the bigger of the other two men, knowing that his father would enjoy knocking the other one to the sand.

"Did you kill him?" Richard asked Francine.

She knelt beside Ronald Barnes and handcuffed him. "No. I only put a bullet in his shoulder low enough to drop him. You got here just in time. I knew I couldn't handle the three of them unless I killed them without giving them a chance, and I didn't want to do that. My boss is over half an hour away." She put handcuffs on the other two men, straightened up and blew out a long, heavy breath. "Thank God, that's over."

She extended her hand to Harland. "I appreciate your helping me out, sir, and I'm glad to meet you."

"I'm certainly glad to make your acquaintance, but I sure didn't expect to meet my son's girl on a beach in a hurricane apprehending thugs. It's been exciting, and I do love adventure."

"Why didn't they shoot?" Richard asked her.

"These guys don't carry guns. If they're caught, they try to lie their way out of trouble, but if they are carrying a gun, they're already felons. Uh . . . I have to stay here with my prisoners until the other officers arrive, but if it's getting too rough out here for you—"

He didn't see the point in glaring at her, because she couldn't see him in the darkness. "It's best we both pretend you didn't say that," Richard said, working hard to keep his voice gentle and soft. When she thought about what she'd said, surely she would apologize.

A federal officer and two policemen arrived and relieved Francine of her prisoners. "We need you there to book 'em," the man he presumed to be Francine's boss said. "You can tail us."

Both of Francine's hands went to her hips. "Not tonight. I've had enough of this weather. I'll probably come down with pneumonia, and just in time for Christmas, too." She looked at him. "Let's go."

When she shivered, Richard put his right arm around her and tucked her close to his body. Could he handle loving a woman who he couldn't protect, whose occupation was too dangerous for the average man, and who loved the work she did? What would he have done if one of those men had shot her? Tremors raced through him at the thought of it. But he loved her and couldn't let that stop him. Tonight, she needed him, and whenever she did, he'd be there for her.

Chapter Fourteen

When Richard walked into the lounge with Francine and his father, the boarders sat precisely as he and his father had left them nearly an hour earlier, every face etched in concern. It was then that he knew he belonged to them and they to him, that the strangers he'd rejected, then courted, and later disavowed because they seemingly had no interest in him had become his loving and caring family. He knew that he could still suffer for his callous treatment of women and for his disregard of others as he strove toward the pinnacle of success, and he accepted that—he had danced with the devil, and he'd pay his dues—but for the first time in his life, he had friends.

Philip Coles seemed to drag himself into the lounge, looked around and knocked his right fist into his left palm, apparently without realizing that he did it. "Where's Jolene? She isn't in her room, so I thought she was down here. She can't be out in this weather." He didn't address any one in particular, but he looked at Judd.

"Jolene called me not long ago," Judd said. "She's staying in Ocean Pines tonight. Nobody can drive in this storm."

Philip let his gaze roam over the group, shook his head, turned and walked slowly back up the stairs, as if dazed. "What's wrong with him?" Francine whispered to Richard.

Richard looked down at her, so close and yet so much farther from him than he wanted her to be. "Like some of the rest of us, Francine, Philip Coles is paying his dues."

She stared at him. "Oh, dear. Has Jolene confronted him?"

"No more than what you heard. It's his conscience, his guilt that's dragging him down. I haven't been an angel, but I couldn't have denied my child, my own flesh and blood, and looked on while she suffered at the hands of a mother who hated *me* and made my child the scapegoat. I pity him."

Even as Richard spoke, Jolene stood with Harper near the main entrance to Long's Department Store in Ocean Pines. "I've never heard such wind," she said to him as she gazed through the glass door at the debris swirling around on the street. "We can't drive to Pike Hill in this storm, can we?"

"It's too dangerous." He took both of her hands. "I'll rent you a room in a hotel that isn't far from here, or you may stay with me. It's up to you."

He stood there holding her hands and looking down at her, and she couldn't figure out what he was thinking. But it seemed to her that the whole world was in his eyes. Unable to divert her gaze, she lowered her eyelids and leaned into him.

"Take me with you."

"Are you sure?"

"I'm positive."

She'd been to his place once before, but she remembered nothing of the masculine apartment with its dark woods and leather seating. She might never have been there, except that her mind recalled with vivid accuracy all that she experienced there, everything that he did to her there.

He made coffee and brought it to her in the living room along with a plate of Graham crackers, which he explained were his favorites. After he spilled the coffee while pouring it and broke the plate that held the crackers, she felt more at ease.

"I'm getting to be a klutz," he said.

She reached out and patted his hand. "Harper, don't be nervous. Nothing's going to happen unless you want it to happen."

She recalled those lines from one of the romance novels she once read so avidly.

As if dumbfounded, he stared at her . . . and stared. Then, he laughed a big air-clearing laugh, picked her up and carried her to his bedroom.

When she awoke the next morning, snug in his arms, he was still buried deep inside of her. She moved languorously and rubbed his buttocks, and immediately she felt herself stretch as he grew within her. She raised her body to meet his thrust, and minutes later exploded around him in ecstasy.

After a while, with her face cradled in his palms, he looked down at her and shook his head as if unable to fathom the wonder of their relationship. "I start work next Monday at the Ryder Furniture Company in Ocean City. I make furniture and finish it by hand. One day, I hope to design it. When the work gets slow, I drive for one of the bus companies around here. They're always willing to take me on, so I'm never out of a job."

He gazed unsmiling into her eyes, and her heart skipped a beat. "Will you have me for your husband, Jolene? I'll take good care of you and our children. Will you?"

She couldn't sit up, because he was lying on top of her, but she had a sudden desire to dance, shout, and flail her arms. "Are you asking me what I think you're asking me?"

He smiled at that, smiled until his face brightened with happiness. "Yes, I am. Will you?"

"I sure will." And then she laughed. Laughed until she shook. Laughed until tears streamed down her cheeks. "Oh, Harper! I will. I will."

On Christmas Eve, two days later, Thank the Lord Boarding House hummed with activity. Judd hung a stocking for each boarder, Fannie, the kitchen help, and the guests. Joe assumed the job of cutting the chestnuts that would roast beside the fire; Percy made wreaths from the fir and holly branches he collected on his last trip; and Louvenia and Arnetha set the tables, some with red and some with green cloths.

Richard took his father and Judd to Ocean Pines to shop for wine, fruit and the ingredients for eggnog, including cognac.

"No point in drinking flat eggnog," Harland had insisted. "The stuff needs cognac *and* rum. It's got so much cream in it that Fannie won't know the difference till she passes out."

"But we have to live with her," Judd said, "and she'd never let us forget it. We'll be lucky if she doesn't raise hell about the cognac."

"What are you giving Francine for Christmas?" Richard's father asked him.

"I'd like to give her a ring, but—"

"Then give her one," Judd said, cutting him off. "You don't think she's gonna come up to you and ask you for one, do you? What can you lose? Last time I saw the two of you together, she was as close to you as she could get. Well, almost. Anyway, if she says no, you can take it back to the jeweler and get your money."

"Right," Harland Peterson said. "That way, she'll know it's D-Day, and she can stop making up her mind, which is something women get a helluva kick out of doing anyhow."

"Hmmm. Not a bad idea." Richard parked in front of Steig's, went inside, and found what he wanted almost immediately.

"What was all the hush-hush about the night of the hurricane?" Judd asked Richard, who told him, and added, "She's finished with that job, so it's no longer a secret."

"Well, I'll be doggone. Cute and womanly as she is, I never woulda guessed it." Judd said. "If your father said his woman was an officer of the law, I wouldn't be a bit surprised, 'cause he's down here on earth like the rest of us. But *you!* I can't even imagine you with your fingers dirty. You look like Harland here, but you're not a bit like him."

"That's because I spent most of my life trying not to be like him. But in the past couple of days, it's become clear to me that he gets more that's meaningful with his ways than I ever did with mine."

Judd cleared his throat. "You want Francine, but will you introduce her to your highfalutin' friends as a policewoman?"

"If you can't do that, you should leave her alone," Harland said. "Francine is a prize for any man."

"What do you two take me to be?" Richard said, becoming exasperated. "My friends live at Thank the Lord Boarding House; other people are acquaintances, and who I marry is none of their business." And to signal the end to that issue, he asked Judd, "Do you want us to visit your sister the day after tomorrow?"

"I wouldn't mind, if it's no trouble."

Alone in his room late that afternoon, Richard walked from one end of it to the other, time and again. Maybe if he wrote her a note. He sat down and began a letter, tore it up and went downstairs. How long would he have to pay for his transgressions? He deserved punishment, and he knew it, but should it last forever?

"If she won't take the ring," he said to Judd, "I'll be devastated. Where's Dad? I thought he was down here."

"She'll be happy to have it," Judd assured him, "so take it easy. Your father is in the kitchen showing Marilyn how to make something called satay that he ate in Indonesia. Be careful you don't get her for a stepmother."

He stared at Judd. "A what? Hell no, man. I'd handcuff my father and lock him up before I'd see him do that."

Laughter rumbled out of Judd in what seemed like gasps. "Well, he's a fine looking man, and he's got Marilyn's prerequisites."

Marilyn didn't allow any of the boarders in her kitchen, so what was Harland Peterson doing in there? He resisted checking on him. His sixty-six-year-old father shouldn't need a chaperon. He tried to enjoy the holiday atmosphere—big beautiful tree and the berry-sprinkled green wreath above the fireplace, the odor of bayberry and pine that wafted throughout the house. Flames danced and crackled before his eyes, spreading warmth and brightening the lounge. A mound of gifts, beautifully wrapped, filled the space beneath the tree. He squirmed in his chair. Where was Francine?

"The odors in that kitchen make me feel as if I haven't eaten in weeks," Harland said when he joined Judd and his son. "Where's Francine?"

She walked toward them at that moment, open and welcoming, and he prayed that he wasn't misunderstanding the signals she sent. He got up and pulled out a chair for her.

Marilyn had roasted a suckling pig and a twenty-five pound turkey with all the trimmings for a traditional Christmas dinner. With two additional tables set, the kitchen staff, Harland, Philip, and Harper joined the boarders and Fannie for the meal.

Fannie stood. "Reverend Coles will say the grace, but I know how gossip flies around here, so before he does, I want you all to remember that this is Christmas, a time of love and forgiving. I've forgiven Philip, and I want all of you to do the same." Philip's grace was more like a prayer, and when he finished, Judd applauded and the others followed his lead.

Richard looked into Francine's eyes, asking for tolerance, understanding and, maybe, forgiveness. Her gaze didn't waver, so he reached across the table and grasped her hand. "I'll be faithful to you, and I'll love you for as long as I breathe."

"I know," she said, "and I promise you the same."

His heart seemed at first to have stopped beating, and then it began a furious pounding in his chest. He recovered his breath, stood, leaned forward and kissed her mouth. He didn't wait for a reprimand for his public display, but reached into his pocket for the ring, took her left hand and slipped the ring on her ring finger. He didn't know what she said, for the deafening applause drowned out her words. But the tears sparkling in her eyes and the smile on her face were all the words he needed, and he bounded around the table, lifted her into his arms and held her. She looked at the ring on her finger and then kissed the side of his mouth.

"I think she just agreed to marry me," he said to those present. "I can hardly believe it."

"She did," Marilyn said. "Now, let's eat before this dinner I cooked gets cold."

"Wait a minute," Harper said. "This guy's got nothing on me. Jolene has agreed to marry me, and we're having the ceremony in February." He stood, slipped a ring on Jolene's finger and hugged her. "Now, we can eat."

* * *

Judd finished his meal and headed for his usual seat in the lounge. Rocking back and forward in his Shaker rocker, his words belied his smile. "Looks like I'm gonna be losing two of m'favorite people."

"I don't think so," Fannie said. "From what I hear, half the town's already signed a petition for Richard's mayoral candidacy, and I'm told Harper lives in Ocean Pines. They'll be nearby. Still, I wish Jolene wouldn't leave me. Jolene," she looked at her niece, "I know Philip's behavior was reprehensible, but the Lord wants you to forgive. Philip will pay for what he's done; you needn't worry about that. Tell you the truth, he's suffering right now."

As if on cue, Philip joined them. "I don't have an excuse, Jolene, and for the rest of my life, I will regret how I've behaved toward you. At least, please don't hate me."

Jolene looked him in the eye. "I won't say it's all right, because it isn't. There were plenty of times when I needed someone desperately, and there was no one. But I've done things that I'm ashamed of, too, and I've hurt others. I don't feel like opening my arms to you, but I don't wish you any harm. In time, maybe we can be closer."

Philip looked at Harper. "I hope you won't keep my grandchildren from me."

Harper didn't flinch from the man's gaze. "Whatever makes Jolene happy."

Judd nodded his head in agreement and when, from his peripheral vision, he saw Richard and Francine gliding arm-in-arm up the stairs, he smiled in contentment, leaned back in his Shaker rocker, and rocked.

Richard walked with Francine to her room and stood at the door gazing down into her soft brown eyes. "I'd give anything if I didn't have to leave you."

"Then don't," she whispered.

"But . . ."

Francine turned the knob on her door, pushed the door open and gazed up at him, telling him without words that the next move was his. "For months, lying in your arms has filled my dreams and imagining what it will be like has dominated my waking hours."

His breathing accelerated, liquid accumulated in his mouth, and he didn't recognize the sound of his own voice when his words came out rough and urgent. "And you think it hasn't been the same with me?"

She looked down at the diamond engagement ring on her finger and then at him. "I won't have to beg you after we're married, will I?"

He could feel the grin spreading over his face as he lifted her, stepped into her room, closed the door, locked it and pressed his mouth to her warm waiting lips.

"Your father," she said. "He knows you aren't in your room."

"My father also knows you just promised to marry me."

Between the satin sheets that she favored, he covered her body with his own, made certain that she was ready for him and they joined.

"What is it?" she asked when he remained still and silent.

"I'm overwhelmed. I can hardly believe what's happening to me. To us."

She tightened her arms around him, and he began to move. Nothing like it had ever happened to him. As if they had been lovers for years, she adjusted to his every stroke, every change in movement. Finally, she exploded around him and wrung from him the essence of himself. He cradled her in his arms. "I love you. Marry me soon."

"I will."

"There're so many things I want to do to you and with you, but we can't be greedy tonight."

"There's still Miami and that hotel overlooking the ocean. How about next weekend?" she asked.

"It won't come soon enough for me."

"Nor for me."

WHEN YOU DANCE WITH THE DEVIL

GWYNNE FORSTER

ABOUT THIS GUIDE

The suggested questions are intended to enhance
your group's reading of Gwynne Forster's
WHEN YOU DANCE WITH THE DEVIL.

DISCUSSION QUESTIONS

1. Are Jolene's grievances against her mother credible?

2. What is the first thing Jolene does that indicates rebellion against her mother and her upbringing?

3. What, if anything did Jolene learn from her mother that is positive and life enforcing?

4. Do you think Reverend Coles and the members of his church should have interfered with Emma Tilman's treatment of Jolene? What could they have done?

5. When Richard Peterson looks at himself as he really is, he experiences an epiphany. What is the principle precipitant of this life-altering experience?

6. When Richard made love to Estelle Mitchell, what was the result for him? For her? Do you think he deserved it and why?

7. What are the circumstances that bring Richard to Thank the Lord Boarding House?

8. What is Richard's reaction to the place and to its occupants? What attracts him? What repels him?

9. How do Emma Tilman's attitudes affect Jolene's regard of men?

10. What accounts for Jolene's casual attitudes toward sex and her failure to value her own body?

11. What does Jim's attitude toward Jolene following their sexual experience tell you about Jim as a man?

12. Judd Walker has a crucial role in this story? What is it?

13. Name some of the ways in which Judd helps Richard find peace with himself and with his environment.

14. What does Richard contribute to the boardinghouse? To the community?

15. What prevents Richard from developing camaraderie with his fellow boarders other than Judd, Fannie and, later, Francine?

16. In coming to the realization that Jolene and Richard must change themselves—each has a critical experience that is life-altering. What are they?

17. Even as she grows as a person, Jolene retains her bitterness. What hurts her most?

18. How does Jolene find happiness with Harper Masterson? Which of her main character traits does she lose in the process?

19. In finding redemption, Richard retraces his old haunts and confronts his lost love. Was time or Francine responsible for his healing?

20. What is your opinion of the Reverend Philip Coles? How did Jolene learn of her relation to him?